TANGLED THREATS ON THE NOMAD HIGHWAY

NEITHER THIS, NOR THAT

Book #6

MariaLisa deMora

Editing by Hot Tree Editing

Proofreading by Whiskey Jack Editing

Photography: Wander Aguiar, Photography

Model: Nathan Van Dyken

First Published 2021

ISBN 13: 978-1-946738-74-5

DEDICATION

"The trouble is, you think you have time."
~Carlos Castaneda

For those who have loved and lost,
and are still rising.

Contents

ACKNOWLEDGMENTS

There aren't enough pages to provide thanks to everyone who supported me through the past few months. Some days it seemed like the hits just kept coming, and it was only those early a.m. check-in calls that kept me moving forward.

Thanks to Megan, for helping with all things social media. Becky and her crew at Hot Tree Editing, thanks for helping make my words represent what I wanted. Much appreciation to Mel from Whiskey Jack Editing, for polishing and letting my story take flight. Mucho thanks to Wander Aguiar for the image on the front cover, and to Nathan Van Dyken for just being your best self, man.

Greatest gratitude to you, holding this book in your hands. If it weren't for you, Dear Reader, none of this would exist out in the world. Your appetite for my stories allows me to write these characters out of my head, and introduce them around. It's quite likely you've helped me retain my sanity, so seriously—thank you!

Woofully yours,
~ML

Tangled Threats on the Nomad Highway

Einstein won't allow himself to believe in fate. His wife and daughter had deserved more than three wizened crones cutting short the fabric of their existence. Fate has nothing to do with the holes in his heart and life. No, those are due entirely to a world he tries to keep in his past. Tries and fails—and now all he has is cold granite to embrace.

As the only nomad for the BBMC, he takes pride in policing all potential threats to the club that has become his home and family. That includes the unwelcome, trespassing shadows from his past.

Marian Threadgill still hasn't become accustomed to her new life. After years spent resigning herself to living as a broken prisoner in her childhood home, she found liberation in the form of unconventional champions: rough-and-tumble bikers who proved to her how deceiving appearances could be. In the months following her rescue, she's developed a strong sense of loyalty to the men who wear black leather and ride steel steeds. She's vowed to herself to defend them against all comers, even threats larger than they might seem.

As danger once again darkens her world, Marian is thrust into an unfamiliar role. She's never seen herself as anything other than an underdog until Einstein demands so much more.

Chapter One

Einstein stood immobile, muscles painfully locked into unforgiving stillness while the first scattered drops of rain patted at the dirt as if with tiny, wet hands. Each droplet raised minuscule clouds of dust that settled back to the surface in an obscuring skin, blurring and muddying pure, clear liquid until it was spoiled, soiled.

Already he missed her. *Lauren.*

The weight of the golden oath on his left hand was a binding promise he couldn't set aside. He imagined he felt the heated graze of her lips on the skin of his neck and froze at the sensation, holding tight to the illusion for as long as he could.

Every memory would fade with time, like photographs too-long exposed to sunlight. Brilliant reality and the gleam from day-to-day life would overlay the stories in his mind until only shadows remained.

Still. Forever he would miss her.

The slide of silken hair in his hand, the undulating glide of skin against skin. Sweet teasing touches intended to rouse and rile, her brilliant smile owning his reactions. *No more.*

Miss them.

The welcome heat and weight of his baby girl resting against his shoulder as he carried her to bed. A burden he'd never shirked or begrudged. The best part of his life had jolted into being on the day Makayla had taken her first breath.

Never again.

"Ashes to ashes." The words drifted through the air around him, as useless in this moment as his efforts to save them had been. Forgettable and harmless, except that the sounds served to mark the beginning of the end of a journey.

My family. My girls.

"Dust to dust." He didn't lift his gaze from the mud rapidly developing underneath the soles of his boots. Watched as the dirt changed texture, becoming something innate to its nature, but an evolution nonetheless. He didn't want to see what was in front of him. Didn't need to see. She wasn't there, not anymore.

All her vitality, the beauty she had carried on her skin and in her heart, was gone forever. The love that had stabilized him through the changes in their lives was already becoming a fallible memory. The heart-stopping pureness of their daughter's love and light—gone. Snuffed out in an instant by a murdering bastard.

Who's gonna save me now?

Weight settled in the middle of his back, a heavy hand bearing down in the same sorrow that coated him. The steady pounding echoed the rhythm of his heart, closed fist thudding against his spine, centered over the patch that was the only thing still holding him together. From nearby, he heard the only word that could bring him back from the dark thoughts circling the edges of his mind.

"Brother."

Chapter Two

Elbows propped on his knees, Jim Dancer leaned his face into his hands, fingertips digging and rubbing across his forehead.

Today.

That's what he'd told himself when he'd risen out of sleep midafternoon, head still pounding from the skinful of forgetfulness he'd sucked down last night—aiming, as always, for oblivion. Today would be the day he'd change his current existence.

That was three hours ago, and the farthest he'd gotten so far was perched at the edge of the mattress, surrounded by rumpled covers.

The paint colors were bright, and on the wall in front of him, a large sticker of a cartoon figure was peeling, the top edge folded over itself. He couldn't stay put. He needed to get up and take a piss, maybe find something nutritious to put in his belly for a change. Only now that it was time to make a decision, it was looking like maybe tomorrow would be a better fit for a shift in trajectory.

Today was too hard.

Eight months not long enough.

Pounding echoed through the house. He shoved up from the side of the tiny toddler mattress to stalk towards the kitchen door, not bothering to pull on pants or a shirt, because whoever this was, they wouldn't give a rat's ass what he wore or didn't wear.

Stumbling over an empty pizza box, he kicked it out of the kitchen doorway and was shocked to see the table and chairs upended, thrown around the space like a child's blocks. Loud knocks clashing with his headache, he struggled to pull a chair out of the way of the door, then thumbed the lock, unfastening the bolt at the same time he turned around, giving his back to the man walking through the door behind him.

"Jesus, Einstein. What the fuck happened here?"

Flinging a hand up to hopefully silence his friend, he responded with, "Don't know, don't care," before disappearing into the bathroom. Accessible from the hallway, it also joined the main bedroom. Blocking the thought from advancing, he ignored the prickles across his skin. That was a space he avoided at all costs. Einstein gritted his teeth and tried to shove the door closed against the wad of dirty towels jammed in the way. He gave up with a grunt and took another step into the room, downturned gaze registering the state of the sink. *Lauren'd be so mad.* Toothpaste, whiskers, blood—the scum was caked on so thick he thought he could peel it off like a leathery skin.

Then his traitorous gaze wandered just a little away from the sink, and every muscle locked in place. A pink, barely used toothbrush stood next to his in a dusty jar. Twins sharing a container, just as its predecessors had, symbolic of his and Lauren's marriage. Only this one hadn't moved in months. She was never coming back.

His shaking hand hovered over it, muscles in his arm shuddering and cramping. In a flash, his fingers clenched, and his elbow bent until he smashed knuckles against the side of his head. Once, twice, a third time before he bent over the countertop, breathing hard through the blooming ache.

"Einstein…Dancer. *Brother*." The pain in Retro's voice was real, bleeding straight through from his soul, and it shattered Einstein's control to hear it. "You gotta let me help you."

Hands to the edge of the counter, Einstein squatted and sucked in great huge breaths, forehead pressing against the smooth wood of the cabinet doors. "I don't know what to do, Jerry." He rocked in place, lightly battering his head against the hard surface. "I can't get past it. Can't do it. Not at all. She's right here—" He smashed knuckles against his temple again. "All the time, man. All the time, and I can't get past it."

"You're not supposed to get past it, brother." A hand landed on his to deflect the next blow; then an arm wrapped around his waist and lifted. "You're never gonna get past it. But I promise you, it'll get easier." Still a dead weight in Retro's hold, Einstein let himself be guided to his feet. At the last instant, he scrambled for the jar, knocking it into the sink before his fingers landed on Lauren's toothbrush. Plucking it from the shards of glass, he cradled it to his chest as he stood more upright but still leaned against Retro. He felt his brother's shoulders lift in a pained sigh. "Come on, brother. Past time for me to get your ass outta here."

It took an hour, but eventually, he was dressed and standing in the living room. He stared at the couch, remembering the visible terror on Lauren's face over the gag shoved into her mouth. Einstein's nail raked against the bristles of her toothbrush before he tucked it into the inside pocket of his vest, fastening the button closed with a forceful push of his thumb.

"Come on, man." Retro's hand landed in the middle of his back, discharging heat through the leather and into Einstein's spine. "Let's go for a ride."

"Fuck, man. Don't know if the bike'll even turn over after this long." He stepped into the kitchen, surprised at the sudden order that had been restored. The table sat in the corner near a bench he'd built specifically for Makayla, the few unbroken chairs lined up on the other sides, pushed underneath as if ready for a hand to claim them. Smashed dishes and pieces of shattered wood had been swept to the side, dented pots and pans placed in the sinks. "You didn't have to do this, Jerry."

"Bike'll start." Retro kept up an insistent pressure, pushing him towards the outside door. "And you know I don't do anything I don't want to, brother. Now come on."

The door closed behind him, and he was startled at the heat and humidity rolling through the air. He looked around, shocked how nothing seemed familiar. His bike was in the right place, but instead of bright chrome and dark paint, it was a lump of fabric.

Following Retro over, he watched as the man took off the cover, using edges of the fabric to slap at dust that had settled on the seat. A battery-minder was plugged into a pigtail that hadn't been there before, and the idea of needing a battery charger in Alabama nearly made him laugh. He was familiar with them, sure, because East Coast winters were no joke. *Philly, sure, but 'Bama?*

"You been busy."

Retro tilted his head and cut over a look so filled with anger Einstein took a step back. "You wouldn't let me do anything else, brother. So I took it upon myself to do what you wouldn't see and couldn't complain about." Retro straightened, shoulders going back as he turned to face Einstein. "And the only thing you need to take out of this little sass session is your bike'll fuckin' start, so get your ass in the saddle, man."

Stalking past Einstein, Retro reached out and clasped his forearm, fingers tight around muscle and bone. There and gone, but piled onto the contact from before, it was the most he'd been touched in— *No, I'm not going there.*

The familiar blat of Retro's old-fashioned straight pipes filled the air, and Einstein hustled towards his ride, fumbling with the pigtail as he unplugged and set the cord from the charger aside. Then he slung a leg over the seat in a move that felt as natural as breathing, straightened the bike between his legs, and clicked the knob on the tank to activate the electronics.

Everything looked good.

Tank was full of fuel, neutral was lit up in green, and the whine of the injectors told him the bike was in working order. He strapped on his helmet and bounced experimentally, then leaned over to double-check the tires. Just as he was about to climb off and give them a kick, Retro's pipes blatted again, and he looked up to see his president and friend staring at him, helmeted head shaking back and forth slowly.

"Trust me," Retro mouthed, and Einstein could only nod in response.

He pressed his thumb to the button and the bike turned over as if he'd ridden it earlier that same day, as if there'd been no time between then and now. Einstein shoved that vicious blade deep inside him, holding on to the tiny bit of happiness that nothing would get between him and the wind today.

He'd been doing things the other way for months. Anything that brought him pleasure also carried pain, and up till now, it had been the bloody ribbons of self-hatred he clung to hardest.

He rolled past the two vehicles in the driveway, steadfastly ignoring them, disregarding their dusty condition, more proof that he'd been sucked into a time vortex and hadn't been able to escape. Retro waited patiently at the edge of the road, and Einstein pulled up as if to T-bone the man's bike, leaning far over his handlebars to shout, "Where are we headed?"

Retro stared at him, then shrugged, the somber expression not leaving his face. "No destination," he called back. "Just...forward."

Einstein kicked his bike back a few inches and nodded, rolling onto the pavement behind Retro as they rode up the street.

This? No decisions, no reminders of what he'd lost, just paying attention to his brother's signals and rolling free. He could do this.

I've had worse days.

***

Hand slackening on the throttle, Einstein allowed a gap to develop between Retro's bike and his, having only now realized where this section of the road would take them.

It had been a good day. They'd run two tanks of fuel through the bikes, gone nearly state to state in their west-to-east and back-to-west trek, and played for hours on the small, curving roads through the national forests surrounding Birmingham. Lunch had been cold beer and hot burgers at a roadside diner where the matronly waitress served up the food along with a side of jokes and good humor.

And now, they were two minutes from rounding a curve after which the clubhouse would be on the right-hand side of the road.

Einstein had no doubts the route was intentional. Oh, not during the ride. That had been pure chance, flipping coins occasionally to pick a left- or right-hand turn. But now Retro was going to demand something from Einstein he didn't know if he could pay.

You can and will, he imagined himself saying to someone else. *Brothers don't stop being brothers because of a loss.* Einstein knew if he walked into the clubhouse, there'd be no dancing around him on eggshells. His brothers would take his presence at face value and assume it signaled a willingness to resume his former life. They wouldn't squawk over feelings, or how shitty it was to lose loved ones. They'd be as supportive as he allowed, their love as good as gold.

I don't think I can.

Retro twisted around in his seat and glowered over his back fender to fix Einstein with a long, firm gaze.

Bossman thinks I can do this.

He nodded and rocked the throttle, closing the distance within seconds. The whole time Retro kept that stare pinned on Einstein's face, until his front wheel was in line beside Retro's rear wheel. Only then did Retro return his gaze to the road, opening up in a curve in front of them.

A couple of minutes later, Retro's left hand lifted, palm forwards, and Einstein downshifted as they steered into the clubhouse parking lot. Up near the building, he paused, waiting as Retro backed his bike in. Then Einstein took his turn, parking three bikes down the row in what had become his spot, and clearly had been held open and waiting for him, as no fresh wheel tracks disturbed the dust and gravel.

These Bastards. He shook his head as he removed his helmet and goggles, letting them dangle from the handlebars by their straps. After standing up off the bike, he took two steps towards Retro to meet him in the middle and wrapped tension-filled arms around his brother. *God, this hurts. Why does it fucking hurt?* "Thank you, Jerry. I didn't—" He stuttered, voice cracking on every word. "Fuck, man, just thanks."

"I got you, brother." Retro's hold on him tightened, then released. As Einstein stepped backwards, Retro lightly smacked him on the side of the head. The blow stung in a good way, the physical pain nearly welcome after so much emotional turmoil. "*We* will always have your back."

"I know." Einstein tipped his head to hide the wave of emotion crashing over him. Thumbnail against his brow, he pressed hard, then sniffed, and sighed heavily. "I know, brother. All I ever need to do is reach out my hand and the club will be there. All this is on me, and I get where I fell down. It's just fuckin' hard." The flight portion of his panic was in full bloom, and he fought the urge to run, to climb back on the bike and go fast.

"Did you know my first old lady died in a drive-by? That's how I'm tied to Petr Volkov. Did you know that bit of my past?"

The segue didn't make sense, and still struggling to contain his emotions, Einstein simply shrugged, not certain how to respond. Forcing himself to pay attention, he offered, "Only pieces, brother. Stood in your house as you glared down Chulpayev. Heard the bits that were tossed around there."

"She died because her father was ambitious, and it was common knowledge that he was working to hook me deep, even before I met his Clara." Retro's throat muscles worked, jaw clenching tightly. "*My* Clara."

The declaration burst out on a rising tone, and Einstein paid attention as Retro lowered his shoulders, stretching out the fingers of each hand before continuing.

"My first love. I had to say goodbye to her in a fuckin' ICU, denied my chance to be at her side when she passed." Brow deeply furrowed, Retro leaned close, hand on Einstein's shoulder as he gripped hard. "It *is* fuckin' hard. Consuming. I don't know your brand of hard, but if it's anything like mine was, it'll tear you up. Make you wish for peace. Any kind of peace, even one that's fuckin' final. Thing is, that peace you might find will surely leave scars behind for everyone else. So when I say we have you, brother, I mean we fuckin' *have you*. Good or bad. You get fucked up in your head so bad you can't breathe, and we'll breathe for you. My hand to God on that, man. We're here, and we're not goin' anywhere."

"All right." Pressing his lips together tightly, Einstein stared at the ground. Retro's scarcely contained anger and pain resonated inside him. Even if he'd been toying with the idea of bailing and just going home, there was no way he could do so after Retro's speech. *Might as well get it all done in an evening.* "All right," he repeated. "Let's go inside." Swiping the back of a hand across his forehead, he cleared his throat and muttered, "Wanna get out of this heat."

"Yeah." Retro sounded surprised, as if he'd been ready for more of a fight. "Let's head in there." He hesitated. "You ready, brother?"

"Fuck no." Einstein's head wobbled from the force of his headshake. "Fuck no, I'm not ready for any of this. But I need it, and I know that now."

"Yeah." Now Retro's tone was more sober, resigned. "Yeah, you fuckin' do," he said, and pulled open the door, gesturing for Einstein to precede him inside.

It took a minute for his eyes to adjust to the dimness inside, but by the time that had happened, he was surrounded. Mudd pulled him into an embrace, the shorter man cradling Einstein's head in his hand, pulling him down for a whispered, "Well met, brother." Then he was gone, and Marlin took his place with another tight hold around his shoulders and a pound against his back, and then Crazy Mike stood there, followed by another member, and another.

Few words were exchanged, no emotional sentiments delivered, but still the depths of shared pain these men held resonated deep inside him. *Validation's for parking,* he thought, trying to distract his brain, and yet it circled back around. Understanding that these men realized what he'd lost, knew even if they had never experienced the same, told him that they wouldn't hold his months-long silence against him. *Maybe it's just the support—* He cut off that lying thought too. It wasn't the way these men supported him that made the club special; it was the men themselves. Every one of them had a story, some that like Retro's might be surprisingly similar to Einstein's. Regardless of that story, the way each man cleaved to the club and their brothers was what made the Bama Bastards the best motorcycle club in the state. *Hell, in the nation.*

Einstein followed Retro farther into the room. "Thanks, Retro." *For getting my ass out of the house, for the ride, for giving a shit, and for forcing me to take off my blinders and see my brothers clearly.* Grinning knowingly, Retro flipped a hand at him in dismissal, then lifted two fingers to his mouth and blew out with a piercing whistle.

"Need to unass and get me a fuckin' beer, prospect. Points to whoever makes it to me first." Mouth snapping closed after his verbal challenge,

Retro stared at him with a grin, one hand stretched out to the side, waiting. By Einstein's count, it was less than a minute before a bottle pressed to Retro's palm, but his president still shook his head. "New boys never gonna live up to your brand of hustle, brother." Einstein accepted a bottle from the same unfamiliar prospect, nodding his thanks. "Let's get settled. Got some shit you're gonna be interested in, no doubt."

Aiming for a cluster of seating along the wall, Retro led the way across the wide room, but even while traipsing through the middle of the crowd, Einstein didn't feel like he was on display, something he'd been worried about. After the greetings near the door, the other members had scattered, going back to their interrupted activities as conversations slowly returned to normal levels. Mudd trailed along with them, a step behind Einstein, his presence and location a familiar comfort.

Got my back. He knew that was the silent message and appreciated how each of the men had handled his abrupt reentry into their lives. Settling into an overstuffed chair, Einstein propped one boot against the table placed in the center of the furniture, watching as Retro and Mudd took their own seats. "What am I going to be interested in?" Might as well lead with the teaser Retro had thrown out at him. "And why exactly do you think I'd be interested?"

"We got a line on Scar."

Einstein's lungs quit working, and he struggled to blow out the breath he'd just sucked down. Throat burning as he choked, head buzzing, he bent double, chin to his chest, and forced out a tiny stream of air.

Scar was also known as Lou, also known as Dominic Scarloucci.

Scar, president of the Monster Devils MC, out of Philadelphia. Einstein's old club, the one he'd taken a beatout from to move his family to Birmingham.

Scar was a man Einstein had last seen months ago. Eight, to be exact. The man's mouth had been forming broken words of regret that had meant nothing as he'd placed Lauren's dead body next to a bound and gagged Einstein. Helpless on the floor of a van, Einstein could only watch as that was followed by Makayla's tiny form. Both of his girls' faces had been flushed pink, almost as if they'd been too long under the summer sun, something Lauren never allowed, always slathering sunscreen on their daughter's delicate skin.

At some point before the funerals, he'd found out his girls had succumbed to unintentional carbon monoxide poisoning. They'd been transported to Florida separate from Einstein, so he'd only seen the rusted-out car once, but the memory was enough for him to assume a faulty exhaust system. Parked inside a building or somewhere out of view and reach from the wind, however it had happened—and no matter the men holding them captive hadn't intended it—his wife and daughter had died.

Lauren's lips had been bright red. He remembered that in his dreams. His dead wife's voice issued from between lips that looked like she was ready to go out on the town. *"Why?"* And damn him, but he had no answer.

Scar was the reason for their deaths. He might not have pulled a trigger or slashed across their throats, but if he had just left Einstein and his family alone, nothing would have happened.

After the funerals, Einstein had asked Retro one thing: *"Any news?"* The answer had been a slow headshake, nothing more or less than he'd expected. Scar had always been notorious for beating the odds, and the fact he hadn't been present when the Bama Bastards, along with four other MCs, had engineered Einstein's rescue meant he'd had foreknowledge they were coming.

Salt water dripped off Einstein's nose, and he clenched his jaw until the creaking of his teeth echoed inside his skull. Head down, Einstein stared at the chair cushion darkening from his streaming tears. Fingers like pinchers latched onto the outside of his legs in a search for enough physical pain to push past this, not finding it. Trying to retain any semblance of control, he was losing the fight to get through a series of wracking sobs that threatened to tear him in half. *Right in the middle of the fucking clubhouse.*

A hand landed on his shoulder, and he shrugged it off violently, not able to stand the touch. *It's better if I'm alone.* At least then, there wouldn't be anyone to blindside him like this.

"Brother. Jesus, man." Retro's voice was close, right in his ear, and he was tempted, so fucking tempted, to haul off and slug the man. Elbows to his knees, he folded in on himself, yanking on his hair in a painful cadence of repetitive movement.

"Brought me here for this, Jerry? I can't fucking do this. God, I hate you right now." Low and rough, his voice scratched across the air separating them. "You couldn't do this at my fuckin' house?"

"No, I couldn't, man. The man I chased out of that wrecked house this morning wasn't ready to hear anything to do with the tragedy that had split his heart in two. That man couldn't have stood to listen to me about anything." Retro's hand rested on his shoulder again, fingers digging into the leather, holding on against Einstein's repeated shrugs. "The man in front of me can handle it. I've got faith, brother. I got news and wanted to give it here, where you've got nothing but support. Every goddamned man in this room, in this club, only wants good for you. The best. That's what we can offer. You can and you will, man."

Fighting through the tears, swallowing only about half of the sobs twisting their way up his throat, he remained in his hunched position. And Retro stayed with him, unmoving, crouched next to the chair, hand on Einstein's shoulder, mouth next to his ear as he continued the litany of encouragement and chiding, alternating by turns as Einstein worked through the wreckage of his emotions. *Of my life.* He clenched his fingers in the fabric of his jeans, clamping hard enough each finger warped the fabric, seams stretched to the max as individual threads popped and snapped.

Something poked his ribs and he jerked sideways, deflecting hand flying up to slip inside his vest, straightening as he stroked over the toothbrush in the interior pocket. He moved it to a better position and rolled his back upright, his chin the last thing to lift as he sniffed and choked. *I hear ya, baby.* Lauren had been a fan of pinching his side, sometimes leaving bruises if he hadn't wanted to listen to her. *Like she's here.*

"What do you know?" Voice cracking on the final word, Einstein cleared his throat and reached for his beer, not surprised to find it warm. He grimaced and left it sitting on the table, glancing around as he reclaimed his seat. Mudd's expression was bland, showing neither annoyance nor sympathy, and Einstein nodded his thanks. Between Mudd's easy acceptance, and the realization no one was crowded close and staring, Einstein's next breath pushed out more steadily in a question, "That bastard raise his head somewhere?"

"We got word of a guy who saw him. I'm tracing it now." Retro lifted a finger, and a few seconds later, the same prospect who'd served them earlier was there with replacement bottles, gathering up the nearly full ones without comment. "Only problem is we got a second sighting that would put him in two places on the same weekend. El Paso and Philly aren't within waving distance of each other, which means one of these is bullshit."

"Home turf and that of the Silent Deaths?" Einstein sniffed and cleared his throat, pushing away the last vestiges of the grief that had nearly overwhelmed him. Ever present, but in this headspace it was manageable. He shook his head before he took a long swallow of the cold beer. "Given how things sit, neither is a healthy choice for Scar."

"True words," Mudd interjected. "We don't really believe either of them, which leaves us wondering where the man might really be headed. We are getting traces on that, too, best we can."

"If he's throwing down fake trails…" Einstein shook his head, surprised at how fuzzy his brain felt. *Fucking exhausted.* "Any thoughts on what that might mean?"

"Means he knows we're payin' good money for any lookie-loo reports of his ass, and he's just trying to give himself more time while costing us moola." Retro sipped his beer. "The question is for what reasons?"

"Stay out ahead of retribution?" Einstein tipped up the bottle, surprised at the enjoyment he was getting from this quiet back-and-forth with his friends. "Has he run through all his landing spots yet?"

"And then some." Mudd shifted in his seat. "Past few months it's been a cat-and-mouse game with him."

"Yeah," Retro agreed. "He pops up his head and we take a whack at him. Then the man disappears for a couple of days or weeks until we catch wind of some other lead. Few leads as specific as these two recent ones, though, even if only one of the sumbitches can be right."

"Who do you have chasing the reports?" He loved that he didn't have to question whether the club was committed to finding and wreaking chaos and destruction on the asshole who had cost Einstein so much. Even for the weeks and months he'd been sidelined by his own grief, it never crossed his mind to wonder if the search continued—because he knew it would. "Anything I can do, Retro?"

"Buzzkill's routed through Texas right now. He should rock up at the SDMC clubhouse tomorrow. We're doing an uninvited, unannounced visit." Retro grinned, the expression lacking any humor. "So to speak."

"And the Philly rumor?" He glanced around, looking for faces he recognized. Einstein was shocked to see three men he didn't know. One of them turned to face away, and instead of a probation bar across the top of his shoulders, the man had a full patch, only lacking the location rocker at the bottom. Einstein kept his surprised gaze on the man, who stood and chatted easily with Marlin.

"Nugget headed out this morning. About the time I rolled into your driveway." Retro's tone pulled Einstein's attention back to him. "And you don't know him any more than you know Dadwarc over there. Or Throttle. Or Wings. Changes happen, man." His tone was conciliatory but firm. "Things don't stop for anything or anyone."

"In eight months you patched four new members? They rounded through their prospect period and made it to patched member in that time? What the hell?" Einstein knew his tone was abrasive, even recognized he was too loud. *Don't give a shit.* "Who's the new probie, then? When's he patchin' in? Tomorrow?"

"Alex is in month three of his scrub period, so don't give him too much shit. He's doin' well, given the situation under which he raised his hand." Retro stared at him, not showing any frustration or anger at Einstein's questioning. "Nugget is a patchover, and there's been a few of those in the region. We picked him up from a Michigan club, but he's got close ties to the Rebel Wayfarers, good ones, which is never a bad thing. Throttle is over by Crazy Mike, mostly because he's just as much of a numbnut as Mike ever thought to be. Nugget, Throttle, Dadwarc, and Wings are members, but can't vote yet. I took a page out of the CoBos book with how they dealt with Po'Boy. They've got too much time and energy already spent in the life to prospect with grace, but for political reasons, they're also not yet enough of a known quantity to give them a voice." Now Retro's voice held a tiny edge of anger, but Einstein didn't know if it was the act of him questioning or if the need for answers was reminding Retro that Einstein hadn't been here to take part in any of the decisions. "I'm not stupid, Einstein, as much as you might think so."

Shit. He stared at the beer bottle in his hands, thumbnail raking up one edge of the label before he smoothed it down. *Now if I can just smooth this as easily.*

"I know you're not stupid. I didn't mean to imply anything like that, bossman. Just took me by surprise." He chanced a glance at Retro's face, finding only patience there. "Shit. I wasn't thinking. Tied up like I was for as long as I was? Gone deep down into my own shit. Shouldn't be a shocker that things change. I just need to learn to shut my trap until I wrap my head around it all."

"Brother, if you can't talk to us, then we've got problems." Mudd shrugged and winked at Einstein as he swung his gaze from Retro's carefully controlled face. "I for one am real glad to see your ugly mug in the house again. We've fuckin' missed you, man."

"I missed you too." Einstein leaned back as he realized the truth of that statement. Deep in the throes of grief, he might not have recognized the feeling. Now, removed at least slightly from the events, he realized losing his wife and child might have started his tip into the unstable field of agony—but losing the club at the same time had only added to it in great shovelfuls of pain. Didn't matter he'd done it to himself. Pushing his brothers away had been a mistake. "I've been struggling. Didn't even know how much." Blinking fast, he willed the heat at the back of his eyes away as best he could, clearing his throat painfully. "Feels really good to be home."

"And we're happy to have you." Retro leaned forwards, elbows on his knees as he stared at Einstein over the tips of his steepled fingers. "Gonna need you to listen to me for a minute. Just listen before you react. Seeing you like I got to today, I really don't think you'll do well if you go back to that house right now. I've taken the liberty of having a few of your things transferred to my old suite upstairs. School just started up again, so it'll be a rare day me and Trina have the luxury of a night away from the kiddos. Much rather use the space than have it stay empty."

Retro gestured towards the stairs, and Einstein cut a glance in that direction, then back to Retro's face, studying his features. With an expression turned calm and determined, Retro radiated patience mixed with a little bit of stubbornness, and Einstein knew any arguing would be futile.

"I'm not going to disagree. Clear statement of fact, brother." Might as well be graceful about his acceptance of Retro's high-handed behavior. "I don't need much in the way of things." He angled forwards slightly. He needed his friend to hear and comprehend his next words, because just the idea made him sick. "But I sincerely want people to leave my shit alone at home. I'll go through their things when I'm ready. Don't try to push me there, brother." His grief swelled, choking him, and he forced out the rest. "I won't have anyone touching Lauren's things but me. Makayla's either. That's on me, you hear?"

"Heard and understood, brother." Firm fingers wrapped around his hand, holding on tightly. He stared down at them, bemused. Rough, clean as working hands ever got, with calluses that reflected the hard labor the owner was familiar with. Retro shook his hand slightly, and Einstein brought his gaze up to meet that of his friend. With an earnest expression, Retro said, "I will *always* have your back, no matter what you need. I've got you, brother. On my life, I've got you."

Einstein stayed downstairs for a few more minutes, but when he made his excuses, he wasn't lying about being tired. It seemed weird he was as exhausted as he'd ever been, just from a few hours of riding and jawing with friends. *And being out of that house.* As much as he tried to ignore the truth of the thought, he couldn't. If he'd stayed home, he would have slept much of the day, so with that context, it did make sense that doing anything else would be taxing.

Door closed and locked, he studied the suite carefully, sweeping the room with his gaze. As anonymous as any hotel room, the space had only a small duffel bag on the foot of the bed to add any personality. Einstein unzipped the bag and shuffled through the few items inside: just enough clothing to span a handful of days, a half-full can of shaving cream, a razor and blades, bottle of shampoo and bodywash, and his toothbrush.

Einstein dropped the duffel and shoved his hand inside the vest pocket, his breathing coming jagged until he had the firm plastic stick in his grip. Running his thumbnail across the bristles, he stared around the room again. It was the work of moments to put everything away and kick the empty bag underneath the bed, hidden by the drape of the comforter. Toeing off his boots, he let them stay where they'd dropped as he turned to sit on the edge of the mattress.

He leaned backwards, allowing his torso to fall heavily onto the bed. Bringing one hand to rest on his chest with a sigh, he settled it between the panels of his vest and curled the clenched fist over his heart. Closing his eyes, he ran the edge of his thumbnail across the bristles again.

"Night, babies." His whisper fell flat in the room, air as empty of energy as a battery left unprotected in the coldest of winters.

"Love you."

Chapter Three
Marian

Crouched on the kitchen floor, Marian Threadgill cautiously rose to her knees and peered over the windowsill. The van was still parked in the front drive, two large men remaining seated inside the shadowy interior. She'd been able to see enough during her snatched glances to know they hadn't stopped staring in her direction, not since they had first pulled up in front of the house she shared with her father.

The screen door creaked. Then there was the thud of a tool belt hitting the floor, and finally a muffled curse followed by a canine cry of pain. All of these noises from the back of the house told Marian her father was home. He would have driven in the back drive, coming down from the church on the mountain instead of up from town like their visitors. *His visitors.* She didn't have anyone to visit her.

Not anymore.

Until a few months ago, Marian's younger sister Myrtle had been dropping by. Infrequently, but still visits Marian had come to anticipate. And until a couple of weeks ago, their younger brothers would have been wrestling their way through the house, but not now. Marian knew without being told what had happened when old man Sallabrook had driven away with Luke, Thad's head popping into view over the top of the pickup truck's tailgate. Since then, the silence in the house had only been interrupted by her father's fits of anger, growing in frequency.

Now he was home, with visitors in the front drive, and Marian wondered if it was finally her turn to be sold or given away.

"Papa." Her call was quiet, solemn, as far away from strident as she could make it. "There're men in front of the house."

"What are you doin', girl?" Floyd Threadgill paused in the doorway before striding quickly over to where she crouched in front of the window. Marian pointed out the glass to where the two visitors were climbing out of the vehicle, as if in answer to some silent signal. "Cowering like your momma." The boney part of his knuckles hit the side of her head almost desultorily, a casual strike she didn't have time to avoid. Ears ringing from the blow, she still heard his snarled, "Useless cowards."

"Yes, Papa." Marian rolled her lips between her teeth, holding still with the mouse's hope of not being seen. The next hits were across her upper back, fists landing hard and fast, overbalancing and sending her sprawling with a cry.

Her father moved away, leaving the house by the front door as Marian pulled her feet back underneath herself. Wheezing with pain, she'd stayed in place, crouched behind the windowsill, and hadn't quite found the courage to move from her place when the front door reopened.

This is it.

She didn't bother to turn around, didn't dare glance towards the movement, not until she realized there were only two sets of footsteps.

Pivoting slowly, she lifted her chin and stared up at the most frightening men she'd ever seen. With their broad shoulders, thick, dark hair, and hardened faces, they could have been brothers. They smelled of fuel and smoke, and the air around them reeked of danger.

Marian couldn't move. Couldn't breathe. She waited for her father to enter behind them and finish what had to be a handoff. He needed money, she knew, the phone message machine lately filled with calls from men with hard voices and blatant demands.

He did it. He finally did it.

She'd expected him to leverage her existence years ago, but he hadn't, and things had stayed in a rut. A safe rut compared to what had happened to her sister. A painful rut when her father remembered the useless nature of having a daughter like Marian, meek and retiring, with a voice too soft to listen to and little to no skills in housework, according to him. Useless and a burden.

"Marian?" The one with longer hair spoke her name like a question, his voice deceptively gentle, but she stayed frozen. "Myrt's sis? Are you Myrtle's sister?"

Her heart pounded in her ears, head gone dizzy with a sudden escalation of fear. "Is she okay?" She slapped a palm over her blurting mouth, mind veering to the worst possible scenario. *Oh, God. She's dead.* Listening at the door when old man Sallabrook had come to talk to her father had given her part of the story, enough to know Myrt had been alive when she'd left the old man. But Myrtle had been gone for weeks and weeks. On her own for days and hours filled with risk and danger, all alone out in the world. "She's been gone so long." Biting her lips, Marian tried to steady her voice. "Is she okay?"

The man who'd spoken to her smiled, the soft expression changing his features, taking him from brooding to beautiful in an instant. "Yeah, Myrt's good. She's real good. She's here in town. We came to pick up your brothers, and I promised her I'd stop by and check on you."

"Asshole's stirring, brother." The other man spoke, his voice deep and rough, like gravel in a streambed. "Why don't you get Myrt on the phone, let the girls talk. I'll go deal with this piece of shit."

"Good idea, Gunny." As the one called Gunny exited through the open door, the first man hunkered down near Marian. He kept his gaze fixed on her face as he pulled a phone out of his pants pocket. Tension flooded her muscles, and he made a cooing sound. "Shhh. Be easy, Marian. I'll get Myrt on the phone. She can tell you what's going down." While he fiddled with the phone, she heard a cut-off shout from the front of the house, but when Marian would have risen to look out the window, he dropped a hand on her shoulder, the unexpected contact and light pressure enough to keep her crouched. "Baby, I'm here with Marian. Yeah, she's okay. She looks okay. Scared to death of us, but she's good. Wanna talk to her and explain what we're doing?" The tiny pauses in his words were just enough to indicate the coherence of a conversation, but Marian couldn't hear anything from the other end. "Here." He thrust the phone her direction. "Myrt said, 'Don't be scared,' and she wants to talk to you."

The tears started bubbling over before she had the phone next to her head, so her voice was unsteady when she asked, "Myrtle?"

"Oh, Marian. Yes, it's me." Her sister's voice held a tiny hitch as she responded. *Joy, not sorrow.* Marian had become adept at telling the difference and was surprised to hear joy from her sister. After the years Myrtle had spent at Sallabrook's beck and call, true sorrow had often suffused her words. This was a change, and a welcome one. "The man with you right now is Bane. He's good, Marian, so good. True blue, just like we always talked about."

"Really?" True blue would have been the best of the best, according to their moonlit giggling conversations, before the world had begun collapsing in on Marian in all the worst ways. "You trust him?" Swiping at her nose with the back of her hand, Marian sniffled. "He's good?"

"So good, Marian. More than I knew a man could be. He and his friends have been everything I needed, all along the way. I've got Luke and Thad here, and I'm taking them away with me. I won't leave them for Ian. I can't believe our daddy could do that to these boys. Won't let it keep happening." Steel laced Myrtle's voice, a trembling rage that sounded barely banked. "I want you with us. Want you to come back with us. Leave our daddy. I miss you, sister. Will you come with us?"

Marian stared at her knees pressed to the bare floor. A floor she'd scrubbed with harsh soap and a handheld brush every week since she gained double digits. *Decades.* She didn't have to see it to reflect on the room around her, walls filled with cheap dime-store plaster quotes about a good life mixed with the mounted heads of dead deer. Taxidermied deer and fish held pride of place. Not a picture of her or her siblings existed in this space, nothing to say they were valued or treasured. Nothing to say the lives of their mothers had been noteworthy.

Tears ran down her face freely, pattering on the fabric of her dress, dampening the cheap weave. The week-old bruises across her back ached, and she knew if she didn't make a change, more of the same awaited her this week or the next. The fact her father would use his feet and fists on her was inevitable. *What if it wasn't?*

That was what Myrtle offered. A chance to change the course of her life.

"Yes." With a broken sob, Marian accepted, praying it was the right choice.

She lifted her gaze to see the man Bane staring at her, understanding and a reflected pain visible on his features. Myrtle was crying as Marian handed him back the phone. She watched as he curled around the device as if he could physically comfort her sister, like it killed him a little not to be able to right whatever was wrong in her world.

Marian pulled in a hard breath, waking the pain of her spine and ribs more acutely, and embraced the knowledge that this was the last time she'd bear bruises from a man. *Never again.*

"You ready, Marian?" Bane tucked the phone back into the pocket of his pants, then climbed to his feet. Towering over her, he held out a hand, and Marian knew it was symbolic, but she clasped her palm to his anyway. He pulled her upright. "Let's get your shit." Glancing around the room, he pointed over his shoulder at the hallway leading towards the back of the house. "Your room back there somewhere?"

She began walking, listening to the echoing footfalls following her. He stopped in the open doorway without an actual door as Marian scooped her small selection of clothing out of the cardboard box shoved against the wall. A few shopping bags hung on a hook near the door, and she took them down, ignoring how her fingers shook. It only took a few minutes before everything she treasured was bagged and ready to go outside.

Bane took it all from her, not letting her carry anything. He steered her through the house and out the front door, placing her belongings near the threshold. His hand was gentle on her arm as he angled them past where her father stood near the front porch, shouting garbled words at the sky. Gunny stood close beside him, massive hand clamping her father's wrist in a tight twist up against the middle of his back.

Bane didn't move from her side as he said, "Her shit's inside, brother. Get it, yeah?"

Gunny did something to pull a pained cry from her father before shoving him to one side. Gunny turned towards the house as Bane opened the side door of the van, his hand out to steady her as she stepped up into the vehicle. His voice was soft when he told her, "Don't look, honey. Not anything you want to see, promise."

Marian stared at him as he pulled the door closed between them, then angled to look out the windows opposite where the house stood. She kept that position as the back doors opened, plastic rustled and rustled again, and the doors slammed shut. Gunny climbed in the front seat and positioned himself to fill the space, reducing her field of vision even further.

"Good girl. Don't look, Maid Marian. There's nothing left for you here, and you don't have to give an ounce of yourself to that asshole ever again." Gunny's words swelled in volume as he continued talking, filling up the passenger cabin until no sounds from outside could penetrate. *He's making sure I don't hear whatever Bane's doing to Daddy.* "Sharon, my wife? She's down in Florida with our friends who are also helping Myrt. I can call her if you need a woman's voice, honey. Breathe easy. Just breathe easy. There's nothing to fear with me and Bane, promise you. Stop shakin', honey. You're safe." Marian folded her fingers together, pressing tightly to hide the trembling.

"I'm safe." She mouthed the words as she kept her eyes aimed out the windows she'd already chosen, holding herself tightly until Bane opened the driver door and levered himself inside.

"Yeah, honey. You're safe now. Fuckin' promise you're safe. Only gonna have good from here on out. You're gonna love Sharon. Vanna and her old man Truck, too. Myrt loves them already." Gunny spoke about people using strange terms and names, as if she'd known them her entire life. The way he normalized Marian needing rescue from her own family loosened the noose around her neck, letting each breath come a little easier. "Vanna stumbled on Myrt when the gal was sleeping rough in a park, similar to how I met the woman. Her trail name is Peepers—Vanna, not Myrt. That woman's a gem, and she's got a thousand stories about her hikes. You'll have to ask her about them, Maid Marian."

"Old maid, maybe." Marian spoke her truth. "Thank you both."

"Maid to me, and there's nothing to thank us for. We're just doin' the right thing. The human thing. Takin' care of someone who's got a need. It's how I was raised. Plus Vanna, she'd have my hide if I did anything but. We're not blood, but she's like a grandma to my kids. Me and Sharon have three so far." Gunny kept talking, still loud, still leaning back into her space as if she might float away if he wasn't there to keep her focused. "Vanna rescued my Shar, too. You should know that. Woman is too good for this world."

Marian smiled and nodded but stayed silent, still looking out the window. She kept to the same as they drove away. Looking ahead, never back.

About time.

***

Einstein

"When'll you be back?" As he asked the question, Einstein glanced over the bags Retro and Mudd had slung against the wall near the front door. "You got any idea, or is this an open-ended run?"

It wasn't typical for their president and VP to head out together, not since they'd made the run to bring him home. *Almost a year ago.* Not that he was aware of, anyway. At least not in the three months since he'd moved into the clubhouse. They'd both been around a lot, seemingly working their agenda of keeping Einstein busy.

Einstein hadn't been idle since moving in. Far from it.

He'd thrown himself into helping any of their brothers with any stated need and had forced himself on a few who hadn't wanted to acknowledge what they had going on. Bike repairs, general home maintenance, bodyguard work—anything was better than sitting in the upstairs suite alone with his memories.

"Need a third?" He took a backwards step towards the stairs. "I can be ready in two minutes."

"No idea how long, probably no more than a week, and no, I need you *here,* brother. Need you takin' care of shit like you've been doin'." Retro gestured towards the prospect and called, "Get me a soda, yeah?" He turned to Mudd. "Brother, you want anything?"

"Water'd be good." Mudd walked towards the furniture grouping they often used for their conversations. "Wet my whistle before gettin' in the wind." Einstein trailed behind him, glancing over his shoulder to verify Retro was following. Mudd continued, "We're headed to the panhandle."

"Texas?" Einstein was surprised. They were friendly with clubs in Texas, but mostly east and south, with El Paso being the farthest location of which he was aware. "Amarillo? Who you talkin' to there?"

"Naw," Retro drawled, taking the bottle of soda from the prospect with a nod of thanks. The pause was enough to heighten Einstein's nerves. Retro didn't look at him as he finished with, "Florida."

Every one of his muscles locked tight. He attempted to swallow and couldn't. Tried to breathe without success. Struggled to look away from the expression of sympathy on Retro's features but was forced to watch as it morphed into alarm. "Breathe, brother." Retro gripped the side of Einstein's neck hard and yanked him forwards, a heavy weight on his shoulders folding him in half. "Fuckin' breathe." Retro's voice held nothing but fear, and the idea he was causing that emotion in his best friend was enough to break the stasis.

Air rushed from Einstein's lungs in a giant whoosh. That was followed by an embarrassingly loud pant for another breath, and another. Slowly, he pulled himself back under control, straightening as he looked around the room, eyes directed anywhere except focusing on the two men who had witnessed his moment of weakness.

"Oh, brother," Retro said softly, leaning his head to press their foreheads together. "When you gotta fall apart, this is the safest place to do it, and you know it, man." Eyes closed, he whispered, "We got your back in everything."

"Even when I'm a weak-ass coward?" He pulled away and glared at Retro. If they'd asked him to ride with them now, he would have refused. Florida was a no-go zone for him and likely would be for the foreseeable future. "Shit, man, that just caught me by surprise."

"I get it. I do. But that ain't why we need you to stay here, man. Need you here because you're what's needed for these new members and our prospects. Everything's lookin' up since you agreed to take on the clubhouse like you have." Retro reclaimed his seat and gestured around the room. "Love what you've done with the place."

"Take on the clubhouse?" Einstein refused to think beyond the moment when they'd leave today. If he could play ostrich, it would be okay. No more embarrassment for him, no more difficulty for anybody. Just keep up the easy softball questions until they walked out the door. "What does that even mean?"

"Saved me, brother." Mudd drawled out the words with a trace of laughter at the end. "You know how much I hate the scheduling and ordering, and you took it on like a champ. Entirely happy with how that turned out for me."

"True story. This man is a born organizer." Retro nodded. He spoke to the prospect who still hovered nearby. "Bring Einstein his usual, yeah? Then you can be released." The man scurried away, a hustle in his steps that made Einstein proud of his coaching. "That's all on you, too, Einstein, and don't think I don't know it. Having a persistent presence around here that's willin' to enforce what's needed like puttin' men in the 'round when they deserve it—that'll give us better members in the end. Thank you, brother."

"I'm just doing my part." He held up a hand, taking the energy drink can from the prospect. "Make sure the downstairs bathroom is stocked, pros. From the chatter I've heard, we have a bunch of brothers inbound. Stay ahead of stocking the bar, too, yeah?" The man nodded and flashed him a smile before trotting straight to the hallway that held the club's private office and public bathroom. "That reminds me. Does it bother anyone that the door to the bathroom is across the hall from the office? We could open up a door from this room and close that one off. Would mean visitors wouldn't have any reason at all to be close to the club's office. Easier to keep track of folks."

Retro pursed his lips as he nodded slowly. "Had that thought myself many a time, but never had someone I felt would be responsible for the project." He leaned forwards and slapped his palm against the low coffee table that separated their chairs. "Make it so, Einstein. Make it so."

"Gonna hit the bank on our way out of town. I'll get them to send you a signature request. That'll let me put you on the account. That way you don't have to wait on my ass before you write a check for shit." Mudd twisted the top off his water and took a long drink, ending on a loud, "Ahhhhh." He grinned. "Make my life a fuckton easier, I tell you what."

"We all do whatever's needed." Einstein opened and drank half the can in one go, holding still as he waited for the zing of energy from the chemicals and natural ingredients in the mixture. It was early in the day yet, but if he ingested enough of the drinks, he'd guarantee himself a sleepless night. *Which means a dreamless one.* His heart rate sped up, and he nodded. "Happy to serve the club, brothers."

Retro stared at him, the expression on his face searching. Einstein locked their gazes together, trying to project confidence and steadiness. By Retro's headshake, he didn't think he'd been successful. "You sleepin' at all, brother?" And by that question, he knew he hadn't.

"Yeah." Einstein shrugged. "Some. Probably not as much as I should, but more than I was at first."

That was no lie.

The first few weeks of staying in the clubhouse had been a reverse reflection of his previous depressed hibernation existence. Instead of too tired to do anything except breathe—and some days that had been questionable—beginning with the first day he'd woken in the strange bed, he'd been filled with anxious energy—an unbroken desire to stuff every instant of every day with activity. The clubhouse had definitely benefited, and he didn't think anyone would complain.

"Still losin' weight, though. You gotta eat, my man." Mudd's statement wasn't finger-pointing, just stating truth as he saw it. "Belt of yours doesn't lie."

Einstein didn't bother glancing down, knowing exactly what Mudd was talking about. The heavily worn and creased hole where his belt had notched for years was two beyond where he currently wore it, and that current hole was nearly too loose. *Is already too loose if I got much change in my pockets.* He nodded and paid lip service to what he knew Mudd and Retro wanted to hear. "I'm workin' on it."

"Well, work harder. Don't make me sic a prospect on your ass." Retro slapped the table again, then sat back in his chair. "Because I'll have a motherfucker set a timer and remind you if I gotta."

"Yes, boss." Einstein glanced away, looking at the members gathered near the bar and pool tables. "Anything special going on here while you're gone?" As long as he didn't focus on where they were headed, he could keep breathing. "What's the goal with your trip?"

"Rebels and Riders are arguing about territory. If what happens that I think'll happen, Bastards need to be there to not only witness, but stake a claim ourselves." Einstein's attention snapped back to Retro, who held up a palm. "Not in opening another chapter. Fuck no. I do not need that shit, man. But if either of those clubs or anyone else who's going to be present think to open a charter, then they'll need patchover men to fill the ranks. IMC's gonna be there, too, and you know how Twisted is about his territory. He's already got a panhandle presence, but with the Rebels takin' over the Jailbreakers, those two are butting up against each other all the fuckin' time now. Personally, I'd like to see Blackie win the toss, because not only is he a stable leader, but he's got good men under him."

"Why's the focus on that area?" *Fuck, I can't even say the state now?* Jesus, he was being ridiculous. Huffing out an angry breath, he forced out, "Florida, I mean."

"Rebels have a member who lives there in Baker. Truck doesn't spend his time in Little Rock anymore, preferring to keep close to home. He and Vanna have a place there." Retro laughed. "A couple of places, but Blackie doesn't like to talk about the second home they're not using. Whatever."

"So Rebels are looking to start a new chapter?" If only a single member was in play, that would explain the need to do patchovers to fill in the gaps. "That doesn't make a lot of sense."

"Well, Bane is one of Blackie's boys in the Freed Riders. And Gunny's in play now, so that's two Rebels to one Rider." Mudd shook his head and drained his water, crumpling the plastic in one fist. "And our master of information here forgot about the CoBos also comin' to play. Gonna be a pocketful of players all jostling for position."

"You're thinking of throwing one of our members into the mix, too?" Einstein ran names through his head. "Can't think of anyone who's already got a…a Florida connection." The state's name came easier that time, rolling off his tongue with hardly a hesitation. "Who you looking at?"

"Who you lookin' at?"

Mudd's attempt at mimicry butchered Einstein's accent, something he hadn't realized had thickened while they spoke. It only came out these days when he was stressed, and since he knew the men around him saw it as a barometer, the Philly accent was something he tried hard to control. "Fuck you, I don't sound like that."

"Fuck you." Mudd tried again, then laughed hard. "Too easy, brother. You're too easy sometimes. Monday."

Einstein flinched. Monday was a fairly new member, well over his year of integration, so he was a full patch with a voice, always well received by the members. "Would hurt to lose him, man."

"Love his connections, and we wouldn't lose him. Not really. He'd answer to a new president, but the intent would be to keep those lines of communication as open as possible, without compromising his honor or affiliations." Retro shrugged. "Like Po'Boy being a full member of the CoBos but still tight with his old friends. IMC hasn't hurt for him patching out. If anything, it's tightened the already close relationship between the two clubs."

"Gotcha." Thoughts rolled through his head, and he picked out the most troubling. "Any idea which club will come out on top? Rebels are allies, but man, they're exploding overseas, too. Does it make sense for them to spin up a new chapter there when they've already got the other ones nearby?"

"Like I said, I'm personally rooting for Blackie's man. We'll see." Retro stood and stretched, his head swinging side to side as he surveyed the inside of the clubhouse's main room. "Leavin' my house in good hands." A palm fell to the top of Einstein's shoulder, gripping tightly as Mudd stood too. "Faith in ya, brother."

"I'll keep it safe." He pushed to his feet and walked towards the front door, depositing his empty can next to where Retro and Mudd placed their trash. *It's the little things.* Clearing their own garbage meant respect to the club, but also respect to the men aiming at a better life as a Bama Bastard, because otherwise, the prospects would be on cleanup duty. Einstein nodded his approval at how easily Retro and Mudd modeled the kind of club they wanted from the ground up. "My oath, brothers."

Their bikes grew small in the distance by the time Einstein turned to reenter the clubhouse, finding Crazy Mike standing beside him. "Brother," he offered, meeting the extended fist with a closed-knuckle bump. "How you doing?" *Shit, there's my accent again.* Einstein shook his head. "Don't start, man. Mudd already gave me enough grief for two men. Let's go inside."

"Not sure Einstein is the right name for you, but couldn't any one of us argue with Retro when he picked it." Crazy Mike followed him through the door, closing the distance as they entered the main room. "Bronx woulda been better."

"Except I'm not from the Bronx." A quick sweep of the room showed him everyone was still in pretty much the same places they'd been before. "Philly, born and bred."

"I knew that, but we can't call you Philly. That's a female horse. That'd be weird, brother."

"That's a different— Know what, never mind." He sighed. "Something you needed, brother?"

"Yeah, I didn't want to distract Retro with it."

Einstein stiffened, because Mike starting a conversation like that wasn't conducive to continued relaxation. "Oh?"

"Yeah. Got some word from Georgia." Mike lifted one shoulder. "Might not be anything."

"His extended family?" Retro's old lady had family in Atlanta, and yet another branch that wrote in Cyrillic. "Which Georgia, brother?"

"The States version. Not sure what it means, just that Chulpayev is asking for information on the group on the East Coast."

Swinging slowly to face Crazy Mike, Einstein narrowed his eyes and waited.

"He's digging into info about Scarloucci, man, but not Dominic. His old man."

"And you didn't think to raise this as a topic before our president and VP rolled off the lot on a little bitty road trip?" Not attempting to modulate his tone, Einstein made certain everyone within earshot—

which was anyone on the main floor of the house—could hear not only every word but the incredulity flooding his system. "Are you fucking insane? We call you Crazy Mike because of how you are with a little booze in you, man. Not because you're certifiable. What the fuck, brother?"

"I tried to tell Retro before you came downstairs. He was focused on whatever shit is happening with the RWMC and IMC." Crazy Mike gave Einstein wide eyes, looking utterly deranged. "Told me to talk to you. So that's what I'm doin', brother. Talkin' to you."

"Okay, let's head into the office." Einstein gestured towards the hallway. "Bossmen are stopping at a couple of places before they get out of town, so if I think they need to come back, we've got a few minutes at least." He opened the office with the key Mudd had given him weeks ago and made his way around the desk, taking a seat before he spoke again. "Shut that," he said, pointing first at the door and then towards the straight-backed chair facing the desk. "And sit." Once Mike was perched on the edge of the seat, Einstein leaned back and stared at him. "Talk."

"Chulpayev put out a call that has made its way into our network." Mike started the kind of efficient info dump Retro had drilled into all of them through the years. "The ask is for info on Luciano, not Scar and not Franco, the grandfather. Unsure what the interest in the unblooded generation is."

Franco was old-school, second-generation mafia, first-generation immigrant from the old country. He'd hung around the Monster Devils just enough for Einstein to know him on the surface. If Einstein had given any thought to the old man after Scar had taken him and his family, it would have been to wonder at what reaction he would have given to the idea of bringing family into the argument as Scar had. His focus hadn't been on the old man, though, and he'd paid absolutely no attention to the man who stood between the generations.

Luciano had disavowed the associations his own father treasured, moving well out of the line of fire by political positioning as well as geography. He'd married a woman from the west, another thing that further divided him from his father. Franco had turned his back on his noncompliant offspring, focusing his attention on the tight-knit group of men in his crew.

As Don, it should have been an embarrassment that his only child had disavowed the family business, but somehow, the old man had turned it into a positive for his outfit. That had only grown when his grandson Dominic had angled his way back into the fold, making his bones as underboss for a capo of a splinter group. Then Lou had brought that splinter home and carved out his own piece of the pie in the form of the Monster Devils, an MC with an enviable sense of being untouchable.

That was the group that had drawn Einstein in, back when he'd still been just Jimmy. The club had made him feel invincible. Young and stupid, he hadn't paid enough attention to the jobs they were asked to do, things that had nothing to do with the club itself and everything to do with the older Scarloucci's business. Even after he'd met and married Lauren, he'd stayed in the club. Turning a blind eye to the inner workings of the club's leadership, he'd spent years defending the club to his wife, until the birth of Makayla had set the tone for his exit.

Leaning over the bassinet, Jimmy stared down at the tiny bundle of blankets. He dipped a finger into the folds—pink and white, so soft to the touch— and drew back the edges until he could see his daughter's face. "She's so small," he whispered, unable to pull his gaze away to look at Lauren.

Laughing, she told him in a normal voice, "She's not little. Nearly seven pounds, honey."

"That's little, Laur." The small face scrunched up, and the little girl made a sound. "She's scrunchy." He kept staring. His daughter opened her eyes and blinked. "Hey there, little girl." Her face scrunched again, and she emitted a small wail. "Oh, no no, baby girl. Shush, now." Glancing up at Lauren, he asked, "What do I do?"

She smiled. "She's probably hungry. Bring her here."

He looked at the legs of the bassinette, finding them flat and unhelpful. He tried to grip the sides, but the molded plastic felt slippery, and he was afraid he'd drop the whole contraption. Using his feet and hands, he scooted it a few inches towards the bed where Lauren was.

"Silly. Just pick her up." Lauren was giggling now, not trying to hide her amusement.

"How?"

Lauren made a scooping motion with both hands.

He looked back down, measuring the distance between the bottom and top of the blanketed bundle. "What if I drop her?"

"Don't," she stated, as if that was something entirely under his control. Another glance at his wife showed her smile had spread ear to ear. "Just pick her up, Jimmy."

So he did. Slowly, he wedged his hands under the squirmy body and lifted, adjusting carefully as he held her a few inches over the bottom of the bassinette, ensuring he had a secure grip.

"Hold her against your chest," his wife coached, and he'd brought Makayla tight to his body as emotions flooded through him. "Now, bring her to me."

Jimmy shuffled the few feet to the bed, then rebuffed his wife's attempts to retrieve their daughter from his arms. Makayla was snuffling now, turning her head towards him, and he stared at her face, mesmerized by each sound and movement. "She's so pretty." Lauren's hand covered Makayla's chest, a finger dragging the blanket down a little farther, and a hand peeked out, tiny fingers curled around the edge of the fabric. "Oh, honey, she's so pretty."

Noises in the hallway had him handing over the baby fast. Lauren had scarcely taken their daughter when the door burst open, a handful of men spilling into the room, Scar at the head of the group.

"Where's my goddaughter?" His question set up a racket in Jimmy's head, because in no way did he want his daughter connected with this man. With any of these men.

"Get out." Arms outstretched, he urged the men back towards the door. "Get the fuck out. Baby's sleeping. You assholes are gonna wake her." He glanced over his shoulder at Lauren, who stared at him, anger and fear plain on her face as he walked away from her, their future in her arms. It killed him, but he didn't turn back, instead telling her casually, "Back in a bit, Laur."

He'd lasted another five years. Five years before he could honestly say he'd begun looking for an exit. Another year and a half before he took the plunge and braced for the pain.

Scar hadn't held back on the beatout, organizing multiple men Jimmy'd had to work his way past, taking blows that should have leveled him. When he made it through, Jimmy had been faced with a fresh and angry Scar waiting at the end.

The two weeks recovering from that day had been worth it all to see the relief on Lauren's face when he told her they were out. Well and truly out, never going back to that kind of nightmare.

So six months after they'd moved to her family's hometown north of Birmingham, when he'd told her he was interested in approaching another motorcycle club, her reaction hadn't been surprising. It had taken multiple weekend parties to convince her the Bama Bastards were for real, and even then, she hadn't entirely warmed up to the idea of the club. More of a trust and willingness to believe him when he said it was what he needed. That the brotherhood filled up something inside him, a hole in his heart he couldn't fix any other way. The give and take of the men and the way they cared for each other felt similar to a relationship, but he would never have told her so. He'd never given her any reason to doubt his love and trust and faithfulness was hers alone.

And here he was, closing in on a year after she'd been forced from his side, taking their little girl with her, and the Scarloucci name was raising its ugliness to stare down at him.

"What's Chulpayev willing to pay for news?" Einstein stared down at the desk, tracing along the path of an old scar with the edge of a fingernail. "He put a price on anything? That'll tell us how critical it is in the grander scheme of things."

"No top end. That's what I heard."

"Fuck," Einstein gritted out, pulling his phone from the pocket of his jeans. Resting it faceup on the desk, he tapped an icon, triggering the app the club had sourced from Myron, the Rebel Wayfarers MC's resident geek. "Make sure that door's closed good, yeah?"

Mike leaned back and pushed against the door, grunting when it snapped shut. Three rings and the call connected, black at first, then fuzzy as the camera on the other end engaged. The camera on his phone would show just the club's logo, painted on the ceiling of the office for just this reason, an instant identification of location.

"'Sup, brother? We're not even out of town and you're already giving me a ringy-ding? That's some serious crushin' you're doing, man." Retro's expression was loose and easy, and Einstein hated he'd be the one to change that. "Tell me, brother."

He picked up the phone and turned in his chair, angling it so Crazy Mike was over his shoulder and captured in frame. "Mike found out some intel I think you need."

"Talk." Nothing more or less than the simple demand came from Retro, but every muscle shown on camera tensed in preparation.

"Chulpayev has an ask out for info on Scar's father. Not the grandfather, but Luciano. His request doesn't have a price cap, boss. That's him looking for some precise information. If he were looking for generalized stuff, he'd use a lower offer, make it more of a scattershot effort to get the most bang for his buck, and I'd have dug a bit before calling. Knowing he's willing to shell out serious money for whatever he's looking for, that's worth interrupting your road trip." Einstein stopped there, knowing from experience that Retro could interpret and assimilate at a speed unrivaled in the club, but even Retro would need a minute.

"Find out what the specifics of the ask are. Watch for Volkov's involvement. If Chulpayev is looking for gold, you can bet your sweet ass that Volkov won't be far behind." Retro sighed. "Had another message that's the reason we're not on the road right now. Mason called and said Gunny's asked for nomad status. He's inclined to approve but wants to see his man once Bane and Gunny get back from Kentucky. That'll be a first, an officer ducking out of that plate and picking up the nomad rocker. So there you go, info for info, as is ever the way."

Einstein chuckled. "Got it, bossman." The unspoken request was to also listen for any rumblings of how other clubs would take the idea of a powerful and connected ranking Rebel member going nomad. "We'll run the info, check the numbers, and I'll let you know if we have anything to report." He hesitated. "I'm also going to put another two men on your house, Retro. These assholes don't play by the rules." Swallowing hard, he swung around in the chair so it was just him looking at Retro. That way Crazy Mike didn't have to see the pain Retro carried for Einstein. That shit was quietly soul-piercing, and Einstein didn't want to share it with anyone. "Take it on myself if needed."

"Brother" was all he got in response, but he didn't need anything else.

He disconnected the call, quit the app, and locked the phone, shoving it deep into his pocket before he lifted his gaze to meet Mike's across the desk. The man looked away first, fleeting expressions of regret and pain flashing across his face.

"Got our orders. Good job you brought that in, Mike. Now we just gotta find out a little more." Einstein gestured towards the door. "Send Buzzkill in, would ya?"

The speed with which Crazy Mike vacated the office said a lot about how uncomfortable he'd been, and Einstein shook his head. It was the same for a bunch of the members. They loved him like a brother, had his back without question, but couldn't look him in the face without flinching. He knew the cause. His unhealing presence was a reminder that life was fleeting, and in him, they saw their own families lost and gone. He probably seemed a token of death itself.

Knuckles rapped on the doorframe, and Buzzkill peeked inside. Einstein lifted his chin, calling Buzzkill in wordlessly. They'd done their prospect periods together, and having spent so much time working alongside the other man had done a lot to develop Einstein's respect for him. Something had bugged Einstein, though. He couldn't wrap his head around how one of them had risen quickly to officer status and the other remained a steady brother, seemingly content to stay in the background.

"Crazy Mike said you wanted to see me?"

Einstein searched Buzzkill's face for any trace of discontent or jealousy, finding none. He tried to force aside the memories that once the beatout was done, Scar hadn't shown any ire directed his way back in Philly, either. Then the man had shown up in Einstein's house, having put his hands on Lauren, and was the catalyst for both Lauren's and Makayla's deaths. *Buzzkill isn't like that, though.*

"Einstein? You okay, brother?"

Nodding, he banished those thoughts to the back of his brain, determined not to go looking for trouble. *If it finds me, however, that's a different fight.* "Yeah, wanted to know if you had time to do a long watch squatting at Retro's house. Could go into a few days. Just while we look up some info." Einstein didn't look too closely at his reasons for not divulging the rationale behind the additional security. "Can I count on you, brother?"

"Uh, Retro's *house*?" Buzzkill shook his head. "Not sure I'm the right man for the job, brother. He still hasn't forgiven me for Nelda's crush and shit."

"That was two years ago, man." Einstein stared at him, disbelief lifting his eyebrows to his hairline. "Surely Retro doesn't hold you responsible for that shit."

"Uh, yeah, he does." Buzzkill leaned forwards, shoulders square with tension. "There's a reason I still do my oil changes at the shed here on the lot, brother. I don't go to his house unless there's a big group of us going over. Not worth it, not even close. All it would take is for Nelda to say some shit about me being there, and Daddy Retro'd have my balls on a platter. He wouldn't even knock me out before he cut 'em off."

"Are you for real?" Einstein couldn't imagine the crush still being an issue. He'd noted it back when they were both prospects, but a summer away from Birmingham had cured Nelda of her attraction to Buzzkill. He was certain of it.

"Yeah. Oh, hell yeah. I'm partial to all my parts stayin' where they're supposed to be. I'm happy to take over whatever other jobs you got, but you putting me at his house when he ain't even home is askin' for shit. Sucks, but it is what it is." Buzzkill's eyes were wide as he nodded, and it was his hopeless frustration that convinced Einstein.

"Well, shit. Okay. I'll figure something else out." He choked on a laugh. "Seriously? After all this time? You're shit-scared of Retro losin' his mind?"

"Have you seen him when whatever's going on has anything at all to do with his family?"

Einstein winced and nodded. "Yeah, I have. I get your point." He flipped his hand towards the door. "Marlin should be near the pool table. Tell him I'm lookin' for him, yeah?"

"Yeah, I can do that, brother. Sorry about the other." Buzzkill turned for the door. "Just never want to get in the midst of family shit like that again."

Chapter Four

Dolph

Dolph Chulpayev leaned his head back and rested it on the headboard as he closed his eyes.

His arms were loosely wrapped around his love, as they'd been since he walked through the door four hours ago, drawn there by her voice on the phone. Quavering, the sound had put the lie to her words about being okay with him needing to cancel their dinner, that need caused by business she would never know about. So Dolph had made a call, delegated work he should already be delegating and knew it, and driven straight to her.

He'd loved her for longer than he'd known her, knocked on his ass with his first brief glimpse of Deloris Fainburg seated at a long table in the library, a place he'd frequented not for the same reasons as she for her homework research. She'd been bent over a book, reading while her hand moved a pencil across a piece of paper. Her long, delicate fingers had driven a pace of writing that didn't flag even when she reached her other hand out, exposing the soft curves of her flesh more, to turn the page.

Her gorgeous, thick hair was pulled into a twisted mass over her shoulder. He'd only had a moment to take in the promise of beauty in her profile before he'd been called away by his associates. Just that single glance and Dolph had been gone for her, needing to know all about the woman who had so easily obsessed him.

Months followed with more of the same. Dolph had made the library a second home on the off chance he'd catch sight of her. He'd spent nearly as much time digging gently into details about her on his own dime to find out every known aspect on the woman who'd so captured his heart and mind. Everything he uncovered, he liked. Deloris was smart and well-liked, and had been spoken highly of by everyone he cautiously interviewed. At the time, she'd been only weeks away from her high school graduation, giving rise to the only thing he didn't like: a realization that there was nearly a decade between their ages.

Deloris had proven herself consistent in her actions and attendance, reenforcing the vast differences between their lives and worlds. The routine was the same every time she came to the library, with her choosing an out-of-the-way nook that afforded a semblance of privacy. That same kind of solitude he'd quickly decided he also wanted immediately, but for wildly different reasons.

Standing in the shadows of the library stacks, he'd consistently talked himself out of making an approach, successful on a half a dozen tries. But the heart wanted what it wanted, and even after telling himself he wouldn't, one day found him boldly walking towards her table.

Dolph had been only yards away when she looked up, and at the first close-up view of her face, he'd been at a loss for words. Figuratively knocked on his ass, Dolph stared as his cock stiffened in his pants and his heart jumped to a racing beat previously only experienced during a chase. This was a chase, too, but of a very different kind.

Distance viewing and photos had not done justice to her loveliness, and he'd been mesmerized while beauty unfolded in front of him as a slow smile blazed up at him. She'd stared back at him, lips curved in amusement, the pink of her tender tongue dancing behind white teeth.

Chin, nose, cheekbones—everything fit together in a way that rendered her magnificent. Eyes snapping and dancing, she'd given him a nod, then said, in her always-direct way, "I wondered if you'd ever come talk to me."

They'd talked that day. Only spoken to each other, something she told him later had disappointed, because she'd been as attracted to him as he was her. But in a conversation that waxed and waxed, never waning, not even when the library attendants came around to shoo them out at closing, during the times of listening to her musical voice, he'd found love. Four o'clock in the morning had seen them sitting in an all-night diner, him laughing at her gravy-covered fries when she'd cut a glance up at him, a subtle unease in her gaze.

"What, beauty?" He'd reached across the table and covered her hand with his. "What is it?"

"Why are you here?" Deloris had asked her question softly, keeping her voice low so the server wouldn't hear. "With me?"

"Because I find you fascinating." Dolph had given her honesty, something he normally held close to the vest. "Because you interest me. Have since the first time I saw you."

Gesturing at the table between them, she'd arched an eyebrow and asked, "And this is all you want?"

He'd reminded himself of her age and probable innocence. "No." Honesty had kept her in her seat; he'd thought it might serve him again. "I would like much more, should you choose to grant it to me." He reached out and waited, palm up, fingers curled. "The choice is always yours, Deloris."

The first tentative touch of her hand on his had driven the very air from his lungs. Her verbal response had provoked a different physical reaction. "And if I already know I want to choose you, Dolph? What happens then?"

Dolph shifted in the seat, wishing for the solitude he'd imagined in those hours watching her at the library. The rest of their conversation played out in his memories. *"Then, you finish your schooling. And you select a college to attend. And we have many more dinners such as this one, but maybe not in so public a setting."* His main message was one of satisfaction with who she was, and Dolph wanted to make certain she understood. *"I don't want you to change the trajectory of your life for me, Deloris. I want a chance to find where I fit in alongside you, see where we can find an us, perhaps."*

Dolph tightened his arms around Deloris, holding her tight to his chest. *So much for my youthful musings*, he thought. She shifted, and her head dropped back as she stared up at him. "My beauty." He kissed her forehead, murmuring endearments in his native tongue, words she wouldn't understand but helped him stay true to the love he held inside himself for her.

"You had to go somewhere." As Dolph smoothed the lines between her brows with the pad of one thumb, she reached up and caught his hand. "Didn't you?"

"You needed me here."

"I dreamed you caught me."

"I'll always catch you, beauty."

She settled against his chest again, and her sigh this time was full of sweet trust and a belief in his love.

If only she could remember.

When their daughter Katrina had been born, Deloris had been articulate and bright, overflowing with love and adoration as she held the infant to her breast.

Ten hours later, she'd barely been holding on to life itself. That had hurt so much, stealing the breath from his body, knowing she was an innocent casualty of a war within his own family. Then had come the pain of finding out it was a relative who had called the hit, hoping to undermine Dolph's hold over Atlanta. Leveraging his love against the brutality of the bratva, and he'd come out the loser.

It had taken years of the best rehabilitation practices he could buy to bring Deloris back even a little to herself. And in the mix, she'd lost any memory of what they'd been to each other. He'd been wiped from her brain as if he'd never existed. Her beauty unchanged, but her mind forever different. Fear had suffused him, caught up in the what-if world that surrounded him then. He'd been holding Katrina when he'd made the hard decision to follow the path Deloris' mind had blazed, hopefully taking any hint of target from the backs of his two girls.

Money had altered Katrina's birth records to remove his name. More money had set fire to the document storage. Even more money had bought an apartment building where he could install Deloris and Katrina, rent money moved to an account that fed back into Deloris' bank. Necessity had him installing a nurse who doubled as a nanny, one loyal only to him.

Everything to keep his girls safe.

He'd then taken on a role defensible in Deloris' altered memory: family friend and near uncle to little Trina. It placed him close enough to take part in many of her milestone moments, but still provided a barrier to keep his enemies at bay. Not close enough, though, as Trina's current arrangement had brought home nearly two years ago.

There were rumblings of more activity directed at her chosen partner's club. Rumblings delivered by independent sources as well as Dolph's nephew, Pooka. Rumblings that were as solid as rumors could be.

Dolph measured everything in his life. Risk versus reward was the least complicated calculation.

To keep his girls safe, he'd do anything needed.

Tightening his arms around Deloris, he pressed another kiss to the curve of her forehead, skin warm against his dry lips.

Even reach out to Retro.

Chapter Five

Einstein

"Be there in a minute." Dragging a hand roughly down his face, Einstein forced his eyes open and yawned as he blinked wearily at the darkness shrouding the room. The knocking at his door resumed, and he pushed off the bed, stepping into the jeans he'd discarded last night. "Hold your goddamned horses."

At least the room had become familiar over the past months, so he was able to make a beeline for the door. Yanking it open, he stared into Alex's bleary eyes. The prospect's hand was lifted in preparation to resume the pounding, and Einstein reached out and grabbed it, stopping the forward movement.

"The fuck you need, man?"

"Popova is downstairs, wants to talk to Retro." Alex ducked his head, failing to hide a wide yawn behind his shoulder. "You're next in line."

"Popova? Gregory Popova? What does he want?" Einstein yawned again and stretched his neck side to side. "What's he here for?"

"Figured I'd leave the hard questions to the big boss." Alex hooked a thumb towards the stairs. "I'll go let him in and keep him in the main room until you get downstairs."

"Good call letting him cool his heels outside." Einstein praised the man's decision as he stepped back into the room and snatched open a drawer, pulling a shirt from inside. "I'll be down in a minute."

Alex disappeared from the open doorway, and Einstein walked to the attached bathroom. He took a few seconds to splash water on his face, wiping away the droplets and yawn-forced tears before he put on the shirt. Back in the bedroom, he yanked on socks and stomped into his boots; then, just before he walked through the door, he settled his vest on his shoulders. The welcome and familiar weight let him breathe easier, and by the time he'd descended the staircase, he'd pulled on his club persona completely. His brothers might know how vulnerable he was after the death of his family, but no way did an outsider need to see anything other than a perfectly composed member left in charge.

Popova stood near the bar. While Alex was nearby, it didn't look like the two were talking, which was good. Alex had clearly exhibited he knew what was and wasn't acceptable, so that wasn't a surprise. Popova, though? Total wildcard in this situation.

"Pooka." Einstein used the nickname he'd heard Retro employ on numerous occasions. Always when the conversation was either easy or incredibly difficult. It was "Greg" otherwise. "What warrants the invasion of our clubhouse at zero-dark-thirty." Flashing a smile to indicate no offense, he was pleased when the expression was returned.

"Einstein." Popova stretched out his hand, and Einstein met it with a meaty smack before clamping on and shaking up and down once. "Well met, my friend." *Well, that's a good sign.* The representative of the mob in Birmingham didn't call people his friend often, and it was usually a signal of comfort. "I hated to have to wake you." *No apology, no surprise.* Apologies in the mob were symbolic of weakness. He'd heard both

Popova and Retro dance with words enough times to understand the avoidance. "I'd hoped for Retro, but by your presence, I'm assuming he's unavailable."

"You tried to call him first." He didn't know for sure, but half of the dance in the information business was making informed assumptions. "Him not picking up should have been a clue." *I didn't get an alarm from Marlin, so that means—* "Smart idea not going to his home second."

"My thoughts exactly. My little cousin's husband is a family friend, but showing at his home unexpectedly isn't a tactic a man should employ." Popova ducked his head, fingers running up the back of his neck. "Not and remain welcome." He lifted his chin and stared into Einstein's eyes. "Which is why I'm here."

"Do we need privacy for the conversation?" Einstein didn't shift and would not be the first to break their locked gazes. *No weakness for the mobster.* "Or are we good here?"

Popova's face registered a flicker of apprehension, and Einstein wasn't surprised when he dropped his eyes and offered, "Private would be good."

"Follow." Spinning on his heel, Einstein led the way to the large office used for outside meetings. The club had a smaller war room that was protected against electronic eavesdropping, but they kept the knowledge of that space close to the vest, only allowing phone calls in there, no video, and no in-person interviews.

He whistled low, then high, then higher in a tonal progression, grinning when he heard the prospect respond, "Got it, boss."

Retro's always been a step ahead of everyone in the region.

Using vocal orders versus verbal ones kept their guests guessing. At multi-club meetings, he'd heard more than one wanna-be attempt to utilize the same communication tactic. The only one successful so far was the IMC out of Louisiana. Their territory might be the full Gulf Coast these days, but the area around NOLA would always be their home base. It was important to continually update personal impressions and internal responses, so he wouldn't be caught off guard by any progression in territory or information.

Another Retro tactic, he thought, hiding his grin as he swung through the open door into the office and stepped to the far side of the table. Popova closed the door with a thud, then thumbed the deadbolt installed above the doorknob. Einstein frowned.

"Not sure anyone other than the prospect is awake, but whatever makes you feel better, man." He gestured at the table, pulling a chair away and standing there with a hand on the back. "Wanna sit, or we doin' this on our feet?"

Popova's hand drifted to the inside of his jacket, and Einstein froze. He hadn't marked the unseasonable fashionwear and hadn't patted down the man, nor had he asked the prospect to do it. Einstein's gun was upstairs, resting on the nightstand farthest from the door. *Well, shit.*

"Might want to go a little slower with that pull, man." Tensing, he evaluated his options and settled on the chair underneath his hand. He could lift and throw in a few seconds, and if Popova's piece hadn't cleared his holster by the time the chair was airborne, it would buy him enough time to go over the table and take the man down.

"What?" Popova looked down, seemingly surprised. "No." He lifted his gaze, alarm clear on his features. "No, no. No, man. Nope. Not in the clubhouse." His head shook as his hands spread wide in a gesture that had his palms out in a clear stop sign. "Not outside of the clubhouse either. Not in my lifetime. I wouldn't dare incur Retro's wrath like that." He held up a finger and thumb, folding his other fingers against a palm in a minimizing gesture. "I've got something you need to see, man. Not bringin' the heat to you. No threat here, man."

"Good to know." Einstein twirled a finger. "Still, go slow."

"You got it." Popova plucked the inside edge of his jacket to pull it away from his body, folding it back to expose the interior pocket. Using the pincher he'd made, he dug around in the tellingly flat pocket until coming out with a piece of paper. "Here. This is what I brought. It's a transcript of a conversation my uncle thought you should know about."

"A transcript?" That implied it was something premeditated, if there'd been time to put a recording of a call or meeting into place. "Of what?"

"He got a heads-up about a meet." Popova confirmed Einstein's assumption as he let his jacket fall back into place. "There's activity surrounding the Monster Devils."

Einstein's muscles locked up, tense and tight enough it was hard to pull in a breath. He managed, then blew it back out slowly, knowing he'd not been able to hide the shift from Popova. *Dammit.* "Tell me."

"There's an outfit lookin' to leverage Scar's connections. Mafia side of things. They're lookin' for a way to deal with him in his grandfather's footsteps. Word is Scar can't be found, and you and I know he's being very careful about covering his tracks. This—" He shoved the paper towards Einstein. "—is them becoming impatient."

Accepting the folded object, he teased the edges apart, smoothing the creases away until he could easily read the contents.

"Have you read this yet?" He glanced up to see Popova's head moving side to side. "Okay then." *Blind handoff. Huh.* Studying the words, he began reading. "Subject one: There's got to be a way to get to the asshole. Have you looked at everything? Subject two: Looked at all his crew, yeah. Subject one: And his family? You look there? Subject two: Mommy and daddy are removed. They got no gains from the family biz. Waste of time to follow through there. Subject one: And the brother?" Einstein stared at the paper, then lifted his gaze to Popova's face. "What brother? I never heard Scar talk about a brother. Who are these people? Who was at the meeting?"

"No idea on any front." Popova shrugged lightly. "But this isn't the first time I've heard mention of a second grandson of Franco's. It's come up occasionally, but I never had anything to wrap my fingers around when it came to digging. There and gone again, you know?"

"How long have you known the Scarlouccis? Not known about the outfit, but Franco and Scar?" Einstein raked through his memories but found nothing to support the idea of a brother. "I'd have thought Scar would be shouting for his brother to join him, given how he feels about family."

"My family has dealt with the Scarlouccis for years. They run Philly and control two major ports on the East Coast. They're a staple when it comes to negotiating anything through there." Popova chewed on the inside of his bottom lip. "Uncle Dolph knows them better." A phone came out of the front pocket of his pants, and he looked at Einstein. "Okay if I text him?"

He approved the contact with a nod, surprised when Popova received a near-instantaneous response. Looking up from his phone, Popova scowled. "He said he hadn't a clue about a brother. If Dolph hasn't heard anything, and the Bastards' network hasn't turned up anything, should we even consider there's anything there to pursue?"

"Why did you need to get this to Retro right away?" As important as the message was, as a standalone tip, it didn't warrant that kind of urgency. "What labeled this red for you?"

"Keep reading."

Einstein lifted the paper, not willing to lower his gaze. "Subject two: Lost him in Montana. Understand he's in Alabama now, so we're looking there." He pulled in a slow breath and repeated, "Alabama," softly as he shook his head. "Subject one: Watch out for those bastards—I'm assuming that should be capitalized?"

"My thoughts too."

"Subject one: Watch out for those Bastards; they've married into the competition." *Katrina Fainburg.* "Subject two: Yes, sir." He turned the paper over, finding the other side blank. "That's it? The sum total of what you got?" Popova nodded. "Sounds like they know Retro's old lady is Uncle Dolph's daughter. You catch that?" With a grimace, Popova nodded again. "Yeah, good call to bring it straight here. I'll get on it now." Einstein gestured towards the door. "Anything else to report?" He knew the phrasing would irritate Popova, making it seem as if he was subservient to Einstein and, by extension, to the Bama Bastards. "This is good, Pooka. Good job."

From the scowl on Popova's face, Einstein might have ground it in a little deep, but he didn't care. This was a potential threat to Retro's family and needed his attention immediately.

"Nothing else. Uncle Dolph told me to pass on that if he finds out anything more, he'll be in touch. Either through me"—being made a messenger boy was clearly an irritant, something Einstein banked for future use—"or directly. We didn't think it should wait for daylight."

"Agreed." He stared at the words typed on the paper again. "You get any kind of lead on who this is, we need to know. Without knowing the players, it's harder to plan for eventualities."

"I hear ya." Popova stepped backwards to the door, not taking his gaze off Einstein.

He fought a smile at the man's caution and sense of self-preservation. *Been in business in Birmingham for years and is still alive. Maybe he's got a right-sized sense of things.* "Be a stranger." Rounding the table, he walked through the door in front of Popova as if leading him from the room. "Unless you got more for me."

"I'll pass your sentiments along," Popova said quietly.

When Einstein glanced over his shoulder, he saw Popova's head was on a swivel, moving as if the room were filled with threats instead of a sleeping prospect at the bar and Einstein. "You do that." He stopped in the middle of the room and kept his gaze on Popova as the man moved past, noting how he angled his body to never give Einstein his back. "Healthy fear you got there."

"Keeps me upright."

The door banged closed, and Alex snorted, picking his head up from where it had been pillowed on his forearms. "What?"

"Nothin', prospect. Sleep on." Covering the distance to the door, he opened it a crack, just enough to see Popova stepping into the back seat of a dark sedan. Einstein closed it, armed the alarm, and turned back to see Alex staring at him. "I'm going to be in the quiet room for a bit. You're good to catch some sleep. I'll see anything on the cameras."

"Not going to argue it." Alex walked to a couch and flopped onto his back, one arm coming up to cover his eyes. "I'll take the chance to catch some shut-eye, but I'm gonna be here if you need me, boss."

"Good man." Einstein strode up the short hallway to the interior room the club had modified for this usage. "Sleep easy. I got this watch, brother." *Alex has a month left; time to start talking about support for his patch.* If Einstein threw his weight behind the prospect, he knew other members would give the man more serious consideration. With how many members Retro and Mudd had added over the past year, there'd been less focus on the prospect than normal. *Gotta fix that for him. The man's putting in the effort—the club better match every fuckin' ounce.*

Door closed and lock engaged, Einstein turned to the computer setup along one wall. He used the scanner to quickly transmit the transcript to the device, the process transforming the image to typed words. He then set the conversation running through a database they'd built up through the years, logging thousands of meetings to create enough data for software they'd acquired that performed diction pattern recognition. Clicking various additional prompts started the process of distributing the information to key BBMC members, prefaced with his brief description of where and how the text was acquired. It would send in a priority order, waiting for recognizable activity on the member's device before transmitting. That left things less vulnerable to sniffing and disruption. Most of the members had become adept at managing their online time, utilizing the Plane Mode to keep their devices offline until needed. In any group there was always one member who would assume the always-on position, ensuring access to everyone.

Once upon a time, Einstein had believed the efforts were overkill.

Not anymore.

Not after seeing what Mudd could dig out of an idle phone, or what Myron could do. He was the Rebel Wayfarers' head tech guy and a certified genius, the author of several software packages the BBMC utilized. *Including the pattern recognition stuff.* Their day-to-day communications were behind an encrypted set of code that the government was still trying to crack. Myron had told Einstein they'd come close a couple of times, but his built-in alarms had given the necessary warning, giving him time to modify enough to not only stay ahead of their efforts but to leapfrog them based on what Myron called the "attack vector." Treating the government as unwanted hackers and bad guys helped keep things in perspective, solidifying the us-versus-them mindset all members needed to survive.

Picking up the landline bolted to the wall, he dialed Marlin's phone from memory.

"Yeah?" At least Marlin sounded wide awake and ready for action, leaving Einstein to shake his head.

"Get your text?"

Marlin made a grumbling sound, then grunted.

"I'm going to get in the wind, come over. We'll do two-by-two shifts until we know more." Einstein flicked on another monitor and clicked over to the camera views from Retro's house. "Where are you?" He rotated through several feeds without finding Marlin. "Brother, you're still at the house, right?"

"Yeah." A sigh followed by the sound of water. "Takin' a dump. Headed back outside now."

The door of the small pool house opened, and Marlin stepped into view. "Got you. I'll be there in a few."

"You sure this is warranted? Send a fuckin' prospect, man. You're supposed to keep the clubhouse up and running." Marlin waved at the camera, and Einstein snorted. "I know Buzzkill won't work the detail, but there's others, man. You don't gotta do everything."

"Shut up. I'll be there." He ended the call, snorting again when he saw Marlin flip off the camera.

The software hadn't indicated the checks were complete, but he looked at the output on the screen anyway. Like with fingerprints, diction matching could only do so much, requiring a human for the final comparisons. The number of potential matches was twelve, not the expected zero, which meant they'd have some audio to listen to. Crazy Mike did well with that, and Einstein sent him a quick message to reach out as soon as he was cogent. "At least that looks promising."

Out in the main room, Alex had flipped to his side, knees pulled up with one hand speared between his thighs. His other hand rested in front of his face, and something about the positioning had Einstein pausing to look harder. He snorted, then choked on a laugh. "Jesus. Linus. We'll see what he thinks." He kicked the side of the couch, biting back another laugh when the man rolled to his back, his hand following but staying an exact distance. Einstein shoved the side of one boot against the couch and gave it a push, the legs scraping across the wood floor.

"What?" Alex sat up facing away from Einstein, his head jerking back and forth. "Who's there?"

"Me, asshole."

Alex nearly fell off the couch as he turned towards Einstein, gaze filled with bleary confusion.

"I'm going to Retro's to finish out the night with Marlin. Crazy Mike'll be here in a few hours. Tell him to check his messages if he hasn't already." He waited, but Alex didn't respond, just stared up at him. "You in there, Linus?"

"What?" Alex ducked his head, palms scrubbing across both his cheeks. "Hold on, give me a minute to wake up." His head rattled back and forth in a brisk arc, and then his feet landed on the floor with a thud. "Shit, what time is it?"

Einstein consulted the clock on the wall. "Three o'clock. Time for good boys to be on their best behavior." He had to bite the inside of his cheek to keep from laughing. "Isn't it, Linus?"

"Who the fuck is Linus?" Alex yawned, mouth open wide with a stifled groan. "God, couple hours' sleep is worse than none sometimes."

"True that." Einstein backed away towards the front door. "You awake, for sure? Want you to set the alarm after me. You remember what I said about Crazy Mike?"

"Yeah, check his messages. You're spelling Marlin?" Alex pushed up, stretching, the ill-fitting prospect vest sliding around on his shoulders. "Everything okay, bossman?"

"Not spelling him, augmenting the watch." The heat that rolled through the door underscored the oddness of Popova's jacket earlier, and Einstein rethought his easy acceptance that the man hadn't come into the clubhouse carrying. "If Popova comes back, make him take his coat off outside. Pass it on." Just before the door closed, he turned and called through the narrowing gap. "Set the alarm, Linus."

"Who the hell is Linus?" The question was easily audible through the door, and Alex's honest confusion had Einstein still laughing as he slung a leg across his bike. Hand going to the clutch automatically, he disengaged it, started the bike, and toed the shifter up into Neutral before he released his grip. Getting his helmet into place didn't take long, and the loping roll of the engine had him anticipating the stretch of highway between the clubhouse and Retro's house.

Einstein rolled off the lot with a wide smile in place.

***

Marian

From her place in the back row of the van, Marian watched over her brothers.

Luke was in the front, a position Gunny called shotgun for some reason, and hadn't stopped plying the big man with questions. About his tattoos, his vest, the patches—some of which were vulgar, and it amused Marian when his ears would go red as he tried to avoid explaining the meaning—where they were going, what Gunny's role was in the club—a term she noted Luke never got wrong—and if Myrt was really following them on a motorcycle.

Thad had stretched out across the long seat in front of Marian, courteously kicking off his shoes before propping them high on the wall of the van. He'd slept a great deal, which wasn't surprising, given the ordeal the boys had endured. When Thad hadn't been subject to Sallabrook's torture and abuse, he'd been protecting his older brother. *Probably not a lot of rest for him.*

Myrt had talked to Marian about her time under Sallabrook's thumb, in painful detail. But it had been necessary to share an understanding of what had brought them to that point, huddled together on a bed in a motel, the boys sleeping uneasily nearby. Marian had seen the pain in her sister's expression as she revealed the past. Agonizing, yet blunted somehow. Then Marian had seen Bane with her sister, and everything had come clear.

Myrt had denied anything, saying a relationship wouldn't be in her future, but Marian had plied her with strong words of advice. Bane was clearly a good man who worshiped Myrt, and Marian had done everything she could to help open her sister's eyes to the fact.

Myrt didn't have time to be wary or mistrustful of fate. Pregnant and dependent on the kindness of others, she needed to see what was right in front of her.

Marian's situation was significantly different, and that wasn't her being obtuse.

Gunny's wife and children awaited at the end of the trip. She might be harboring a tiny bit of hero worship for him but not *that* kind of emotion. His gentle nature with the boys would have won her over alone. Then Marian had the experience of him soothing her while they waited in this very vehicle as Bane took care of business. She'd overheard Bane's response to Myrt's questions, and the muttered "you'll never have to worry about him or Sallabrook again" had told her everything she needed to know.

Knights.

These men were protectors through and through, their instinctive reaction to right whatever wrongs had been shoved down the throats of the unwilling or weak. *Off-white knights*, she thought, covering her mouth with one hand to hide the way her lips curled in a full-bodied smile. Scary upon first encounter, both Gunny and Bane had quickly proven themselves ready to do anything to shield Marian, Myrtle, and the boys from badness.

"Y'all ready?" The van slowed as Gunny spoke, turning left onto a small oil-top road. It bumped and swayed as Luke chortled a laugh. "We're here, Maid Marian."

Rolling her eyes at his continued use of the ridiculous phrase, she craned her neck to see the upcoming house on the right-hand side of the road. She was nervous. *Like the boys are.* All of them were curious about where they'd be staying, and if Marian were the only one worried about any kind of repayment? Well, that was okay. The boys shouldn't have to worry about shelter and safety. *I can take that on.* She'd done it all her life. Trading labor for full bellies and a protective room for her siblings. All the things that should have been a given coming from a parent but weren't.

The driveway was wide and well-maintained. From here, the house looked on the small side. It was a two-story structure with a broad front porch, but there was a wide groomed yard along the side and back, as far as she could see. Through the trees beyond rose the outline of a larger house, about a quarter of a mile farther along the way.

As the van rocked to a stop, a woman burst through the front door. She had a child on her hip and was followed by two more, the door scarcely landing in its frame before it opened again and an older woman exited.

Gunny's reverent, "Shar," cemented the identity of the younger woman, as did the childish screams of "Daddy, Daddy."

Marian and the boys stayed put, stuck to their seats as Gunny bailed out of the vehicle and swept his wife into his arms. One of his hands left Sharon's back to drift down and find the back of each little head where the girls had encircled one of his thighs with their arms.

This is what love looks like.

Marian swallowed hard and dipped her face, intent on giving the family privacy. The vehicle's side door opened, and she looked up to find the woman who'd followed Sharon outside standing in the gap. "You must be Marian. You're Thad, no doubt, got that look about you. Luke, is that you up in the front? Did Gunny keep you amused for the drive down? Come on out. I'm sure you're all tired of being cooped up in this van. I've got snacks in the house. Marian, are the boys allergic to anything? Come on, slide out. Luke, can you open the door from in there?"

Luke tumbled out of the seat and latched on to the woman, face buried against her shoulder. "You're Vanna Mom. Myrtie told me all about you."

Vanna's laughter was soft and sweet, and Marian loved her in that moment, at how the woman walked the fine line of finding humor in his words but careful not to laugh at Luke's reaction. "I am. You can call me that if you like. I'm so happy you're here, Luke. You too, Thad. Come on inside. I don't bite."

"Don't let her lie to you, boys." Gunny's laughing voice carried from where he was still in a close embrace with his family. "She bites hard when she's pissed."

"Well, I'm far from pissed right now, so I think everyone's safe from my chompers." She clacked her teeth together, and Luke giggled.

Marian leaned forward and gave Thad a tiny shove against his shoulder. "Out we get. I'll come back and grab our bags in a bit. Let's stretch our legs, little brother." He looked back at her as he moved, the lack of trust he felt clear in his expression. "Test the waters. I don't think Myrtie would steer us wrong. Just test the waters, Thad."

"Okay." The word was grudgingly given, but it was thrown out as Thad started moving. Marian followed him through the door, unfolding with a groan as her bruises pulled and ached.

"Welcome, welcome." The booming shout alarmed Marian, and without thinking, she quickly moved both boys behind her, stepping between them and whoever this new potential threat was. She kept one hand on Thad's shoulder, ready to shove him to safety.

"*Jesus*, Truck. Tone it back, brother." Gunny rushed to a stop in front of Marian, and she focused on the image sewn to the back of his vest. A skull with a key clenched between its teeth. She startled as she realized it was different from the one Bane had worn. *Huh.* Gunny turned and crouched slightly, his face in line with Marian's. Earnest concern pulled the features of his face taut. "Shit, Maid Marian. He's harmless to you and the boys, promise. He's loud but harmless. Wouldn't hurt a woman or a child, no matter what." His gaze darted past her, and she glanced over her shoulder to see Thad had done much the same as her, putting Luke behind him. "Goddamn, your family fucked you guys up." The whisper was tortured, and Gunny shook his head while Marian watched, rocked by his statement. *He's right, though. His family is so different from ours.* Louder, he continued, "Thad, I swear you're safe here. Luke's safe here."

"No harm will come to you or yours, Marian." Marian looked away from Gunny to see a mirroring expression on Vanna's face. "My old man wasn't thinking, is all. Look at him." Marian did, easing to the side to see beyond Gunny. The man called Truck was leaning against the porch railing with both hands, arms straight, and his head hanging low. "Man's sorry as anything he startled you so badly."

"Okay." *Myrt trusts them.* She shifted to stare into Gunny's face. *Gunny trusts them.* If Marian were being honest, his approval held more weight than her sister's avowal. Myrt had been as sheltered as Marian, but Gunny's many stories had revealed the breadth and width of his experience in the world. "If Gunny trusts you, that's good enough for me."

"Me too." Thad moved around Marian, Luke in tow, and positioned them both next to Gunny.

Sharon stepped into view, and the wide grin on her face surprised Marian. "That's my man, makin' friends and bein' everyone's savior. It's in his DNA, swear." The words were teasing, but Sharon's tone held nothing but love and pride as she took up a place on Gunny's other side. "Here, take your hunk of child, big guy."

Gunny's arm extended and wrapped around the boy Sharon had been holding. He slung the child over his shoulder, locking the little thighs in place with one beefy arm as the boy giggled wildly. "I got him." He stretched his other arm across Thad's shoulders and latched onto Luke's shirt with his hand. "And I got you guys, too. Let's go find food."

Marian watched them walk through the grass to the steps, Gunny not letting the boys hesitate before making their way up and onto the porch where Truck was waiting. He crouched down and extended a hand to Thad, and Marian held her breath until her brother responded to something the man had said, reaching out to shake solemnly. Luke was bouncing on his toes by that point and quickly responded to the man when the hand was extended in his direction. Truck's laughter at something one of the boys said was quiet but pleased, and he opened the door, stepping back to let Gunny and the boys through first.

Vanna appeared in front of her and, with a wide gesture, wrapped her arms around Marian gently. "We've got you, sister."

A lump the size of a crab apple developed in her throat, blocking her words but not her sobs as Marian allowed herself to begin believing.

***

Dinner preparation was hectic, the two men and three boys paired with two little girls. All of whom were underfoot as they looked for scraps and nibbles. It was a happy occasion, unlike any meal Marian could ever remember, filled to the brim with harmless teasing and laughter. Each time Thad or Luke joined in on the antics caused her heart to hitch painfully in her chest, their hesitating movements and words gradually gaining confidence throughout the evening. Her brothers began to bloom in ways that should have always been part of their lives. Dread and a sense of loss filled the space around her like white noise, though, making it hard to hear conversation. She'd missed a dozen direct questions, her inattention forcing the person to ask again, and the idea they would go to the trouble was enough to floor her emotionally.

The food itself was plentiful and good, something Vanna called comfort food. She'd made savory meatloaf and extra-creamy baked macaroni and cheese as the main dishes, and sides of mashed potatoes and brown gravy were paired with mixed vegetables Vanna explained came from her garden. That was followed by a casserole dish filled with peach cobbler, Marian's sole addition to the meal. Cheap and easy to make, it was something the boys were familiar with, and it pleased Marian to have the dessert declared a winner by even Gunny and Truck.

She'd stayed close to Sharon, watching the woman to take cues from how she behaved. That had led to some confusion as Sharon acted more like it was her house than Vanna's. And then, after dinner, when the kids were all watching some movie on the living room TV, Marian had learned why.

Gunny had shared that Myrt wasn't the first person Vanna had rescued. What he hadn't mentioned was how Sharon had lived in this home for years, helping Vanna care for her son, Kitt. The young man now lived on his own in a suburb of Atlanta but had placed a stamp not only on the house but on Sharon's interaction with his mother.

Marian perched on the edge of her chair, and as Sharon related her version of the story, she kept track as Vanna's expression changed. Love was the overriding emotion, but much like Sharon was with Gunny, it was mixed liberally with pride.

"And that's how I came to call her Vanna Mom." Sharon scooted her chair closer to Marian, and before she could wave Sharon off, had leaned in and cinched her arm tightly around Marian's body.

Gunny's "Sharon, no," wasn't in time, and all Marian could do was groan as the tight hold woke the pain. She wavered, held in place by hands on her shoulders, and tried to struggle free as her shirt was flipped up, exposing her back.

"Don't." Her request was too late, based on the shocked gasps from Sharon and Vanna. "Please." She tried to slide her clothing back into place, each movement waking the pain more. "No."

"Who the hell did that to you, girl?" Truck's question boomed through the house, and Marian heard heavy footfalls immediately approaching the kitchen from the direction of the living room.

"Let go of her," Thad shouted, and Marian bent over, hiding her face in her palms. "Get your stinkin' hands off her."

"Thad, it's okay," Gunny responded, as the hands on her shoulders disappeared. "Buddy, it's okay."

Blocking out everything happening around her, Marian tried again to restore order to her clothing and failed. A body bumped into her side, and Luke whispered, "I'll help," as the shirt lowered to hide her shame.

"Leave her alone," Thad shouted again, and a hand she recognized as his landed on top of her head, the boy knowing from long experience it would be a safe place to connect, unlikely to cause pain. "Leave us all alone."

Shouted arguments between the two men were echoed in Thad's voice, Sharon and Vanna nowhere to be heard. Marian carefully measured each breath as enough to stay conscious but not enough to trigger a cough or pain, the broken ribs complaining loudly about the strain of holding her body together. "Nugh." Mouth opened wide, she sipped at the air, each exhale releasing a little more pain. "I'm okay," she tried to reassure Thad, but he snorted his disbelief. "No, I am. It's not bad. Just took me by surprise."

Hands still in place over her face, she sat more upright, careful not to lean backwards. "Tissue?" Something soft drifted across the back of her hand in response, and she clutched at it blindly. Eyes wiped free from tears, she dabbed at her nose, knowing from experience that blowing it would tear down all the progress made so far. "I'm okay."

Thad's hand was replaced by another, fingers gently threading through her hair. She blinked up to see Gunny standing next to her. "Fuckin' knew I should have taken you to the doc." His expression was tortured. "I'm sorry I failed you, Maid Marian."

"I wouldn't have gone." She gave him the truth and heard Sharon snort from behind him. "Nothin' against you, Gunny, but I wouldn't have. This isn't bad."

"God *damn*, girl." Truck's voice was raspy. "You're breakin' my fuckin' heart."

"I'm sorry, Marian." Sharon popped her head around Gunny's side, teeth worrying at her bottom lip. "I didn't know."

"I didn't want you to know." They deserved the truth as she saw it. "It's never going to happen to me again. I'm here, and you, all of you, have saved me." Air rushed into her lungs on a groan, and Gunny's hand tightened in her hair. Shaking her head slowly, she reminded him, "You saved us. Like with Sharon's stories, the bad is in the past, and there's only good in our futures."

Vanna replaced Gunny, and she stretched out both hands, guiding Marian to her feet. "I'm thinking a hot shower will make you feel tons better, then we'll get you into bed. Truck," she called over her shoulder. "Earlier, Marian set their bags just inside the front door. Bring them up to the guest suite. We've got the pull-out in there the boys can sleep on." Focusing on Marian, she murmured, "I suspect you'll rest better if you know they're close by."

Marian straightened, forcing her shoulders back as she nodded. "You're right." Looking at Thad, she gave him a smile she knew he'd see straight through to the pain beneath, and recognized she'd been right when his brows wrinkled. "Take the little ones and go finish the movie? That'll give me time to get ready for bed. Vanna Mom's right. I'm pretty near wiped out."

"You call out, I'll hear you. This house ain't too big." He stepped back and looped his arm around Luke's neck. "We'll be up in a while. Give you a little bit."

"Sounds good." She shuffled forward and dropped a kiss against his temple before he could shrug away. "Love you, little brother. Love you too, Lukie."

With a glare at Truck over his shoulder, Thad guided Luke out of the room, and Marian relaxed a little more. Without turning around, she told him, "Mr. Truck—" That generated strained laughs, but she'd been told Myrt called him that, and the telling had sparked amusement, so any laughter meant she was on her way to successfully deflating the tension in the room. "He's not a bad kid, just protective. Give him half a day and he'll warm up to you."

"That's something worth working towards, Maid Marian." Gunny's nickname for her in Truck's thick accent made her want to laugh. "Keeping the whole of your little family safe is an even better goal. Myrt and Bane will be here in another day. He'll loosen up then, once he knows she's good."

"You've got a good intuition about you." She spoke to Truck as she accepted Vanna's extended elbow and leaned lightly on the older woman. "I think you're a big ole softie with an even bigger heart."

"She's got your number, old man." Vanna's pseudo whisper had the people in the room laughing, and that was such a pleasant sound Marian almost didn't want to move away.

The promise of an ache-easing hot shower was ample draw, though, and she followed Vanna's guidance up the stairs. Pausing in the doorway to a large room, Marian took in the bed and other furnishings. Larger than any she'd ever seen, and she'd already thought the motel beds were huge, this bed held a novel number of pillows propped against the heavy wooden headboard. A full-sized couch sat along one wall, and a TV mounted on top of a dresser would be easily visible from either of the main pieces of furniture. Tables and plants were scattered around, and Marian thought it looked more like an apartment than a guest room.

Noise on the stairs had her moving to the side of the door, and she watched as Vanna disappeared into a doorway across the room just as Truck walked in the entrance. Without asking, he identified the bags and dropped the duffels for the boys on the couch, carrying the trash bag that held Marian's things to the bed.

"There you go, girl." As he passed her on his way back out the door, Truck lifted his hand and gently tucked a strand behind her ear, then was gone, only a spicy scent left in his wake.

Knights in black armor.

Vanna leaned around the doorframe and waved Marian forwards. "Shower's running. It'll be hot by the time we get you out of those clothes. Grab your pj's while I get you a towel and me a chair." She walked into the room. "Oh good, he listened." Without asking permission, she unraveled the string holding the bag closed. "Just need panties and a big shirt to sleep in."

"I can do that." Mortification unrooted Marian's feet, and she closed the distance, jerking the bag out of Vanna's hands. "Please. I've got it from here."

"Okay." Passing over control of the bag, Vanna backed away a step. "I'm here if you need me."

"Yes, ma'am." The honorific came naturally, easier than calling the woman Vanna Mom, and Marian's shoulders loosened a tiny bit. "I'm okay. You don't have to stay."

"I'm sure you are, but staying will ease my mind."

Marian pulled out the clothing needed and turned to the bathroom. "I'll be back in a minute."

"I'll be here." Vanna's declaration held weight, the words hovering in the room like a profound statement.

Marian paused and slowly turned, not sure what to do or say.

"I will never understand a man like your father. Carelessly creating these tiny lives, little people who should be looked upon as gifts from God. But instead, a man like him sees these trusting, perfect children as assets to be used. Playing games with their well-being, with their futures, and only caring about how it impacts him in the end." Vanna's face twisted, features collapsing into a mask of grief. "A parent should love their children. Love and cherish them. I want you to know you aren't alone, Marian." Vanna's shoulders lifted and straightened, and she stared Marian in the eyes. "I'll always be here for you. You're home now, girl."

Blinking back a sudden wash of tears, Marian could only nod, the movement going on for what felt like hours. She accepted Vanna's words of censure for her father and his treatment of not only her but all her siblings. Took on the knowledge that Vanna understood what it was like to be forgotten until there was value in skills or the attractiveness of a growing body. Validated Vanna's read on how badly she and her siblings needed someone to be in their corner.

At the end, her head buzzing from the rapid rocking up and down, Marian turned and entered the bathroom. Face wet, she placed her clean clothing on the counter and dropped everything else to the floor. Shoulders heaving, she climbed into the shower and stood directly under the pounding flow of water. Biting her lips, she cried in silence, releasing all her bitterness and rage, imagining every moment was another pound of anger flowing down the drain.

All her life she'd wanted better. For her. For Myrt. For the boys.

It doesn't matter how it happened. Better is here, finally.

She vowed to embrace this offering with both arms. Take hold of the chance they'd been given and work it until everything was in place for her loved ones. She'd accept the help, their new place in a found family, and make sure no one ever had a reason to regret what they'd done.

They'd been past due for a change in luck, and in this house in Florida, surrounded by strangers, she and the boys had found something worth holding to.

Lucky me.

Chapter Six

Einstein

"Head out." Einstein flicked a finger towards the door. "I got tonight."

Marlin stared at him for only a single beat before laughing. "I'm not going to ask you if you're sure. Gonna head home and sleep in my own goddamned bed for a change." Shoving off the couch, he glanced towards the kitchen, then back at Einstein. "Call me if you need anything, or if anything changes."

"Will do, brother. Rest well." Einstein's gaze followed Marlin's, taking in Trina hovering over Retro's boys seated at the table. "See you tomorrow."

Retro's old lady had taken their presence better than Einstein had hoped, not questioning the reasoning for upping the security levels at their home. The only thing she'd really said about it had been a plea, but not one Einstein could lay a promise to. *"You'd tell me if he was in danger, wouldn't you?"* His response had been a flat stare, and she'd turned away with a huff of frustration.

She knew. They all knew. After the events of the past year, none of them were safe.

Chatter in the kitchen pulled his attention, and he rose from the couch, making it to the door in time to watch Marlin give Jimmy a high five, followed by a low five to Saya, then a quick side-hug to Trina. Einstein lifted a hand and waited until the door closed behind Marlin before turning to Trina and gesturing towards the living room with a tilt of his head.

Once they were out of earshot of the boys, he told her, "Just me tonight. I'll bunk downstairs, but don't worry if you hear me movin' around." He stared over her head back into the kitchen, seeing the two boys already clearing the table. "Stick to your normal routine, just like you did with Marlin. We've got you, Trina."

"I wish I knew what warranted this level of protection." She held up a hand between them like a stop sign, shaking her head. "I'm not badgering you for info. I know Retro wouldn't ask for this if it wasn't necessary. I just hate being in the dark."

Einstein took a moment to compare what he imagined Lauren's reaction would be to Trina's calm acceptance and shoved that thought aside. It didn't matter if one would have argued while another agreed. Each answer was valid, and neither was wrong.

"I understand, but in this instance, the answer can only come from Retro." Pasting a regretful expression on his face, he lifted a shoulder.

"And he's on the road, I know." She flashed him a grin that didn't reach her eyes, faking an easy response just like he had. "I'll pester him soon as I can talk to him. That way you're off the hook."

"That'd be best." He took a step towards the front door. "I'm going to do a circuit, check things outside while you get the kiddos buttoned up and ready for bed. Then I'll shut the house down and set the alarm. You wake up worried, just give me a call. Phone's always on me."

"Okay." She didn't move, staring hard at him. "I worry about you, Einstein."

"I'm good, little sister. No worries." The pat answer rolled off his tongue as it had so many times in recent months. "Don't gotta worry about me. Club's got my back."

"I worry." That grin reappeared, then faded. "If you ever need anything, I hope you know all you have to do is let us know. Retro would move heaven and earth to get you anything. Between him and me, we've got you covered."

"Nah. No need." He hooked a thumb over his shoulder. "Doin' my rounds." His hand was on the knob, escape only a moment away. "Back in a few."

"I know you have to miss her. I only got to meet her the once, and we chatted for moments before she was called away, but she really seemed like a good woman. I can't imagine not having Retro in my life, not after what we've shared." Her voice cracked and broke. "And your little girl."

"Don't."

He flattened a palm against the door, resting his forehead on the cool wood as rage swelled inside him against this woman who meant so much to his friend. The problem with her sympathy was it wasn't her grief she was stirring up. Wasn't her hurt she was laying bare again. Wasn't anything other than a misdirected unspoken gladness that she still had her family, her husband, their children—while his was gone. In an instant, he was furious at her fumbling attempts to console herself.

"For God's sake, don't."

"Jim."

A breeze drifted like a touch across the back of his neck, and he whirled, expecting her to have invaded his space, but Trina was clear across the room from where he stood. "Stop it."

"It's okay to not be okay." Her mouth didn't move, and the soft words seemed to come from the air around him instead of her lips.

Without another word, he whirled and flung open the interior door, fighting with the latch on the storm door for the space of a dozen mental curses. Then he was on the front walk, stalking away.

"I'm sorry." He never knew who he expected to hear his regret when he said it like this, alone, in the dark. The wetness on his face turned cold in the night air. "I'm so sorry."

Ignoring the ache in his chest, he made his way around the house and verified all the windows were closed, the garage locked, the pool house the same. When he reentered the house through the back door, only a nightlight remained on in the kitchen. On the countertop near the full coffeepot, he saw a plate and walked over to find a piece of cake and a note.

I'm sorry. It's not my place to bring up painful things. I know you're a night owl so made you coffee, and Saya said this is your favorite cake. ~T

"Dammit." *Why does she have to be so nice?* It would be easier if he could just stay mad at her, but with a few words, she'd acknowledged the very things that had so angered him.

Einstein filled a mug he pulled from the cabinet, taking in the scent of the dark, rich coffee with pleasure. He lifted the plate, holding the fork in place with his thumb, and turned to the table. A face hovered in the darkness outside, near enough to the window to be recognizable. "Motherfucker." Returning the mug and plate to the countertop, he looked at the man outside again. "Son of a *bitch*."

Keying in the alarm sequence, he opened the door only wide enough that Dolph Chulpayev could grab it and keep it from slamming shut. Backing away, he reached behind him to where his gun rested in a waistband holster, releasing the strap holding it in place.

"The fuck you want?"

Trina's father could be evicted from the property. That was a truth he knew, because he'd been here more than a year ago when it happened the first time. He'd heard about additional events that went down while he'd been holed up in his grief. Over the past months, however, it had become clear that Retro had an uneasy truce with his father-in-law. That meant Einstein needed to at least hear the man out before he pitched him back through the door.

It shocked him when Dolph walked in alone, locking the door behind him and casually keying in the alarm code. *That is something he should not know. Dammit.* Another note to file away in his head. He would deal with it only once this man was gone from this space.

Einstein looked through the windows, but no shadows moved. Nothing appeared out of place. Shifting around the kitchen towards the outside wall, he kept part of his attention on the door leading into the rest of the house. If Dolph had the code, he could have his men coming in the front door, ready to flank Einstein. Nerves fired along his spine, and he straightened, glancing out the windows again.

"Yes, I am alone," Dolph answered his unasked question. "I waited for Trina to retire. I should commend Retro on the diligence of his men. If I hadn't been watching for you, I would never have seen you patrolling. Your other members—" The way Dolph's mouth twisted said it all.

"What do you want?" He ignored the slight against his brothers' stealth abilities.

"I have information Retro will want." The pause was pregnant with tension, but Einstein opted to wait him out and force Dolph to continue. "It concerns the group responsible for your..." This pause was filled with Dolph's heavy sigh. "Trouble." The man's accent gave the word a guttural tonality that resonated throughout Einstein.

"The club's trouble?" He had an intuition of what Dolph meant but wanted it spelled out. *No guessing games, old man.*

"*Your* trouble."

Nail on the head. That's what he'd expected, but it still caused his stomach to lurch. Einstein cleared his throat, suddenly unsteady. "Which group? There were a couple of parties involved in my...trouble."

"Old money backing Dominic and his men. The dons are not happy he failed to pick up the reins."

"If you're talking about the info dump on Luciano, we already got that flagged and are pursuing." The way Dolph's eyes widened was gratifying. "Is there more?"

"Yes. They have upped the ante in the past day. Franco is missing. His associates assume the worst, so they are dictating the son step in and step up. If he declines, they will pursue Dominic. If Dominic fails to satisfy, they will search for the brother."

"Old news, old man. Already got that too." Folding his arms loosely over his chest, Einstein leaned back against the wall. From this position, he kept up his surveillance outside, through the door to the living room, and continued to observe Dolph closely. "You're keeping me from my cake. If you don't have anything new to offer, then kindly hie your ass back out the door."

"Did you ever meet Scar's parents? Luciano and Pearl?"

Einstein didn't react, keeping his gaze flicking between the window, door, and man in front of him.

"She is Native American. Luc met her in school and somehow convinced her to leave her family and move to the East Coast."

"What tribe?" This was new information, and Einstein could kick himself for not having anyone look deeper at the mother. They'd focused on the male-dominated relationships because of the Italian connection, and that now felt like a mistake. "She still with her old man?" The ease and familiarity with which Dolph spoke of Luciano didn't escape Einstein, which was another note to keep and follow up on later. *Calling him by a nickname wouldn't be a mistake, so it's something Dolph is expecting me to catch.* "What about the brother? Are you saying he's going to be found with family?"

"Your questions are many." One corner of Dolph's mouth pulled back. Not a smile, but not a disappointed grimace either. "Unfortunately, I only have a few answers. She's Crow, the only one to have moved away from the Montana family home. As far as her relationship with Luc—"

There's that diminutive again.

"—that is and always has been tumultuous. William—"

Ohh, got me a name, keep talkin' old man.

"—was seen there a few years ago, but apparently dropped off the face of the earth afterwards. He had a bad experience with a club—"

"Club?" Einstein could have kicked himself for interrupting, but all of this was brand-new information.

"Yes, a motorcycle club. Seems he and Scar are somewhat more alike than they'd like people to know, in that one way. The clubs—"

Clubs, as in plural. If they lost him in Big Sky Country, that means he has more than one organization in his background prior to the disappearance. More ground to cover. Maybe it's tied to that Michigan connection in the transcript.

"—William has been in are nothing like the Monster Devils, however. Which means he's yet unlike his brother. I've known Luc—"

Knew they were tight. He fought a smile at the blooming sense of satisfaction in his chest.

"—for years, and by all accounts William is a good man, much like his father."

"Tell me about his bad experience."

A grimace flickered into and out of existence on Dolph's features with the admission, "I do not have all the details."

Damn, that had to hurt to admit. Dolph's nearly as anal as Retro is about getting all the dirt.

Expression smooth again, Dolph continued, "But it surrounded a woman."

"You think the Italians factor into that situation at all?" A memory flashed through Einstein's head. There and gone in an instant, but Lauren's face was clear as day, closed eyes, ruby lips, chest still.

"No. That was pure human stupidity." Dolph stilled, his gaze drilling into Einstein. "She yet lives."

Pain cinched around his chest, and he fought to hide how those words had hit him. *So they kill my wife and daughter but spare the woman of a favored son.* "Good." That would be all Dolph got out of him on that topic, and Einstein pressed his lips together.

A slow exhale preceded Dolph's next question. "Do you know the full story of my history with Katrina's mother?"

The unexpected segue had Einstein's head shaking before he could think. "No." *What the hell does this have to do with anything?*

"I saw her. My attraction to her was unexpected, because my family had arranged for a marriage for me. I'd known from my teens what my path would be. Learn as much as I could in America, strengthen the family's hold on the southeast, and marry the woman groomed from childhood to be my wife. She was from Kiev, and the arrangement would solidify an agreement my family had with hers." Dolph pulled in a hard breath through flaring nostrils. "I would not have fought the course as laid out had I not conducted business in a library one day. Deloris"—Dolph's voice changed, dropping, so it was quiet and soft—"stole my heart without knowing or trying. I needed to know her, and then once I learned about her nature, I couldn't live without her."

Searching through his knowledge of Katrina's mother, Einstein offered up the only detail he could remember. "She was attacked after the birth, right?"

"Killed. She was killed following Katrina's entrance to the world. Killed in a hospital, surrounded by my bouquets and gifts, with our daughter in a bassinet next to her bed. A nurse interrupted the man and resuscitated my Deloris. Brought her back." Dolph's nostrils quivered as he sucked in another breath. "The damage was significant. Many said it would have been better if she hadn't survived." He leaned forward an inch. "They were wrong. I will always take her however I can have her, and the injuries inflicted didn't diminish my love for her."

"Why are you telling me this?" *I don't think Retro knows as much as the man just laid out for me.* "I don't get what that has to do with Scarloucci. Not sure what you want me to do with this."

"It has shit all to do with that cursed family. This is about me and how I relate to you. People I loved tried to kill my woman. Would probably have moved to my child next, if they hadn't gotten the results they wanted. People who had once meant the world to me, trying to gain my cooperation with their plans, caused pain and suffering for my family. I'm telling you so you know you aren't alone. The sense of betrayal never goes away. The anger—the rage will continue to eat at you inside for a long time. It could kill you if you let it. It will." Straightening his shoulders, Dolph lifted his chin and stared down his nose at Einstein. "Do not let it. You...you are a good man. Right now, you see everything through the lens of your grief, and that is to be expected. But you will one day have a moment where the rage leaves you, and what I want you to take away from this conversation is that it is okay. All of it, those emotions, they will come back but be lessened. That too is okay. Natural. Over and over, in its own timeline. What you have to remember is the natural way of things has life moving on. When it happens, let yourself be moved with it."

Einstein kept his gaze on the man as he keyed the alarm sequence again and opened the door. The broad back never slumped, the shoulders stayed rigid, and the tall man with questionable wisdom disappeared into the darkness.

***

Einstein

The sun rose, rays of brilliance spearing into the shadows inside Retro's home where Einstein occupied a kitchen chair, still awake. He'd made a second pot of coffee about an hour ago, when the first shades of pink and blue had appeared along the edge of the sky. There wasn't much more than dregs left. With a laptop in front of him, he took a moment to scan the camera feeds again. Moments away from retreating to the pool house, he leaned forwards and tapped on the keyboard, changing the display.

A message from Retro had come in during the night, the vibration of his phone signaling the communication. Now reading it a second time in the app installed on the computer, Einstein shook his head.

Baker, Florida. A tiny town not far inland from the Gulf Coast, it held nothing to pull the Bama Bastards.

Except.

He snorted and leaned back, scratching along the edge of his jaw, scruff bristly against his fingertips.

Except it was the home of a Rebel Wayfarers chapter officer, Truck. And a frequent vacation spot of another RWMC officer, Gunny, recently petitioned to become a nomad. That knowledge had set tiny seeds growing in Einstein's brain. In the next few hours, tiny Baker would become the new location of an RWMC chapter, folding in those two men as well as members from a variety of clubs—including the Bastards.

At least that was the plan for now. *Shit changes with the wind.*

Rolling his eyes, he flipped back to the ranks of camera videos and looked at each closely. Reassured that no bad actors waited outside, he exited the software and closed the laptop with a click as he rose from the table. Mug refilled, he dumped the rest of the old coffee, then set up a new pot for Trina to kick off when she woke.

Disarming the back door with the new code he'd input hours earlier, Einstein stepped outside and walked closer to the garage, peering through the large window in the last bay at a scatter of bike parts. Retro encouraged members to work on their rides here, and most of the men took him up on the offer. Einstein thought this might be Mudd's project bike, something he'd been sourcing parts for over the past few months, broadcasting both his enjoyment and frustration to anyone who'd listen.

Phone in hand, he tapped into the app, then connected with Retro's information, waiting through the silence until the speaker beeped. Voicemail. Didn't matter. He would deliver his update regardless.

"Hey, man, had a visitor last night. Chulpayev dropped by. He provided intel on the asks swirling around Scar. The Italians are going after family. Franco's missing, Dominic's in the crosshairs, and if he balks, sounds like they'll deal as they usually do and then go after the brother. Chulpayev had info about Scar's mother that was interesting and might provide a solid lead on this mystery family member. I want to track it down, man. Would require a road trip or two, so I'll wait for your word."

He swallowed, hoping the sound didn't pick up on the phone. "But I want this. The brother, he's in the life, man, but sounds like he's at odds with how Scar runs things. Might explain why he's not a MDMC member and is in Montana instead. I want this, Retro. Nomad makes the most sense. Know we don't normally patch for this, but I'll do whatever you want, man. Call me back when you can. Oh, and get this, Chulpayev had the security code. I've got that locked down, brother. Got your back, always. Glad you got there safe, and fuck—sounds like you've got your work cut out for you there. Who the fuck are you going to pitch to the RWMC wolves, man? Still Monday? I can't see him or anyone else wanting to pick up and move away. Glad that's all on you. Be safe, brother."

Disconnecting, he stood and watched the rippling water of the pool until lights came on in the main house.

Through the windows, he saw Trina pause at the coffeepot. She read his note and was turning towards the door when she paused and looked behind herself. Arms extending, she caught Saya in midleap, hugging him tightly against her body with a sway. Jimmy followed, slower, yawning, but he went to Trina for his own hug. Retro's daughter was the last into the kitchen, and like her brothers, Nelda made greeting Trina with arms wrapped around her neck her first stop.

Pain sliced through him, and with Dolph's cryptic statements fresh in his mind, Einstein studied the feelings, dissecting them.

"Nope, still hurts like fuck."

***

Marian

The sound of motorcycles seemed unending, the machines rolling into the driveway every few minutes over the past hour. Individual men, groups of them with club affiliations—each time Marian glanced out the window, the sea of black leather had grown.

Well-mannered—and she didn't know why that surprised her—they first greeted Truck, then Gunny, and then each man presented himself at the kitchen door asking for Vanna. Tall and broad, or thin and small—it didn't matter, their arms were opened wide for the woman who seemed to mother everyone, even those who were arguably older than she was.

Each interaction was a revelation for Marian. Some of the men spoke to Vanna as if they'd talked last week, comfortable and easy in their conversations. A few of them had remarked on the time passing since their last meeting, but still easy with their treatment of Vanna. And she gave it back to them as much as they dished it out. Snark and sarcasm were like subtext languages, defining their connections.

Some of the men clearly held more of Vanna's heart, and when Marian recognized one from the photos arrayed on the living room wall, she paid closer attention. Blackie pulled her close, and Vanna went willingly as they whisper-talked about someone named Peaches, who would be following soon—of course Marian had come to realize that soon might not mean today, but two weeks from now, or a month—and Blackie claimed Vanna's son as his own, something Marian didn't think was true, but showed again how interwoven this kind of found family could be. The affection between the two was sweet and strong and didn't diminish when Truck made his way up behind Vanna, wrapping his arms around her chest to tug her against his strong frame. Blackie didn't change the way he spoke to her at all, and Marian understood their friendship wasn't something they tried to hide. Vanna had love for both men, in different ways, and was proud to be their focus of attention.

Then Gunny had arrayed himself at Vanna's side, and that affection had expanded to include him, highlighting how right Marian was in her assessment.

What would it be like to have friends like that?

For the next few hours, she'd experimented. Hovering close to Sharon when she accompanied Gunny outside, Marian had been introduced to a multitude of men. Bikers in leather and denim, with long hair or short, bearded or smooth-shaven—they were unfailingly polite in a sweet way. Confidence oozed out of every man, and when Gunny would tell his story of meeting her, they each looked at her differently. Not bad different, not like the pastor's wife had the few times Daddy's marks had been on visible skin.

The different they offered was more supportive. Gunny would say she'd been in a "bad situation," and without asking for any specifics, the men would stand taller, adopt a more alert posture. It was as if each man took her safety upon themselves and had immediately embraced her in their inner circle of people worth protecting.

A few of the men had asked for more details, and Gunny would wait for her slow nod before responding. Then he'd explain about her and Myrt's father being a "douchenozzle" or "worse than a creek turd" and gloss over the fact he'd sold one of his children, then supplied two more of them to a heartless old man who'd proven ruthless and cruel, vicious in his treatment of Myrt, Luke, and Thad. He'd focus on Marian's rescue and emphasize how none of the siblings would ever be going back to the hell they'd lived through.

After hearing Gunny's rendition at least a dozen times, Marian had to excuse herself, retreating to the upstairs bedroom. Behind the closed door, cupping both hands over her open mouth, Marian had screamed in horror. She let the realization sink in that as bad as her life had become, she'd clearly escaped the worst the mountain had to offer by not having to go to Sallabrook's home. Unwanted emotions flooded through her, rushing along until her ears buzzed. Hands shaking, she admitted to herself that the unwarranted jealousy she'd harbored for her sister so long had shown how ignorant she'd been.

"I would have helped her." A broken mutter split the air, and Marian flinched from the sound of her own voice. "I swear, I would have. I didn't know."

"No one's blaming you, honey."

She whirled, stumbling away from the door. Slowly Gunny's face swam into focus, and Marian's knees unhinged, toppling her into a pile. He'd come in behind her and heard everything. "Oh God."

"If you didn't know what Myrt had been dealing with, then you can't be pissed at yourself for not helping her." He entered the room and closed the door behind him, then folded into a squat, balancing himself with a knee on the floor. "You can't take that on, Marian."

"He *raped* her." The words were hard to push out, a verbal acknowledgment of the horror her little sister had suffered. "She was just a child. Thad is *still* a child." *My baby brother.* Fists pressing to her temples, she bent over her lap, muffling her scream against her knees. "I want to *kill* him."

"Would you? Given the chance, would you take things into your own hands?"

"Yes." No time to think, no time to wonder if she spoke the truth, the word burst forth from her lips. "I want to. I want to go back to that mountain and hurt him. Kill him. Make him feel a fraction of the pain he's given my family."

"And your father? What would you do to him?"

Lifting her head, she leveled a glare at Gunny, knowing he'd understand he wasn't the true target. "I'll kill him, too."

"If something happened to them both, would you want to know? Want to hear the truth?"

She pulled her chin back, feeling the harsh expression on her face softening. *He did something.* "Yes." Hoping he wouldn't have noticed the instant of hesitation, she pushed forwards. "I'd want to know everything."

"Would you feel justice had been served, even if not at your hands?"

"If they were both dead?" She swallowed hard and held out her hands, showing him how they trembled as with a palsy. "I'm so angry, Gunny. If they were here, I'd tear them limb from limb. *They hurt my family.*" Marian straightened, realizing she'd bent forward with the force of her shout. "They need to pay."

Silence stretched between them until Gunny blinked, the corners of his mouth curling upward. "Fuckin' bloodthirsty woman. No wonder Shar likes you so much. Two of a kind." His head traveled side to side once, left, then right, then back to center. "They paid, Marian. Paid in blood and pain. It's done, honey. And you'll never have to worry about them again." Deep, sonorous, his voice wrapped around her, the fierceness in his tone holding her upright. "They fuckin' paid."

"Good." Lifting her head, she stared into Gunny's eyes, not flinching away from the anger she saw there. "No regrets from me."

"How often did your daddy beat you?"

"As often as he wanted." The pain in her body had been pushed aside during the emotional exchange and now came roaring back. "Since my momma passed. Even when he had Myrt's momma, he'd turn his frustration on me."

"Oh, darlin'. That's a shit life, woman."

"Yeah." Her laugh could score glass, rough and brittle. "Yeah. It really was."

"Now that? That sounds really good."

Marian narrowed her eyes, lifting a brow as she stared at him.

He grinned. "Puttin' that shit in your rearview. Past tense means you're startin' to move past it."

"I'm going to miss you and Sharon when you go home." Forcing a smile on her face, she could only hold it for a few seconds before she had to look down and clear her throat, blinking back tears. "How does it work that I just met you but feel like I've always known you?"

"Don't matter. Just matters what is. Shar and I are the same. We talked about it last night. You're a little sister at this point." He huffed out a laugh and stood. "Come on, woman. Shar's prolly freakin' out, and her losin' her mind ain't good, not for me at least. She's gonna wanna make sure you're okay."

He held out a hand, and Marian accepted the offer, meeting his palm with hers and marveling at how his swallowed hers whole. He gave a tug and she was on her feet.

"If I'm the little sister in this scenario, does that count for Sharon too?" He nodded and opened the door, stepping back to allow her to pass through first. "Hmm. I think a person can't ever have too much good family."

"That's a true statement if I ever heard one, lady."

They walked down the stairs with him a couple of steps behind, surging ahead when they got to the first floor so he could open the front door. Sure enough, Sharon and Vanna both were on the porch, keen gazes locked on Marian as she came through the opening.

"She's good." Sharon made a noise at Gunny's statement, and he held up both hands. "Swear, baby. Plus, you gals are two sticks, one fire. She's got a retribution streak just as wide as yours is." He pretended to wipe away a tear. "Made a brother proud. Real proud."

Marian snorted and moved into Vanna's arms, held wide to gently embrace her.

"You good, girl?"

Marian's nod moved her face farther into the crook of Vanna's neck, and tears threatened again just because this—a level of motherly concern and affection she couldn't remember ever being on the receiving end of—was almost too much. "I'm good."

Heat enfolded her as Sharon's voice came from next to her ear, and she understood the woman had pulled both Marian and Vanna into her own hug. "Even if you aren't right now, you will be. Saw a shirt the other day that resonated with me. Said 'It'll be fine in the end. If it's not fine, it's not the end.' We just gotta get past this mess, and you can settle into a life surrounded by people who love you for you. You and your sister."

Sharon's laughter was low and filled with as much affection as Vanna's hug. "Birds of a feather. You deserve so much, and we're going to make sure you get it all."

"Is it too soon for me to get in on this?" Vanna and Sharon squeezed tighter around Marian, and with a groan, she looked up to see Gunny had wrapped himself around all of them. "Shit, sorry, honey. It was a bonding moment, and I didn't think about your ribs. Still, I'm a proud brother all over again."

Laughter was a great tension eraser, and as the group hug fell apart, they were all laughing so loudly a couple of men nearby called out in irritation that they weren't in on the joke, whatever it was. Their complaints only made Marian laugh longer, each round of rising sound met by one from Sharon or Vanna.

"Time to start lunch," Vanna declared, stepping towards the door. "I'll take any helpers you can find for me, Lane."

"You got it, Vanna Mom." Gunny turned with a wink. "You wanna eat, you gonna help cook." Leaning against the porch railing, he bellowed the instructions out across the crowd, and Marian was shocked to see friendly waves returned to him, along with a general movement towards the house.

"There's not that many men. I can take care of lunch if you want."

Vanna's head was shaking as she entered the house. "Any help they offer is accepted, always. As is your offer." The call over her shoulder was accompanied by a come-on motion of her hand. "Let's get things started and see where it goes."

A couple of hours later, Marian's stomach was still complaining about the quantity of food she'd eaten, and like many of the group, she had found a comfortable position lounging in a chair. She was in the kitchen, which was where the women and older men seemed to cluster. The younger men and kids all gravitated to the living room, where someone had put on an animated movie. She'd expected objections from the men, but everyone seemed engrossed in the cartoony drama, with Sharon's and Gunny's kids—Cade, Kitten, and Josh—perched on various laps around the room.

She heard something and cocked her head slightly, listening closely. Another bike was approaching. Looking at Truck, she saw he'd heard it too, an anticipatory expression on his face. He stood and angled to look out a window, then called out, "They're here."

It took her a moment longer than the other people in the kitchen to understand what he meant, so she was behind the first flood of people exiting the house. Still in time to see Bane assist Myrt off the motorcycle, watching as her sister's face beamed a smile. Luke and Thad encircled her, and when Marian reached them, they immediately pulled her into the embrace.

"You're here." Luke's whisper communicated he'd been worried without saying anything, and Marian felt a pang of guilt at not reassuring him better. "All of us together. *Here.* It's so good here, Myrtie. Everybody is nice. Truck showed me how to help him change his oil, and never once did I mess up. I did it right from the beginning. I never had that. It's so good."

Thad snuffled wetly and pressed his head against Marian's shoulder. "I'm glad to have you here with us. Lukie's right. It's good here. Can we stay? Do we get to stay here?" He angled his head to look up at Marian, tears streaking his face. "We don't gotta leave, do we?"

"No." Myrtle's reply was immediate and firm, convinced in her response. "We live here now. Nobody's going to make us leave, Thad. We live here now."

Staring at her sister, the lines in Myrt's face making her seem older than her years, Marian was struck by the reversal of their roles. Myrt had suddenly become the sister with all the answers, the leader of their little family. She felt a weight fall away, a burden she didn't even know she'd been carrying leaving her reeling a little as it began to disappear.

"Vanna said we'd have a place as long as we wanted." Marian threw her tiny reassurance into the mix alongside Myrt's confidence. "Gunny said we're part of his found family. I don't think he'll let anything happen to us ever again."

"And Bane is the same." Myrt returned Marian's glance with a shy grin. "I'm with him."

"Like Bane's your boyfriend?" Thad straightened as his expression threatened to turn from happiness into a glower. "Is he good enough? Man's got to be good to be good enough for my sister. When did that happen? Is that why you didn't come with us? Wanted to be alone with him?"

Marian froze and waited to see how Myrt would react to the rapid-fire questions their brother had lobbed at her.

Myrt lifted her hands and cupped Thad's cheeks, pulling him in so she could kiss his forehead. "Bane's a good, good man. I love him." He deflated a little, the protector fleeing as hope returned to his features.

I shouldn't have worried.

"Gunny's good, too." Luke's interjection had Marian laughing aloud. "What? He is."

"Gunny's also married." Marian stepped back, grasping Myrt's hand in hers. "Let's get inside. You've been on the road for a while." Myrt rolled her eyes and then froze in place with a groan.

"Get me a chair with a pillow? I want to hear everything, but my bottom hurts like the devil."

"You heard her." She tapped Luke's shoulder and gave Thad a tiny shove in the direction of the house. "Get a cushion for one of the kitchen chairs." The boys rattled up the steps and through the door as Marian turned back to her sister, giving her hand a tug. "Come on, you can lean on me."

They'd gotten to the top of the steps when Luke gave a cry. Myrt squeezed her hand before dropping their hold. "Go see what happened."

Marian left her behind and entered the living room. Luke held a bare pillow, the covering in Thad's hands. "Boys." The grin on her face belied the attempt at scolding, and they both knew it. She took the pillow and case, reassembling it as she made her way to the kitchen.

The next hours flew by, talk interspersed with laughter followed by more food. Marian made herself useful when she could, keeping an eye on Myrt where she sat at the table, surrounded by women who'd ridden in with their men. The names were too many for Marian to keep track of, so she didn't try, except for those Sharon specifically introduced her to, like Peaches, who was married to Blackie, who was Bane's boss. Then the house was filled to the brim with men as they finished whatever business they'd had outside.

When the cacophony of noise became too much, Marian would go upstairs to the room allotted her and the boys. Just having a closed door between her and the rest of the people helped, and she was never alone long. Sharon and Gunny took turns coming up to keep her company, their quiet acceptance of how overwhelmed she felt a solace in itself.

One trip upstairs had Vanna come to find her, and they sat, listening to the shouts and laughter from downstairs.

"It'll be loud here all night." Vanna's smile said she didn't mind, and Marian steeled herself to be okay with it too. "Truck owns the house just down the road. It's been waiting for a family to claim it. I thought it might be Sharon and Gunny, but she's found a bigger place just behind ours. Adjoining property lines. Bane's moving down here to be with Myrt, and we sent them over to the empty house a while ago."

"I didn't get to say goodnight." Marian's breathing grew choppy. "I'm sorry I haven't been more help, Vanna Mom."

"You and the boys will be headed over in a bit."

"Oh."

Vanna's lips curled in a knowing smile and she waggled her eyebrows. "The new couple needed a little alone time."

"*Oh*." Marian's cheeks were hot as fire, and she ducked her head, staring at her knees. "He's a good man?"

"One of the best. Truck wouldn't stand for what's happening between them if he didn't think he could trust Bane with her life." Neither of them spoke for a beat; then Vanna continued. "These men, they look rough on the outside, but you won't find a more loyal and loving group if you tried. Gunny's a fan of Bane's. I'm sure you saw that up in Kentucky. You trust him, right?"

"Yeah. A lot. More than I should, probably."

"No, girl. There's no one I'd trust more than Lane." She laughed softly. "Well, except for Truck, of course. But Lane? He'll bend himself into a pretzel to help someone he considers family, and that's how he sees you and Myrt and the boys. He's said it, I'm sure, and it might take a while to completely understand what he means, but it boils down to the fact he'd die before he let someone hurt you. That's not an exaggeration, either. I've seen the man throw himself into situations where the outcome wasn't certain, to make sure his people, those he loves, were okay."

"I get it. We had a talk, and I listened to what he said and didn't say. I know what he did for us." She lifted her head and stared at Vanna, watching for any consternation or condemnation, ready to stand up for Gunny if needed.

"Oh, honey. Looks like you've got a protective side to you too."

"If I'd known what was happening—"

"You don't have to defend yourself here, Marian. Not against something that was out of your control. No one here will criticize you for that." Vanna's expression made Marian's breath catch in her throat. "We all have guilt about things that happened where we could effect no change. Just gotta get past it and see the good in what's happening today." Slapping her palms against her thighs, Vanna pushed to her feet. "Ready to go see your new home?"

"Home?" Standing, she turned to face Vanna, who was moving towards the closet. "We're going to stay there? Not here?"

"Honey, you'll be less than a quarter of a mile away. I'm just a shout from the porch over there, and you can be here as much as you want." She disappeared inside the closet, and Marian heard rustling, then a soft, "aha." Backing out, Vanna had a suitcase in her hand. "Let's get you packed up. Boys' bags won't take long. I'll do those"—she tossed the suitcase on the bed—"and you can get your stuff gathered. The men are waiting downstairs to walk you all over."

Marian stepped over to the bed and stared down at the suitcase. Another example of the generosity of these people, this woman. *We're so lucky Vanna found Myrt.* "I think I love you, Vanna Mom."

"Oh, Marian. It's just an old suitcase. I don't use it anymore. You're doing me a favor, honestly. It's just been cluttering up that closet. But I love you too." The boys' bags thumped against the floor in rapid order, one after the other. "Done here. You need some help?"

"No. I've got it." Marian had transferred her things from the garbage bag to a single drawer in the dresser along the wall, and it didn't take long to retrieve and arrange them in the suitcase. She shook her head at Vanna's attempt to reach for the boys' bags and looped the straps over her shoulder. "Ready."

Downstairs, Gunny and Truck waited with Blackie and another man, each of them armed with a large flashlight. Marian glanced at the windows and realized she'd been upstairs long enough for night to fall. Clenching her teeth against the urge to apologize, for what she didn't know, she forced a pleasant expression. That morphed into a true smile when the boys walked into the room, Thad his accustomed half a step behind his brother. *He's protecting him.* She recognized that for what it was now, having seen it modeled by each of the men in the room.

With only a modicum of conversation, they went out the back door of the kitchen and made their way through a field, coming to the other side and weaving between trees.

"Should get my brush hog out here, clear a path." Truck's light flicked back and forth.

"I can do that in the morning." Gunny's voice came from behind her.

"Not too early, me and Peaches gonna be up late." The drawled words were Blackie's, and she realized his lewd meaning when the men around her laughed softly.

"I got you, brother." The beam from Gunny's light kept a steady trail in front of Marian's feet. "Watch that tangle, little sister. Careful now. Gimme that." The suitcase slipped from her fingers. "Shoulda noticed it back at the house. Boys, get your own bags. Your sister shouldn't be haulin' your stuff around."

Every light in the woods zeroed in on Marian, and she froze. Thad stepped into the spotlight and took the bags from her, handing one behind him to who she assumed was Luke, but the lights were so brilliant she couldn't see beyond the glowing circle. Chin down, she tried to escape scrutiny and knew she was unsuccessful when a hand landed on her shoulder.

"Little sister." Not Gunny, and the unfamiliar man touching her made every hair on her body stand on end. Marian stumbled sideways, out from under the light grip, lifting a hand to shade her eyes. "Hey now, it's okay. It's Blackie. I won't hurt you."

Marian tripped over an unseen obstacle, her plunge to the ground halted painfully by a sudden grasp of her upper arm. Struggling futilely, she quickly subsided with her head down, elbows next to her sides as she gasped for air.

"Let go of her." Thad sounded too far away, and Marian struggled to stay in control. "I said let her go."

"It's okay." Crackling branches accompanied someone's approach, the grip on her arm not easing. "I'm fine." As she pushed those words out with a little more force, it seemed they'd heard her, because the footsteps stopped. "I just got turned around with the lights. I'm fine."

"Little sister." That nearby repeat of Gunny's name for her was not in his voice. "You don't know me, but trust that if we're this close to you, I don't pose any threat. None at all. Sweet lady, I just didn't want you to fall, that's all." The hand on her arm slipped down, cupping her elbow. "I'll be your guide until your eyes readjust, if you'll let me."

"Who are you?"

"These reprobates call me Horse. I'm with Blackie, and as close to Bane's best friend as he'd ever find. You're safe with me." She tried to take a step, finding herself still tangled with whatever had first tripped her. "Just a sec." He came into view at her side as he knelt, one hand still anchoring her elbow, the other working at her ankle. "There, that should do it. Gunny, you need some help with the mowing, I'll be up and at 'em early enough. Just give me a wave. This isn't safe for folks walking back and forth."

"Well, I foresee that there's going to be some traffic between the houses. We'll get it done early, no matter what your president has to say." Gunny's snort expressed his attitude well.

Laughter bubbled up from Horse as he walked next to Marian. "Watch who you piss off, man. I heard the plans."

"Yeah, but it ain't in effect yet, so I'm safe."

"T-minus eight hours and counting." Without the lights shining in her eyes, Marian could make out the faces of the men walking all around her and the boys. Blackie's grin was broad and looked genuine, revealing that whatever they were all talking about, it made him happy. "Cannot fucking wait."

"You good, Marian?" She chanced a glance at Horse's face, finding worried eyes turned her way. "That was a near tumble, but seemed to pack a punch even if you didn't land."

"I've—" Her mouth wouldn't cooperate with her mind's intent of glossing over, and the fight with her tongue tied it into silence.

"Her old man beat her black and blue. She's got some fractured ribs, if not clear broke." Flat in timbre, Gunny's voice still conveyed the depths of his fury, at least to her ears, and Marian was surprised the trees didn't go up in flames at the hotness of his rage.

"Oh, shit." Horse pulled her closer to his side, his hand slipping away and curling around her shoulders. "I've got you, little sister." Fingers threaded between hers in a gentle hold that somehow steadied her more. "Won't let you fall, promise." His hold on her didn't change, but his voice was rigid as steel as he asked Gunny, "You deal with the motherfucker?"

"Aww, yeah. He's dealt with, and I raised the stakes until he couldn't pony up."

"*Gunny.*" She craned her neck to look over Horse's shoulder, wanting Gunny to shut up before the boys overheard.

"No worries, Maid Marian. They're at the house already, well out of earshot. Far as I know, Myrt doesn't know either. I knew you could handle it, but you want to hold it close, that's fine with me." The beam from his flashlight flicked up and traced the bodies already on the porch of the rapidly nearing house. "You wanna share, that's also fine with me. I trust you, lady."

"Maid Marian." The words flowed from Horse, his voice low and coarse, ruffling her nerves like a breeze would ruffle her hair. "I like that."

The open door shed light onto the porch and down the steps, illuminating the final distance to the house. She straightened and tugged discreetly, but Horse didn't relax his hold, keeping her tucked against his side.

"I'm good now, thank you." Stopping in place seemed to trigger something for him, because his hands fell away immediately. "Gunny, I can take that."

"No you can't. Not if I don't let you." He lifted his lip in a fake snarl as he moved past her and inside the house. His "Bane, brother, where's Marian's room?" filtered back outside.

"That man." She looked over as Horse ostentatiously cleared his throat. "Yes?"

"He's married." Horse gestured back into the dark where they'd come from and Marian narrowed her eyes as she waited for him to elaborate. "In case you didn't know."

"Oh, I know. Married to Sharon, and they have three kids that both Vanna and Truck claim as their own. I'm not sure what you're implying." Her ribs hurt badly enough she had to fight the urge to shuffle, not wanting to show this man any more weakness than he'd already seen from her. "He saved my life. Not for any kind of payment, but because it was the right thing to do. He and Bane rescued me, when I'd long ago thought any escape was impossible. What you're not saying is something that would hurt him. What about me makes you think I'd do that?"

"Firecracker. I just…" He scoffed and made a frustrated noise. "Way you looked at him, that's how some of the girls look at a man they want. Thought you should know."

"Well, thanks for that grace, small as it is. I have no designs on Gunny." Wrapping her arms around herself, she lost her struggle against a groan. "No designs on any man." Turning, she made her slow way up the steps, taking them with an even stride. Through the open door, she saw Luke and Thad with their arms around Myrt, and Bane and Gunny standing to the side. Bane was looking at Myrt with that expression Marian had seen before, like something about Myrtle solved the world's mysteries in his eyes.

Gunny was looking at her, then flicked his gaze to the doorway at her back. "Horse go back to the house?"

The headshake she gave him was small and confused and probably showed every ounce of hurt that was still bubbling through her at Horse's words. "I don't know."

And don't care.

Chapter Seven
Einstein

"You're sure?" Slowly sinking onto the edge of his bed, Einstein stared at the partly open door leading to the hallway. "It's him? He's been under our noses all this time?"

"I wouldn't label it as under our noses. Man's been patched into Blackie's crew for a while now, but we don't make that many trips their direction. When he comes this way, Blackie usually brings the same couple of men. Just not been an opportunity to make his acquaintance thus far." Mudd's drawl was missing, the words clipped and spoken at a quick pace as he delivered information efficiently. "Retro said you should come here first. Might be a reason to head west, but for now, he'd like you down here."

"When?" Easier to give in on this, especially since it was Mudd and not Retro. He knew from experience how frustrating it could be when—as the message bearer—the instructions were ignored.

"How about now?"

"Shit." Einstein let his head drop forward, stretching the muscles of his upper back. "I'll take thirty minutes to grab some lunch and a shower, and I'll be on my way. Call you as I go along, or just show up?"

"I'll text you the address."

The call disconnected, and a moment later, he had the location for the map app on the phone.

"And that's shorthand for don't stop, don't call, don't take a shit—just ride." He stood and, in the space of a few minutes, had packed a bag, including spare ammunition for his preferred gun. Staring around the small room that had become home, he hummed and sighed, the sense he'd forgotten something as irritating as losing a word on the tip of his tongue. "Whatever it is, it can't be that important."

He was nearly halfway down the stairs when it hit him, and he headed back up, taking the steps two at a time. In the bedroom suite, he went directly to the bathroom and scooped up the toothbrush he'd kept all this time, tucking it into the inside pocket of his vest and securing the fastening to keep the pocket closed.

"*Oh, honey.*" Lauren's voice was exactly as he remembered it, and he spun in a circle, heart in his throat.

"I'm goin' fuckin' nuts." Staring at himself in the bathroom mirror, he took a long look at the changes wrought by nearly a year. The grizzle in his beard was more pronounced, lines in his forehead deeper, and his lips had settled into an enduring scowl. Lauren hadn't been a fan of his tattoos, all gained since they'd first married, and the leather vest over his bare chest showed them off in full glory. If he were to meet her for the first time right now, she probably wouldn't give him the time of day.

Don't fuckin' matter anymore, does it?

Shaking his head, he trotted down the stairs and hunted through the rooms until he found Marlin in the kitchen, talking with Crazy Mike.

"Glad I caught you two. I just got off the horn with Mudd. Retro wants me to come to Baker, interview one of Blackie's men. Turns out Scar's brother is in the life, but one more like ours and less like his fucked-up family."

"Are you shittin' me?" Crazy Mike's hands rose, fingers closing over his palm, making a grasping fist. "That close, and we couldn't get our hands on him?"

"Guess he's not advertised the relationship much. I'm assuming Blackie knew, but you know what they say." Einstein adjusted the bag over his shoulder. "Headed out now. The only update call they want from me is knuckles against the door when I get there. You both aware of the arrangement they've all made in Baker?"

Marlin stretched his neck. "Yeah. Monday's going to be our offering. Sucks, man, he's good."

"Agreed. Wasn't displeased when we took him on from the Freaks." Ryman had been a fringe member of a nearby club called the Borderline Freaks MC and had arranged to patch over to the Bastards following some personal drama. He'd wanted a move and a clean break, and the Bastards had given him that. As former independent security hired out by the military, he was disciplined and intelligent and able to analyze a situation almost as fast as Retro—which was saying something. "Saw how he was when he took on his patch for the Bastards. Loyalty earned by trust, and that tells me we can't assume he'll be an inside lead on anything going on in the Freed Riders, man. Admire that about a man when he joins us."

"When he leaves us? Not so much." Crazy Mike eyed a clock on the wall. "You got about three hours, add a few for fueling. Boss man calleth."

"And the men followeth." Einstein tapped a finger to his temple. "I know how the man works. I'm headed out now. Just wanted to give you the info so if he needs more from up here, you're up to speed. Give you a chance to fill my rotation at Retro's house."

"Obliged." Marlin's top lip curled in a tiny grin. "Be safe, brother. You need one of us with you, we can be ready in ten."

"I'm good." Forcing himself to meet their gazes, he let the smile he had plastered on fade. If the wince Crazy Mike gave was any indication, he might have let too much honesty slip through. "If I wasn't, I'd ask. No worries, brothers."

"Hmph. I'm guessing that's not as reassuring as you'd like to think, man. But we'll take it at face value and trust you to make that call. Even if you didn't in the past, I for one gotta believe you've learned." Mike leaned close, hand extended, and Einstein met it with his own tight grip. Pulled off-balance by a tug, he landed with his shoulder in Mike's chest. Then he was held in place by an arm around his neck. "Fuckin' love you, brother. I find out you needed me and didn't make that goddamned call? I'm gonna be one pissed-off Bastard."

"You and me both," Marlin chimed in as Einstein pulled away from Mike. "Don't hurt me anymore, man." The pouting expression he pulled was hilarious, and the kitchen filled with laughter.

"Jesus, give it a break. I *will* ask, I fucking swear." At the door, he paused and glanced over his shoulder. "Make me proud."

"Sure, Daddy."

Einstein was glad he'd already turned away so Crazy Mike wouldn't see how that—just that word, spoken so casually—tore him up inside.

Not yet, Dolph.

He double-checked to make sure his tool kit was safely stored in the bottom of one saddlebag, then strapped his duffel to the bike, pulling on the bungee netting to verify the tautness. Helmet in hand, he straddled the seat just as his phone buzzed, so he shoved one hand in a pocket to retrieve the device.

The screen told him what he needed to know, and with a tap, he sent the call from his in-laws to voicemail. It would be his mother-in-law, and she'd want to know what he planned for the one-year anniversary of

Lauren's and Makayla's death. *Nothing, that's what I've got on tap.* In a way, this trip was a godsend, because by not being here, he could honestly tell them it couldn't happen. *Not right now, not ever.* Any kind of memorial would feel like a celebration, and he wasn't ready to find the goodness in the end of their lives, couldn't see his way clear to that kind of a gathering. *Probably not ever.*

Helmet strapped tight, he checked the contents of his pockets as he placed the phone back where it belonged. Wallet on a chain and clipped to a belt loop, phone tucked deep, he verified everything and then made a final pat against the front of his vest, the hard cylinder of the toothbrush safely stored away.

Three and a half hours later, as he followed the directions read through at the last fuel stop, his gaze flicked from the odometer to the upcoming turn onto a narrow country road. *That's it. Nearly there.* The ride hadn't been onerous, with light traffic and sunny weather, but he was ready to be still for a while, this being the longest trip he'd made in more than a year. Riding around Birmingham for hours wasn't the same as a long-distance highway trip, and one—conducted with friends at his side—was significantly less wearying than the other.

Even if he hadn't memorized the distance to Truck's house, he could have easily picked it out from the crowd of bikes spread out in the yard and a field adjacent to the structure. A truck and trailer were parked perpendicular to the road, and Einstein eased his tires up past the rig, scouting around to find Retro's bike. Seeing it in the field behind the house, he rolled that direction, feet down in case he needed to balance the bike.

By the time he'd parked and removed his helmet, he could see Mudd already headed his way. With a quick stretch, he hung the helmet from the handlebars and adjusted his wallet, quickly patting the pockets of his jeans and front of his vest to ensure nothing had been lost. As he met Mudd halfway, they greeted each other with gripped wrists and fists thumping solidly against broad backs.

"Brother. You made good time."

"You kinda implied it was in my best interest." Einstein pulled a face, breaking character with a grin. "I do what I'm told, boss."

"That true? News to me, but I'm sure Retro'll be glad to hear it." Mudd indicated the house with a tilt of his head. "Let's go introduce you. Shit's already gone down, and get this…Rebels pitched two heavy hitters into the mix with both Truck and Gunny patching over. I'd expected Truck, but Gunny was a surprise. Twisted's offered up a member, Coolaid, most recently in his Big Bend chapter. Shit's movin' fast with this one. Monday should be down here within the week, and Retro's gauging interest from a couple of RC members we know."

"Interesting. I think I'd rather have Gunny here as a member than roving as nomad." Einstein slowed Mudd with a hand on his arm. "Retro tell you about Chulpayev showing at his house, and what he gave us?"

"Yeah. Glad as fuck you were there. Making it a rotation was a good idea. How the hell'd he get the code for the alarm?" Mudd's scowl showed he was as unimpressed as Einstein had been. "That's some shit, man."

"No idea, but we're doing a rotation on that now, too. I also put the secure app on Trina's phone, and we're sending the new code that way. Hey." Einstein turned partly away, not wanting to see Mudd's expression. "Retro tell you the rest of what I left in the voicemail?"

"Yeah, and you'd get a flat no if you'd asked me that shit, brother." Mudd's headshake echoed his dismissal of Einstein's request. "We just got you back, man. Not ready for you to roll off down the road yet."

"Which way is Retro leaning? You know at all?" With Scar's brother identified and located, he didn't know what was pushing him on this, why he'd keep asking if there wasn't a demonstrated urgency. *Even if this is his brother, that doesn't tell me where Scar is.* "Tearing me up, man." A little truth could go a long way to sway Mudd his way. "This brother, if he's as good a man as I'm hearing, I'm not sure how Scar went so wrong. Don't know, but I need the man to pay." Breath whistling in and out like he'd run a footrace, he propped fists against his hips. "He's got to pay."

"And that right there is why I think you goin' nomad is the wrong path, brother. You get a lead on him and you'll be off to the races, not wastin' time to make a call, no matter how at risk it might put you." Mudd's gaze lifted to the sky, and he heaved out a lungful of air. "You fuckin' matter to me. To the club." Chin dropping, he locked eyes on Einstein with a glare. "You don't see it because you're inside it, but we fuckin' need you. I might be Jerry's oldest friend, but you're yards and yards closer to him now than I am. He's still tore up about how shit went down with Lauren and your little girl, and I know him—that man's gonna grant your ask. Gonna let you ride your ass off into the sunset as you look for a man who's a master at bein' a ghost. You ever think the reason we can't find Dominic is because he's no longer in the country? He's got family on two continents, and nothin' to say he didn't go to Italy. I know the Jersey boys are looking inland for him, chasing the matriarchal side of things, but my gut tells me if he were there, we would have located him by now."

"His blood brother hung under the radar for years, Mudd. What makes you think we'd be more successful long-distance at finding Scar? I gotta talk to this Bane to make up my mind, but if he spent time in Michigan and then the frozen north without us raising a trace of him? Scar'll have access to more resources, better intel, and his motive for staying hidden is a fucking better one than just turning his back on his blood." Einstein muffled his scoff, the sound coming out as a grunt. "Finding the brother was the catalyst for me wanting nomad, but now I see the need even more. This is how I'll find Scar, I feel it."

"By puttin' a nomad rocker on your goddamned vest? By divorcing yourself from the help of your brothers?" Mudd began to stalk away. "God bless, there's no talkin' sense into you. You're gonna fuckin' kill yourself, and this is the way you'll do it. Not gettin' my vote, I tell you that now." Angling his neck, he yelled over his shoulder, "You wanna fuckin' die, then pull the trigger where we can mourn you, man. Don't prolong the agony like this. Retro needs you, but if you don't want to hear that, then you do your thing, brother. I'll miss you when you're gone."

Einstein watched as Mudd angled through a gate and ducked under a clothesline filled with sheets and towels, disappearing behind the fabric. A door opened in the distance and closed, and apart from the grumbling rumble of voices from the front yard, he stood in silence.

I'm not trying to kill myself.

Closing his eyes, he jerked when an image of Lauren's face swam into focus, rising out of the darkness. Her, dead in the van, inches away, but he couldn't break his bonds and touch her. Couldn't check on her or their daughter, and that struggle had nearly cost him his sanity. *Why can't I remember her alive?* Tucking his chin to his neck, he searched for a memory, only able to capture flashes of events in their past. Her smile on their wedding day, the flash of her eyes as she told him they were expecting, the grip of her hand on his as she pushed their daughter into the world—pieces, broken from the whole, shattered in such a way that he'd never be able to put them back together.

I just want Scar to pay.

Not believing his own lie, Einstein opened his eyes and looked around, taking in the whole scene for the first time. The house was encircled by tall pine trees, and the scent of sap was strong in the air. A donkey heehawing nearby was followed by raucous male laughter, and he tracked that sound around the house, rounding the corner to the front yard to see a dozen faces he recognized.

The subsequent greetings were subdued, something he'd become accustomed to over the past few months. Men who knew the story would be avoiding bringing it up, wary of the conversational topics they were uncomfortable with around him, and men who didn't know would be looking at their friends with puzzled gazes, but still following their lead.

Retro walked out of the front door and trotted down the steps, bootheels noisy on the wooden treads. Mudd appeared in his wake, moving slower, his gaze pinning Einstein in place. Retro stepped between them, his signature mane of hair loose, telegraphing to those who knew him that he expected to remain here for a time. If it had been braided, that would have put forward a different nonverbal dialogue, and Einstein smiled as he welcomed him, enjoying that he knew his friend so well.

"You made good time." Retro pulled back from their one-armed clinch, eyes narrowing at Einstein's laughter.

Still chuckling, he explained, "Same thing Mudd said."

"Well, just goes to show you how great minds think alike."

Shit, did Mudd already talk to him? Retro's words played through Einstein's head. *He's not going to allow it. Dammit.*

"Did I take a shit on your plans? No, sir, I did not." Retro clamped a hand on Einstein's shoulder and pulled him to the side of the house, away from the larger group. "I haven't even addressed your request yet, man. Stop making that face."

"I just thought—"

"If that's how well you think these days, then my answer's gonna wind up a flat no. If you're gonna be the Einstein of a year ago, I'm a maybe. A could-be-convinced maybe." The corners of Retro's mouth turned down, expression sour as if he'd tasted something vile. "You with us, brother? Body and soul? Your mind tuned in to what we need to pay attention to?"

"Yes."

"Don't seem like it. You standin' here like this, lookin' like that? It's makin' me question even having you make this run." Tongue poking at the inside of his cheek, Retro scanned him down and up, gaze lingering on Einstein's face. "Am I wrong about you? About where you are inside your head?" He held up a hand, palm facing Einstein. "No, don't answer fast. You take a fuckin' minute and work through things. Hold your tongue until you understand where I'm comin' from, man. Anything less won't earn my confidence."

Noise swelled in the background, laughter as the donkey brayed again and again, the ludicrous soundtrack impossible to ignore as he dug deep inside himself to find a way to reassure both Retro and Mudd.

I need to find Scar. That was a given; the man had cost Einstein his family. *He needs to pay.* It might not have been his hands that killed Lauren and Makayla, but he'd been the originator of the fucked-up situation. Scar, who'd already taken his pound of flesh directly from Einstein's hide, demanding a beatout that could easily have been fatal.

I knew him. Maybe too well. Scar who'd pursued ex-members with a vengeful hatred, something Einstein had seen again and again while still a member of the Monster Devils. Nothing was enough for the man. He saw every man who patched out as a deserter, branded in his eyes by what he claimed was weakness.

Shit. This was the first time he'd forced himself to dig so deep, the litany of retribution loud in his head for so long he hadn't been able to see past it. *I knew him. Knew what he was capable of.* Einstein rocked back on his heels, putting as much distance between him and Retro as he could without having to take a step away. *I should have seen it coming.*

"Even when he sent the message, I didn't give it enough weight. He'd gone after previous members before, no matter if they'd gone out good or were out bad. Status didn't matter. To him, they were traitors. I told you about what he'd said and gave you my evaluation of the threat to the club, but I discounted what it might mean for my family." Angling his face to the side, he stared at the boot-churned ground, not finding any refuge there. "He was cold. So fuckin' cold, and didn't give a fat shit about anyone but himself. I shoulda been more careful." Lifting a hand, he scrubbed it across his cheeks, surprised to find the skin dry. "I feel like it's on me as much as him. But that doesn't change my need. He's got to pay."

"That's the kind of introspection I can get behind. I don't agree with everything you just said, but I see where it might weave that story in your head. Understand, this is why you've got to talk to us, brother. You get inside your head and fuck up your mind, and we—me and Mudd at least—we can help you unfuck that shit. Scar took you and your family. It's his actions that caused Lauren and Makayla to be where they were, and ultimately what happened is on him, not you. Not you. Fuck no, not you." Retro laughed, the anguished sound causing Einstein to look into the man's eyes. There was no recrimination there, no hard dismissal. "You got to get with the program, find a way to believe in what I believe. Then, if we can keep movin' forward like this, you'll be okay."

Mudd shuffled closer. "None of us gave his message the weight it needed. It was positioned as a cry for help from a club's president and something entirely unheard of for the man Scar had always shown himself to be. Why would we believe a lick of it, knowing the kind of hard-ass shit he'd pulled in the past? No." Mudd shook his head. "I still trust in our process. We digested, pulled it apart and put it back together, and came up with a logical thesis for the situation. That means between the time he messaged and when he showed up in your house, something changed. He wasn't there right away, wasn't there even a week later. Whatever it was, it took a while to set things in motion. Maybe that needs to be the first thing you look for, to find that trigger, see what knocked him loose from his mooring and aimed him your way."

"Good thoughts," Retro agreed, straightening his shoulders. "I'd be all over it, but I trust Einstein to know his path." He leaned closer, tip of his index finger thudding against Einstein's sternum in an insistent beat. "I also trust your ass to check in like I tell you to, and if you don't, then I'll haul your ass back home. No in-between bullshit. You do it my way, or you'll be on the highway back to where I can kick said ass."

"You're—" Einstein wasn't sure what he wanted to ask.

"Yes." Fortunately, Retro didn't have any trouble reading him. "Yeah, brother. I told you I'd do whatever you needed. Did you think so little of me to believe I'd lie about something like that?"

"Bastards haven't had a nomad before." His grin broke free, and he worked on taming it back. It couldn't hurt to show how much it meant, but wouldn't bode well if he looked like he'd lost his mind. *I probably look worse than Crazy Mike on a three-day bender.* "You always said that wasn't in the cards. That you wanted to keep things close to home."

"Well, it's high time we got with the program, then. All these clubs here have managed to do it and survive. Yet, here I am, ass hangin' out and suckin' hind tit, because you slackers never forced me to up my game." Retro's easygoing expression said he wasn't serious. "Y'all are assholes. Alla y'all."

"Maybe." Mudd's chuckle broke the word into pieces, but the laughter also let them slip effortlessly into place. "Not like we would front that shit, man. You've got to be more self-aware than that."

"Come on," Retro urged, flicking his finger against Einstein's chest a final time. "Let's go do a meet and greet with the man of the hour. Never seen Blackie as high on anyone except Horse, and you know I like that man. I fielded a few requests from him through the years, ran the first couple past Blackie to ensure the veracity of the request. He was always on the up and up. From where I sit, Blackie's a good judge of character and reads people nearly as quickly as Mudd here does. If he's not only vouching for him but putting him forward to lead an expansion chapter two states from home, then this dude is someone worth getting to know."

"What happened to this being an RWMC chapter? That'd been all I'd heard talked about, and then all of a sudden, the tide changed. Got ideas on that?" He followed Retro, only a stride behind him, able to hear his words without straining.

"Not sure who fronted the idea to begin with. Seen more posturing in the past two days than at many a formal sit-down. Even before Bane rolled in, he'd been pulled hither and yon without his knowledge, everybody wantin' him in their corner. Says a lot about him and also about the placement of Baker in general. Great stopping-off point for back-and-forth traffic, and a welcoming community is always a good thing. Bane rolled in asking for what you have, wanted to go nomad, rule the area in opposition to Truck's longtime residency. Should have been a slam dunk, except that left the territory up for grabs." Retro slowed his long strides, and Einstein matched his pace, knowing the shift would allow the delivery of the full story before they gained the group of men tens of yards away.

"Blackie was the naysayer, touting a variety of reasons, but the most compelling was his desire to plant his flag here. There was some wavering between FRMC and their support group, the Iron Riggers." Retro lifted a finger. "Remember that name; it'll come into play again in a minute. Once Blackie had said it straight out, first Mason, then Twisted and Wrench backed the idea of rolling up a direct charter as opposed to a support group that wouldn't be welcoming to big boys like Truck and Gunny. Skyd, president of the Iron Riggers, was more than down for Blackie's backtracking to the FRMC charter idea, and I don't blame him. Rolling up a chapter here would have stretched his resources thin, being a smaller support club to begin with. We also found out Mason's Rebels were looking to patch over the IRMC, something that was guaranteed to have pissed off Blackie. If they'd spun up a charter here, Mason would have just gobbled them up faster. So this, as it shakes out, is a win-win all around." Retro lifted a hand as someone called his name. "And that's you being up to speed, much as I can get you in ten-point-two seconds."

Einstein laughed as they stopped near a large group of men, the ring expanding to include their three. He grinned and acknowledged faces he knew, nodding at those he didn't when they were introduced. A lot of men he'd never seen before, and he worked to commit names and associations to memory, expecting a quiz from Mudd later. *That's just how we work.* It struck him then, how going nomad would remove him from this kind of exchange. One where he had faith in his patch brothers and knew they were backing him up.

Doesn't matter.

Scar needed to be brought down. No matter where he'd run to, Einstein would find him. *Find him and deal.* Didn't matter what the end looked like, as long as things came to an end.

***

"No, no. That's not how it was." Gunny's disappointment was clear as he argued against something Mason had said. "Jesus, Prez, you can't tell a story worth shit."

"That's because I tell the truth, not a story." Mason's chuckle was low and quiet, matching the mood of the men surrounding the dying bonfire.

Blackie and Mason had set men to building the beginning of a formal campground in a small field between two houses. The path connecting the two homes had been freshly cleared, chopped bits of brambles and stinkweed scattered across the track. A second, shorter path wound between trees to this field, which was backed by a creek. Bikes had been wheeled into the area, kickstands blocked up with pieces of wood and rock to keep them from sinking into the soft ground. A score of tents lined the field, with most of the people who'd arrived today opting to stay on site after hearing from yesterday's arrivals that the local motels were all full.

Retro had laughed about this turning into a mini-rally, likening it to the kind of ragtag gatherings he'd attended decades ago. Blackie had stared at Truck, the two men immediately moving to the side with their heads together, and Einstein assumed the gathering would become an annual event. *Birth of something new, right here.*

He was glad everyone seemed pleased by all that had happened today, because from his side of things, it had been a bust. Bane didn't know anything about his blood brother over the past several years, having pretty much avoided him like the plague. Their shared parentage didn't mean a lot, with Scar sticking to the Italian side of things and Bane more open to exploring his mother's heritage. He claimed his trek up to Montana had been an attempt to find family there, but something in his stories just didn't ring true for Einstein. *More there to check up on, for sure.*

A pause in the conversations pulled him from his thoughts, and he watched as Gunny stepped around the fire to stand over Horse. The look on Gunny's face wasn't humorous, and the tense way he loomed shouted he was seconds away from dealing with whatever had pissed him off. Horse had his hands up in a defensive posture, but he wasn't trying to get away, wasn't even trying to get off the log he sat on, and the way he gave all the power in the exchange to Gunny said he understood clearly that there were only moments left to stop what could be a bloody encounter.

"Gunny, stand the fuck down. Don't do this, man." Mason's voice cut through the low chatter. "Man didn't mean anything by it."

"She's not the topic of your fuckin' jokes." Gunny leaned closer. "Not now, and not ever."

"I get it."

"No, you don't. You didn't see her, man. Didn't see the way she cowered but accepted that she'd probably been sold to me and Bane. Her eyes gave everything away. She'd come to believe that everybody was a threat, but we weren't gonna be one she could fight against." His hand rose, finger and thumb a fraction of an inch apart. "She was this close to giving up. This fuckin' close, man. We brought her back from that. If she's going to come out of this a winner, she doesn't need people around her who are gonna keep tearin' her down."

"It's not tearing her down to say I find her attractive." Horse's head went side to side in negation. "Fuck, man. You're taking things entirely the wrong way."

"How should I take it, you sayin' she'll be too much trouble for any man, being as she's so damaged? How should I take it, asshole?" Muscles bunching in Gunny's arms illustrated what Einstein couldn't see—the big man was clenching his fists, hard. "How should I take those words?"

"I didn't say she'd be too much trouble. I just said a man would need to know what he had on his hands, that's all." Expression telegraphing he'd had enough, Horse jackknifed up from the log, standing close enough his chest brushed Gunny's. "I was talkin' about myself, you fucking dick. Thinkin' out loud, because I can't get her out of my head."

"What'd you say to her last night? She ran from you, got into the house still lookin' over her shoulder. Ratcheted her up big-time, you apparently bein' an asshole." Gunny leaned harder into the contact with the other man. "What'd you say to her?"

"Told her the truth. She was lookin' at you like you hung the moon. Didn't want her getting partway down a path that didn't have a good end for her, so I reminded her you were married." Horse sneered. "Big man. You always gotta play the hero, doncha?"

"The fuck is that supposed to mean?"

Mason moved in behind Gunny and gripped his shoulder, a hold Gunny shrugged off, only settling slightly when Mason's hand insistently returned to the same position. Einstein could see how deep Mason's thumb dug, and knew the man was using a painful grip to settle his officer. He glanced at the patch on the vest and revised his mental assessment at the reminder of today's proceedings. *His previous officer.*

Sure enough, Bane was on his way and wedged himself between Gunny and Horse, forcing both men back on their heels. "Back the fuck off, brother." Face pushing into Gunny's space, Bane snarled the demand. "Right now."

"You want to be her hero, Horse? Don't act like an ass." Even as he took a step backwards, Gunny shouted over Bane's shoulder, "Don't assume you know anything about this thing between her and me. Something my old lady not only knows all about but is entirely in favor of, seeing Marian like a sister." Gunny whirled and glared across the fire. "Old man, you need to have better taste in your goddamned officers."

"Now, no need to denigrate your president that way, big man." Blackie didn't shift from where he sat in a folding camp chair, a bottle of beer tucked into a mesh holder built into the armrest. "He's gone from a chapter officer to a new charter president, so you might want to watch your mouth."

"You see Marian's face today? See her for more than a half a minute, unless you went to Bane and Myrt's house? No, you didn't, and I suspect it's because she was afraid she'd run into that"—he flung a hand out behind him, middle finger extended to point at Horse—"asshole."

"Woman's choice. Nobody made her stay away from the festivities." Blackie leaned back, kicking both feet out in front of him as he angled one ankle over the other. "Maybe she likes takin' care of kids like she was. You talk to her and ask her what was goin' on? No, you didn't. I don't even need you to answer me. Get your head out of your ass and listen to Horse, and you'll hear a different tune than the one you put inside your own head. Fuck, Bane, you got your work cut out for you." Blackie didn't miss a beat as he turned his face from Gunny to Bane, then to Mason. "And you? You're a far more tolerant fella than I thought."

"Horse." Truck's voice was cutting as he projected it across the firepit. "What was your intent when you told the girl what you did?"

Einstein noted lines of stress around the older man's upper face. The beard made it easy to hide any tension around his jaw and mouth, but the tightened muscles of his forehead and eyes made it clear as any beacon that the answer to this question meant something to the man. He swung his gaze to Horse and noted the same markers. Both men had some kind of stake in this conversation, and it was more than just Gunny's physical challenge.

"Marian's had so much shit in her life, she deserves something good. Way she is with Gunny, I was afraid she'd latched on to him in an unhealthy way. I didn't want her to get more hurt if she followed a route that wouldn't end well." Horse stepped towards the fire and held out his hands as if cold suddenly. "She'd had a kind of anxiety attack in the woods. Everybody looking at her, and with the darkness, she couldn't get away. Her face, man. She was genuinely terrified but pulled it together and kept walking. That's a woman with some strength inside her. Then she looked at Gunny, and it was like all the fight went away. Marian's gonna need that strength. Gonna need all the fight she can get, digging her way out of the things her family did to her."

"You want me to believe you had her best interests at heart when you went at her that way?" Gunny's anger hadn't flagged; his shout was sharp and vicious.

"Fuck, man. I didn't go at her. I went gentle, aimed for sweet." Horse didn't look away from the fire. "And yeah, I only want good things for her."

"What the fuck are we fighting for then? That's all I wanted to hear. You started off like she's the butt of some damn joke in your head, and I wanted to set you straight. All you had to do was say so, man." Laughter burst forth from every man around the fire, and Gunny's head swung side to side as he looked at every face. "What?"

His confusion was clear, and Einstein took pity on him. "You went about it bass-ackwards. Shoulda started with a less confrontational tone." He glanced at Blackie. "Gotta say, you've groomed two very levelheaded officers, brother. Well done."

"I work with what God gives me. Trust me, not alla my men are capable of the same." Blackie put a hand beside his mouth as he lowered his voice, pretending to whisper. "That's why they're not here. Can't really take 'em out in public. These two are the cream of the crop, and I'm fuckin' proud of them."

"Are you sayin' I shouldn't be out in public?" Gunny dropped into the chair he'd abandoned to tackle Horse. "I'm wounded, old man."

"Call 'em like I see 'em."

"As do I," Truck piped up. "Hey, Einstein, I didn't see a sleeping roll on your bike. You set for somewhere to lay your head?"

"I hadn't expected the hotels to be all full up. I'll figure something out. I got a tarp, keep the worst of the dew off me." Unfolding his arms from around his knees, he propped them behind him, leaning backwards as he stretched out his legs. "Sleeping rough isn't a big deal. No worries."

"There's a couch downstairs. Be more comfortable than rough." Bane pointed at the second house, the one Einstein hadn't yet visited. "Feels weird inviting you into a house that ain't mine, but needs must, right, man?"

"I'd appreciate it. Like I said, I hadn't prepared for not having a cot." He yawned, then watched as a dozen men around the fire followed suit. "Would you mind if I headed over soon? Need to text your old lady and let her know you'll have a guest?" The women who'd been with the group had retired hours ago, Myrtle among them.

"Yeah, I'll do that, but you go on soon as you want. There's a closet under the stairs with blankets. Grab one if you need it. Boys slept in decently this morning, even in a new place with new beds, so hopefully nobody'll bug you too early." Bane pulled out his phone. "Sweetheart," he cooed into it as soon as he lifted it to his head. "We're going to have a visitor crash out on the couch tonight. Just wanted to give you a heads-up in case you hear him come in. Good guy." Head angling down, Bane grinned. "Yeah, one of Retro's men, that's right. Good girl."

"Man, he's got it bad." Mudd's whisper was awed, not mocking, and Einstein nodded in agreement.

"Yeah, he seems to. It's a good look on any man, showing the world they're owned by their better half." Einstein shifted until he was on one knee, then pushed upright with a groan. "I do appreciate the offer, brother." Staring at Bane, he let the reality of the situation sink in. *There's nothing of Scar in him. They don't even look alike.* Talking to the man today had revealed an entirely different mindset, one more like Einstein's, and he fully understood why Bane had gone about as far as he could from the club Scar had started. Nothing in that setup would appeal to him, and it embarrassed Einstein that he'd been sucked in and swallowed the lies. He should have known better, should have trusted his instincts, but he'd wanted the community, the brotherhood that had been promised. *All I got was shit.* Bane's story had shown he'd had to fight free from family to get where he was today, just like Einstein. "Catch you in the morning."

He detoured by his bike to grab his bag, then made his way along the path to the second house. Similar in construction to Truck and Vanna's place, it boasted a wide porch that was begging for a swing. The light was on, a handful of bugs swooping lazily through the bright heat. The doors were unlocked, and he entered a quiet house, standing near the door as he closed it and looked around.

A glow from the kitchen slightly brightened the darkness downstairs, showing him the outline of furniture—a couple of chairs and the couch Bane had promised. The banister of the stairs gleamed in the low light, and he marked the darker shadow underneath, knowing that would be the door to the linen closet. The silence wasn't complete. Shouts of laughter made their way inside from the group, muffled but audible. He could hear a clock ticking, not loud enough to be annoying, but standing out in the quiet that surrounded him.

Einstein slipped off his boots and placed them and his bag near the end of the couch. There were cushions and pillows he could use to rest his head, so when he made his way to the closet, he only retrieved a couple of blankets. Dropping those off at the couch, he took only a minute of further exploring to locate a downstairs bathroom, which he used without turning on a light.

He flipped out one blanket, then the other, and shoved a pillow to one end, then stretched as he unfastened his belt. He removed that and his wallet, digging his phone and knife from his pockets, and deposited those into his boots for safekeeping, draping his vest over the collection, confident that in this house, no one would touch it even while he slept.

Stretching out with a groan, he had curled up on one side, back against the cushions, when the front door opened. A dark figure came inside, pausing much as he had while they closed the door behind them.

"Bane?"

"Yeah, man. Sorry to wake you."

"Just resting my eyes." That earned him a snort, and he grinned. "Thanks again for the couch."

"There's a bedroom, but it's next to Marian's."

"Say no more. I get it from hearing Horse and Gunny talk. It's a good thing to want to keep your sister-in-law safe, man. No worries." He was surprised to find his words were the truth. If he'd found out another way that there was a regular bed not offered, he'd probably be offended, but knowing it was next door to a woman who'd suffered so much—it was a no-brainer to avoid upsetting her more. "Night, man."

"Yeah. G'night." The dark figure moved out of view, the creaking stairs identifying where he'd gone.

Einstein followed his progress through much of the house by the sound of footsteps, loud in the stillness. Water pipes groaned, then more creaking, moving away until it was lost in the distance.

"Good man."

Adjusting against the pillows, he closed his eyes and relaxed. Sleep wasn't too far behind.

***

Marian

Old habits die hard. Marian shook her head at the thought. *I need to remember that it's been a matter of days, not months. Of course I'm still waking early and making my way to the kitchen.* Didn't matter it was a different kitchen; since she was here, might as well get the coffee started and then see what was in the refrigerator to use for breakfast.

Pausing, she bent to look through the window towards Vanna's house. *No lights.* That would probably mean they wouldn't be doing a big feed this morning for those who'd stayed another night. Yesterday the adults had flocked to Vanna and Truck's place, and the kids all wound up here. It had been fun staying with the kids, listening to them play, and watching as they folded Thad and Luke into their group.

Grinning, Marian dumped the water she'd drawn into the coffeemaker and finished prepping for coffee, then pulled out the flour, milk, and eggs for the second day in a row. Turning on the range, she positioned a heavy skillet in place. Pan-a-cakes, as Luke called them, cooked quickly and kept well with a covered pan on them, staying warm in the stove without drying out. Also, if whatever kids were still here found out she'd made pancakes again, they'd probably come to eat, which would give Thad and Luke someone closer to their age to talk to.

The smell of brewing coffee had her breathing deep with a sigh. "Few things smell better than fresh coffee first thing in the morning."

"I'll second that thought."

She whirled, the two eggs in her hand flying free to smash against the lower cabinets. One hand clutched at the neck of her shirt, the other held out between them, she faced the man who'd spoken. He took a step backwards, his hands held harmlessly down at his sides.

"Hey now. Hey." He took another step backwards. "You're Marian, right? I didn't mean to scare you." The man moved so the kitchen island was between them. "Bane let me sleep on the couch. I didn't come prepared to camp out, so he basically saved me from an uncomfortable night. I'm sorry I scared you."

Dressed in just a pair of jeans, which were unfastened, the man stood with the half-mast zipper the only thing keeping the garment hanging off his hips. The man's bare torso, tanned and rippling with muscles, gleamed warmly in the low light. He had lines on his skin, dark tattoos mixed with color until he looked like a walking riotous canvas. Hair on his head shorn nearly as close as the scruff on his face, he was frowning, a furrow between his brows. Marian watched his eyes and his hands, knowing from painful experience that the one would telegraph what the others would be doing next. Instead of being clenched into pounding fists, his fingers flexed and straightened, arms down at his sides.

"I didn't mean to scare you. Thought for a minute you were talking to me and that you knew I was here." Mouth twisting to the side, he offered an expression that was as much grimace as smile. "Forgive me?"

Pulling in a steadying breath, she lowered her gaze before answering, "I'm...I'm Marian." Grabbing a couple of paper towels from the roll, she dampened them at the sink before squatting near the wasted eggs, scooping up what she could in one hand before wiping at the mess with the other.

He murmured something she didn't catch, focused on cleaning up. A trash can appeared next to her, and Marian dropped the shells and slimy eggs into the container. Water ran in the sink, and another handful of wet paper towels came into view. She held up the other, and it was plucked from her fingers. Courtesy came to her like second nature, and she murmured, "Thank you." Finally happy with the way the cabinet door looked, she rose and dropped the last bit of trash on top of the rest. Still without looking at him, she explained, "I was going to make pancakes."

"What can I do to help?"

The matter-of-fact way he assumed she'd have a job for him was disarming, making him less terrifying. She was still frightened, heart pounding half out of her chest, but it lessened somehow. *He's like Gunny.* Bane allowing him to sleep here should have been all the recommendation Marian needed, because he'd proven to be amusingly proactive in his protectiveness of Myrt. Marian had watched from the windows yesterday as he'd come up behind her sister over and over, wrapping himself around Myrt's frame as if to safeguard her from the world. He would never place Myrt in a position where she might be threatened.

"They're easy, not much to do." Retrieving another couple of eggs, she cracked and added them to the bowl. "Thanks, though." She didn't want him to think she wasn't grateful for the offer. Marian kept her back to the man as she worked, whisking ingredients together until they blended smoothly, then flicking droplets of water into the skillet to test for readiness. A dab of oil, and moments later, three pancakes bubbled as they cooked.

"Here, Marian." Turning, she accepted the container he'd extended. "It's oven-safe, so I figure will work to keep breakfast warm for the lag-a-beds." He'd dressed, a shirt and vest now covering his chest, pants done up and held in place with a leather belt. She noted he wore socks without boots, and glanced towards the door to see them lined up alongside Bane's. "I'm Einstein." He nodded to the skillet. "Those are looking good."

Turning back to her cooking, Marian flipped the browning circles, trying not to jump when a tub of butter slid onto the countertop nearby.

Attempting to focus on the pancakes, she kept getting distracted listening to the rattle of drawers and silverware, plates clinking, and the rasping tearing sound of him making napkins out of the roll of paper towels. That earned him a smile he didn't see, aimed at the skillet instead. *Nice of him to not expect me to wait on him.*

She heated a second skillet before dropping the first batch of pancakes into the waiting container. Lifting the bowl, she spooned out another set of batter circles.

"Bacon?"

She nodded at his question, heard the refrigerator door open and close, then the metallic snick of a pocketknife opening. A moment later, an opened package slid onto the countertop next to the butter.

A third skillet joined the others, and she cracked, then beat eggs into a froth. After dropping a spoonful of butter into the skillet, she waited for it to pop and spit before stirring the scrambled eggs onto the hot surface, sprinkling cheese over the yellow mix.

They worked together like that until the meal was prepared. He'd retrieved place settings for two, arranged on either side of the island. Syrup sat alongside two cups of coffee, with sugar and cream nearby, and there was room between for her to set the container of food. Einstein busied himself with something on his phone while she served herself, then took the tongs from her to do the same.

"Thanks for cooking." His head bent over the plate as he efficiently cut the pancakes with the edge of his fork, fingers lifting a strip of bacon to his mouth.

Marian nodded, following her mouthful of food with a swallow of coffee she'd doctored just right, two spoons of sugar and a dollop of cream. "Thanks for getting everything ready."

"No big deal."

He laid his phone on the table, eyeing the screen. The rest of the meal passed in silence, scraping of forks against plates interspersed with his phone vibrating against the table. Marian's seat allowed her to look out the big window towards Vanna's house, and she watched a steady flow of people trek from the field to the house and back again. Engines rumbled in the near distance, and Einstein's head lifted, listening.

"Sounds like some of them are about ready to head out." He made no move to rise, stealing another slice of bacon from the container. "Did you get to meet everyone yesterday?"

"A few." She drained her coffee, arranging her fork across her plate. She picked up the lid and slid the container closer to him. "Want anything else? I'm going to put it in the oven to keep warm."

He took another pancake and a scoop of eggs with a grunt. "Thanks. I got here after the festivities." Randy the donkey brayed in the distance, and his mouth twisted sideways. Einstein chuckled. "Do you know what the deal is with Gunny and that donkey?"

She'd found out yesterday that Randy had belonged to Sallabrook. While Myrt hadn't been attached to the animal, Thad had developed an affection over the course of the days he and Luke had spent at the man's farm. On their drive to Florida, Gunny had listened to the boy's stories, really listened. During one stretch when her brothers were sleeping, she'd overheard Gunny call a local sheriff's deputy, Heame Junior, and arrange to have the beast brought down. The truck and trailer had arrived yesterday, and the expression on Thad's face when he saw the donkey being unloaded had been pure joy. Somehow Gunny had instinctively known the donkey might be pivotal to Thad's healing. The over-the-top gesture was one of the most touching things she'd ever witnessed. When she'd asked him about it later, Gunny had laughed and said sometimes animals were better listeners than people. For him it had been dogs. They'd gotten him through a tough time, something he'd categorized as "a fuckin' dark and despairing period in my life." The expression he wore while watching Thad, the boy's mouth running a mile a minute as he led the donkey around, told her Gunny's dark days might not be completely behind him.

"He found out Randy meant something to my little brother Thad." She didn't qualify the explanation.

"Got it. Gunny's a good guy." Finished with his breakfast, he followed her example and arranged his fork across his empty plate. "Definitely one to have in your corner."

Stacking their plates, she rose and went to the sink, rinsing off the remaining syrup before loading them in the dishwasher. When she turned around, she was surprised to see her coffee mug had been refilled, the top swirling with just the right caramel color to say cream had been added. When she sipped the hot liquid cautiously, she found it was also sweetened. "Thank you."

Einstein's shrug barely lifted one shoulder. "No big deal."

Footsteps approached the stairs, and Marian looked up to see Bane with his arm wrapped around Myrt's shoulders, his mouth pressed to her temple in a sweet kiss. Partway down, they paused, and Myrt sprinted back upstairs, Bane watching her with a frown before turning back to come down the stairs. Once on the main floor, Bane turned them towards the kitchen, grinning. "I smell bacon."

"I ate it all." Einstein's flat delivery had Bane's smile dimming. "Just kidding. Marian made plenty."

"Pancakes and eggs too." She stood and opened the stove. A man's hand reached past her and gripped the hot container. She took a step back and turned to watch Einstein place it on the island counter. He opened a drawer with one hand to pluck out two forks while pulling a cabinet door wide and scooping up two more plates. She retrieved the roll of paper towels and ripped off two sections. He reached out a hand without looking, and she passed them over, amusement bubbling in her chest. She didn't want the moment to go without comment, so she murmured, "Thanks again, Einstein." He flashed her a grin over his shoulder just as a clinking sound made her glance at his hands. There was a broad band on one finger, a golden, gleaming wedding ring. *No wonder he's so handy in the kitchen. His wife's a lucky woman.* She turned away to ask, "Did you sleep okay, Bane?"

The blush that overtook his face made Marian stare long enough for Einstein to snicker. The sound made Marian realize what might be so embarrassing, and she dropped her gaze without asking anything else.

"Yes," the man finally squeaked out, the sound nearly as damning as the blush had been.

Okay, time to change the subject.

She opened her mouth only to close it when Einstein asked, "Bane, do you know what the plans are for today?" He'd seemed to have the same thought, and she smiled her appreciation at him, surprised when his brows drew together. She barely had time to think, *What did I do?* before he continued. "I heard something about a cleanup in town?"

Bane held up one finger and swallowed, reaching back to grab a coffee mug, pouring it full, using the same extended stretch that allowed him to stay seated. "Yeah, we've got a clubhouse now, but it needs a fuckton of work. We'll welcome any willing set of hands, because it'll be a lot for the three of us. There's more members incoming, but some won't be here for a week or more."

"Worth everything in the end. Having a place where everyone can come is key to keeping the cohesive relationships you need for a good club, a good charter. I got nowhere to be, and anything I can do to help, I'm happy to."

Nowhere to be?

Einstein's words were a curious puzzle, but the rest of their discussion had nothing to do with her, so after giving the two men a tiny wave,

Marian made her way to the stairs. They continued to talk behind her, their voices trailing after her all the way upstairs. Sounds in the boys' room told her they were waking, smells of bacon and pancakes lingering on the air doing the work. Sounds in the bathroom attached to Myrt and Bane's bedroom told her the scents hadn't been kind to her sister.

The bunk beds the boys were using had youthful coverings, and the framed posters on their walls were perfect for them. She smiled at the memory as she closed the door of the bedroom she'd been using, looking around at the neutral furnishings. This was more of a blank canvas, and the idea made her pause. *Will I be here long enough to warrant decorating?*

Then the reality of her situation hit her.

As it had each time, the knowledge that she had no money, no job, nothing to offer anyone—took her breath away. Her very existence here was dependent on charity. Truck, Vanna, Bane, Myrt—they belonged here, making an extended family through the men's relationships, and the mothering nature of Vanna. The boys would be okay. Marian couldn't imagine anyone turning them out. Myrt alone would fight tooth and nail for them, and her paired with Gunny were all the champions their brothers needed.

Me? She was less confident that the same kind of grace would be applied to her situation.

And why should they have to carry her? She was a grown woman, able to work. Maybe she didn't have any marketable skills other than cooking or cleaning, but there had to be something in town she could do. *I don't know how to drive.* How would she get to town even if she could find a job?

Suddenly aware of the clammy sweat coating her palms, she scrubbed them against the pants she wore. Even these pants were a symbol of the charity that had been granted her. Jeans awaited in a drawer, donated by

Vanna, who had insisted Marian needed more than the thin cotton pants she had always sewn for herself.

Stumbling to the bed, she turned and toppled, holding herself upright on the edge with effort.

From their brief discussions back in the hotel, Marian knew Myrt had invested months of planning in her escape, slowly saving up enough of a sum to get her by. The relationship with Bane meant Myrt had a partner now, someone to help carry that burden. Something he seemed all-in on, his love and affection for Myrt making it clear he'd go to the ends of the earth to keep her.

I've always been a planner.

It was why the church ladies always asked her to lead their dinners and projects. As long as Marian could get it down on paper, she could make nearly anything happen. For the first time in her own life, everything depended on Marian finding a way forwards, even when starting with nothing.

Myrt's pregnancy would mean she'd need help around the house, but that was easily something Vanna or Sharon could do. *Of course, Sharon has her own kids, and Vanna's older.* Marian could selectively take on the harder jobs, leaving them to mother Myrt as needed. She'd seen the remains of a largish garden behind Vanna's house. Dirt work was something Marian was well accustomed to, so contributing to that effort would be something in the positive column.

Bane's comment about needing all the help they could get to help prepare the building downtown for the intended purposes danced along the edges of her mind. She didn't know what a clubhouse was used for, but if it was a mess inside, then there'd be walls and floors to scrub, windows too. All of that was within Marian's meager skill set. She supposed she could paint. Lifting her head, she glanced around the spare bedroom. It would take time to get things done at the clubhouse. Maybe she could test her hand out here first, gain confidence in picking out colors or whatever was needed for that kind of thing.

Her childhood home had been styled by a dozen hands, her father along with his many dead wives, their efforts piling on until the walls should have groaned at the weight. The only room that had been bare was hers. Tiny, tucked behind the pantry near the back of the house, it had originally been a mudroom.

There was a room in this house that was similar.

Marian froze in place.

Bane had put his friend on the couch last night because Marian was taking up the main guest bedroom.

I could make out it was my choice. Say that this room's too big, too bright.

The mudroom would suit her fine. Couple of wooden boards and she could make a bedstead. Thad's bunk bed had an extra mattress on top of it, something that had caused laughter about looking like the princess bed and claiming he needed to watch out for peas.

Mattress on the floor would be fine to start.

The more she made herself small, the less likely it was people would notice her. The more she helped, the more they'd appreciate what she could offer. If it never earned her a dollar, it was still worthy, and working for bed and board something she was well acquainted with.

The trick would be to do all of that without someone realizing how desperate she was to stay. To be around so many people without letting them see the panic inside her. The fear driving her forwards.

I just have to hide in plain sight.

Should be easy.

***

Einstein

"What'd you say to her?" Bane's question had an edge, and Einstein looked away from the stairs where he'd been watching Marian make her way up them.

"Me? I didn't say anything. Woke up and she was starting breakfast. I startled her at first, but explained who I was." He sipped his coffee. "Set the table while she cooked, helped where I could, but she seemed to have her routine down. She was fine."

"She was quiet." Bane looked down at his plate. "After that bullshit with Horse, the last thing I need is Gunny on my ass about Marian again. I'll get Myrt to check in with her today, make sure she's settling in okay."

"Sounds like a plan." He realized he was looking at the stairs again and tore his gaze away.

"You serious about hanging around to help out downtown?" Bane shoveled the last forkful of eggs into his mouth, staring at Einstein.

"Hell yeah. I got nothin' goin' on back in Birmingham. Retro and I had the conversation I needed yesterday, so I can hang around for a few days. I've worked construction before, if that's any help."

"Big-time help." Leaning back in his chair, Bane grabbed the coffee carafe again and topped up his cup, then Einstein's. "Appreciate the fuck out of it—" Mouth twisting, Bane shook his head. "Okay, that sucks. I don't do sensitive very well or bother with assumptions. I was about to call you brother, but then stuttered my way out of it because with everything I've heard, I don't know if you'd take it from me."

Einstein laughed, straight from his gut, because the expression on Bane's face said this not knowing hurt him somehow, and the idea was ridiculous. "That's okay, man. I'd take it. Stories I heard from Blackie— who my president trusts with his life—is more than enough to set you on a different stage from what might have been." He pointedly glanced at the ceiling, then back to Bane, one eyebrow up. A quick headshake in response told him everything he needed to know. Myrt must not be aware of Bane's family, not the gritty details at least. "No worries, brother. Ain't no big. You be you, and I'll do me. I suspect we'll get on well enough that way."

Footsteps sounded overhead, a loud clomping that couldn't be Marian. Einstein turned to the stairs in time to see two boys making their way down. One was early teens, the other slightly younger, and both wore cautious expressions. *The brothers.* He had seen them at a distance yesterday, trailing around with the donkey in tow a couple of times. As they approached the kitchen, from up close he saw a resemblance with Myrt, but not so much Marian. *Wonder why?*

"Luke, Thad—ready to have some breakfast?" Bane stood with his arms out, and both boys arrowed directly to him and ran into his embrace. He liked that Bane didn't hold back his affection, giving each boy a close hug and leaning near to say quietly to both of them, "Marian made pancakes and bacon. Eggs are all gone, but you snooze, you lose." He grimaced as he released the boys. "Myrt had to head back upstairs, but I don't think she'll be ready to eat for a while." Bane moved the empty plates to the far end of the counter, as if they were offensive. "She'd already puked once this morning, so I didn't think about it as we came down."

Morning sickness? There'd been a couple of comments yesterday that weren't quite specific enough to point to a pregnancy, but Bane's statements didn't leave much room to question. They'd only known each other for a handful of weeks. Einstein frowned and looked at Bane. If she'd gotten pregnant right away, she still wouldn't be experiencing morning sickness.

As if feeling Einstein's scrutiny, Bane turned to face him. Taking in Einstein's expression, Bane mouthed, "Later."

Good enough for me. Even if there was a story here, it wasn't his to get involved with anyway.

"I can get a scramble going." Moving with the familiarity working alongside Marian had provided, he retrieved the eggs and set the previously used skillet on a burner. Listening to the boys and Bane chatting while he scrambled up and served another batch of eggs had him gritting his teeth. They seemed oblivious to their missing sisters upstairs, going on about the people they'd met over the past few days, Bane chiming in with little details that turned each name into a fuller version of a person.

He deliberately pushed aside his annoyance, focused instead on taking advantage of the unexpected opportunity for information gathering.

"Horse is one tough son-of-a-gun." Bane's chuckle told volumes about his respect and brotherly love for the man Gunny'd been ready to go to pound-town on last night. "Back when I was trying to join the Freed Riders, they initially didn't want me."

"Why didn't they want you, Bane?" Thad's question was asked through a mouthful of eggs and bacon. The boy had foregone the pancakes, leaving them for Luke, who was plowing through syrup-soggy bites rapidly. Thad swallowed as he shook his head. "They were crazy. You're awesome."

"Well, thanks for that." Bane reached out and gripped the boy's shoulder in a quick gesture, pulling back to give Luke's arm a squeeze too. "I don't blame them one bit. I was kind of a mess back then. Looking for something and finding everything except the one thing you want will do that for you."

"What were you looking for?" Luke reached for another slice of bacon, shoving it into his mouth in one go.

"Something better than I had. I grew up in a dysfunctional family, afraid every day that I'd somehow manage to catch their brand of crazy." He shrugged and glanced at Einstein, the direct look telegraphing Bane knew he was listening. "I'd just about run the breadth of the country looking. Found a variety of people I'd connect with, but there'd always be something not right. Something missing. I'd heard about Blackie and his crew, and the stories sounded too good to be true. Then I got there and found out everything I'd heard was right. They felt right. Like a family. A true one."

"Did your daddy beat you too?" Luke's low question had Einstein's breath stuttering in his chest. The matter-of-fact way the boy had opened the door on his treatment at home was devastating. Glancing at Bane, he saw evidence of the same dismay. "If he did, then I wish you'd had a sister like Marian. She'd stop him every time she caught him doing that to either of us." He gestured towards Thad, whose fork was frozen midway between plate and mouth. "Didn't matter she'd get it worse for not knowing her place. You shoulda had a sister like Marian."

Bane cleared his throat, Einstein following suit, glad the boy hadn't asked him a question.

"Not my daddy, but my grandpa. And my brother. I didn't have a sister like that, but I got real good at running and hiding." Bane's hand curled around Luke's neck, and he pulled him close. "Found out early that there's no shame in turning tail if it'll save me gettin' my ass whipped for no reason. That's what was different about Blackie's crew." He paused, throat visibly working. "Found something worth fighting for in them. And now, I've found the same with you four. You guys, your sisters—it's my honor to have you be part of my family."

"Not everyone had someone to step in and keep them safe. Myrtie didn't." Thad's fork clattered against the edge of his plate, ringing out a staccato beat of bad memories.

"I'm sorry I wasn't there." Bane's words trembled with an ill-suppressed rage, bringing both boys' attention back to him, and Einstein watched as Luke's face softened while Thad's developed hard lines. From what he'd seen so far, that reaction typified the boys—Luke the empathetic one and Thad everyone's protector. "I'd give anything to turn back the clock."

"You had your own row to hoe." Thad's headshake looked older than his years, a reluctant acceptance of things he couldn't change. "You want to turn back the clock? I want to turn it forwards so I could have been old enough to save Myrtie."

Luke's bottom lip dropped, and he turned his face, burying it again against Bane's chest. The silence around the table grew, elongating until it was heavy in the air. Einstein needed to change the subject before one of the boys innocently asked about his family.

That frantic fear drove him, and his... "Bane, what kind of plans do you have for the clubhouse today?" might have been louder than normal, but he needed to be sure his topic change would stick.

The grateful expression on Bane's face said he welcomed the question, and he rattled off a dozen tasks he deemed most pressing. Their conversation flowed naturally. From the corner of his eye, he watched as Luke pulled away, and the boys slowly went back to eating, finishing their meals without prompting. He gathered the empty dishes from the counter as Bane continued, rinsing and placing them in the dishwasher while asking clarifying questions about details.

Walking around the end of the island, he paused with his back to the room as he listed various suggestions. It was clear Bane hadn't worked construction, making Einstein glad he was here before they started tearing down and building back. He finished with, "We'll need to map out the load-bearing walls and beams, and ensure they're left intact, even as we open up the bottom floor as much as possible like you want. There's a lot of planning into that part, but we can do a good portion while we're clearing out the trash. No big."

"I want to help." He turned to see Marian had come back downstairs and was nervously rubbing her palms against the sides of her thighs. She'd changed pants, and wore boots now, hair scraped back from her face. Her glance at him was pleading, but it was Bane she spoke to. "Myrt needs to rest and shouldn't be around the chemicals anyway. I can clean while you do the other stuff."

"Not turning down offers of help." Bane's easy response surprised Einstein. "But don't feel like you have to. Nobody's asking that of you."

"I know." Her smile was fleeting. "There's not much to do here. I'm used to keeping busy."

They all turned at the sound of the front door opening, and Einstein watched the man from the bonfire last night, Horse, walk inside. *Not my house, not my place to ask why he's here.* Gunny's words resonated through his head, turning his instant on-guard a match for Gunny's wariness. Last night Einstein hadn't yet met Marian, didn't know how fucking terrified she was, hadn't understood the threads of people-pleasing warring with a bone-deep anxiety inside her. *An hour working alongside her don't make me an expert, but she's a woman who'll need careful handling.* If Horse was aiming at an old lady, he'd have an uphill battle to fight by picking Marian. *And she's going to need to want it.*

"Hello the house," Horse called, an easy smile on his lips. His eyes darted from Bane to Marian and stuck there. Einstein watched as warm color slowly tinted Marian's cheeks, her gaze pinned to the toes of her shoes.

"Hey man," Bane returned easily, reminding Einstein that these men were patch brothers and had known each other for years. He thought about the stories circulating of how Bane had reacted to Marian's plight, the way he'd dealt with her and Myrtle's father—and Einstein relaxed a hair.

"Thought you might need an extra pair of hands today." Horse continued walking until he stood near the table, gaze swinging back to Bane. Even without his scrutiny on her, the blush Marian wore deepened.

Her hands are trembling. Anxiety or excitement, it was hard to tell which from the few clues she'd provided. He scooted farther around the counter, moving towards Marian as he made space for Horse, blocking the man's view of her. Close enough to hear her take a heavier breath in followed by a slow exhale, he leaned his forearms on the edge of the island and stretched a leg back, tapping her ankle with the toe of his boot. Another slow breath in and out, and a brief pressure appeared against his foot.

Maybe she just needs to know someone's in her corner.

"Gunny's gonna be there." The warning look Bane leveled at Horse spoke to his memory of the near altercation at the fire last night, too.

"Already talked to him this morning. Cleared the air." Horse scoffed. "Man's got a hero complex, big as a barn."

"He's my SAA, brother." The tone of Bane's voice had changed subtly, dropping an octave as it became an admonition. "Don't need no shit." He stood, and Einstein matched his movement, shuffling a half step towards Marian. If Bane was expecting to throw down with his patch brother, Einstein wouldn't be in the middle of it, but he'd make sure the woman was well clear.

"What's SAA?" Luke's question broke the silence, and when Einstein looked at the boys, he found Thad standing in front of his brother. The similarity to his positioning with Marian was striking.

No surprise there.

"Means he stands at my back. Helps keep me and our brothers safe." Bane's explanation didn't encompass the full duties of a SAA but was close enough. The implication that Gunny might have to protect Bane against Horse was interesting, but maybe Einstein was the only one who took the words that way.

"Against threats outside the club, or from inside if needed." *Maybe not.* Horse's response said he'd understood Bane the same as Einstein. The rigidness of his shoulders spoke to how the warning had been received. "Which won't happen, because brothers have each other's backs, too."

"How about you, Einstein? Where do you stand on the topic of brothers having other brothers' backs? Hmm?" Bane's gaze didn't budge from where he had Horse pinned, and Einstein wasn't certain what motivation was behind trying to drag him into their argument.

Not playing your games. "My take on it is narrowed to the reality within the Bama Bastards. I try not to think about other examples I might have experienced. With the BBMC, hell yeah, we have each other's backs, come hell or high water. Other clubs?" He shrugged, and Bane turned to look at him, eyes wide and brows lifted. "Some, not so much. In my experience, it is entirely dependent on the leadership. Knowing Blackie as I do from the stories about the man, I'd expect him to cultivate a supportive atmosphere. Good men do that." *Can't forget who his family is.* Lifting his chin, he stared at Bane, shifting into a more aggressive stance. "Bad men, not so much."

They remained like that, silent shouts rocketing between them as Einstein tried not to shove it into Bane's face that he knew where the man had come from. That wouldn't do any good, nor would fixating on what that history had done to Einstein. *And my girls.*

"I'm going to go and get Myrt settled in upstairs. Crackers and clear soda will help her past this morning's tummy issues." Marian's quiet voice broke the oppressive silence, and her arm brushed Einstein as she moved past him, her fingers trailing across the back of his hand in a supportive move. Bane turned his back on the room to look out the kitchen window.

Marian reminded him, "I'll be back down in a minute, Bane. I still want to help."

"You got it." Bane's response was flat and quiet.

Unfazed, the boys moved around him, then the treads creaked as their footsteps thudded upstairs.

"Well that was fun." Bane shuffled to face the room as he spoke, and the man's gaze moved over Einstein before it landed and stuck on Horse. "Won't stand for shit bein' shoveled against people who haven't deserved it, brother. Gunny hadn't done a damn thing except take a chance on me, same as Blackie, and I'm bustin' at the seams to live up to their trust. Won't start this whole thing by having someone I've been brothers with not exhibiting that same amount of trust in me, or in them." Bane's features tightened, his voice turning rough as it lowered, stern tones matching the tension in his face. "You not down with me being the new charter's president? Take it up with Blackie. Not down with the men I've patched over into *my* chapter? Then you and I will have words, and I'll see your back as you ride away."

"Jesus, brother. Wasn't my intent. He's taken Marian on as his little sister, finger in my chest and jutted jaw as he extolled her virtues while threatening me if those virtues don't remain intact. His old lady was standing behind him, grinnin' and shakin' her head, and when he was done, told me about him adopting anyone in need. She made me promise not to take it personal." Horse shook out his arms and hands, then forcefully shoved curled fists into the front pockets of his jeans. "I came over to offer my help, but if you don't want or need me, then I'll be on my way home. But, just sayin', man—anything that happens between me and Gunny don't necessarily have a damn thing to do with you. I'll keep my fuckin' mouth shut from here on out, let you make your own observations without me contaminating anything with my words."

"Shit." Bane strode around the island and straight to Horse, and wrapped his arms in a hug, returned as soon as Horse had struggled free from his own makeshift hobbling. "Shit, man. I'm fuckin' on edge, brother. This is big, so fuckin' big."

"Yeah, but you got it in you to deal." Horse lifted him with a groan as Bane shouted laughter. "Knew it early on. You're a tenacious fucker, and I'm proud to call you brother."

"They sort themselves out?" Marian had snuck up alongside Einstein, and he glanced over at her whisper, offering a quick dip of his chin. "Good. Myrtle doesn't know many of the men like she does Gunny. Proximity and opportunity will fix that for them, I'm sure. My understanding from Gunny is that Horse is as close to a brother as Bane will claim."

"Bane already had a bad hand dealt him on that front. I'm glad he's picking better family than the universe saw fit to give him." He shook himself. "Forget I said that." He took a step and glanced over his shoulder. "See you at the clubhouse in town."

"Can I ride with you?"

He didn't lose a beat as he clipped out, "No," continuing to stalk towards the door on suddenly numb legs. "I'm on a bike."

He'd never had a woman ride second seat.

Never.

Lauren had been totally uninterested in the lifestyle, outside of where it benefited them as a family by providing a large circle of support. She'd never snuggled up against him and wrapped her arms around his waist. Never leaned her head against his spine and trusted that he'd keep her safe.

He'd wanted.

Lord God, how I'd wanted, once upon a time.

Had coaxed and cajoled, then Makayla had rounded out their family, and it'd seemed like testing fate to have both parents riding, so he'd stopped asking.

Slamming through the door, he rattled down the steps and into the dusty grass of the front yard. His bike was still parked at Truck's house, and he made his way there without pausing. Along the trek, he passed Gunny's oldest girl running after a donkey, her yells of, "Randy," shrill and loud, but laced through with amused laughter that said she might not mind chasing the beast. Shaking his head, he got to his bike and stopped short. He'd left his bag at Bane's house. *I can get it afterwards, see if Truck's got room for me tonight.*

"Einstein." Retro was seated on the porch swing, socked feet up on the porch railing as he pushed himself back and forth. "Heard you're going to help with the clubhouse cleanup."

"How the hell did you…know what? It doesn't matter. Yeah, I was planning on it, unless you've got something else in mind?" Propping a heel on a stair tread, he leaned an elbow against his knee, stretching out muscles suddenly tense and complaining. *Back wasn't hurting when I woke up on the couch.* "I can be swayed."

"Nah, just make sure you catch me before I head out tonight. We got a few more things to iron out, you and me. Wanna make sure I do it right before I hand you a rocker for your new status."

The donkey rounded the corner of the house, hilariously carrying what looked like a sleeping bag in its teeth. It paused when it saw Einstein and Retro, not much, but enough for Gunny's girl to grab the lead rope dangling from its halter. "Got you," she shrieked, then waved at the two men as she led the donkey off at a fast trot, sleeping bag trailing behind them.

"Don't give it much mind." Retro's laughter couldn't be contained, bubbling over each of his words. "I've come to understand that kind of shit happens a lot around Gunny."

"Tell me what you know, old man." Einstein quirked an eyebrow at the door in silent question.

"Everybody's either in the kitchen or out saying their goodbyes. By noon it'll just be you, me, and those newly patched into Baker's first official MC, plus maybe one or two who'll hang around today. By nightfall, that count will be down by at least one, and the rest is up to you." Retro's feet disappeared, and he bent double, long hair flowing down to hide his face as he tugged on boots. "I'm going to ride west with Blackie's crew, eat lunch with 'em, then hie my ass back here." His neck angled, and he shot Einstein a grin. "Mostly I'm gettin' out of cleanup duties. Not my clubhouse, no reason to add my sweat equity to the mix. Monday'll be down here in a few days. He can represent all he wants." Retro straightened. "As can you, from today forward. Gonna be weird as fuck not knowing by the day what's goin' on in your head, brother."

"You'll hear from me on the regular." Einstein took the stairs in three strides and settled his vest, working his shoulders until it swung freely around his hips. He closed the distance between himself and his president, his brother. "Wouldn't be right not to. If Monday's representing down here, then what I'm doing is representing out there, on the road. Man needs to know what he's thrown out into the world, and I'll keep you in the know."

"Fuckin' right you will." Retro slapped a meaty palm against his shoulder, the sting not mitigated by the thin shirt Einstein wore. *Motherfucker.* "You will, or I'll have your ass. Won't be no 'in the round' conversation. I'll tell you again tonight, but I have two fuckin' rules for this bullshit."

"Lay 'em on me, man." Shoulders back, he waited, gaze locked with Retro.

"One, you check in every couple of days. Me, Mudd, Marlin, Crazy Mike, don't matter. Checking in will consist of a location, garnered information, insights, and outcomes. I want to know where you are, who you talked to, what you gained from those conversations, and where they're taking you next. I know finding out Bane's the brother throws a crimp in your initial thoughts, but something in my gut says you were on to something. Probably be good to follow that up." Retro stepped closer, the tips of his boots overlapping Einstein's. Leaning in, he shoved his face within inches. "Second, you fuckin' keep breathin'. You have more than a passing thought otherwise, you give me a call and I'll come to you. Won't matter where or when, so don't give a bullshit excuse of me bein' busy. You breathin' matters to me, Jim. That's the only way this'll work."

"What happened to my family isn't your fault." This was the first time he'd seen the depths of guilt hiding in Retro's eyes. The heaviness was crippling, stripping his breath away, so his words were weak, without force. "Not a bit of it is on your doorstep, Jerry."

"You can say that all you want." Retro swung his head side to side slowly, hair quivering as it trailed over his shoulders. "Won't make it a lick truer than it was the first time. I shoulda given more weight to the man's ask. Shoulda looked deeper. Shoulda dug until I hit blood and bone." Muscles in Retro's jaw quivered and flexed. "I didn't. Had shit goin' on that felt more pressing. My own shit with Trina and her old man, shit with the cartel, pressure from the north to suck in a couple of riding clubs and clean up their mess—and in retrospect, wasn't any one of those things more important than looking into a club's president asking for sanctuary."

"You couldn't know." The muscles in his throat tensed, chokingly tight as Einstein tried to swallow. "Nobody could have known just from what he gave us then."

"I shoulda. What's the Bible say? 'Pride goeth before a fall?' Ain't right you took that fall in my place." The sideways wrench of Retro's mouth was painful to see.

Man has got to understand.

"Coulda been your kids. Little Saya or Jimmy? Are you looking to trade eye for an eye? Say no, brother. *Please God,* say no. I can't stand the idea.

Not saying I can stand the idea of my Makayla gone, either. Neither way makes a bit of sense. You losing one of your kids isn't right." They needed to move on from this topic or Einstein wouldn't last. "You've gotta understand, it's not on you. Man came after me, and I've got to believe I did everything I could. That it's not for lack of trying that they died."

Casting his glance around, Einstein saw a bundle of flowers along the front edge of the steps. "Like those white lilies there. High traffic area, but they've prevailed. Man comes along with a shovel and digs 'em up by the roots, there's nothing they could do. All that work, that striving—and it's not enough. Someone persistent enough, someone dogged in their desire to destroy the beauty in their path? Not a lot someone not in the moment can do. Even if Vanna was standing right here, stave in her hand, they could get close enough to do a lot of damage. Might salvage one root, enough to transplant and save. Would take work, and that's where you came in on this tale. All there was left was me, and me alone. I would have withered and died. Eaten a bullet. But you wouldn't let it happen. Coddled me, set me on a path of salvation even if I can't catch up to the healing part yet. So you saying it's your fault? Fuck, brother. I don't know, but it isn't right. Take the win you fought for. Take it and run."

Wordlessly Retro stepped forwards, arms wrapping around Einstein's shoulders like they never planned on letting go. Tight grip, almost fierce in the angry pain that still rolled off Retro. A big hand cradled the back of Einstein's head, moving him so Retro's mouth was at his ear.

"Count myself lucky that you're still with us, brother. The pain, Jesus God. I cannot imagine. Won't. My fuckin' heart breaks in two every time I think about it. Losin' my kids would kill me, which makes you a stronger man than me, because you're still puttin' one foot in front of the other. Trusting you'll keep on that path, brother. My brother. Gonna be the one and only nomad on books for the Bama Bastards. Fuckin' hope you find another brand of happy out there, man."

"Me too, Retro." Wrapping his fingers around the edges of Retro's vest, he pulled his friend closer. "Fuckin' me too."

Chapter Eight

Marian

Rolling her shoulders didn't ease the ache that had built all afternoon. She paused and propped the fist holding a scrub brush against her hip, using the back of her other wrist to push hair away from the sides of her sweaty face.

Listening to Bane speak in general terms about the state of the building hadn't prepared her for the reality. The club—and she mentally gave herself a high five at remembering to call it that—had purchased an old retail store located along the downtown stretch of highway. Driven out of business by a big box store one town over, the previous owners had sold down to the bare walls, fixtures and all. So that was a plus. But they'd left behind anything without value, which meant their first few hours in the building had been spent hauling boxes of unidentifiable stuff to a dumpster outside the back door.

Einstein had talked Bane into focusing on the downstairs first, so they were at least able to see the dent they'd made in the mess. She was glad. She'd toured the upstairs. It was a different kind of disaster.

Earlier, Marian had been in a small room along the farthest edge of the balcony that overlooked the main downstairs area. Probably some kind of office, with the windows on two walls and grooves ground into the floor from something sliding back and forth—maybe a chair? Next to one of the windows had been a thin mattress, something similar to what she'd used at her father's house. More a foam pad than anything else, it was spotted with indecipherable stains. She'd been toeing at some unique-looking trash that littered the floor nearby when Einstein walked in.

He'd choked and called her away from where she stood. She'd made her way over with a frown. Then he'd managed to embarrass and educate her within a few words. The things she'd touched with the tip of her shoes were condoms, used during sex. *Ugh.* Someone, likely the local high school kids, had been using the room to hook up with their boy- or girlfriend.

Just remembering the way Einstein had looked at her had Marian's face going scalding hot again. It had taken her about a half a second to vacate the room and the floor, racing down the stairs to position herself within a room already cleared of debris, scrubbing brush in hand.

Her stomach grumbled, and she gave it a pat, frowning down at the dark mark left on her shirt. Doing a top to bottom clean on something like this was dirty work—she glanced around the room with a sense of satisfaction—but worth it when the end results looked so good.

"Marian." Someone called her name from the main room, and she walked to the door. She was surprised that there were only two men present and looked around for the others. The last time she'd been in the room, the overlapping voices of nearly a dozen people had been overwhelming, driving her back into her self-assigned chores.

"Told you she didn't leave with Bane." Horse gestured towards Marian. "I don't think he realized you were still here. No one remembers seeing you at lunch."

Hands clasped in front of her waist, she shook her head. Lunch had come and gone, a buffet of pizza and wings that had smelled really spicy, so after peeking out of the room, she'd passed on making her own plate.

"Give me a minute, I'll call him back." Einstein lifted his phone to his ear, chin angled towards the ground. "Bane, yeah, man. Come back and pick up Marian." His gaze cut to where she still stood, in the doorway of the small downstairs room. "Yeah, she's here. I'm lookin' right at her, man." His neck bent, head dropping farther towards the floor. "No man, we're on bikes."

"I can give her a ride, if he's tied up." Horse's grin her direction was slow and confident, but all she could think about were his previous words, detailing what he saw as her stupidity.

Shoulders curving in on herself, she shook her head. "It's okay. I can walk. It's not a far stretch."

"You're not walking," Einstein shot at her, then groaned. "Seriously, man? You can't—" He groaned again. "Yeah, if your old lady's not feelin' it, then you need to stay with her. I get it. We'll sort things here."

"You can call Gunny." Marian was surprised by Horse's laughter, low and rolling. "Maybe Sharon or Vanna can come get me?"

"You can ride with me." Einstein poked at the surface of his phone with a rigid finger. "Unless you have a problem with it?"

You were the one with a problem earlier. What changed? Marian tried to keep the question off her face.

"Seriously, you can ride with me. Stop lookin' at me like that." Shoving the device into the front pocket of his jeans, he shrugged. "It's no big deal. Long as you feel safe with me."

Clearly she'd failed.

"I'd feel safe."

"And me over here feelin' like chopped liver now." Horse laughed again. "Not that I blame you, Marian. But I want you to know I'm sorry if

I offended you before. In my own way, feeble as it was, I was tryin' to look out for you."

"It's okay." Marian shifted her gaze between the two men, finding matching expressions of annoyance. "I'm not offended, Horse."

"Maybe you should be." Einstein stalked away towards the front of the building. "But either way, come on. We've got to lock up and get back to the houses. Vanna and Gunny are doing some grilling." Her stomach gurgled again, this time louder. "And from the sounds of it, you need something to eat."

"See you there." Horse swung past where Einstein was in the doorway, staring back at Marian. His mouth split in a broad smile, and he gave her a wink as he told Einstein, "Have fun, brother."

"Come on, Marian." As she approached, Einstein held out a hand, and she accepted it. Only afterwards did she realize that hadn't been his intent, her grip on his broad palm a surprise. He didn't shake her loose, however, just angled himself to grab the door with his other hand, pulling it closed behind her.

Without releasing her hand, he turned a key in the padlock, then pocketed the keychain and turned, using their joined grip to lead her towards his bike.

This morning he'd been so adamant that he didn't allow passengers, his anger and pain a palpable force that had pushed him from the room, from the house. It had been hours later when she'd seen him again, upstairs here. That kind of reaction shouldn't have changed in such a short time, and she considered her words as they watched Horse's motorcycle angle out of the parking lot and onto the highway, the deep blat of his exhaust quickly diminishing in volume.

"I really wouldn't mind walking." His fingers tightened around hers, the rejection of her words immediate and unmistakable. "This is something that makes you uncomfortable, and that's the last thing I want to do, Einstein. You've been unfailingly kind to me."

"No, I haven't. I wasn't nice to you this morning, and it's bugged me all day." He turned and stared at her, expression somber. "This gives me a chance to apologize and fix it."

"You don't have anything to fix." Other than his refusal of her spur-of-the-moment request this morning, he'd been nothing but nice. "It's okay."

"No, it's not." His roughened fingers gave hers another squeeze, then dropped away as he retrieved a helmet from the backrest of the bike's seat. "I've got just the one lid, but we'll get it tight on you, keep you safe."

"Who'll keep you safe?" *If a helmet is required, and he only has the one, doesn't it make more sense for the driver to wear it?* "Don't you need one, too?" She angled her body away. "I feel like you've been trapped into something you didn't want. That's...that won't work for me." Marian backed away and looked over her shoulder at the road and dark buildings, sun already lost behind the tall pine trees to the west. "You go on back, and I'll make my own way."

He groaned from behind her, and footsteps approached as she struck off along the edge of the road. "Are you this much of a pain in the ass for everyone, or is it just me?" Marian didn't answer him, adding a little speed to her stride—matched by an increase in his footsteps. "Jesus God, woman, I already said I want to fix this. You hoofing it won't do a damn thing except piss off everyone else at me. Anyone not already there will be by the time you walk all the way back out to Bane's place." Fingers tangled with hers, and he tugged, pausing her progress. "Swear to God, Marian. Hold up."

"It's okay." She tried to retrieve her fingers but found them in an immovable hold. "Honestly, I'm happier walking than riding."

"You already said you'd feel safe with me. Me, and not Horse." A quick pull had her spinning to face him, staring up into his eyes. "It'll take us fifteen minutes max, and I promise to ride safe as if it were—" His lips pressed together. "I promise to ride safe."

The interruption of his speech was abrupt, and she wondered what he'd been about to say. "Why does it matter to you?"

"Because I wasn't as nice as I could have been earlier, and that made you doubt me. I just want to redeem myself." He narrowed his eyes. "Don't be afraid of me, Marian. I'd never hurt you."

"I'm not afraid." That was a tiny bit of a lie. Standing alongside the dark highway, with shadows of nighttime falling all around them, just the knowledge that they were alone carried fear. *He could do anything.* Marian swallowed hard. "You'll show me what to do? I want to keep you safe, too."

"Yeah." His fingers curled around her hand, slipping his palm against hers. "I'll show you."

***

Einstein

Mother. Fuck. The easy way that Marian followed him back to the bike belied the speed at which she'd tried to leave only a few minutes ago. No matter what he tried, he seemed to mess up with her. Being the sister of the new Freed Riders president's old lady meant she would wield a certain amount of influence in the future, if she wanted.

That's the only reason I'm so adamant to get her home safely.

The lie burned in his gut.

It didn't have anything to do with leveraging today's kindness against some far-flung moment of need.

No, the thought of leaving her here, or having her walk home, or having her ride on Horse's bike—all twisted through his chest like the gut punch of a fishhook swallowed deep. He didn't know what it was, didn't like it, and surely wasn't about to cultivate it—but he also couldn't just let her walk away.

"First the helmet." He held up a finger. "And before you argue, don't. You're wearing it, and if you ride with me again"—*what the actual fuck am I saying*—"I'll make sure I have two, one for each of us, so we're strictly legal." There wouldn't be a second time. Shouldn't be a first, but he'd boxed himself in neatly with his arguments. *But for sure, no second ride.* "I'll get the bike running, then you come up on this side, like a horse. Puts you opposite the pipes, which will be hot. It's good you've got jeans and boots on. They'll protect you a little bit against quick brushes against them, if it happens. Just be careful." She stared up at him from underneath the rim of the helmet, eyes open wide as she listened closely to every word he said. "There're two little pegs for your feet, to keep them from getting tangled in anything they shouldn't. As long as you stay on behind me and keep your boots on the pegs, you'll be fine."

She nodded, and he finished tightening the helmet, tucking the extra length of strap back through the D-rings to keep it out of the way. With the bike started, he settled in and then gestured towards the seat behind him. Marian stared at him, then at the space between his ass and the back of the seat, and back to his face. He could tell she was wavering, reconsidering the decision to ride with him, then caught the moment when her shoulders went back and her spine steeled. She hopped on one foot to get her boot over the seat, taking his offside hand with a death grip when he offered it, levering herself into place with a bounce of the bike's suspension.

"Where do I put my hands?" The side of the helmet thudded against his head, and Einstein couldn't help himself. He laughed aloud, turning with a grin still on his face to see a matching one on hers. "Sorry."

"Hands at my waist, hold on to my belt. That's best." One of her hands settled into place, and he patted the hot spot he'd instantly become acutely aware of, telling himself he was just ensuring she secured her grip. "Literally your only job is to not let go. Can you do that?"

"Oh, I expect I can manage." Her smile was wide and genuine, and held enough amusement to light up the sky.

"Then let's go home."

***

Marian

Quiet steps carried her into the kitchen, and she flicked on the coffeemaker, watching for a moment to ensure it began its job. Careful not to make too much noise, she began gathering things for breakfast, smiling as she thought about the previous morning. It had been nice working alongside Einstein.

The ride back had been nice too. His cautious maneuvering of the bike increased her confidence in him with every turn and curve, and by the time they'd ridden up in front of Truck's house, she couldn't hide her wide grin.

Gunny had been on the porch, apparently waiting on them, and his gentle, "Little sister," as greeting had warmed her insides.

Found family, she thought now, staring down at the eggs as she whisked them into a scrambled froth.

Footsteps on the stairs pulled her attention, and she watched as Bane wandered down, yawning wide.

Glancing at the couch, she realized she couldn't see anything of Einstein and stared harder.

"He was up early to talk to Truck."

Bane's words were a surprising blow she didn't understand, and she busied herself with breakfast to hide the reaction.

"Oh?"

"Yeah." Bane poured himself a cup of coffee, only seeming to notice Marian's lack at the last minute. "Want a cup?"

Einstein wouldn't have asked; he'd have just poured and doctored it. He'd learned in the space of a few hours that given a choice, Marian never asked for anything. Him just doing for her had been a nice change, something she'd miss when he left for good.

"That's okay. I'll get it in a minute."

The eggs popped loudly as she poured them into the ready skillet. No time to wonder if she was the reason he'd left the house early.

She had things to do.

Chapter Nine
Einstein

He stared out at the groups of men dotting Truck's yard. They'd spread out and grown over the past half an hour, early arrivals coming out to greet those who'd just gotten here.

In the four months since he'd left Baker in his dust, things had changed here on the homesteads. What had been a rough field with uneven camping had turned into a cultivated space complete with thick grass. Someone had crafted more fire rings, and large logs had ass-sized scoops shaped out of them, creating seating at each.

Through the gossip grapevine, everything had sounded good—sometimes too good, as if the storyteller wanted the new chapter to be a grand success. In person, he found that the stories had actually been downplayed somewhat.

"Einstein." Laughter wreathed the sound of his name, and he turned to see Horse was the one who'd recognized him. Lifting a hand, he gave a wave in response. Horse gestured and called, "Come on over, brother."

Brother.

That right there was the one downside of the nomad rocker. Bama Bastards was a small club, tiny when compared to the bigger players like Incoherent and Rebel Wayfarers. Even Freed Riders was a larger club, with multistate chapters as notches in its organizational belt. He hadn't realized how much he'd miss being around people he knew...and trusted.

"Horse, good to see you." Their palms slapped together; then Horse adjusted his grip, pulling Einstein into a one-shoulder clinch. "How is it I'm back in Baker and you're back in Baker? You stalking me?"

"No. If I was gonna do that kind of shit, I'd have just locked you down when you came to visit a few weeks ago." Blackie and Horse had given Einstein a warm welcome, offering a room in their clubhouse for him to rest his head. "You look a little better now than you did then."

"Asshole, I'd just run through a hailstorm."

"So you say. I'm not convinced the black and blue you were wearing were caused by itty-bitty balls of ice, but whatever you want to believe. Whatever." With a final thumping hit against Einstein's back, Horse pulled away, still grinning. "You know you're welcome anytime, right?"

"I know. Know and appreciate the trust, brother." He thudded his fist against Horse's shoulder. "Tell me what I've missed."

"Clubhouse here is done-done. Fuckin' finally. I didn't think Bane'd ever get it finished to his satisfaction. Your drawings and information helped out a fuckin' ton, man. Great job there." Stepping away, Horse leaned against a tree. "Gunny's settled in better than anyone expected. Man's a menace, but he's also kinda a fuckin' genius when it comes to dealin' with Bane's patch-overs and prospects."

"I've heard only good things about him." Einstein paused and considered. "Well, mostly good things. He had a moment a few years ago when he was helpin' RWMC deal with some shit. Heavy-handed, but it all sorted out in the end."

"Brother, we've all got those kind of stories in our rearview." Horse's chuckle was wry. "At this point, if you don't have shit stories about you somewhere in your past, you're probably too much of a lightweight to play with the big boys. Too much happening in our world between shitty clubs, RICO, and bullshit overseas beefs coming home to roost."

"True. Some of us more than others." Glancing around at the clustering men, he picked out several women standing close to their better half, either legal or of the moment. "Hey, you ever meet Bane's old lady?" It had become a running joke before he'd left Baker. Neither of them had met Myrt officially. Caught glimpses of her from a distance, but between her exhaustion and morning sickness from the pregnancy, she hadn't made many appearances. "She's about due, right?"

"Should be. As you know I've been runnin' my ass off between the two chapters but stayin' at the clubhouse here when I'm in town. So nope, haven't met her to speak to."

Movement in the distance caught at Einstein's attention, and he grinned as he stepped towards the wide path between the two houses. "Hey, Marian's on the front porch. You said hello yet?" Horse lifted a shoulder. "What? You ghosting her for some reason?"

"She's not the reason I come to Baker, brother." Narrowed eyes stared at him. "Business comes first."

"Always." Angling his head to the side, Einstein took another step away from Truck's place. "Stay here if you want. I've got no reason to steer clear of Marian. She's a good girl."

"Woman."

"What?" The flat statement pulled Einstein up short. "What does that mean?"

"Means she's no little girl, much as Gunny'd like to pretend. Woman who can make up her own mind on what she wants." He lifted that single shoulder again, the black leather of his vest swinging heavily against his hips. "If she wanted to say hello, that door swings both ways."

"She ghosted *you*." The realization had tension in his chest easing. He glanced at the porch, disappointed to find Marian had disappeared. "What'd you do?"

"Why does everyone immediately go there?" Horse pushed off the tree and turned, walking next to Einstein as they made their way towards Bane's house. "I didn't do a damn thing."

"Yeah, yeah."

A couple of RWMC members he knew fell into step with them, and they shared quick greetings.

He blinked at a small woman waddling their direction, preceded by a round belly. "Is that Myrt?"

"Looks to be."

They stepped to the side and gave her respectful greetings. Those bits of conversation quickly turned into a rescue of sorts, Einstein and Horse crafting a carry chair with their arms. That moment then morphed into a request from the woman, one that had Horse smiling wide in agreement.

Hours later, Einstein was lounging to one side of a low-burning fire, elbow on his knee as he tried to decide where he'd sleep tonight.

"I heard that was some funny shit today." Einstein looked up, surprised to find Retro standing across the circle. "Bearing the queen on her portable throne so she could toss a question at her old man. Classic stuff, brother. Material that'll still be makin' the rounds years from now."

He scrambled to his feet and rounded the pit, wrapping his arms around his best friend. "What the hell, man. I didn't know you were coming in."

"I like to keep ya guessin'." Retro returned the embrace with the same amount of strained strength. "Fuckin' miss your ugly mug, brother."

"God." Einstein squeezed tight, feeling somehow steadier just knowing Retro was here. "I miss you, too."

"Tell me."

"Tell you? Tell you what?"

"Every-fuckin'-thing, man. I want to hear everything over the past two weeks, since we last spoke." Retro gestured towards the log Einstein had leaned against. "Let's pull up a seat, have a chat."

Making his way back to where he'd been seated, he ran the memories of his journey through his mind, trying to isolate the pieces that Retro would be most interested in. "I've already reported all of this through Mudd, you know. If you didn't get the memo, then you need to take it up with your man."

"Oh, no worries for your little head, he told me everything." Retro settled next to Einstein, folded fist pounding against Einstein's flexed quad. "Nothin' like gettin' my info straight from the source, though. Me and Mudd think a lot alike, but we aren't twinsies. You just gotta fuckin' deal."

"Yeah, can do." He fell into the stories then, letting Retro guard them against eavesdroppers, corralling the tales into linear additions to what they might have already known about any given situation. How the Silent Deaths were breaking from the Machos, and what that might have to do with a different Machos affiliation to the Legends from up in Wyoming. Legends had absorbed the club that Bane had given up on years ago. Through the confusion of the takeover, their records hadn't been updated well, or at all. It had taken Retro a full week to suss out all the names of members like Bane who had left. At least now he was reasonably confident Scar wasn't among them. While there, though, he'd isolated information about two Jackals who'd routed through the northern states on their way to the East Coast, an odd arrangement, given they were chartered south of San Diego. That had jumped out at him as a desire to avoid certain clubs and had garnered its own week-worth of investigation.

By the time he finished talking, his throat was dry and scratchy, voice hoarse from sucking in wood smoke and breathing out secrets.

The look of pride on Retro's face?

Worth anything.

"I'm impressed with myself for the first time in a while." Retro leaned back, stretching his legs straight in front of him, soles of his boots aimed at the guttering fire. "Makin' you take that nomad rocker is the best idea I've had." He got his feet underneath him and stood, looking down at Einstein as he held out a hand. "Come on, brother. I copped Bane's couch for you tonight."

"Where are you sleeping?" He accepted the assistance and groaned as he rose and stretched. "Jesus, shoulda realized my ass was numb."

"I'm in the guest bedroom. My understanding is we'll be feted breakfast early, then we'll head into town to do the main business." Retro took a slow breath, regret etching lines on his face. "You heard about Marlin, right?"

"Patching over. Never woulda thought it, man. The Baker chapter is solid, though, a great group if a body was looking for a change of scenery. Did he give you a reason behind the request?" Einstein paced beside Retro as they walked towards Bane's house. "This feels sudden."

"Same info as Monday, needs to vacate the Birmingham locale. I didn't press him beyond finding out that it wasn't club related. If I'd denied, I think he would have stayed." Retro shrugged.

"Yeah, but how unhappy would he be in a few weeks or months. Sometimes you just gotta know when it's time to cut losses and move on." Since his plan was following select bikers as they moved through the community, picking up and putting down patches as they went, Einstein felt like he'd seen it all by now. "He'd either bury himself inside the club in an unhealthy way, or he'd start staying away if it meant being in proximity to whatever has his hackles riled up. You ensuring he does it right will always keep the door open for him to come back someday."

"Oh, yeah. And we're doin' it right. You should know that about me for sure."

Retro stomped his boots against the flagstone at the bottom of the kitchen steps, a feature that hadn't existed before. Einstein followed suit, noting other changes since he'd been here last. The railing was new, sanded smooth, and stained a dark color to match the older treads. In the darkness, it looked like the paint around the door had been touched up, too.

Light flooded out as Retro opened the door and went inside, Einstein a stride behind him. The party in the house hadn't yet flagged, with the kitchen and what he could see of the living room packed with bodies.

"So much for getting some shut-eye soon," he murmured to Retro, gesturing towards the couch currently seating four couples, women on the men's laps.

"I'd offer you my bed in exchange, but—" Retro laughed aloud, grinning broadly. "I don't wanna."

"Asshole." Einstein thudded a fist against Retro's shoulder. "I've got my tent. I can head back out and set up."

"There are two guest bedrooms." The soft female voice had Einstein spinning with a grin. "I saved one of them for you, Einstein."

He held out his arms, pleased when Marian immediately moved in for a hug. "Woman, it's good to see you." He stepped back, hands sliding down to curl around her wrists. "You look good."

"The rooms are ready if you're tired now." Rolling her eyes, she brushed off his compliment. "I heard what you and Horse did for Myrt earlier. It was very sweet."

"Weren't you in the other room upstairs?" Einstein remembered Bane's explanation of why he needed to bunk on the couch the first time he'd stayed over. He dropped his hold on her arms. "I'm not taking your bed, am I?"

"No, I've moved to a room on this floor." She tipped her head to the side, eyes tracking across his face. She snorted a quiet laugh at whatever she saw. "And yes, before you even ask, it's got a lock on the inside. I'm not sure why men with such honor believe others with the same are untrustworthy, but I'm not going to argue."

That question had been on the tip of his tongue, but he just gave her a grin. "We cookin' breakfast in the morning?" Most of the days he'd spent in Baker had all begun the same as the first, with Marian out of bed before the rest of the house, and Einstein happy to assist in whatever she was making for food.

The pillion motorcycle ride back to the homesteads had done more than broken whatever remaining reticence had her holding back. She'd gone from giving lip service about trusting him to giving him a glimpse into her bone-deep belief in his goodness. He'd held on to that through long nights since, when his doubts of his worthiness surfaced. Regret at how he'd failed to save Lauren and Makayla still bubbled along under his skin, but something about Marian's explicit trust helped salve the wounds.

"Eggs and meat. One thing I've learned is that Bane's friends can eat copious amounts of meat." She grinned at him, then offered a shyer one to Retro. "Hello again."

"Hey there, Maid Marian." That had her rolling her eyes again, Gunny's nickname for her still making her flush a delicate pink. "I'm going to head up. Assuming Myrt and the boys are already in bed?"

"They are." Marian looked over her shoulder at a call from someone. "I need to go back and help out." She jabbed a thumb at the kitchen.

"Go see what they need. Just make sure you're safe and smart." Einstein reached out and brushed a finger across the back of her hand. "I'll see you in the morning." He watched her walk away.

"She's a good woman." Retro's words made Einstein realize he'd blanked on the man. He turned and glanced at Retro's face, surprised to find a puzzled expression there. "Looks like you've got a good friendship brewing. Maybe something more?"

His head jerked back. "What? No. Hell no. We got into a routine when I was here before and got familiar. She helps out so much, people don't even realize, so I took on a little bit of that for her. That's all." Suddenly uncomfortable, he reached for the doorknob. "I'm going to grab my bag off the bike. See you in the morning?"

"Yeah, brother." Retro's hand landed on his shoulder, fingers gripping deep against the leather. "See you then."

Einstein fled the house. There was no other word for it, and he was self-aware enough to own his actions.

No way.

Retro was wrong. What he held for Marian were respect and friendship. When he'd first met her, she'd been just off her rescue, literally days from being under the thumb of her father. It had been gratifying to watch as she gained even tiny amounts of self-confidence. The effortless way she trusted him after the bike ride was a great memory, sure. Even if he'd steadfastly ignored the physical feelings of her thighs on either side of his hips. Closeness was a necessity when riding double. Then, after he'd left Baker, when he'd called Bane's house it hadn't been to speak to her. There'd been business behind every single call, and he'd conducted that with Bane, as intended. Of course, if she answered, they'd spend a while on the line, just talking through their days, but that didn't mean anything. Her seeking him out tonight didn't mean anything either. Neither did his desire to see her safe and cared for.

There isn't anything else here.

Retro wasn't wrong often, but he had been with his speculation tonight.

Einstein touched the front of his vest, the ever-present hard plastic of the toothbrush safe in the inside pocket.

I love Lauren, doesn't matter she's gone. Love my girls.

Einstein leaned his ass against the seat of his bike, head bowed. With his eyes tightly closed, he worked to pull up the memories that had at one time often swamped him.

Lauren's terrified face, the gag painfully pulling at the corners of her mouth. The blanket-covered bodies on the floor of the van in Florida. The day of the funeral, Lauren's mother and father audibly weeping while Einstein stood over the graves as rain pattered down, as if even the sky cried for the loss. Those all came to him easily, raking their blades through his insides until he was bleeding and weak.

He pushed himself further, looking back to when he'd first met Lauren. Those were still harder to surface, and the most he could get was the soft expression on her face as she held their daughter for the first time. He fought for something, anything, unable even to come up with the feel of her skin against his.

Then his brain supplied the tender sensation of Marian's hand, hot against his fingertips as he touched her gently.

His dick twitched.

"Fuck   no."

***

Marian

"Marian."

Retro's call surprised her, since she'd just left where he'd stood with Einstein. Turning, she saw he was alone. She glanced at the stairs, expecting to see Einstein making his way up them. Instead, it looked like he'd disappeared. Retro gestured, calling her over with a smile.

"Yes?" The dozen strides felt like a country mile, taking forever, because she knew from Bane that this man had a high ranking in their world. A world she existed within in only an ancillary fashion, along the edges. "What can I do for you, Retro?" Through the months, she'd decided the complicated protocol of Bane's world boiled down to two things. One, don't approach a man who hadn't initiated a conversation, and two, apply respect in every interaction.

"Wondered if I could pick your brain for a minute." Retro's gaze on her was unwavering, his sharp eyes locked on her face for some reason. "Einstein's stepped outside for a bit. Will the door still be unlocked later, or should I text him to call him back now?"

"With so many of the FRMC in attendance, it's unlikely Bane will lock the door." She gestured at the room behind her. "Any of the members would be better to ask than me."

"But I'm asking you. Seems like you've slipped into a tailor-made role here. Carved out a place for yourself." Retro's mouth smiled, the expression not reaching his eyes, and the observation made her uncomfortable. "Sweet deal, if you ask me."

"I'm only doing what's needed." Threading her fingers together, she hid the way her hands shook at his questioning. *I'm not a fraud.* The reminder made her rebuttal stronger than it might have been a moment before. "Swear, I'm not pushing into anything that's not my business."

This man is important to Einstein, even more so than to Bane. "Promise, I'm not in anything I shouldn't be."

"Oh, I've no doubt of that." He waved a hand expansively, stirring the air between them, that careful distance she was always careful to maintain. *Except with Einstein.* "Do you think I should call Einstein back now or let him wander outside?"

"I thought he was going to bed soon? Why would he have gone back outside? Did he forget something?" She glanced at the door, failing to penetrate the darkness beyond the glass. "And as far as what you need to do, Retro, I wouldn't presume to try and dictate that, especially not where it involves Einstein."

"Do you know his history?" The question seemed casual, spoken in a soft voice, but if anything, Retro's gaze sharpened, piercing her through and through. "Know what happened to him?"

"If I did—" *I don't.* She picked her words carefully, not wanting to give offense in her defense of the man she'd come to think of as a friend. "Then it still wouldn't be my place to relate those stories. People's business isn't mine, and I try not to insert myself where I'd be unwanted." If Einstein had something in his past he hadn't shared with her, while it might hurt because of that friendship she'd imagined, maybe him not telling her wasn't intentional. *I'll ask him tomorrow.* "Retro, sir."

"Oh, well done, lady." This time Retro's eyes shone with amusement matching the curve of his lips. "You'll do for my boy, Marian. You'll do." He held out a hand and waited, stuck in that pose until Marian lifted her palm to meet his. "This is our pact. We'll do what's needed to get our boy to pull his head out of his ass. I'll work on my side of things, and you—" He laughed softly, in a way that made her feel included in whatever the joke was. "You just be yourself. It'll all work out in the end."

Releasing her hand, he turned and made his way to the stairs, going upwards without a backwards glance.

What in the world did he mean by that?

She moved closer to the door and peered out, only seeing vague shapes of trees silhouetted against the orange of faraway flames.

Retro wanted her to help him keep Einstein safe. *I can do that.* She glanced at the rowdy crowd in the living room and kitchen, then gave them her back as she made her way down the back hallway to the little mudroom she'd turned into a private sanctuary for herself.

This close to the outside door, she'd be certain to hear the comings and goings of everyone. She locked the door and undressed, pulling on her sleep clothes and climbing into bed. Without meaning to, for as long as she stayed awake, she kept her ears tuned to the door opening and closing. Finally, the sound was followed by footsteps making their way upstairs.

Only then did Marian turn on her side and close her eyes, sinking quickly into a dreamless sleep.

Chapter Ten
Marian

Rising to her toes, Marian felt the pull of tense muscles as she waved, hand still moving long after the disappearing figure would have stopped looking.

She rocked backwards, thudding painfully to her heels as she pulled in a long, slow breath.

Einstein had been here for three days. That totaled up to three shared mornings, orbiting around each other as they moved through the kitchen. Six rides sitting behind him, back and forth to town. In the year since she'd first met Einstein, Marian had been careful to keep her side of the relationship exactly as he seemed to need it. Loose, casual, and easy. Still, a dozen times she'd caught her gaze on him a little too long.

"You gonna tell him how you feel?" Retro's voice startled her, and Marian whirled, staring up at him.

It took a long set of breaths in and out, but she finally found the words she needed to say. "I don't know what you're talking about."

"That's what I was afraid of." The man headed back inside, leaving Marian to glance over her shoulder at the empty road.

It's the only way I can keep him as my friend.

Chapter Eleven
Marian

Laughing and looking up into Horse's face, Marian let her imagination take her on a tiny trip. One where they were more than friends. She suppressed the shudder that rolled through her body. In the two years since she'd fallen into this enchanted life, her body and emotions still seemed to only react to one man, and it wasn't Horse.

"Never met a girl who liked fishing." Horse continued their conversation, not noticing Marian's sidetrack into never-happening land. "You're one of a kind, little sister." His shoulder bumped against hers, rocking her sideways. "Whoever catches you better realize how much of a keeper you are." He finished tying a new lure to the line and tossed his hook into the water, picking up the cane pole with one hand, the other patting her thigh gently.

"If there's ever anyone fishing for something like me, they'd need to be bold enough to get past Gunny." She finished piercing the wriggling cricket with her hook and swung the line out, dropping the hook into the deep end of the swirling pool of water. They were on the bank of the creek that ran behind the houses, at a spot where the water had eaten away at the bank, carving out a place where it grew wide and deep. "Not seeing that happening anytime soon, my friend." Even with the open invitation to call him brother, she never took advantage of the offer. That word meant too much to the men in the clubs, and she would never hijack it for her own benefit.

"He does present a formidable barrier. What if…" The tip of his pole dipped, and he froze, fingers spread on the handle in anticipation. It stopped moving and he relaxed. "What if I could find someone that he'd approve of, would you be interested in dating?"

With a shake of her head, Marian cleared the images from her mind again. "I know you aren't talking about yourself here." His laughter made her smile, and she was glad he hadn't taken her words as an insult. "Gunny's made it clear what he thinks of that idea."

"Oh, yeah. He has done that. No doubt about it." Horse chuckled again. "No, I was thinking of this guy in town. I've seen him hanging around the club. Seems like a nice guy. Maybe date material?"

"I don't know." Her pole thrummed, bending nearly in half, and she was up in a flash, working the line up and down, creating momentum. "I got one." With a final hard pull, she dragged the catfish free of the water and swung it over the bank behind them. Just in time, too, because it spat out the hook, cricket still in place, and fell to the dry ground. "He's not bad."

Horse thrust his pole into her hands as he stood. Capturing the flopping fish with one hand, he hooked fingers through its gills and brought it back to the edge of the creek where they had their stringer anchored. Just then, the tip of his pole dipped again, and Marian felt the rushing thrum through the cane pole that indicated there was a fish on the line.

With a whoop, she dropped her pole to the ground and anchored it with one foot, starting the same pull-and-release movement with Horse's pole.

"Are you fuckin' kidding me?" He looked out at the water, then back to her with a deep line between his brows. "Ten fuckin' seconds in your hand and the fish are basically jumping out of the water? What the everlovin' hell?"

She wrenched on the pole, lifting hard, and propelled the fish from the water, watching as this much larger catfish spat the lure out like the other one had. It flopped around in the dirt, and she whooped again. "That's ten pounds if he's an ounce." The hook swung over the water, and she nearly dropped it back in before deciding to look at the bait he'd used. "What are you fishin' with? They like my crickets well enough, but I'm only getting ones that are a couple of pounds." She'd caught eight so far to two of Horse's, but the final filleted weight would be fairly even between their two stringers.

"Don't—"

Line in her hand, she ignored Horse's bit-off shout, staring down at the shiny lure. "Is this what I think it is?"

A gruff, "What is it?" made her look up. Gunny stood nearby, and she saw his kids were playing in the water farther up the creek, where it was shallow enough to wade across. "Show me, little sister."

Wordlessly, Marian held out the lure, still attached to the line. The rose gold cock and balls dangled upside down, tiny clusters of tied-off feathers affixed to the head.

"The fuck?" Gunny whirled to where Horse stood, hands on his hips as he surveyed the sky above. "You put a dick on her fishin' pole? What kind of pervert are you, asshole? I knew I didn't like you."

"Shut up, man. That's my pole and I'll use whatever I want, dillweed. The fucker works." Horse began chuckling, and she could scarcely make out his words. "It's a—" He broke off, laughing again. "It's a one-eyed winker. Good for one fish."

"The fuck?" Gunny choked and started laughing. "One-eyed…what? You mean it's here for a good time, not a long time?"

"Yeah." Horse had bent over, still roaring. "It's a jerk bait." His hands flapped towards where Gunny was folded in half, laughing. "Not a trawler."

The pole under her foot shook, and she looked down to see the tip vibrating. Tossing Horse's pole to the ground, she ignored their raving in the background as she fought this newest catch to a fatigued standstill. With a final twitch, she pulled and lifted, the pole bending deeply as she swung the catfish to drop at Horse's feet. The hook was embedded in its lower jaw, and Marian had her pliers in hand quickly, holding the fish still as she worked it free.

The hook was bare, and she grumbled, "He took my cricket."

"Marian?" Still red in the face, Horse bent next to her. "Lemme get the stringers. With this one, I think we've got enough for supper." As he leaned closer, his gaze darted from her eyes to her mouth and back again. His lips parted, tongue sweeping his bottom lip, and she stared at him in confusion. "Marian, I'd like to change my earlier—"

"I'm not done talking to you, asshole." Gunny's laughing bellow interrupted whatever Horse had been about to say, and he shot her a grin instead.

"Talk to you later, little sister?" Horse stood and stretched a hand to her. She accepted the help, climbing to her feet slowly.

"Sure."

Walking back to the houses with Horse and Gunny carrying the fish and Marian toting the tackle, they held a quiet but active conversation about the local diner. Each of them having a different favorite gave them opportunity to try and convert the others to their preferred meals. Of course Gunny kept circling back to Horse's choice of tackle, finding it by turns amusing and revolting, and then hilarious again.

They rounded the corner of the house and Marian spied a familiar motorcycle parked near the back door. "Einstein!"

He stood up from where he'd been crouched next to his bike and turned, immediately finding her with his eyes. His wide smile was welcoming.

Marian dropped the tackle and left it lying in the dirt as she ran to him with arms outstretched. "I didn't think we'd see you for a couple more months."

Mouth next to her ear, Einstein's murmured, "Marian," told her as much as the tight hug. Einstein had been lonely on the road. *I'm glad he's got here to come home to.* "Wanted to see my favorite girl."

She stepped back to let the men greet each other, surprised at the chilly reception from Horse. She'd thought they were good friends. The sad expression Horse turned her way was also surprising, but she didn't have a chance to ask him about it. The evening was taken up in conversations about Einstein's travels, Thad's sports, and the latest achievements of Myrt and Bane's baby.

It was only later that she remembered Horse had wanted to talk to her. *I'll have to find him and see what's up.* Already in bed, Marian pulled the covers up as she turned to her side, snuggling into the pillow.

Einstein's here. That meant their morning ritual tomorrow.

She fell asleep with a smile on her face.

Chapter Twelve
Einstein

"Still not sure what you're aiming at, man." Einstein tapped the wood of the pool cue against the edge of the table, knocking a few drifts of blue chalk loose from the tip. "Ain't no way you're going to make that shot."

He lifted his lip, giving this stranger the fake and easy smile he'd learned to cultivate. *Talk to enough bullshitters, some of it's bound to rub off eventually.*

The bustling bar surrounded them with noise and movement. In one corner, a jukebox belted out decades-old chart-toppers as men and women swayed on the tiny parquet floor, each weaving couple pretending they'd had enough to drink to make hooking up a given.

The click of pool balls brought his attention back to the table, and he offered the same smile when he saw the stripes and solids counted up to the same total, just moved around a bit.

"Aw, dammit," the skinny cowboy groused, shoulders rounding as he leaned heavily on his stick. "Thought for sure I'd catch at least one of them."

"Gotta know what you're after before you let loose with the hit." He lined up on the cue ball, leaning over to give it a tap. It hit the solid ball near the corner enough of a glancing blow to knock his ball in, then angle off the cushions to roll back to where it began. "See what you want to happen in your mind, then let go." Striking the cue ball a second time, he split the difference between two solids near the middle of the table, directing each into a corner pocket. "Once you have it in your mind, you can do nearly anything."

The cowboy grinned good-naturedly as he flipped through his wallet and pulled out a bill, holding it out to Einstein as the eight ball rolled slowly to drop into the side pocket he'd called. "Next time I need schoolin', I'll give you a call."

"Keep your money." Einstein waved it off, then sidled a step closer. "Instead, what if you tell me everything you know about Marcus Littlelight?"

Proving himself perhaps more astute than Einstein had given him credit for, the cowboy grimaced as he tucked the money away. "Buy me a beer and a shot, and everything I got in my head is yours."

Three hours later, Einstein lounged on a motel bed, back to the dubiously padded headboard. He'd kicked the comforter to the floor when he'd entered the room and had only removed his cut and boots so far. Flipping his phone from one hand to the other, he eyed the clock on the nightstand. Another hour before Retro'd be home from the game. Jimmy was developing into a savvy and talented tailback, and the junior high team had played their cross-town rivals tonight. The game might have ended a bit ago, but Einstein knew their routine as well as if he were there enjoying it alongside them. The drive home would include an obligatory visit to the pizza place where the team would rehash every play. Tales of their prowess would grow with each rendition, until the next time he talked to Jimmy, he might have well won the whole thing singlehandedly.

So no Retro yet.

That left him with a short list of additional contacts he'd want to spend any time with, even from remote like this.

Monday was a given. The man managed to always be amusing and yet still provide a deep well of compassion. But he and his latest beau might be snuggled up about now, and alone time was sacrosanct to the man.

There was Bane, but he'd be dealing with nearly the same as Retro. Thad had turned into a sports fanatic over the past couple of years, and the last time he'd spoken to Bane, the family had been in-between two different sports events—on the same day. Luke still would rather spend his free evenings at the library or arcade, either of which was more Myrt's speed, so she'd take her and Bane's little one with them and leave Bane to Thad's mercies.

Gunny had turned into a surprising friend, one who could offer insights with composure one moment, then segue off into one of Sharon's wild-haired ideas the next, laughing the whole time. His kids kept him busy, too, and he'd been making loud noises about another baby since Josh was going into junior high next year. Einstein always tried not to interrupt family time for the Robinson household.

Forcefully steering his mind away from the other person in Baker he liked being around, he glanced at the clock again, mentally calculating the time it would take him to run there from this bohunk Mississippi town.

"Fuck it." Spending yet another night in a no-tell motel wasn't the greatest of his options, and if it hadn't been for the uncertainty of sourcing the most recent rumors, he wouldn't have checked in at all. "Four hours puts me there at midnight. I know where the key is if it comes to that."

Swinging off the bed, he stamped into his boots and grabbed a long-sleeved Henley out of his bag. Tugging it over his head, he threaded his way through the fabric, then reached for his cut as soon as he had a hand free. A final glance around the room confirmed nothing left behind, and he slung the bag over his shoulder, fingers gripping the woven nylon handles tightly.

Another five minutes to check the bike over, retrieve his helmet, and strap the bag into place—then he was astraddle of the saddle, feet firmly on the ground as the engine rumbled underneath him. He smiled. *Hope I never get tired of that feeling.* Even after so many years, just the sound and sense of the bike represented freedom, and most recently, a sense of healing.

Angling his wheels out of the motel parking lot, he settled back for the ride and selected his route from memory.

Time had been kind to him. Time and separation.

It wasn't that he missed Lauren and Makayla less acutely, because the knowledge and understanding that they were forever gone would still strip him of breath and strength when it hit him unawares. But as he'd traveled the road under the guise of his nomad rocker, he'd found that distance helped—both physical and regarding passing seasons. It had become a certain kind of freeing to be around people who'd never met his girls, never understood what precious gems he'd held in his hands— and so never knew what he'd lost.

Like this run, because even with folks at the end who intellectually knew what had happened, Lauren and Makayla wouldn't be top of mind for them. Those graceful buffers between what had come before and what he was building with every mile underneath his wheels had become something he'd longed for.

Just blessed that I've friends who give me the space I need.

And that was another reminder that he should at least text Retro from his first fuel stop, so the man would know where he headed tonight.

Another five hours had passed before he rolled the bike as quietly as possible into the curving driveway, the relatively new asphalt pavement secure under his wheels when he glided to a stop in front of the big house.

Retro hadn't been placated with a simple text. *Of course not.* Which had meant Einstein had found himself seated at booths reserved for paying customers inside an all-night gas station. Their quiet conversation had been refreshing, as they always were, topics ranging from what Einstein had found on this run, to Retro's family, back to the club and their most recent gathering, then away to how Retro's oldest was doing in college.

"Nelda's on fire, man. She banked enough credits throughout high school that she could graduate now with her associate's, but the program she's lookin' at needs her to kill these last couple of classes before swinging into the next level of shit." Retro's fond tone held enough exasperation to be amusing. "Fuckin' glad the girl knows her daddy ain't made of money, because if it wasn't for the scholarships and grants she's gotten, she wouldn't be considering moving on towards graduate school at all."

"She's a good girl." Einstein chuckled, remembering back to the long-ago time when Retro had moved his family into the clubhouse for a few weeks. "Even when she was askin' way too many fuckin' questions about Mudd and Rhonda's toys she found tucked behind the bar."

"Oh, God, don't remind me of those days." Laughter, warm and rich, flowed through the call. "Now that was an awkward conversation I never expected to have to have with my teenaged daughter."

"And you wouldn't change a damn thing. Be honest."

"You're right, as always. That's why I call you Einstein. Smartest man among us, always."

"Yeah, yeah. I'd like to point out that she's still a teen, for another while at least." Grief hit him in an instant, coming out of nowhere to sideswipe his chest, throat, and eyes on its way past. Choking, he ground out, *"Hold on to that with both hands, brother."*

"Fuck, Jim." Silence followed by a quiet clearing of his throat, and Retro asked, *"How old would she be today?"*

Einstein didn't need to ask who.

"Not quite fourteen. Close. Couple of weeks."

"And you're headed to Bane's for a bit of time off the road?"

He grunted in response, unable to roll vowels and consonants into words.

"Jimmy's got a game next weekend, but then we've got a break. I'll load up some brothers, and we'll come down. Truck's been asking me to give him a date when he could plan to do a big feed. Maybe we'll call in some other folks, make it a big to-do. Just another Baker Mini-Rally." He could hear something in the background, and away from the phone Retro said, *"Just a minute, baby. On the horn with Einstein."* There was a soft sound, like the echo of a kiss, then Retro whispered, *"Sure thing, I'll give him your love."*

"Tell her it's coming right back at her." Trina was a great old lady for Retro, understanding of the time needed to keep the club healthy and the members engaged, and happy to take care of not only her man but their extended family. *"She's a good woman, Retro."*

"I got lucky." Heaviness gone from his voice, Retro chortled. *"Call me a lucky, lucky man."*

"I'll see that lucky man in a couple of weeks. We'll sit and chat, but in the meantime, you know where to find me."

"That I do." Another silence hung between them, this one less painful. *"Be safe, brother. Roll easy and keep the rubber down."*

"You know it." He disconnected the call and threw the remaining rancid coffee into the trash, lifting a hand to the guy boxed in behind the counter. Then Einstein did what he always did these days. He got in the wind again.

The sun wasn't close to being up. He spied a scarce line of lighter darkness along the edge of the world as he swung a leg off the bike and stood, stretching. Above him, a light flickered on in the kitchen window, and he caught a glimpse of a figure moving out of sight towards the door.

With any luck, it'll be—

The door swung open. There was a pause, then a vibrating, *"Einstein."* It was too shadowy to make out her face, but Marian's pleased call of his name made him grin. Her bedroom was near the kitchen, in a little room along the back wall of the house, so pulling up where he had, it wasn't surprising he'd woken her. He'd earned the sharp edge of her tongue more than once when he'd tried to creep in silently to keep from doing the same, so these days, he just followed her repeated directions. "Come in. This air is cold on my feet." Sure enough, she was barefooted, the hem of her nightgown sweeping against the skin of her ankles.

"If you'd wear socks to bed like any sane person, your feet wouldn't be cold now." The bag on his bike was retrieved with a few economical movements, and he paused on the bottom step, taking the edge of the door in his hand. "Mornin', Marian."

"Come in," she repeated, and this time he was close enough to see the welcoming smile stretching her lips. "What can I do for you? Breakfast and coffee, or want quiet, blankets, and the guest room?"

He paused by the door and toed off his boots, bending to set them to the side. "Depends. If you go back to bed, you think you can sleep after I woke you?"

Marian had a job in town at a flower shop. According to his memories from the past year, they did a brisk business during the fall, so she probably had to go in today.

She yawned behind a hand, shaking her head as she moved towards the coffee maker. "I'm up now. Randy'll start his nonsense soon as it gets a little lighter outside. That fool is better than an alarm clock." A flick of a switch and the machine started humming. "Was an early night for me. Everyone was out of the house for a change, and I fell asleep reading before they got home."

Through the years and months, he had developed a strong friendship with Marian, built on his understanding that she was as true in her heart as she was strong and resilient. His faith in her never wavered, even if hers did, and for a while, it had been him holding to that knowledge until she would accept it as truth.

It all began that first day as he'd watched her fall into a natural caregiver role around her family; then, recognizing how he'd felt, she'd taken on trying to make him less of an outsider.

Marian was the glue that held the house together, whether she'd admit it or not.

During his many visits, they'd cooked for the house, standing at the counters hip-to-hip preparing meals, Einstein quickly falling into a comfortable routine. In their conversations, he'd uncovered her deep-seated fears of being a burden, something that couldn't be overcome with arguments.

Once he had a grasp on the issues, he'd helped her plot out a path that would move how she saw herself to the other side of the line. Everyone he'd enlisted in the efforts had willingly assisted, in whatever way made sense. Over the following months, he and Horse had taken turns teaching her to drive, then cheered her on when Truck had bought a subcompact car for her use. That had led to her applying for a job in town, excited as a schoolgirl when they'd hired her, then sick with nerves before reporting for her first day.

"No, I'm serious. I don't know what I was thinking. I don't know anything about flowers or arrangements, and I don't know people in town to even recommend something they might like."

Einstein had taken a chance that she'd still be up, hearing through thirdhand accounts that she was nervous about her first day at the flower shop. Now, recognizing the tension in her voice, he was glad he'd called.

"You got the job because you showed them you were willing to learn and could work hard." When she didn't respond after a second or two, Einstein forged ahead. "You told me they had a test, even if they didn't call it that, and if you'd flunked out they wouldn't have hired you. Trust, woman. Trust in yourself, yeah?"

"I won't know what to do."

"They'll tell you, I'm sure. Don't sweat it, Marian."

"What if I mess up?"

"You will. It's inevitable. Everyone messes up. The difference is that you won't be afraid to own it, and then will be all-in on fixing whatever it was." Einstein grinned down at the toes of his boots, shoulder propped against the outside wall of a Montana bar. "You're a fixer if I've ever met one. Ten'll get you twenty that within a month they'll be asking you to work more hours."

"I'm not taking that bet."

"Because you know I'd win." He chuckled quietly. "And that's because you know I'm right." A door opened to the side, and he looked up to see the man he needed to talk to walking out of the building. "Shit, Marian. I gotta go. I'll call real soon and see how you did, but I'm not worried about it. Not at all, and neither should you be." He straightened, glaring at the

man while he kept his words and tone soft. "Sleep well, and do good things."

Their history was filled with hundreds of those kinds of conversations, with the insecurity and need for reassuring eventually going both ways as Einstein found himself opening up to her more and more.

"Tell me what's new." Socks still on as protection against the chill of the floor, he wandered towards the kitchen, following behind Marian. He idly watched the way her nightgown swayed with every step, gaze trailing up her legs to the curves of her ass. Then he realized what he was doing and yanked his attention to the window, focused on the line of only slightly brighter light along the horizon. *Shit.* Fumbling for a topic, he tried to remember what he'd last said to her, deciding on a safe, "How's work been?"

Marian glanced over her shoulder with a smile, unaffected and sweet. "Work is work. I love it, but it's not rocket science, so hasn't changed since the last time you asked." A tiny line appeared between her brows. "You okay? I didn't expect you in tonight—" She gave him a tight smile. "This morning. Usually you call first."

"I've got my tent. Girl, you know I can camp out."

"No, that's not what I meant. Just usually I hear from the boys that you're on your way inbound. No chatter this time means I'm wrongfooted on my welcome." She turned, the coffeemaker burbling behind her. "I'm glad to see you as always, Jim."

That was a new development over the past couple of months. During one of their late-night conversations, he'd asked her to call him Jim, throwing it out as if it weren't important. It had become a deep regret, because in moments like these, it meant she held more power than she knew.

"Marian, your welcome is always on point." He shook his head, then felt the vibration of his phone. Dragging it from his pocket, he looked at the screen and frowned. "I need to take this."

"I'll just be in my room for a minute," she said, already moving across the kitchen towards the short hallway.

Einstein once again watched her walk away, gaze fixed firmly on her ass as it swung side to side with each step. He connected the call as she disappeared, then answered gruffly, "What?"

"Man, I thought you should know." The whining tone of this contact immediately set him on edge. "Heard he's on the move. Heard he's in Kansas, aimin' east at KC."

"How did you hear?" Einstein considered this particular contact disposable, because he wasn't known for the veracity of his information. Einstein had kept him active because he was sometimes useful for establishing the truth of someone else's info.

"Heard from a man who knows Zipline. Zip was plannin' on bailin' on the Silent Deaths, and Smoke pushed him out early. Accepted his resignation with immediate ejection. Now Zip's headed to KC from the southern side, plannin' on meetin' in the middle." The pause between words was filled with the man's puffing breaths. "What's it worth to ya to know what the topic will be?"

"Dillweed, you know how this goes. We've done enough business that you already got a clue I won't pay out for anything I can't verify." He grabbed two mugs from the cabinet and poured coffee into each. "How do you expect me to verify something if you won't finalize the details?" He took a spoon from the drawer next to the sink, measuring and stirring two overflowing spoonfuls of sugar into one of the mugs. "Gotta give me what I want, and then I decide if you get anything."

"I don't know why I call you with this shit."

"Because you know that if you do bring me something worthwhile, I'll be fair with my money." That was true, and the man understood it, because he'd been on the receiving end more than once. "So spill. Why are Scar and Zipline going to meet up in Kansas City, where neither has allies or a friendly club chapter to give him sanctuary?"

"Word is Zip isn't happy with how the Machos are drillin' into the SDMC profits. He wanted more cashola than Estavez was willing to part with, and Smoke wasn't holdin' the line. Scar just wants more discontents to fill his ranks." The huffing sounds slowed and deepened as if the man were holding his breath between. "Scar's been looking for those stupid enough to stand behind him, and if he convinces Zipline, then he'll have a base. He might be unwelcome on the East Coast these days, but the center of the country doesn't have the same kind of memories."

Opening the refrigerator, Einstein asked, "Why you think he's unwelcome out there?" This was the first confirmation Einstein had that men loyal to Scar's grandfather might be breaking ranks with their exiled prince. If it were true, then that could have two outcomes. One, Scar would be less dangerous, losing the leverage of his family line. He paused, creamer in hand. *But the second might prove Scar more dangerous, as he's pushed into a corner not of his choosing.* "They've always held the door open for him."

"Not anymore. I heard from a guy who knew a guy who knew Scar back in the day. They're pissed he hasn't produced for them in so long, and they're not likely to give him a chance to reinvent himself." A grunted laugh came through, the sound making Einstein wince, nearly spilling the cream as he poured a measured amount into the already sugared mug. "So whadda think? Worth anything?"

"I've got your number. Once I take a couple of days to verify the info, I'll give you a call. Hopefully we'll come to an agreement." He shoved the creamer back into the refrigerator and turned. Lifting the mugs one at a time, he placed them on the kitchen island countertop. "Don't call me back for the same. But if you get more info, be sure to pass it along."

"Will d—"

Call disconnected, he returned the phone to his pocket and walked to the hallway. "Marian, you decent?" A soft sound pulled him closer to the door to her room. It was open slightly, and he lifted a palm to push it wider, stopping in his tracks.

Acres of bare skin greeted him as Marian bent over to drag a pair of delicate-looking dark red panties up her smooth, tanned legs. Her fingers settled the waistband into place just above the delicate curve of her ass, dimples still in clear view. *Jesus God.*

He must have made a sound, because her head whipped sideways, wide eyes catching and holding his gaze as she reached out for her discarded nightgown. She lifted the garment as she turned, keeping it in front of herself, the draping fabric effectively blocking his view.

Einstein was breathing heavily, muscles of his jaw tense as he kept his gaze on Marian's face. "I'm—you're..." *So fucking beautiful.* "I just wanted to tell you the coffee's ready." Whirling on his heel, he brushed past the door. "I'm so sorry."

"Einstein." The demand in her tone stopped his feet in place, but he kept his back to her as he waited. "I'm not upset at you."

"Maybe I'm upset at myself." Shaking his head, he tightened one hand into a fist. "I should have knocked. An open door isn't an invitation."

Stuck there, he waited, listening to each breath echo through his head. In and out, and again, and again. She sighed and finally said, "I'll be out in a minute."

Mug in hand, he plotted a dozen different conversations he could introduce as soon as she came out. Safe topics, things they'd discussed before, nothing risqué and nothing personal.

That all went to shit as soon as she came back into view.

Einstein's mouth dried up like the Sahara.

Marian was wearing shorts that hit high on her thigh and a shirt with a wide neck that drooped off one shoulder, leaving her collarbone bare.

His first instinct was to look around the room to ensure no one was there who might creep on this view of Marian. Then he checked the windows, then the stairs, and finally dropped his gaze to his half-empty mug, focusing on the shifting liquid as if it held the secrets of the universe.

She closed in on the island near him, and her hand appeared in the edges of his vision, lifting the mug of coffee he'd prepared for her.

"Mmmm."

Her soft vocalization of pleasure sent the tingles that had been dancing through his chest and belly straight to his dick, taking him from slowly thickening to fully hard within one breath and the next. Mug to his lips, he tried to take a sip but choked when the sound came again.

"So good. Mmmm."

The bottom of his mug thudded against the countertop, rattling edge to edge before he could still the trembling. Einstein flicked a glance at Marian, then back to his mug, but in that instant, something about her face stuck out at him. He angled his eyes upwards again to take another look, freezing when he saw the broad grin.

"Oh my God." She burst out laughing, bending over the countertop and continuing to belly-laugh until each breath turned into wheezing. "Your face."

"What the hell, Marian?" He watched her rearrange her clothing, the collar now covering her demurely. She bent over, and when he glanced around the island, he caught a glimpse of fingers working to unroll the hem of her shorts. "Why would you do that?"

"Because if I didn't do something to knock you out of your head, you'd wreck our friendship." Surging upright, she angled her chin at him defiantly. "What we have means a lot to me, Jim. The relationships I have with Bane, Horse, Gunny, or Truck—those're important, and I'd do a lot to make sure they stay strong." The smile she gave him was strained, corners of her mouth pulled down. "But for you and me? I'd do anything."

"I saw you naked." He reared back and thudded against the edge of the counter with one fist. "Naked."

"It's just skin, Jim. I've seen as much and more with most of the boys who wander around here." She lifted her mug and sipped, this time refraining from making the obscene sounds. "Like I've heard Truck say a thousand times, 'It ain't no thang.' Not to me." She slowly lowered the mug. "Hmmm. Now, if it had been one of the others, like Horse, I don't think I'd be as okay with it."

"What? What does that mean?" *Does she not see me like that?* Why did that thought bother him so much? "That I'm okay but he's not?"

"I can only give you what I have in my heart, Jim." She carried her mug towards the refrigerator, setting it down on the side counter. Opening the door, she surveyed the contents without looking back at him. "And that tells me confusing things sometimes. Yes, if one of the others had seen me like that, I would likely avoid them for at least the near future." Her head disappeared inside, voice floating out to where he stood. "I just knew I had to fix it fast, before you built it up into something it wasn't."

"I'm still sorry." He stepped to the side of the island and stopped in place. Her apple-ass was right there, muscles of her calves bunching and flexing as she moved items around inside the refrigerator. Swallowing hard, he stepped up beside her like he normally would and held out a hand. Striving for a voice as close to normal as possible, he asked, "What are we making this time?"

"Eggs and sausage." She nudged the back of his hand with the egg carton, and he took it, then the package of pork. "Thad has early practice, so he'll do a shake instead of real food."

He shuddered at the idea, then twisted to set down the items. When he looked back, she was holding out a container of cheese, so he took that and placed it alongside the eggs.

"Maye loves scrambled eggs."

"How's she doing?" Maye was Bane and Myrtle's daughter, born following an early, short labor not long after Myrt proposed to Bane. The little girl was adorable, and from the pictures Einstein had been sent through the most recent months, was growing like a weed.

"Maye is her mother's daughter, full of sass and vinegar." Marian turned from the refrigerator, a couple more items in her hands that she placed on the counter as the door closed silently behind her. "Did you hear the good news?"

"Apparently not." Rummaging through the cabinets, he found his favorite bowl for the eggs, bringing that and a whisk with him as he returned to stand next to Marian. "Clue me in, friend."

"We'll have another little one in a few months." He couldn't help himself, his gaze sweeping down to graze across her belly. Marian caught the glance and laughed. "No, silly. Not me. Why would you even—" She huffed a laugh. "No, Myrtle is due just around Thanksgiving. This one snuck up on her. No morning sickness, so she didn't pay close attention. Would you believe it was Bane who put two and two together?"

"I would. That man is smart as a whip." Unsettled by Marian's dismissal of his consideration, Einstein felt unbalanced. "Do you not want kids?" Poking around in his memories, he couldn't find any recollection of having that kind of conversation with her before. "I'm surprised."

"Not a lack of wanting." She spoke easily as she laid out the pans while he cracked eggs into the bowl. "More a lack of opportunity."

"Do you not date? I thought you went out with that guy a while back." The fishhook twisted in his gut to the point he lifted a hand, rubbing knuckles against his hard sternum. "I know Bane didn't like him, but if you did...?"

"I went on one date." Back to him, she rearranged the pans on the stovetop. "My first date."

Sour spit pooled in his mouth, and he was glad she couldn't see his expression.

"My only one."

"What was wrong with him?" Blood pounded in his head as his jaw clenched tightly. He didn't try and examine his reaction this time, instead focused on listening for her answer in case there was an asshole in town who needed the shit beaten out of him.

Marian shook her head, the braided tail of hair brushing her shoulders.

"No, honey." Looking away, he stared out the window as he tried to slow his racing thoughts. He wanted—*needed*—her to talk to him, to know she trusted him with her secrets. *She's my friend, that's all.* "Something must have happened if you didn't want a repeat."

"He was okay." When she paused, he glanced over at her again to find her looking at him, a strange expression on her face. "It was good."

"I'll take you on a date." The offer that categorically didn't feel throwaway was out of his mouth before he could clamp his lips shut, and panic swelled through him.

"You're a hoot, Jim. I'm fine, though."

Marian's response didn't do anything to settle his nerves. *Am I not what she'd like in a man?*

It was a struggle, but Einstein managed to hold her gaze. "He didn't hurt you or try anything?" Her immediate smile and headshake reassured him. "You'd tell me if he had?"

"And risk you going to jail defending my honor?" Marian's laughter was light, belling through the room. "I'd sell tickets to the event."

"That's my girl." He seasoned the egg mixture and dropped the whisk into the bowl. "Ready for you here."

Their conversation steered itself into less personal topics from there on out as they fell into comfortable routines, working around each other in a complicated but easy dance. Einstein wasn't sure if he was upset or glad when the door opened and Gunny walked in, because that signaled a different change in the discussion, one where Marian would occasionally interject but was quieter. Then Bane descended the stairs, and upon seeing Einstein, called back upstairs to rouse Myrt and the boys. Within minutes, the kitchen had become the bustling center of the household, and once Truck and Vanna walked in, followed closely by Gunny's family, a sense of completion swept over Einstein.

With a plateful of food in front of him, he listened to Gunny while stabbing another bite of eggs when he felt something. An awareness, like a ghost touch along his skin. Lifting his gaze, he met Marian's from across the island. Luke was next to her, pattering on about something, just as Gunny still was next to Einstein—but for an instant, a brilliant moment in time, it felt as if he and Marian were the only two people in the world. Her full lips curved into a smile, tiny and delicate, but real. A smile she seemed to reserve just for him. The corners of her eyes crinkled, and he watched pink sweep up her cheeks as she broke their gaze, looking down at her own plate. *So fucking beautiful.*

"Hey, man." Something jostled him, and he looked away from Marian to find Gunny staring at him with a puzzled expression. "You need rest before we ride?"

"Nah, nah. I'm good." He shoveled a bite into his mouth, then gestured a go-on to Gunny. But attempting to keep his focus on the man was harder than it should have been, since Einstein found himself hyperaware of every movement Marian made.

She lifted a biscuit to her mouth and his jaw muscles clenched as if he were the one biting into it. Her lips met the rim of a glass of milk, and he salivated watching her throat muscles work to swallow. He blinked and his imagination filled with the image of her bare. The long lines of her back drew his gaze down the curves of her silhouette, a tempting glimpse of the tease of breast only visible from the side.

The fuck is wrong with me?

Angling himself more towards Gunny, he cut off any line of sight he had to where Marian stood, determined to bring his focus back to where it should be. These men were his brothers. Maybe not under the patch, but individually and as a group they'd taken him in and kept him safe, just like Retro had.

Catching feelings for Bane's sister-in-law wouldn't be looked on with approval. Which meant even if he could get past his own sense of betrayal to Lauren for looking at another woman, he couldn't go there. Dolph's long-ago words would never come true.

Just as well I'm not attracted to her in that way.

***

Marian

Ducking her head, she murmured to Myrt, "I'm headed out. Make Thad help with the dishes. I'll be taking Lukie to the movies after, so we won't be back until late."

Corner of her lip smeared with jam, Myrt glanced up and nodded. Then her brows drew together. "I didn't know you worked today?"

"I'm not on the schedule, but after a late away game, it's a fair bet at least one of the girls will call in." Licking the pad of her thumb, she cleaned away the jam. "You're a mini-mess, Myrtie. Love you."

"Love you too." The immediate response made her smile. In the years since they'd been reunited, the sisters had worked hard at their relationship, finding their way past any misplaced anger at their father and others to a place where they were both comfortable. She turned and lifted her hand, Gunny and Vanna returning the wave.

Einstein was engrossed in whatever Gunny was telling him, not even looking up when Gunny paused in his spiel. *Dang it.* He was still being weird about the awkward moment this morning. Even after all her efforts to make him comfortable, she was afraid he would twist it in his mind further than he already had.

Shoes on and purse in hand, she made her way outside and to the little car that was hers to use, still fussing over the dilemma. *Wasn't like he saw anything important.* Joking with him had been the only way she'd concocted to move them past what had happened. In her mind, the moment had happened, wasn't a big deal, and they should be just like normal. But after she'd peeked into the kitchen and seen him staring into space, she'd just known he was making his unintentional invasion of her privacy more in his mind.

Since Marian had moved in with her sister and Bane more than three years ago, her world had expanded in unexpected ways. There was being with her siblings plus their add-on family, in the form of the groups living in three houses set close together. Then had come her job and learning the skills necessary to make her efforts at being less of a drain successful. The confidence-bolstering recognition that she was a contributing member of the household was good.

Another area that had been stunted while living with her father was access to TV or shows, or online entertainment. His idea of her expanding her brain had been to learn a new recipe from a lady at church. Marian and Myrt both had soaked up various pop-culture classics, and one of those had given Marian the idea for this morning. It had been the work of moments to adjust her clothing, and the hardest part had been pretending to be clueless about his response to her over-the-top actions.

It had been embarrassing but worth every second. Einstein's smile, his laughter, and falling into their more typical joking comfortable routine afterwards—she'd do it a hundred times over, just for that.

Parking behind the shop was effortless after so many trips just the same, and she hesitated only a moment before exiting the car and walking inside.

It wasn't uncommon for her to check in on days when she wasn't scheduled, and she hadn't been lying to Myrt earlier. The two girls who did the greenery prep for pieces were both cheerleaders, which meant they were out as late or later than the players.

The only thing hard to predict was Noah Penrose, the owner of Penrose and Peonies. They'd become friends over her time working for him, and with the information he'd pried out of her during their conversations, he'd be sure to know why she'd escaped home this morning even before she opened her mouth.

No time like the present. The sooner she got inside, the faster she'd be able to get her fingers into the flowers and stop worrying.

Pushing through the back door, she stepped into a typical scene of happy chaos she'd come to love. Noah's voice came from the front of the shop, a bouncy, excited tone he reserved for people who were customers but not friends. He'd told her once that he had to be "on" for certain sectors of the community, fulfilling their expectations of how a gay florist acted. Closer to hand, Whitney, one of the older part-time assistants, looked up sharply, her face relaxing as soon as she recognized Marian.

A glance around the workroom revealed her instincts had been right. The other two spots that should have been busy creating arrangements for two funerals today were empty and still, with nothing in prep.

She stepped close with a quick side-hug for Whitney, who whispered, "He's in a mood."

"When is he ever not?" Marian joked back, earning a grin. "I'll let him know I'm here, then be right back to get started. Get done with that one, and then lay out the work orders for me?" Whitney nodded, gaze already back on the arrangement she'd been working on when Marian came inside.

She pulled the swinging door back and peeked around it. Noah was behind the counter, which meant he was either about to ring up a sale or had just finished, and by the way the elderly customer was tucking away her wallet in an agonizingly slow ballet of movement, they were in the final stages of the exchange. Three people had lined up behind that customer, gift items in their hands. Each would need packing and wrapping, and she mentally gauged the size of the items as she called out, "Noah, I'm going to get started on things." Noah's head whipped around, and he glared at her, proof of his mood mentioned by Whitney. "Ohhhkay. I'll just"—she thumbed over her shoulder—"be back here."

Prepping the necessary items on the packing table, she left an array of them in the order Noah would need when he came back to deal with the process. Over at the flower table, Whitney had placed a fan of printed orders arranged near Marian's normal station before moving on to a second simple vase arrangement. Marian picked through the requests, sliding a couple of the easier basket container instructions across the table for Whitney, who didn't look up, just nodded as she continued working with the greenery in her hands.

Then she got to work.

From being certain she'd be hopeless at the job in the beginning to the self-confidence that drove her fingers today, she'd created a lot of arrangements. There'd been simple vases of adorned roses for wives and girlfriends sent as apologies from their partners, as well as elaborate funeral sprays requiring not only precise placement of the requested greenery stems but also an eye towards the critical timing for the presentation. Florists used ampules of water to keep individual large stem pieces from drying, but knowing the flowers would be on display for days meant they waited until the last minute to actually apply the stock to the arrangement. Everything was a careful balance of beauty and function.

When Noah walked into the workroom with the first gift item in hand, she and Whitney had already finished with a couple of the orders. Marian looked up to see the lines on his face ease and knew she'd done well by ensuring he could see even a few completed items. While not quite feast or famine, like all small one-owner businesses, Penrose and Peonies was subject to economic swings, and funerals were big business, steady as life and death. They might be the only florist directly in town, but many of the larger shops in neighboring communities were willing to deliver even though it was a fair distance, and as Noah had often reminded her, they had to remember their customers always had options.

"Hey, bossman." His grimace made her grin. She'd picked up the phrase from the FRMC members who called Bane their president, and Noah knew it. "Looked like sales were brisk out there."

"Yes, well. It's been an okay day so far." Pausing in front of the packing table, he glanced over his shoulder. "Thanks, doll."

"Anything for my favorite guy." Marian spun the design she was working on, the turntable moving smoothly underneath her direction. The shears she loved to use were comfortable in her hand, and she used them to cut a new stem to the right length before threading it between the tape stabilizers already in place on the vase. "I figured the girls would call in later than normal with their lame apologies."

"I'm paying you for today." Noah stopped in the doorway, hand out to catch the door. "And you're not going to argue with me about it. I'm in a mood."

"So I heard." She kept her retort quiet and waited until he was back into the front of the shop to grin to herself when Whitney giggled.

It was several hours later before they caught up with the morning's influx of orders. The calls and drop-ins had continued, keeping Noah busy up front and her and Whitney sticking to their normal frantic pace in the back. As arrangements and vases went through the door to be handed off to their buyers, Marian experienced the same sense of awe and excitement she always did. People would be looking at things she'd made and smiling. With arrangements intended to stay fresh for days, the work she did today would help lift their spirits for a span of time they might not otherwise enjoy. Even the funeral flowers were a work of love for her, ensuring that someone's loved one was sent off with a visible reminder of how much they'd mattered.

"Marian, you've got a visitor." Noah's singsong announcement was followed by the swinging door opening wide. "I'm just sending him straight back."

Einstein walked into the room, glancing around at everything before his gaze landed on Marian.

This is new. He'd been in town countless times since she'd started working at the florist, but even though the clubhouse was only a couple of blocks away, he'd never visited.

"Hey." Not pausing in her work, she cupped the rose bloom in one hand, using the thorn stripper with the other. "What's up?" Moving swiftly through the array of stems in front of her required attentiveness, so she only flicked glances to where he was prowling along one edge of the room. "Everything okay with Myrtle?"

"Yeah. Myrt's fine." He reached the corner near the back door and turned to face the room. "You don't have any security cameras in here?"

Caught off guard, she slipped, and a rogue thorn caught a jagged edge against the inside of a finger. "Ow." Lifting the offending stem, she glared at it before finishing stripping the thorns. "No, no cameras." Whitney giggled, and Marian gave her a grin. "Why, you planning on doing something bad?"

"No." He seemed to move between blinks, appearing next to her and holding out his hand. "Let me see." His hands cradled hers, lifting. "That's not too bad." His thumb caressed tenderly before bringing her digit to his lips. "I think you'll live." Dry heat hit her skin as his mouth molded to her finger.

Heat flooded her face and she yanked her hand back. "I'm fine."

"Yes, ma'am, you are." The flirty tone in his voice couldn't be her imagination, and when he reached for her hand again, she shoved it behind her like a naughty child, caught out doing something wrong.

"What are you doing?"

Einstein didn't react to her hissed question. The man wasn't behaving the way he normally did, joking and teasing. He'd practically ignored her this morning after they had company, not even giving her a wave when she'd left to come to town. His behavior now didn't make sense.

"Thought I'd take you to lunch." A glance at the clock over the door to the shop told her it was past time to eat. "Noah said you could take a break."

What the…? He'd asked *Noah* if he could take her to lunch? With Bane and the men of the FRMC she'd learned the direct route was generally the right way to go, and Einstein wasn't any different. "Einstein, what's going on?"

"I just wanna talk to you, baby."

Baby? They weren't into sweet nicknames. This wasn't the kind of friendship Marian had with him.

Einstein's palm skated up her arm and over her shoulder, coming to rest against the base of her neck, where his fingers gave her a squeeze that set her insides trembling. "Let's go to lunch."

Better to play along with him and find out what's wrong. "Whitney, I'm going to lunch."

Looking more like himself, Einstein grinned at her words, and Marian just shook her head, not understanding. "You should break too."

"Yes, ma'am." Whitney moved through the back door so quickly she was already out of sight before Marian could turn.

"Okay, she's gone. Now you can just tell me what's going on."

Einstein bent closer until his face was only inches away from Marian's. "Told you, Marian. Wanna feed my baby." That dangerous flirty tone had reappeared, curling around her heart in a way she liked too much.

She stepped back, breaking his hold, waiting for the laughter she was sure would be coming. "I'm not sure what game you're playing, but I don't like it."

"Come to lunch." His features molded back into the expression she expected from him, pleasant but distant. Friendly. "I'll explain everything."

Tongue tracing the inside of her front teeth, she stared at him. Not finding what she needed, Marian turned back to her station and tidied everything, ensuring all the stems were in water as necessary and trashing the debris from her earlier efforts. "Okay." Without looking back at Einstein, she started towards the back door, brought up short by his hand on her forearm.

"Let's go out the front." His fingers laced with hers, and he used the grip to tug her towards the swinging door. "Come on, baby."

Marian followed him blindly, gaze fixed on where their hands joined them. His hold was tight but gentle, and with bemused amusement, she noticed he steered her deftly around any obstacles in their way, leading her through the shop.

"Have fun at lunch, you two." Noah's lilting dismissal yanked Marian out of her fugue, and she lifted her eyes to glare at him. Nothing but joy radiated from him, so whatever had him so amused wasn't at her expense. She glanced around the shop, identifying two women browsing through the baby gifts nearby as leaders in the local church. "No rush, Einstein. You can keep our girl as long as you want."

Marian jerked her attention back to him, but he'd already turned away to take care of the person in front of the counter. *Our girl?* Marian had no idea what that even meant.

Einstein chuckled and called back, "Thanks, Noah."

On the sidewalk, Marian tried unsuccessfully to reclaim her hand, but Einstein folded their arms together, pressing the back of her wrist firmly against his side. *Hot and cold.* "Einstein," she hissed, glancing around. Downtown Baker wasn't bustling by any means, and she didn't see anyone around who would be impressed by his manhandling of her. "Let me go."

"No, baby." His shoulder bumped hers. Marian looked up to see he'd turned a tolerant smile her direction, eyes dancing with humor.

Baby. Marian wished her heart would stop leaping every time he used that sweet name. She forced herself to remember how he'd morphed back into his normal self in the back of the store. *It's a game to him. He's probably bet Horse or someone that he could get me to sit a meal with him.* That thought sent a wave of heat to prickle at the backs of her eyes. Would Einstein do that? Would he use her in that way? *It's just a game.*

The evidence in front of her led her to believe he would, which changed her estimation of him.

"Lies and playacting aren't my strong suit." Marian yanked at her hand again, pulling hard enough that Einstein stopped abruptly and swung in a half circle to face her. "Let me go." Chin angled down, she kept pulling, twisting as she tried to reject his hold. "Pick somebody else to play your games with."

"Marian." Soft and low, his voice held a weight of some emotion she didn't try to decipher. Fingers gripped her chin and lifted, forcing her gaze to meet his face. "It's not a game."

She stared into his eyes, focus flitting from one orb to the other, struggling to make sense of what looked like pain and grief.

"Ride on the bike with me. Come to lunch. I'll explain everything." His mouth opened and closed, bottom lip caught for an instant between white teeth. "Promise." Einstein leaned in, his intention obvious, and Marian turned her head at the last moment, leaving his lips to graze her cheek instead. "Please." Mouth so close to her ear his breath raised goose bumps along the skin of her arms, he whispered, "Maid Marian."

"I don't know what to say." Marian hated how her voice shook, didn't want him to know how much the closeness affected her.

"Just say yes." Ghosting across the skin near her ear, his words preceded a wave of heat she belatedly understood was his mouth on her again.

"Yes."

"Good girl." Einstein pulled back slightly, still so close she could have closed the gap in an instant to press her lips to his. "Bike's right down here, next to the clubhouse." His fingers gave hers a squeeze. "I'll keep you safe, Marian."

"I know." She stepped away as far as the leash of their joined hands allowed. "I trust you." His body jolted as if with a blow, and she watched his Adam's apple dance under the skin of his neck as he swallowed hard. "Lead on."

He stared down at her, face impassive. "All right."

He guided their steps to where his bike sat along the side of the building, behind the fencing securing the lot. In a move she'd become well acquainted with through the years, he handed her a helmet, his gaze not leaving her as they both secured the gear. She waited for him to straddle the bike before climbing on. Her hands went to his waist naturally, the position as comfortable as ever. She didn't flinch when the bike started with a roar, just scooted closer to Einstein and gripped the waistband of his jeans tightly.

Same as always. The normality of the moment did a lot to settle her nerves. *He'll tell me whatever's going on, and we'll laugh at how funny he was with the sweet talk.*

Nothing was changing.

Same as always.

***

Einstein

He shouldn't like this so much.

Shouldn't, but did.

Marian leaned tight to his back, her thighs riding and gripping along his hips in a move so familiar, and yet totally foreign. He might not have slept with anyone since Lauren's death, turning down offers while riding the line between being kind and an asshole—but he hadn't forgotten the feeling of falling into the cradle of a woman's body. That's what Marian riding behind him felt like. An intimacy he'd never experienced outside of the bedroom.

They whipped past the city limit sign, and when Marian shifted behind him, he anticipated her question.

"Going to Quails." At his shout over his shoulder, her fingers tapped an irregular rhythm along his waist, and she subsided. Firm contact between his shoulder blades was her head and helmet.

The diner in town wouldn't work for the conversation he intended to have with Marian.

He forced his muscles to relax. His phone calls today had uncovered a variety of information, none of it welcome. From everything he could find, Scar was on the move. Through the years, Einstein had received enough indirect messages from the asshole to know Scar was tracking Einstein just as fervently. So whatever this new move was, Scar had to know the information highway would take rumors both ways. Scar's moves over the past couple of days might have been for an unknown reason, but the man had made himself visible in a way that meant he wanted to telegraph what he was doing.

Whatever that is.

One of the more direct messages had been a recitation of an overheard conversation, and as he remembered that reveal, the sweat on his body evaporated, leaving him chilled.

"Man said he'd never heard a voice so filled with rage." Smoke's whisper filled up Einstein's hearing, the information so necessary it overwrote the crackling on the line. "Said Scar was twirling like a dervish at the idea of his enemy finding happiness. You and I know that role is filled by just one person, and I wanted to make sure you heard the stories fast."

"Anything else?" Einstein's fight with the threatening tremor in his voice was successful, his words coming out as if oiled with a rival's blood. "From this fast-tracked rumor mill?"

"Nothing yet, but I've put out feelers, so maybe we'll get something more. Anything I hear, I'll pass on. You know that's true." Hesitation filled Smoke's voice as he resumed a more normal volume. "You heard I lost a brother?"

"We did." Use of the plural was intentional, and the choked sound from Smoke meant he'd caught it. "Hard to lose a member. Harder still to lose someone in the trusted circle."

"Sucks hard, man. I didn't see it comin', either. Means either I had a blind spot because it was him or a blind spot because I'm just fuckin' blind. Haven't sorted out yet who knew what, and when." Smoke cleared his throat. "Be worth it to me if you heard anything along those lines. If the Bastards heard anything." The acknowledgment of what his "we" had meant was gratifying. "Make it worth y'all's while."

"I'll pass the ask along. See what we might have in the books." An intentional veil of mystery over the process the Bama Bastards followed for rumor collection was to indicate they held a cache of information they'd only provide if there was a request. "We're usually content to watch how things shake out. I know Retro and Mudd think highly of you, so might be a chance they've banked something already. Either way, I'll pass it along and you'll hear from someone."

"And if I catch word of anything else from Scar, I'll call you personally."

Smoke's reassuring words weren't needed. Einstein already knew this. Smoke owed him for a favor done last year, and the information about Scar only went a little way towards clearing the debt.

"Appreciate it, brother. I'll revise your tally." Unlike some men, Einstein didn't have a problem calling someone on a favor owed. Revealing that

Smoke's information didn't completely fulfill the need was just good business. "Later."

"Shiny side."

Einstein let his hand drift from the handlebar to where Marian gripped his belt and wrapped his fingers around hers. He squeezed, leaning into the wind when her thighs responded, tightening around his hips.

Scar's message had been clear. He believed Einstein had latched on to someone and was building a life beyond the broken one the man's actions had left him. It didn't take much thought to realize the only person who could fit that bill was Marian. Even if Einstein had just realized it this morning for himself, in retrospect, it probably had been apparent to anyone who witnessed how they were together. Given the number of people who came to Bane's mini-rallies, the tales back to Scar could have started with anyone. Which meant even if he left and never returned—the notion of which made his stomach flip in uncomfortable ways—she might still be in danger.

He needed to attack the rumor at the base, but knowing the potential for hurt, had wanted to talk to Marian first. Then he'd walked into the florist shop and caught Noah's knowing look towards the door to the workroom. Rejecting the emotions she stirred in him was one thing, but rejecting her? He couldn't imagine intentionally hurting her like that.

The idea of the late lunch had come over him in an instant, and he'd rolled with it, because for the life of him, Einstein couldn't imagine riding away from Marian. The sweet, caring ways she brought to everyone in her life had grown to include him from their first meeting. *I can't give her up.* He rolled the throttle a little more, picking up a bit of speed at the idea. *If I can't give her up, then maybe I can figure out if I can take what's in front of me.* The concept of pretending to be a couple was a flash of genius. *I hope.* Test driving this feeling while telling her it was just pretend.

What can go wrong?

Chapter Thirteen

Marian

"I'm sorry. What?" She scooted a little farther into the corner of the booth and away from Einstein's body. Normally if they shared a meal out, they took opposite sides of the table. Today he'd steered her onto the bench farthest from the door of the diner, then followed her in an unexpected move. She hadn't questioned it at the time, just took a pair of menus from where they were tucked behind the napkin holder and passed one over.

Then he'd blown her mind with a request, something she would never have expected. Not from him.

"I need you to go along with a pretext that we're together." One corner of his mouth lifted as he repeated his previous words. "There are good reasons."

"Together-together? I at least want to hear your motives." The approaching waitress looked like salvation. The interaction would give her time to catch up with the conversation, because even though the words were simple, the meaning behind them wasn't. "I'd like a coffee, black." Marian toned back the desperation in her tone. "Um. Please?"

That curl of Einstein's lips spread until he was smiling broadly at her. Without looking away, he told the waitress, "Make that two. And go ahead and bring some cream." He reached past Marian to nudge the container of sugar packets closer to her. "She wants the grilled cheese with cheddar, not American. Throw some bacon on a burger for me. Fries with both." He angled his face towards her, and one eye swooped closed in a slow blink Marian cataloged for later. "That'll do it for us. Thanks."

Marian shifted and stared up at the waitress, hoping if she stopped looking at Einstein, things would return to normal between them. His smiles were usually full of mischief and affection, not whatever his expression a moment ago might mean. And he didn't wink at her. Ever.

The waitress gave her a grin, pen scratching at the pad in her hand. "You got it." Then the waitress also winked at her before walking away.

"Marian."

She scanned the diner, not seeing any faces she recognized. Working in the back of the flower shop meant she occasionally interacted with customers, but not often enough to get to know many of the folks, especially not from out of town. The diner he'd brought her to was two towns away from Baker, and something about that settled her nerves. Whatever it was he wanted, Einstein didn't need anyone who knew them to see them together. Not right now. *Not yet.*

"Baby."

The tender way he said the word had her head jerking his direction, and she took in his features. He was intelligent; she knew that from their many conversations, and from hearing the people she trusted talk about him. Smart and handsome, and if Einstein had decided he needed her to play a part in whatever scheme he was cooking up, she was inclined to go along with it. But the sweet names? That felt dangerous. *To my heart.*

"It's nothing bad, promise."

"Tell me why." Marian pressed her trembling hands against her thighs. She wanted to cover her mouth, tug at an earlobe, or fiddle with her hair, but any of those would expose the nervousness in her belly that had swamped her at his request. *He can't know what I've been fighting.* She'd been around bikers enough to know they were people like any others. Einstein, though? The way he and Retro observed their surroundings and the people around them was different. Like they could just look at someone and know what was in their heads. "I don't understand why you'd need me."

"We're friends, right?"

Marian nodded slowly, then drew back so the approaching waitress could deposit coffee cups and glasses of ice water on the table.

"Thanks," Einstein responded to the waitress, then reached past Marian again to drag the sugar closer. It was the work of moments for him to doctor one of the cups, and Marian didn't miss how he'd gotten it exactly right. *As always.* He even dipped a spoon into the water and retrieved a couple of ice cubes, stirring them into the cup. "Here you go, baby."

Marian closed her mouth and stared at him. That damn grin came her direction again, and the fluttering in her belly got worse than before.

"Is it okay?" He nudged the cup closer to her. "Did I do okay?"

"Yeah." Never taking her gaze off his face, she reached for the cup and lifted it, sipping slowly. "It's good." Licking her lips, she set the cup back into the saucer with a tiny clatter. "We *are* friends."

"Yeah, we are." He leaned closer, his shoulder bumping against hers before she could dodge away. "You're my best friend. Did you know that?"

She blinked, unsure how to answer him.

"Retro even called me on it a while back, said he didn't exist when you were around. Claimed to be hurt and pained by the jealousy his realization caused." Einstein's grin split his face, showing white teeth that moved to clamp on his bottom lip. "Told him he was a damn fool, but I see it now. This morning, I finally understood what he meant. I think we're always going to be friends, Marian. More than friends. And that's why this makes so much sense."

"Nothing about this makes sense yet." She shifted and looked out the window to where his bike sat in the parking lot. *He's in a club, and that holds every bit of his loyalty. This is something to do with the BBMC, I bet.* "Just explain what you need, and I'll tell you honestly if I think I can do it."

"I've been looking for a man. For years now, been looking for him. For some reason I can't figure yet, he's being flushed out of hiding now, and I want him. Marian, I *want* him." Einstein's expression changed, hardening and growing remote as it closed down. "He did something to me, something to people I loved, and after he went into hiding, I've only caught third- or fourth-hand information about him. This is a lot closer than that and feels like he's intentional about being drawn out." The fist he had on the table clenched tight, knuckles going white. "I want him."

"What did he do?" The pain that flashed across Einstein's features made her wish she could call back the words, not wanting to wound this man, and especially not with something she didn't understand. "I'm sorry." She tried to cover the blunder, but Einstein shook his head. He turned from her and lifted the cup of coffee he'd left for himself, taking a series of hard swallows she knew had to burn going down. "Jim, I'm sorry."

"You hear stories about what happened to me?" His gaze cut her direction, then back to the cup resting between both of his hands. "Anyone tell you?"

"No." This was truth, at least. "At first Bane said it was your story to tell, and I understood him not wanting to gossip. Then as time passed, it seemed less important that I know your past, because our friendship was in the now. If that makes any sense."

"Makes a lot of sense, baby."

Marian couldn't stop the way her body reacted to that sweet word, heating up until her cheeks were blazing.

"And I'm a selfish bastard, because I'm glad that my friends and brothers protected me like that. Means I get to be the one to tell you."

He pulled in a hard breath, and she instinctively reached for him, laying her palm on his thigh. His hand landed on top of hers, and like he had when they'd been walking the street earlier, he twined their fingers together.

"You make everything easier, did you know that?" His question didn't need a response, so she just gave his fingers a squeeze. "The man I've been looking for is Bane's blood brother. You should know that up front. They don't speak, don't ever associate with the other. As close to strangers as two men could be. They're on opposite sides of nearly every moral stance that can be taken." She'd been about to speak but closed her mouth as he continued. "My first trip to Baker was to feel Bane out, see what he might know about his brother. Didn't take a hot minute to know they weren't alike. Learning that Bane wasn't like the Scar I knew from the past? Just the way he cared for your family told me what I needed to know. Scar, that's his brother's club name, was my president. Long ago and far away, and almost like a different life."

"What does that have to do with me?" He moved in the seat, and she was so focused on him, the waitress's appearance startled her into pulling away, yanking her hand free. Plates rattled against the table, were slid into place, and then a bottle of ketchup landed on top of the ticket near the end. "Thanks," she called out belatedly, pleased when the woman lifted a hand acknowledging her gratitude. She snapped her gaze to

Einstein and found him grinning at her, the expression happy and guileless. "What?"

"Your default is just so fuckin' sweet." He pulled her plate closer and rearranged the food to make space, then grabbed the ketchup bottle and upended it. A couple of whacks of his palm later, and a gurgle of red descended to her plate. "There you go, baby." He sent her plate sliding; it stopped in the exact place it needed to be in front of her. He conducted the same procedure with his own food, minus the sliding plate of course. "What does it have to do with you?" Einstein dipped a fry into the puddle of red, then slipped it into his mouth. He seemed to be thinking hard as he chewed and swallowed, following it with a sip of water. "Everything, baby."

"Why are you calling me that? Don't do it. That's not nice." Her stomach revolted at the idea of food, and she shoved her plate away slightly. "I never thought you'd be mean."

"Sweetie." The kind tone registered at the same time she felt his fingers wrap around hers on top of the table. "This isn't me being mean. If you agree to what I want to do, you'll have to get used to me talking to you like this."

"Maybe just tell me? I don't understand anything about anything. And that's unsettling."

He released her hand and slipped her plate back in front of her, the scraping grating on her nerves. "Eat, Marian. I promise I'll tell you everything. But I have to start where it began." He nudged her plate closer with the back of his hand. "Eat, baby."

Marian picked up half of the sandwich and took a bite, then directed a glare in his direction. He chuckled and met her tiny bite of bread and cheese with a giant one of his own, leaning close to devour most of what she held in her fingers.

"Got you a start." He pointed to his burger, then lifted and offered it to her. "Fair is fair. You love bacon." Marian fought a grin as she took a dainty bite from one side. "Now, you keep eating, pretty lady. I'll tell you my story." That impassiveness took over his expression again, and Marian steeled herself for whatever he was going to say, knowing it was something he held close.

"I'm married."

She choked on a drink of water. Shooting a glance at his left hand, she didn't try to hide the surprise. She remembered the first time they'd met, and he'd worn a ring. When it disappeared between one visit and the next, she moved it to the back of her mind. *Married? Still?* Then again, that would explain so much, like why he treated every woman in their circle with a careful friendliness. *But then, what about all the "baby" names today?*

"Yeah. Shocker, right? Keep the ring in my bag, where it's safe." He patted the front of his vest. "I keep my memories closer than that. Lauren. She and our little girl Makayla are my life. Love them both so much. They died a little under five years ago."

Marian forgot how to breathe at the pain in his voice paired with the terrible news.

Upper lip curling in a silent snarl, he paused for so long she wasn't sure he'd continue. "Scar killed them. Doesn't matter he wasn't physically present when they took their last breaths—he killed them."

"He killed them?" Marian wanted to comfort Einstein but didn't know if he'd accept anything from her right now. It hurt to hold back, but she wanted to give him whatever he needed. "Oh, Jim. That's terrible."

"Yeah. Really fuckin' is. No reason for what he did. His beef was with me, but he knew taking my girls would ensure I'd go along with whatever he wanted. Anything. But then he didn't keep track of his insurance and they died. Left me standing. That was his second mistake. Man should have killed me right then, not left me breathing."

His burger thudded back onto the plate, and Marian felt an echo of the tremor of his fingers in matching shivers deep inside her belly. She inched closer to him on the bench, plastering herself along his side.

"But he didn't. Took my girls in a way that left me responsible. I'll never get back from that, Marian. There's just no recovering, you know?" The click of his hard swallow was audible. "Been looking for him for years, and you'll ask me what I did that first year and a half they were gone. It's a real question, and I know how it'll reflect on me, but all I did at first was try to find a way to follow them that wouldn't leave Retro and my brothers in the BBMC in a bad way. There's a history between me and Scar, and I'd told Retro about a message from him a few weeks before shit went down." He cut a glance her way, a sickly smile flashing on and off his face. "You know how Retro is. If I made my own exit, he would have taken that on himself. I didn't want to leave him with that."

"I'm glad. Whatever the reason is you held on, I'm glad." Marian draped an arm over his back, the leather of his vest cold against her skin. She curled her other hand around his arm and held tight. "That sounds like a fistful of pain, Jim. I wish I could do something to make it easier on you." She remembered his earlier words, the unexplained request. "Tell me. Whatever it is, I'll do it for you. You really want me to pretend to be your girl? Is that what the sweet words mean? If that's what you need, I'll do it."

"You need to hear the rest." Marian leaned her cheek against his shoulder, shaking it in negation. "Seriously, Marian. This won't be a walk in the park." Fingers covered hers and squeezed. "Eat, baby."

"Tell me the rest of it. What you think makes a difference. Tell me, get it out, and we'll both eat." She didn't move, sticking close to his side.

His chuckle rattled through her. "You're tough."

"The way I grew up, it wasn't a choice to be otherwise." The waitress started their direction but locked gazes with Marian, who shook her head again. The woman turned on her heel and walked the other way. "I've got my own stories, but today, this is about you."

"Strong woman." His fingers tensed over hers, curling tighter. "He took her as leverage against me. Came to my house and had her trussed up like a turkey while they waited on me to come home. This was after I'd done everything right when I exited his motherfucking club in Philly. Took my beatout, and then needed a fucking month to heal up so we could move to Birmingham. Lauren's from there. Made sense for us to come to where she called home. Her folks doted on Makayla. Our little girl can do no wrong." He winced. "Could do no wrong."

The past-tense change hurt her heart. He'd been talking about his family in the present all along, and she hated to hear that shift of acknowledgment.

"Things went to shit for Scar back east, and he was looking for a place to land. Me and Retro wouldn't offer him anything. We shut him out, closed the door on any conversation. So Scar came to Birmingham to try and make his case in person. It meant he wanted me focused on listening to him, so he ensured he'd have my ear. He had it, all right. Promised he wouldn't hurt my girls, so I went with him. Thought he was honorable, somewhere deep in his soul. Willingly gave him my back, let him tie me up, and me talking to Lauren the whole time. Reassuring her. He put us in a van, carried our little girl like a sleeping princess and laid her gentle-like on the floor. She never woke, not then. He had friends, though. They split us up. Makayla was awake by then, asking me what the bad men wanted. Crying as they chained me to seat struts in the van so I couldn't get loose. That was the last time I saw my girls breathing. The doc Retro hired said they'd died of carbon monoxide poisoning. They'd have gone to sleep and never felt anything. There were no bruises on them anywhere, not even around Lauren's wrists. So Scar kept one promise, even as he fucked himself over on another one. Might not have been his hands that killed them, but still they died."

"What can I do?" Marian didn't remember feeling this helpless before. Not even when Myrtle had told her about the treatment survived under Sallabrook had words caused her this kind of pain. That had been in the past, at least. What Einstein was living through would never be a distant memory. *Pain like his doesn't fade.* "Please."

"Let me finish." His arm flexed underneath her fingers. In a tone gone dark and heavy with the memories he'd been reciting, he promised, "Then you can ask whatever questions you have."

"Okay." She'd offer him anything right now, if it had a chance of stripping the anguish from his voice.

"Bunch of clubs banded together to save me. Retro called in nearly every marker he held and then organized the collaborative rescue mission. Included flying to Florida on a private jet, believe it or not. Fact is, I'd be dead right now without what Retro did, because Scar had lost control of his allies. Those men who had come alongside him to take everything away from me. Scar'd known it was a possibility, given who he was turning his back on, namely his family. So when it went down and was sideways, he had a plan, and the bastard bailed, leaving me in the hands of men who weren't inclined to feel kindly towards me.

"Back when I'd been in Scar's club, I'd done everything he asked. No questions. Beat up a guy who didn't deserve it? Done. Push deep into enemy territory and start shit? Done. None of these assholes felt a bit of compassion towards me. I'd already seen the faces of my girls not breathing, cold and still. I wasn't going to fight them too much."

Marian tried to slow her breathing, aware she'd begun panting during his recitation of grief.

"Then Retro entered the building, followed by a couple dozen faces I knew and some I didn't. They were there for me. You'd think that'd be enough to make me second-guess that decision." His laugh was harsh enough to scald her skin. "You'd think wrong. Scar was in the wind, my girls were in the ground, and I didn't want to be anywhere. Retro dragged me back to the present by the skin of his teeth, clawing his way back into my life in a way that wouldn't let me close the door. Then, Maid Marian, I found my mission. To hunt down Scar and make him pay."

"That's where you go when you disappear." So many things made sense now. Every club member she'd met over the past few years stayed a lot closer to home than Einstein did. Plus, she heard through gossip that he never went back to Birmingham even though that's where the BBMC had their clubhouse. "And it's why you don't go home. It hurts too much. You come here instead."

"Smart woman." He patted her hand and let his fall to his lap. "I'm always on the lookout for good info on him. He and Bane, their mother was a woman from the Crow Nation in Montana, so periodically I'll idle up that way and keep tabs on their family. Their father is the only son of an old Italian mafioso, but he disavowed his legacy. That legacy isn't happy about their investment in the Scarloucci family going unused, and they keep reaching out in a variety of ways. Made it so I've opened up lines of communication overseas, ready to get a stamp on my passport if needed. Their family home is in New Jersey, and I have cameras on that around the clock, just in case interested parties come by. At least once a week, Mudd runs that video through some software for me, so I know who's been to visit. Been keeping my ear to the ground, listening for hoofbeats of things that might never matter. Digging through dumpsters looking for diamonds. But today?" He paused and looked at her, upper lip lifting again in a snarl. "Today I got news that Scar's on the prowl. He thinks he can force me into making a mistake. He knows that I come here and not home, just like you realized. Only he thinks you are the reason." Einstein's head shook back and forth. "He's not wrong, but that's not something I want to talk about right now."

"He's going to try to use me to get to you. Leverage a woman in your life." A chill raced along her skin, leaving goose bumps in its wake. "Just like he did before."

"Yeap. But he didn't count on the friends I've made. And he didn't factor in everything that's you." He lifted her coffee towards her, and Marian let go of his arm, keeping her hold around his back as she accepted the cup. He picked up his and clinked the rims together. "You and me, we're gonna make him pay."

Marian thought of the life she lived now, compared to what it had been like back in her father's house. Family was supposed to keep you safe, but she'd had ample experience to know that wasn't how it worked out, not always. Her siblings had been pawns, assets to be bartered, leveraged. There'd been neither love nor loyalty. Those things had only come when she'd left her childhood behind. "I've never felt safer than in Bane's house, surrounded by men in the club."

The expression that flashed across Einstein's face was a shocking show of hurt, smoothed over in an instant. *What in that statement could have hurt him?*

"Sitting here with you, I have complete confidence that you'd protect me, no matter what walked through the door." With that, he—*preened is the only word,* she thought. His chest puffed out, neck arching as he looked directly at her. *He didn't like being excluded from what makes me feel safe. Huh.* "I never had that at home. Seeing how my father treated Myrtle, then the boys, giving them no say in their own lives." Marian took in a slow breath, deliberately unclenching her jaw. "You, Bane, Gunny, Truck, Monday, Horse—I'd do anything for you men. Being your girlfriend wouldn't be a hardship." Another flare of emotion in his eyes made her realize her misstep, and she corrected herself. "*Pretending.* I know it won't be real."

Einstein opened his mouth, and she rushed to fill the gap. "Regardless, I'd do anything to keep you safe, and what you're asking? Small in comparison to what's been done for me." She retrieved her arm and put both elbows to the table as she straightened in the seat. *I'll do whatever's necessary to help ease his pain.* Picking up her sandwich, she took a small bite, staring down at her plate as she chewed. Swallowing, she told him, "I'm all in, Jim."

"Are you sure, Marian?" Now he was the one shifting around, and she leaned against his side when his arm dropped heavily across her shoulders, his hand curling across her skin to pull her close. "It's a lot to ask. We'll need to appear..." Grief warred with some emotion she couldn't name in his face. "Intimate. It'll be intense at times."

"You know how you taught me to ride behind you?" He nodded. "And how to drive the car?" One corner of his mouth lifted along with his brows. "And Gunny taught me how to shoot?" Both brows shot down, a furrow appearing between them. "Well, Horse taught me—"

"What's your point, Marian?" He cut her off as his face came closer, taking up all of her vision. "You saying you'd be my student in intimacy? That I'd be the one teaching you...things?"

Marian thought back to last summer, a lazy afternoon on the banks of the creek, Horse sitting next to her as they both laughed at her attempts to copy his actions. "Horse taught me to kiss, is all I was going to say."

Einstein went rigid beside her. His face flushed, nostrils flaring as his jaw worked side to side. "Horse did what now?" His fingers dug into the upper part of her arm, holding her in place. Not that she would have tried to move away, but with the force of his suddenly fierce grip, she knew she couldn't have. "Did you say Horse taught you to kiss?"

"Yeah." The memory was funny and sweet, and she saw her smile reflected in his eyes. "He was really nice about it."

"Oh, I just bet he was. Gunny's gonna kill him, he finds out."

Marian rolled her eyes. "Gunny already knows."

"Really." Einstein loomed closer, his mouth inches from hers. "You sure about that? Were you a good student? Should I test out how well you learned from him?" Each outward gust of breath was warm, heating her skin. *Is he going to...* "I think I should."

Marian's lids fluttered closed as he leaned in that last bit of distance. She wasn't sure what she hoped would happen. Then his lips pressed to hers, dry and hot and somehow exactly what she'd expected.

The pressure was gentle, the touch of his lips soft as they glided across to drop a sweet peck at each corner of her mouth. Insistent as they plucked at her upper lip, then pulled her bottom one between them. She gasped as her head dropped to the side. He continued on while Marian tried to control her reeling senses, those tiny kisses drugging as they moved from sweet into something bigger, growing until his mouth worked harder against hers.

Scruff prickled delicately against her chin and scraped lightly at her cheeks, stinging tiny arcs of electricity on her lips as he moved across and over. Something wet and persistent relentlessly swiped across her bottom lip, drawing her tongue out to taste. What had to be his tongue touched hers in response to the needy sound that escaped with his gentle exploration. He tasted of coffee and something wild. Then there was a return to the sweet pecks, only now his mouth was hot and wet, feeling like sodden silk as it dragged across her lips to her cheek and then up beside her ear. "So good." The whisper didn't make sense until Einstein pulled back and she opened her eyes to stare up at him. His pupils were dark, edging the color of his irises to a narrow band. "God, Marian."

"That's..." She huffed out a sigh. "That's not how Horse did it." Head lolling against his shoulder, she grinned. "I like your way a lot better."

Einstein's frown made her want to reach up and smooth it away. "How did Horse do it?"

Marian lifted her hand and made a fist, angling her thumb across the edge of her index finger. "Like this." Lazily lifting her hand to her mouth, she made a smacking sound as she touched her lips to it. "But I like your way better."

***

Einstein

"Jesus God." Einstein breathed out, having trouble regulating his heartbeat, head busy tamping down things the kiss had stirred inside him.

Marian blinked up at him as her hand fell back to her lap. Her plush bottom lip caught between her teeth. Her eyes searched his face, gaze flickering from one eye to the other.

Einstein reeled. Every emotion he'd been fighting came roaring to the forefront, arousal not the least of them. "When you said he taught you to kiss, I thought—" *Clearly I was wrong.* Did it make him a bastard that he liked the fact he'd been her first real kiss? *Probably. But do I give a fat fuck? Nope.*

In that instant, he knew he wouldn't have to pretend with her. Nothing would be pretense, everything real, but she couldn't know that. Him developing feelings wasn't what she'd signed up for, and there was no way Einstein would saddle her with someone as fucked-up as he was. Not even as a short-term thing, and especially not when Marian deserved the longest commitment a man could make.

"We should eat. You've got to get back to work." He changed the subject as he slipped his arm free of her shoulders, but couldn't stand to lose contact with her totally, so draped a hand over her thigh. "Then tonight, we can talk more. Hammer out our strategy." A thought struck him, and he winced. "We'll have to pretend in front of everyone, Marian. That means Myrt and the boys, Bane and his men. You sure you're up for that?"

Sometime during his epiphany, she'd withdrawn as well, now sitting straight and staring down at her plate of half-eaten food. "Yeap." She didn't look at him. "Don't like lyin' to folks, but already told you I'd do whatever you needed."

"Marian, what's wrong?" *Asshole, you know what's wrong. You kissed her stupid and then pulled back like it didn't mean anything. Like she doesn't mean the world to you.* "Are you mad?"

"No, just thinking." The smile she aimed his direction didn't reach her eyes. "I'm okay." She tossed his frequently stated words back at him. "No big deal."

"Hey." He crowded closer and tightened his fingers around the muscle of her thigh. "That was a good kiss. Real good kiss for me. I liked it." She didn't look at him, and he wrapped his hand around the back of her neck, pulling her tight against his side. "You're the first woman I've kissed since I lost Lauren, Marian. I'm sorry if I'm out of practice."

"It was my first kiss ever, so trust me I wouldn't know good from bad at this point." Stiffness in her muscles was a reminder that he'd hurt her. "Guess we'll get to practice more, huh?" There was a clear lack of enthusiasm in her tone. "I'm not hungry anymore, so I'm ready to go whenever you are."

"Marian." Just her name, because his brain had stuttered and was in the process of shutting down, not willing to reengage while he tried not to unpack his own emotions. "I really do like you."

"I know. I like you too." Her fingers twisted together in her lap. "We're buds. I'm everybody's little sister, right?" The corner of her mouth moved, lifting into an expression he couldn't quite see, turned away as she was. "I won't forget." Using the surface of the big window next to her as a mirror, he studied her reflected image. The twist of her mouth wasn't a smile, not by a long shot. "Can we go now?"

Einstein shoved away his plate, the burger largely uneaten. He glanced at the window again and turned away from his own expression, one of utter devastation, and caught the attention of the waitress with a lifted finger. She was bustling over as he pulled his wallet out, not bothering to look at the ticket before he handed her a couple of bills. "We've got to go. Food was fine." He lifted his gaze to find hers locked on Marian. "Keep the change."

As he slid out of the booth, he slipped his hand around Marian's and helped her to her feet. "Thanks," she whispered, still not meeting his gaze. "I need the bathroom before we get back on the bike."

Briefly, he contemplated what he could see of her face. "Sure, baby. I'll be outside. Take your time." She pulled free from his grip and turned to walk towards the back of the restaurant. He looked at the waitress again, seeing her gaze had followed Marian. "Check on her for me?" She glanced up at him, and he saw tension lines in her features had eased at his obvious concern. "We didn't have a fight or anything, just a hard conversation for her. I'm in no rush." She pushed past him without speaking.

Outside, he strolled to the bike and leaned against the seat, maintaining a clear line of sight with the front door. He pulled out his phone and checked messages to find he'd missed two calls. Both were from Birmingham numbers but unfamiliar to him. Only one had left a voicemail. Einstein punched buttons and lifted the device to his ear.

"Einstein. *Friend*." The hard emphasis on the second word was unmistakable, and he tensed. "This is Popova, Greg Popova. Been a minute, man. I got a strange message a little bit ago, thought you'd like to hear about it. Gimme a call."

If Greg thought the Bama Bastards would need to be in the loop, he would have called Retro, not the club's only nomad. The fact he'd dialed Einstein's number meant this had to be personal. Russian mob versus Italian was an ongoing struggle everywhere the two groups tried to coexist, and through the decades, their clashes had been historic.

He saved the voicemail to the files folder on his phone, an action that would trigger the club's backup routine to pick it up and push to the main servers, making it easier for him to call Mudd's attention to it. Einstein looked up in time to see Marian swing through the front door, head held high as she walked his direction. An intense examination of her features didn't give him any indication as to her emotions. Her expression was blank and bland, and something curled tight in his chest. *I don't like that. My Marian*—Einstein cut off that thought. She wasn't his anything, except friend. He deliberately pulled on memories of Lauren to burn any ideas out of his head but found them harder than ever to surface.

Marian was at his side before he refocused on her. *Nope. Don't like that look on her.* "Ready?" Instead of reaching out to her, he stood upright and swung a leg over the bike. Lifting it off the kickstand, he balanced the heavy machine between his thighs. She hadn't answered him, so he glanced at her again. "Need a few minutes more, Marian?"

"No." The single syllable didn't give him any indication of where she'd gone in her head, and he narrowed his eyes, surveying her body language instead. Shoulders back, chin up, she looked ready to take on the world. But he knew her well enough to pick out the tension in her neck, cords standing out as her jaw clenched. Fingers morphed into tight fists under his scrutiny, and her face angled away. "As you pointed out, I've got to get back to work."

"Baby." Lines on her face deepened at the word. He heeled the kickstand back into place and dismounted the bike, standing in front of her. "Talk to me." Cradling the hinges of her jaw in his hands, he lifted her face, so she stared up at him. Bending close, Einstein pressed his forehead to hers. "If it's too much to ask, all you have to do is say so. I'll get Gunny and Truck involved, Bane, too, and we'll protect you. I promise I won't let anything happen to you, Marian. Scar won't get close to you or anyone you love. We'll keep everyone safe. The guys already know most of this. They know the history, so we're all on high alert as it is." He decided then. "We're not going to go through with it. It's too much, and I should have known it. Shouldn't have said anything. *Dammit.* I'm so sorry I hurt you."

Her palms landed on his wrists, fingers digging deep as she stared into his eyes. "It's not too much. If it weren't the best way of flushing him out, you wouldn't have suggested it. I can do this, Jim." The muscles of her throat moved under his palms. "I'm doing this—" She faltered, and he waited, giving her time to find her words. "I'm not worried about being safe. I told you. I *trust* you. Trust you with everything inside me. You and me, right? We're a team?" She pressed against his hold and he relaxed slightly, surprised when she lifted to her toes and touched her lips to his. "You and me, Jim. We're doing this...babe, so get used to it."

There'd been only the slightest hesitation before the word "babe," but it was enough to tell him that regardless of her declarations, she wasn't completely comfortable with the ruse. Then she rolled onto her toes again, mouth opened slightly as she kissed him again. He groaned at the feel of her heated breath against his lips and closed his eyes, wanting to etch the moment into his memory.

Deepening the kiss, he stroked one hand over her shoulder and down her back, her arms threading around his neck as he pulled her closer. Less tentative than before, her tongue touched his as he stroked into her mouth, and he groaned again. Heads angling as their mouths worked together, the kiss went on and on, moments elongating as he tasted her deeper. She trembled in his arms, and he wrenched her tighter against his front, her breasts and belly a line of heat everywhere they touched. Fingers curled in his hair and tugged, the sting sweet and burning as her teeth nipped at his bottom lip. She broke away and buried her face against his heaving chest and he curled a hand around the back of her neck, cradling her to him.

"Jesus, Marian. Gonna give an old man a heart attack, kissing me like that." Dipping his head beside hers, he nibbled along the shell of her ear, eliciting a shiver from her he hoped had nothing to do with the wind. "I'm...you're amazing, woman."

"I liked it too." Her chin tipped down, hiding her expression from him. One of her tiny hands fisted his shirt inches away from her face, the other still tangled in his hair. "We're a team, right?"

Her words ripped the satisfaction from him. "Right." This had been a second trial run to see if they could hide the lie when this close to the other. "I'd say we're compatible enough to do this, if you're still willing. I meant what I said before. I'll always protect you, no matter what."

Snorting delicately, she scraped her cheek against his shirt. "We're doing this." Her shoulders lifted in a slow breath. She pushed back from him by a few inches, and her chin came up, face lifted to look at him. Einstein was bewildered as he took in her expression. Anger, arousal, and resignation. "You need to avenge the death of your wife and child."

He clenched his teeth. Stated so baldly, her words sank a knife of pain into his chest. With one sentence, Marian had effectively removed herself from consideration in this deception. "You matter too." Confused, he shook his head. "It's not just about them."

"You're right. It's not." Gaze steady, she stared at him. "I'm doing this for you." She stepped back, and Einstein found his arms reluctantly releasing her to stand on her own. "For me, this will all be for you." Marian turned towards the bike. "I need to get back to the shop."

The entire ride back to Baker was a blur, Einstein's mind more focused on the two kisses he'd shared with Marian than the road. They made it without incident, mostly because he could nearly ride in his sleep, having put so many miles in over the past few years. He pulled to a stop in front of the flower shop, but before he could angle the bike backwards into a parking space, Marian had released her grip on his waist and hopped off. She didn't look up at him as she packed her helmet away in the sidebag where it waited for her in between rides on the bike. The rumble of the bike kept them from any meaningful conversation, but the peck on his cheek and shouted, "See you later," wasn't enough for him.

He reached out and snagged her wrist with one hand, pulling her back towards where he sat on the bike. "Wanna go out for dinner?"

Marian shook her head. "I'm taking Luke to the movies after work."

"See you later, then?" That earned him a nod, quick and brusque, her eyes focusing anywhere except his face. "Marian."

She glanced across him as she lifted one eyebrow.

"Baby."

Lips thinning as she paused and looked at him, she angled her head in a clear question.

"I wanna see you. Sure, we've still got things to talk about, but you need to remember you're the reason I come back to Baker so much. I want to see you."

The corners of her lips curled sweetly, and she leaned closer, brushing her lips across his cheek in a slower caress than before. "I'll see you later."

She turned, and he watched as she walked through the door, not looking back. No final wave. No last glance or smile.

He'd kissed her, finally. Kissed her and made them both weak in the knees, holding her close. He should have been on top of the world that she hadn't turned away, hadn't hesitated in giving him her trust. She'd agreed to help him find and stop Scar.

He should have been ecstatic at the afternoon's outcome.

"Why do I feel like shit, then?"

Chapter Fourteen
Einstein

"Things are heating up." Retro's snort was clear through the call, and Einstein grinned. "Yeah, I know I've said that before, but this is backed up by Pooka."

"Popova called you?" No emphasis on anything in that three-word sentence, but the surprise shone through. "Direct-like?"

"Yeap. This is the first time since I left Birmingham that he's initiated contact. I figure it's worth a look-see to ensure we don't get blindsided by anything. I saved the file, so it's available to be analyzed, pick apart his speech patterns." Einstein looked around the room Bane set aside for him when he was in town, one of the guest rooms up by the nursery. He supposed it was the room Marian had used when she first moved in, but any semblance of personalization had been stripped away long ago. Frowning, he thought about the room she'd picked for herself, downstairs and far away from everyone else in the family. He'd been inside that room recently, during the debacle of walking in on her changing clothes, and didn't remember it having a personality either. *Wonder if that's just how she likes things, more minimalist?* He shook off the mental interruption, focusing back on business. "You're here tomorrow, right? I've got quite a bit to share and might be better in person than on the phone."

"Would this have anything to do with you kissing sweet Marian in the street earlier today?"

Einstein forgot to breathe, every muscle in his body going rigid.

Retro laughed softly. "You were occupied, so didn't see a pair of bikes pass you, but they saw the BBMC patch and radioed home about one of our members being down that way. It came back to me directly, and it didn't take much figuring to sort out who it had to be."

Tell him the truth, or not? Retro deserved his loyalty, and with that came honesty. *Right?* But his feelings for Marian were tied up in the subterfuge, and the thought galled, setting something inside his chest ablaze to deny the truth of what might be. *I need to remember Lauren.* The reminder didn't hold the same unbearable weight it might have a year ago. *Wouldn't have had to remind myself not long ago.* When had things changed?

"Your silence tells it all, brother." Retro broke into his thoughts. "I'd say have a care, but you being who you are, I know you will. My advice, not that you've asked for it—" Retro chuckled, sounding tolerant on top of being pleased. "—get in front of the news now if you haven't already. Bane's sister-in-law holds a piece of Gunny's heart, and that means something, man. You say something to them yet?"

"No. It's new." With those words, he'd sealed the deal. Choosing the path forward of withholding from Retro something he might need to know, would prefer to know for sure. *Hopefully it doesn't come back to burn my ass.* "I don't want to talk to anyone about it. The conversation she and I had today, I told her about Scar and what happened with my girls. That's enough for one day, brother." Nothing in that was a lie, especially the desire to keep the pseudo-relationship under wraps. "Talked a little about some of the things I need to go over with you, because it has the potential to impact her."

"We already know Scar's on the move." Silence pulsed down the line, and he imagined Retro angling his chin up, staring at the ceiling as he mulled over the pieces of information he had in his possession. "You think he's gonna target her. Man, that is one dumb son of a bitch. He's gonna go after Marian." Retro's intellect never failed to impress.

"Yeah, I do. Today was me asking her to stick with me, while telling her all the stories that should make her wave off." He cleared his throat. "She didn't wave off." *Still not lying to Retro.* "I promised her we'd keep her safe, keep the ones she loves safe. She understands the danger and trusts me." *No lies.* "Scar doesn't realize what he's risking by threatening to come here. I'm going to unload a lifetime's worth of hurt on his ass, brother. He won't lay a hand on her."

"Every brother is at your back, Einstein." Retro blew out a stream of air. "You get any intel that says he's making an approach in the next twenty-four hours?"

"No. Last time a body had eyes on him was near Kansas City, yesterday. He's been pacing himself, stopping everywhere he might have allies. Any breaking news about the shakeup in the Machos?"

"Nope. Since Smoke picked up the phone and wanted to gather any info on what Zipline might have been planning, we've kicked off that inquiry, but it has yet to bring home the gold. Are we certain about connecting Scar with Zippy? I'm just not sure those two make fuckin' sense, brother."

Einstein scoffed, the noise hard and echoing in his ears. "Oh yeah, I expect Zipline to be riding with Scar when he shows his face. Scar doesn't have many followers left. He's fucked over everyone he comes into contact with, and, for those he hasn't yet done the honors to, I've reached out and proactively made friendly overtures. I don't think they'd latch on to him without at least a courtesy call."

"Think he's continuing that angled drop this way?" He might sound distracted, but Einstein knew Retro was fully engaged in the conversation. "Or maybe drop due south?"

"Tulsa or OKC? Dallas? Unlikely. Between the RWMC and Blackie's boys, Scar'd be an idiot to try and scoop up any support in those locations." Closing his eyes, he ran through what he knew. "But, there's the fact Smoke's VP bailed. Maybe he's looking to scout help from farther west, all the way out to El Paso? Zipline would have a ton of connections, and we know for a fact he's being friendly with Scar. I dunno. Is that what you're thinking?"

"I wasn't. Not until you put words to it. Now I am." Retro chuckled. "I miss doin' this with you, asshole. If you're looking to lock down that pretty Marian, does that mean you're going to give back the rocker soon?"

Air turned solid in his lungs, his blood seeming to congeal where it flowed through his veins. *Give up being nomad?* "No." His head was already shaking back and forth before he could grit out his response. "No. No, not yet."

"All right, all right. I'm gettin' ahead of myself. But, just sayin', bein' a nomad don't work that well if you're lookin' to put down roots. There in Baker, or here in Birmingham, we could talk." Noise in the background resolved to a bright woman's voice, words not quite intelligible. "Oh yeah, baby. You know I'll be up in a minute. Go ahead and get all warmed up for me. Give me a little show when I get to the bedroom."

"I'll let you go." He sat upright, looking around. "What time is it?" Darkness hovered behind the gap in the blinds.

"Ten or so. Not too late for fun times, if that's what you're trying to say." Retro's laugh was low and knowing. "But you're right, I need to follow my Trina up those stairs right quick. Talk soon. See you tomorrow."

The line went dead in his ear, and Einstein shoved it in his pocket as he stood. There'd been noise from downstairs a little bit ago, and a wave of anxiety drove him to the kitchen, where he found Bane standing and rocking his little girl, who was sleeping on his shoulder while Myrtle bustled around the countertops near the microwave.

"Brother." He kept his voice low but couldn't hide the grin at seeing this doting-father side of the big man. "Would you and Gunny have a minute to chat tonight?" He might not want to discuss Marian as he'd been forced to do with Retro, but they deserved to know everything he'd gotten so far about Scar and Zipline, and what he thought the men were aiming for. He grimaced. "Maybe more than a minute?"

Bane's gaze was flat, emotionless as he studied Einstein's face. Slowly his expression softened, and Bane nodded. "Yeah. Maye's down for the count. I'll take her and Myrt upstairs in a few. Go ahead and call Gunny, give him a heads-up. Let's do a firepit convo. Tell him to bring the beer."

"Sounds like a plan." He indicated the side door with his chin. "I'll be out there."

"Catch up with you soon, man." Myrtle sidled close to Bane, and Einstein watched her fingers curl around Bane's belt, remembering the feeling of Marian's similar grip today. Bane dipped sideways and kissed her temple. "Let's go up, Momma."

"Night, Einstein." Myrtle's sweet face wreathed in a smile. "Sleep well."

"You too, Myrt."

Outside, the darkness had deepened to cover everything. Fortunately, Einstein had been here often enough he could easily follow the pathway in the limited light. He angled the screen of his phone away when he unlocked it, using it to illuminate the grass and packed dirt in front of him. At the clearing, he found a stack of wood off to the side, propped a boot on the splintered edges of the wooden wedges, and dialed Gunny.

"What?" One ring was all it took to have Gunny growling in his ear. "My demon spawn are sleeping, which means I have about half a buzz on already. You need me to go somewhere, it'll take me most of a pot of coffee to feel comfortable ridin', brother."

"Firepit closest to Bane's place. You steady enough to climb the stile over the fence, or need me to come give you a hand?"

"Halfway to the door already, man." From across the clearing that stood on this side of the fence and past the field standing on the other, he saw a bright rectangle appear against the darkness. A form filled the opening, and then the rectangle disappeared. "Whadya need, man?"

"Bane said you should bring the beer." He suppressed laughter at Gunny's groaning sigh. "Hey, he's your president, not mine."

"Damn good thing I got a beer fridge near the jackass shed." There was a forceful exhale; then Gunny grunted, "Shit fire. Fuckin' dogs."

"See you in a few. I'll get the fire started."

"Yeah. I gotta beat me some kids. They're not pickin' up after the beasts."

"Not tonight though, right?" He lifted a partial log, tossing it towards where he knew the fire ring was. "And you can say it all you want, but not a bit of me believes you lift a hand to your so-called demon spawn."

"And you'd be right. Not sayin' I don't want to some days, though." Bottles clinked. "Two sixes enough, you think?"

"Should be more than plenty. I'm hanging up now, Gunny."

"About fuckin' time. I don't know how the hell you expect me to carry the beer and climb the stile if you're insistent on sticking me on this damn phone."

Einstein laughed aloud as he disconnected the call. It took a minute for his eyes to readjust to the darkness, but he set to work and quickly transferred a medium-sized pile of wood and a handful of kindling to the metal ring. One knee to the ground, he stacked the first few sticks over the top of the arranged kindling, then cursed quietly under his breath.

"Forgot a lighter?" Bane's voice came from the darkness, tone light and teasing. "Happens to me all the time. Not sayin' I want more brothers smokin' death sticks, but I've sure found it handy when one of 'em is around."

There was a click, and Einstein watched as the kindling caught fire, tiny licks of flame dancing along the bottom edges of the pitchy wood.

"Gunny should be here soon." He averted his gaze, trying to regain the night vision that had fled at the bright blaze.

"Wanna give me a preview of the topic? Is this a club business talk or one about the spectacle put on in front of a local diner today?"

"What?" His head snapped around, and he stared at Bane across the tiny fire.

"You really think you could lip-lock Marian like that and not have it get back to me?" What he could see of Bane's expression was amused, not angry as he'd expected. "Want my personal opinion? I'm glad y'all finally pulled y'all's heads out of y'all's asses and stopped dancing around each other. Glad you let loose of the idea you weren't allowed to be happy again, after what happened with your wife and kid. I know bringing them up is probably not what you want or even expect, but they were part of you, man. They should never be a forbidden subject. I can't imagine Marian makin' you feel that way either." Bane crouched, poking at the growing fire with a stick as Einstein stared at him, dumbfounded. "She's a good woman who had a shit start, and she deserves someone who'll go to the mat for her. From what I know about you, it seems to me like she found one."

Bane stood and made his way to one of the comfortable wooden seats the club's prospects had crafted out of giant logs. Einstein stayed on his knees next to the fire, following Bane with his gaze. *A forbidden subject?* He didn't know how Bane could think that about Einstein's girls, especially since he'd dedicated the past three years of his life to tracking down the man who'd been the cause of their deaths.

Sure, I don't talk about them much, but that's not because they deserve to be hidden away.

Mostly it was out of self-preservation, at least at first. Being around couples, some of them with kids around Makayla's age, had hurt like a motherfucker. *Survival mode.* Was that honest, though? They'd been gone more than a year before he'd met Bane. *Wasn't that I wallowed, though.* A memory struck him of Retro standing in his kitchen back in Birmingham, staring at a pile of splintered wood that had been furniture. *Dark days, that's all it was.* That had been nearly a year gone from planting his girls into the ground, though. Einstein was honest with himself, had come to grips with the knowledge that if Retro hadn't dragged him kicking and screaming into the daylight, he would have gladly remained in the dark. *I'd have stayed there until the dark was all there was.*

He thought of Marian's face following their first kiss, her seated on the squeaky plastic of a bench in a booth meant for families and lovers. *She's the opposite of darkness.* Softly yearning, her lips had chased his. The love-drunk expression in her eyes when they fluttered open had curled gently around his heart, warming him from the inside out.

"Okay, I have feelings for her." The honesty in his statement literally knocked him sideways, his ass landing in the packed dirt around the fire ring. *No I don't. It's just a ruse.* Bile rose in his throat at the thought, and he knew lying to himself wouldn't be possible. *She thinks it's a stunt, a lie.* Now he wanted to vomit at the idea he was actively taking something so good and perverting it for his own end. "Not sure she feels the same." That was truth, because she'd only agreed to go along with the plan after she'd understood what happened to Lauren and Makayla. *Will we ever be able to get past this into something that's real on both sides?* "I'm going to do what I can to get her there."

"*Brother.*" Gunny's urgent shout came from the darkness. His tone had hair all over Einstein's body raising into gooseflesh. Einstein awkwardly climbed to his feet, aware of Bane doing the same across the flames. "Answer your fuckin' phone already." Heat suffused his voice as he came into view. "There's something happened to Marian."

*****

It was hours later and the words were still circling his head.

Something happened to Marian.

Luke had first phoned the house, and unable to get an answer, had called Bane's cell phone. With the device left on the kitchen countertop, that call had also gone to voicemail, and so Luke had turned to Gunny for help.

Luke and Marian had been at the theater, walking out with the crowd afterwards, when he said his sister had stumbled. He'd caught at her to try and steady her, but a man was there faster. Luke said all he could grab was her arm, because the man already had a hold around her shoulders, keeping her upright as her head nodded. The man hadn't said anything at all, ignoring Luke and steering a mumbling Marian to a van parked along the curb nearby. Luke had yelled as he'd yanked at her hand, trying futilely to pull her from the man's grip.

Luke had still been screaming and yanking at the handle as the van door shut in his face and the vehicle pulled away. Only then did some of the people in the crowd ask what was wrong.

Gunny estimated it had taken less than ten seconds to incapacitate her, probably medically, and then another ten to abduct her in clear view of more than three dozen people. With everyone's attention on the shouting boy, the police didn't have a plate to run, and only the most generic "white panel van" as a description. Luke hadn't looked at the man, his attention focused on his sister, so even the club didn't have a single solid clue to follow.

Einstein knew, though. He knew if there'd been a picture taken of the moment—there were security cameras that potentially had a view of the scene, and Myron of the RWMC was working that angle right now—he'd see the same face that had haunted him for three years.

"Scar." He leaned his shoulders against the outside wall of the house, staring into the darkness from the front porch. There were too many people inside, and he'd escaped out here a while ago, ensuring Bane and Gunny knew where to find him if there was a need.

I underestimated him.

Einstein was gutted that he'd been so confident in his read on Scar's movements.

Again.

In the hours since the calls had come in, he'd had numerous flashbacks to what had happened before. Lauren's terror as she sat on the couch next to Scar. Makayla's fear as she'd asked what was happening. The horror of their silent and cold bodies lying next to him in a van very similar to the one in which Marian had been taken.

Retro's response on the call letting him know what had happened summed up Einstein's world. "Jesus fuck, not again."

Bama Bastards were rolling to Baker in force. As were RWMC from the Big Bend charters. And the last he'd heard both Twisted and Wrench were coming from Louisiana with dozens of men at their backs. Of course, the Freed Riders were here, with more riding in every hour as Gunny rousted their men.

Sour saliva flooded his mouth for the hundredth time. He leaned over and spat into the darkness.

This is my fault.

As fast as word had spread about his display with Marian today, flying north to Birmingham as well as making its way to Bane's ears within hours, he had to assume Scar had heard about it too. That meant if he'd been on the fence with Marian's importance to Einstein, everything today had simply cemented his knowledge and probably pushed him to act.

I promised her I'd keep her safe.

His gut ached, a hot burning buried deep, causing him to bend double in pain.

He'd talked it through with Bane until he ran out of air. Everything except the fact Marian didn't know his displayed feelings were real. The consensus between them had been that Scar wasn't stupid. He could and had learned from mistakes in the past. His mistake in the last engagement had been to trust Lauren and Makayla's safety to underlings. That meant he'd probably keep Marian close.

"I just don't get what he hopes to get out of this whole situation." Einstein leaned back as he talked to himself, head thudding against the hard surface. "Not my cooperation with whatever fucked-up idea he's got; he's not that crazy." Einstein's activity over the past few years had ensured Scar hadn't been able to return to his previous world. He'd forced the man into hiding, putting his life on hold. "Maybe he's—fuck, I don't know. I can't get a read on it."

"Neither can I." Bane stepped out of the doorway, letting the screen door settle gently into place. "I've been over it and over it, and I don't see where the win is for him in this." Einstein's gaze locked onto Bane's face, the man's expression taut and pained. "Unless the win is fucking you up worse than you already are. If he made this personal in his head, then it makes the smallest amount of sense. Even as a kid he was always a bully, always needed to be the winner. Wanted to come out on top no matter what. What if he's trying to break you?"

"Or if he's trying to draw me into the open? If he does and is successful in taking me out, then his life can go back to a closer version of normal." Einstein pressed his folded-up hand against his belly, pushing hard to make the pain go away. "If that's his game, then he leaves Marian alive."

"If it's my version, then she's probably already dead, and he's just biding his time to reveal what he's done. He'll build it up and up, string you along for days, weeks even." Bane tipped his face to the ceiling and clenched his jaw. "Fuck." The growled word held a heavy burden of anguish. "Then he'll drop the hammer, just when it would hurt you the most."

"I don't like that scenario for what's happening. If he wanted to take away my world again, he could have killed her there on the sidewalk. He would have to know that I'm close to the boys, too. Hurting Luke by taking her was calculated, even if the location was chance—I mean, they didn't make plans until this morning." Einstein blew out a slow breath. "She works in the back of the flower shop. That means she had the opportunity to tell only two people not me or her family." He pushed off the wall and stalked to the railing, turning his gaze outwards again, thinking. "What do you know about the owner, and the girl, Whitney? Noah isn't from Baker, right? Where'd he come from?"

"Noah?" Bane's surprised bark of laughter was wrong, and Einstein hated how it echoed back to the porch from the tree line. "No, he's not from here. Somewhere out west. Mesquite, I think?"

"Dallas area?" The door behind Bane opened, and Gunny came out, followed closely by Truck. "That's FRMC area. You know him at all from there?"

"You talkin' about Noah Penrose?" Truck's question came with a tilted head as he tried to catch up on a conversation he'd stepped into the middle of. "Not Dallas. I wanna say New Mexico."

That had the hair on Einstein's arms prickling into gooseflesh. "How close is Mesquite, New Mexico, to El Paso?"

Gunny had his phone out already and was tapping on the screen. He angled the device so Einstein could see the display as he pinched and shoved at the surface with big fingers. The image halted, and Gunny zoomed in long enough to verify the name of the town, then out to show more of the state. Mesquite sat directly between Las Cruces and El Paso, a pipeline of highway between the RWMC chapter and where the Silent Deaths held territory.

Turning to Bane, Einstein said, "Can you get Myron—"

"Already on it." Bane waved a hand through the air. "Myron, it's me again. Got a guy we want some history on. Noah Penrose, owns the florist shop here in town, Penrose and Peonies. He's from Mesquite, New Mexico. This is hot, man. We're looking to see if he has any connection with Zipline." His rapid-fire list of information paused, and he nodded silently, listening. After a few moments, he grunted, "Yeah. Soon as, brother. Thanks."

Looking at the men on the porch with them, Bane shrugged. "It's something to look at, for sure. Whitney is just a kid. She's from here, graduated local. Her daddy runs a bunch of chicken houses for the local packing plant. Jodan Cavanaugh, his wife died a few years ago. She's a real good girl. No boyfriend, something Marian has bemoaned many a time." He shook his head. "I don't see her as having anything to do with this, but exposure to Marian would mean she's been around bikers enough to not have as much caution as your typical citizen. Might make her an easier mark for someone looking for an in. I don't know—that doesn't feel as urgent as finding out about Penrose's possible connection to Zipline."

"Anyone know Zipline's government name?" Einstein glanced around the group, seeing only shaking heads and lifted shoulders. "Retro's on his way down, and Mudd's with him, but they probably left Buzzkill or Crazy

Mike at the clubhouse. I'll get him to dig into our files." He pulled out his phone. "I could do it, but it's a pain in the ass on my phone. My tablet's upstairs." There was one ring and the call connected, just like earlier with Gunny, and he marveled at how things had changed since then.

"Einstein?"

Relief washed through him at the familiar voice. "Buzzkill. I want you to look at Zipline, see if we know what his government name is. We're trying to track through a couple of potential contacts to see where things might land."

"Half a second, brother." Background noise he hadn't noticed until now died away, and he knew Buzzkill had made his way to the secure room used for most information lookups. "I'm sure we've got it. We trace lineages where we can. It's made a big difference in the past, knowing where a man comes from and what's in his rearview. Half a second," he repeated, the silence deepening around those moments when he spoke. "Zipline, originally from Las Cruces. His mother married a man from Mesquite, just south of where he grew up."

The gooseflesh was back, and Einstein interrupted him to ask, "Was the man's name Penrose?"

"Yeah, how'd you know? Oh, hang on, I've got a marker shows we've got more info on the family." The system they used had been stolen from a major genealogy retailer and featured the same abilities to associate various interconnected profiles. "Mother's name was Dorcas, maiden name Terrence. Zipline's name is Walter Terrence, and I don't show a record for his father. Stepfather was Nicolas Penrose, had a son by a previous marriage. Noah Penrose."

"Got it. Can you send that info to Retro and Mudd, so they've got it when they get here?" Movement at the edge of his vision made him look up to see Bane making an us-too gesture at the three men on the porch with Einstein. He nodded. "Loop in Bane, Gunny, and Truck, please. Fuck, send it to my phone, too, so I know we had this convo."

"Brother, if there's anything else. Anything at all—" Buzzkill's voice broke at the end. "Fuck, this is unbelievable, happening all over again."

"It's not happening again. He wouldn't have taken her if he wanted to kill her." Einstein forced the words out with all the certainty he had in his body. He had to keep hold of that thought because the alternative— *Not happening.* "Thanks, brother. I'll dial you back if we need more." His phone pinged and he pulled it away to see it was the requested information. "Stay close, yeah?"

"You got it, Einstein. I'm here, man, anything you need."

He disconnected and looked up, finding each of the men studying their own phones. "Noah is Zipline's stepbrother."

"Fuck." Bane clipped out the word. "How the hell was this on my doorstep and I never knew it?"

"It's hard to find something you don't know to look for." He couldn't absolve Bane of the guilt creasing his face any more than Einstein could offset his own culpability. *Don't mean I won't try. He's more use to us if he's less focused on the coulda-woulda, and more on the now.* "You know where he lives? I bet Zipline's confident that connection is buried, since Marian was working there. If you'd known, you'd have vetoed the job, no matter how she argued. Am I right?"

"I've got his number."

Einstein reached out and halted Bane's action, stopping him from dialing. "No, man. I've met Noah. If Zipline is there, if *Scar* is there and you call, there's no way Noah will be able to hide his reactions to any questions you might have. Even if you wake Noah from a deep sleep, you can bet Scar'd hear the call." Squaring up his shoulders, he stood tall and looked at the men surrounding him. The forced inactivity had grated against every nerve in his body. Not knowing had been paralyzing. But this was a good lead, a clear direction. "We've got our target. I'm rolling right the fuck now. Noah lives just a couple of blocks from the shop. Marian had to pick up something from him once and I took her there."

Moving on instinct, he pushed past Bane and ran down the wooden stairs two at a time, hitting the ground full stride as he aimed towards his bike. Ignoring the legal call for a helmet in Florida, Einstein didn't take the time to put his on, leaving it fastened to the lock on the rear of the frame. Once out on the country road, he looked in his mirrors to see three headlights gaining ground on him and twisted the throttle viciously. The bike leapt underneath him, roaring as he rode into the last piece of night, an edge of light showing along the far horizon.

Please God, keep her safe for me. She deserves to know this is real.

When he found her—because he couldn't stand to think about a possible future where that didn't happen—he'd tell her, first thing. The truth this time.

I think I could love you.

No decision in his life had ever felt so right.

Chapter Fifteen

Marian

The bed underneath her was so soft it felt like she was resting on clouds. She sighed and rolled left, then right, giggling. There was a sharp niggling in her mind, but she ignored it to float on the clouds. "Thees nized." That set her to giggling again, because what she'd meant to say was "this is so nice," but it had come out garbled. "Gargd." More giggling. Something stopped her rolling, and she blinked up to see Jim leaning over her, the expression of concern a weird overlay of the smile on his face.

"Baby, love you so much." His words were strangely out of sync with his mouth, and she tried to focus on reading his lips. "Marian, be still. You're going to fall off the bed."

"No not." She sighed. "Love too." It was exhausting to compare what she was trying to say with what actually escaped her mouth, so she decided talking was overrated. Pushing up on one elbow, she lifted a hand to touch his face like she'd always wanted, but misjudged the distance, and her fingers whipped past, rising to the ceiling. "Uh-oh." Her fingers fluttered like birds' wings, and she watched them try to take flight. "Losin' mah grip." The pun had her giggling so hard it triggered a coughing fit, and she doubled over, hiding her mouth against her knees as she hung over the edge of the cloud-covered bed. "Das bad."

"What did you give her?"

The angry voice shouting near her ear was familiar but wasn't Jim's. Marian would know his voice in a crowd, be able to pick his face and physique out in a lineup of hundreds. The hand that landed on her shoulder to tug her back onto the mattress wasn't his either.

She opened her eyes a tiny slit, guarding against the brightness surrounding her. A man stood next to the bed, and he wasn't Jim. Then he looked down at her, and she saw Jim's face again, but that weird overlay was back. His lips were offset, landing where his cheek should be, and his eyes morphed as she stared at him. His sandy brown hair was disheveled, as if she'd already been running her fingers through the top part.

"Jim?" This time she wasn't certain her own eyes weren't deceiving her and wasn't surprised when his misshapen head swung back and forth negatively. "Who are you?" She jolted away, scrambling to gain purchase in the clouds. Her heels dug in and shot her to the far corner, where she looked down to find her flying fingers clutching at normal sheets. "Where am I?"

"Marian, it's Noah."

She watched in horror as his single eye rolled wildly in its socket as it traversed the width of his head, disappearing around the other side. "Ga no. No no. No oh ah."

"Yeah, Noah." The eyeless being seemed impervious to her panic, lowering to sit on the edge of the bed. It smiled, lips parting to show her sharpened teeth, worse than any terror clown in a horror movie. "I'm your friend."

Marian hung her head, unable to look it in the face any longer. "No no no. No no. No oh ah. Das bad. Bad bad bad." She darted a glance up and screamed. Teeth that should be inside the dark maw were now drifting aimlessly across its face. Her back hit something solid, and she could retreat no farther. "No oh ah."

"The hell did you dose her with, Walter?" Angry voice was back, so unlike Jim's, she didn't know how she could have mistaken it before. "This is like the worst bad trip I've ever seen."

"Special K. She should still be knocked on her ass. Doesn't matter. Either way, it'll be out of her system in a while."

"How long until she's past the worst of these symptoms?"

"Another few hours maybe? I don't know."

Marian shrieked when the clouds underneath her shifted, throwing her against that hard surface again.

"Her heart's pounding so hard I can see it in her throat. In another few hours, she could be dead."

"No no. No die. Nooooo."

"Shhhh, Marian. It's okay. Can you close your eyes for me?"

She nodded, not really wanting to see the no-eyed monster man again.

"Okay now, think happy thoughts."

"Jim."

"Okay, let's think about Jim. What's your favorite thing about him?"

"Sooooo sweeeet." Eyes closed, she thrust her chin out and pouted her lips. "Good man." His story about his family hit her all at once, every detail she'd etched on her mind pummeling her brutally. "Sad man."

"Jesus, can you shut her up?" A third voice joined the other two, and Marian was tempted to look, but the memory of the monster sitting beside her was enough to keep her lids shut tightly. "Shouting the house down, man."

"You both need to go. Walter, I don't know why you thought it was a good idea to involve me in whatever this is. But you're in the wrong on this one. Leave her with me and go. I'll take her to a hospital and say she landed on my doorstep, which isn't a lie. I just won't mention who landed her there." The bed shifted again, and Marian groaned. "Shhhh, Marian. I'm going to take you to the doctor. Okay, honey? I'll get you to the hospital and then I'll call Jim."

"Jim. Jim Jim, Jimmy Jim. Sad man."

"Yeah, sweetie. Jim. Keep your eyes closed and think of Jim. Good. Now give me your hand."

Something exploded nearby, and Marian added her screams to the shouts of the men.

Chapter Sixteen

Einstein

When he saw what was in front of him as he steered the bike around the final corner before Penrose's house, Einstein had a moment to think, *Can Scar really be that stupid?* Two bikes and a white van sat near the curb across the street from the house. He flung up a fist and toed down his shifter, planting his right foot hard on the brake. It was enough to make the bike dance sideways, and as he killed the engine the other three bikes also came to a stop, tires barking slightly on the road. Glancing over his shoulder, he noted Gunny's front wheel was inches away from his rear one, and realized he didn't give too much of a shit that he could have wrecked them all.

Phone in hand, he dialed Retro. Expecting to leave a voicemail, he was surprised when he got the man himself. The lack of wind noise told him that the column was stopped somewhere. "Where are you?"

"Clubhouse on the main drag. Felt better to bring the boys here. Where are—"

"Backtrack two blocks, turn north. That'll be to your right. Two blocks and make a left. We're waiting. Scar and Zipline are here." He didn't give Retro a chance to respond, disconnecting and then dialing another number from memory. The call connected, and he didn't wait. "Myron, what can you tell me about Penrose's house? I've never been inside."

"I can tell you the white van is outside. I've been trying to call you. Never mind, I see you now." Einstein glanced up, not sure what he expected to see. "I'm into a doorbell camera two doors up from where you are now, across the street from Penrose's place. You wanted a floor plan? I can go one better. I've got a high-level asset in place and can"— Einstein's phone pinged—"send you a recent heatmap of the house. This is fifteen minutes ago. They're all near or inside a back room, probably a bedroom, given the positioning. Heatmap hasn't changed significantly since I've been watching."

Einstein pulled his phone away from his face and looked at the message that had just come in. The image reflected everything Myron had told him. He studied the lines of the walls, appearing on the image as a darker gray.

"Einstein," the man was shouting at him, and Einstein returned the phone to his ear. "I do not have eyes into the house, man. Penrose seems averse to anything that might connect to the internet. I'd bet his only computer is at his shop. There's a passive alarm in the house that dates back two decades but is still active." Einstein put the call on speaker. "That alarm can be easily bypassed for entry, and you've got a guy with you who's one of the best at dealing with that kind of stuff."

"He's talking about me," Gunny spoke up, face grim. "Don't matter what alarm he was talking about, you need it and I'll do it, brother."

"Gunny." The relief in Myron's voice was apparent to them all, and Einstein grimaced, shoving his ego aside. Gunny had a long history with the RWMC. It was only natural that someone like Myron would lean towards the big man. "The alarm will just need an alligator clip wire to bypass, but it looks like it's full coverage. You need to treat every door and window as potentially armed."

The sound of bikes swelled in the distance, and Bane took off at a run. Einstein allowed the conversation between Gunny and Myron to fade to the background as he watched Bane meet the column a block back. He gestured frantically for the men who had ridden down from Birmingham to turn off their bikes. Swiveling around, Einstein stared at Penrose's house, which was so close he was suddenly shocked their own arrival hadn't drawn any attention. *Thank God Bane was thinking on his feet.* Marian was the only thing Einstein could focus on for any length of time. She was in there, in that room where the blooms of heat were, trapped inside the house with Einstein's sworn enemy, Scar. *He's got my Marian.*

"Fuck." Shoving the phone at Gunny, he had only taken a single step towards the house before he was yanked back with arms around his chest. "Let me go."

"Not happenin', brother." Retro's murmur was loud as a gunshot to Einstein, and he whirled, not surprised to see a heavy concern on Retro's features. "We got here. We're fuckin' here. Now, what do you know?"

"Myron's got a heatmap of the house. He's tapped into a camera across the street. They've got her inside. They have her inside, Jerry. That van's the one they took her with. Scar and Zipline, they're in there." He realized he was trembling. "She's in there with them. My Marian. She's by herself and in there with Scar."

"Gunny's gonna get us in there." Retro's head dipped and lifted, his face a mask of solemn acceptance of how fucked-up Einstein was right now. It was a relief, knowing he could leave some of this in Retro's hands, trusting he'd have the right answers. "You're going to stay with me, no matter what. Our job is to find your lady and get her out. Mason is at the homesteads. He's gonna hold down the fort there, but he's sending Hoss in with a car so we can get her away from here. Isaiah is on his way, brother. We've got you, man."

A hand appeared on his shoulder, and he turned to see Mudd standing close, the man's gaze fixed on the house down the street. Marlin was right behind Mudd, his scowl focused on Einstein. Along the street in a ragged line were all the men he knew from the club, all the men he called brother. Each of them had dropped everything at his call, and for the first time since he'd methodically sewn it into place, the nomad rocker chafed.

"Okay, we're good to go in. Gunny's got our entrance planned out, him and Myron. Isaiah is only a couple of minutes away. We're good to go." Retro's voice came from a hundred miles away, and a moment after he finished speaking, Einstein rattled back and forth in Retro's grip as he was shaken. "You with us, brother?"

"I'm with you." He stiffened his spine, lifting his head. *Everyone came here because I needed them. My brothers. My family.* "Scar—"

"He's yours, brother. I know."

Einstein shook his head. "No, that's what I was going to say. Whatever happens to him, he's pulled all this in on himself. I know I've been hunting him for a long time, but it doesn't have to be me. Any of my brothers deal with him, they're acting with my hands. My sole focus is Marian. Everything else is noise to me."

"Always knew you were fuckin' smart." Retro glanced around at the men standing nearby. "Are we ready to go?"

A dozen affirmative responses had their boots aiming at the house. Einstein didn't ask what the strategy was, didn't ask who was assigned what; he just followed Retro, knowing his brother and best friend would never steer him wrong.

They came to a halt on the back porch. Einstein stood directly behind Gunny, who already had the screen door opened wide, held there by one wedged boot. He watched in amazement as the man wrenched the molding off the side of the door with his bare hands, a wire contraption clenched between his teeth. Tossing the piece of wood into the yard behind them, Gunny turned back to his work, and a pocketknife appeared in his hand. He used the pointed end of the blade to tease a set of colored wires out of the gap between the door and the wall. On two of the wires, he frayed the plastic covering and attached the clips, one at each location. With a deft twist of his wrist, Gunny snipped through one wire.

Gunny turned. "You're in. I've got to get the front door next. Give me a count of fifteen." Then he disappeared. Einstein was left staring at Retro as he bent over in front of the doorknob, hands held close together, metal flashing as he picked the lock.

"Got it." Retro straightened and moved so his shoulder bumped the screen door, hand on the knob of the inside one.

"Fifteen," Einstein heard from behind him, the voice sounding like Mudd's.

"Here we go."

Inside the house was dark. Only limited light filtered in through the sheers over the windows. Einstein followed the patch on Retro's leather vest, noting the heatmap had been accurate with the placement of the walls as they immediately turned a corner into a short hallway. It was brighter here, the end of the hall illuminated with light that streamed through a doorway.

Shadows darkened the area, and just before he and Retro got to the opening, a man stepped out. Einstein had an instant to recognize Scar. He was older, face more lined, new marks living alongside old ones—then Scar ducked back into the room, and another man appeared, pistol in hand. The brilliance of the muzzle blasts as he pulled the trigger was blinding, loud reports deafening in the enclosed space.

Retro went down with a yell, and Einstein slammed against the wall as Mudd pushed past them both. *Fucking hell, Retro's down!* Then a woman's screams split the air, and Einstein was torn between pausing to check on Retro or continuing. *Oh my God, Marian!* He saw Mudd's trajectory was true as he tackled the man, shoving him through the window at the end of the hall. As the glass shattered, it reflected a final blast from the end of the gun, pointed harmlessly overhead. Immediately, alarms caterwauled around them, shrill and adding to the insanity.

"I got Retro! Go, go, go!" Marlin shoved at his shoulder, and Einstein stepped over Retro's prone form, even as it killed him to do so. He raced through the door and came into the room to see Marian dangling at the end of a man's fist. She was in front of the large form of Scar, held in place by his hand clutching the seam of her neckline. An unmoving Penrose lay on the floor near Scar's feet.

"Back the fuck off." Scar's shout seemed to come from a thousand miles away, echoes of the gunshots still blocking Einstein's hearing. The man shook Marian like a ragdoll as she jerked with uncoordinated movements. "I'll kill her. Back off!"

"You're dead anyway." Gunny's voice from behind preceded the appearance of a pistol over Einstein's shoulder by only an instant. Einstein had only a breath to bring his hand up and cover his ear before Gunny pulled the trigger. A tiny hole appeared in Scar's shoulder as red splashed the wall behind him, both arms lifting as he fell to the side. He was up in an instant and plunging through the glass of a window and into the darkness beyond.

"*Fuck.*" Gunny pushed past Einstein towards the broken window.

Freed from Scar's hold, Marian sagged, and Einstein lunged forwards, catching her against his chest as he sank to the floor with her on his lap.

She looked up at him, her smile brilliant, eyes unfocused and alarmingly aimed in different directions. "There you are."

Her words were slurred, blending together in frightening ways, and Einstein shouted, "*Help.* Someone help me." Marian's head tilted towards him, thudding against his chest with a painful blow. "*Something's wrong.*"

"Be still, motherfucker." Bane's growled instructions had Einstein shifting to place his shoulders against the side of the bed, well away from where Marian had fallen. Penrose was moving, trying to sit up as he held one hand against the back of his head.

Mudd appeared, and Einstein stared at the red on his hands. He darted a glance towards the door, then back to Mudd's face. "Don't worry, brother. I'll always have your back. Folks are takin' out the trash I left on the yard right now. Do you know what's wrong with her?" Mudd looked at Bane, who was smashing the rest of the glass from the window, already halfway out. "Where's Scar?"

"He got out, that way." Penrose lifted his chin to indicate a disappearing Bane. "Through the window. They gave her ketamine. She's been hallucinating."

Einstein clutched Marian closer at Penrose's words.

"I missed you." Marian's lips pursed in a sweet demand, and Einstein didn't hesitate before dipping down to press his mouth to hers. Her cold lips heated underneath his, and a tiny bit of his terror faded away. *She's going to be okay.* He wouldn't allow any other thought inside his head right now. She'd be okay, and so would his brothers.

"Get the fuck off of me." The words from the hallway were clearly audible, spoken just as the alarm ceased its klaxon alert, and Einstein took a deeper breath in, relieved to hear Retro's voice. "I'm not dyin'. Leave me the fuck—god*dammit,* that smarts, asshole. Stop pokin' at it."

"Baby, did they hurt you?" A quick scan of Marian's visible skin didn't show him any bruising, something that wasn't as comforting as it should be. "Talk to me. Tell me you're okay."

Gunny climbed back through the window, a shake of his head answering Einstein's unspoken question.

Fuck.

"Definitely winged him. I'll get Myron to watch the hospitals, see if we can tag him that way. Motherfucker's fast." Gunny's fingers worked across the screen of his phone. "Maybe the drone that gave us the heatmap can track him." He picked up a small bottle from the floor and frowned. "Shit. Ketamine?" Einstein nodded as Gunny crouched nearby, gaze darting between his phone and Marian's face. "Okay, that's not the worst. Not the best either."

"The bad clown went away." She shuddered and clung tighter to Einstein. "Thank you for making him go away, Gunny."

"Clown, huh? Well, that's about right." Gunny snorted. "Let me look at you, Maid Marian." He crouched next to Mudd, reaching out to grasp Marian's chin and direct her gaze towards himself. "Do you see me, honey?"

"Yeah." Her voice was high and childlike. "You're my first friend." She laughed softly, lips curling at the corners as she stared at Gunny. "My first forever friend."

"You better believe it. We're friends for life, Maid Marian." Gunny turned to Einstein, his serious expression belying the amusement in his tone. "Her pupils are jacked, so she's still pretty deep in the K-hole. That clown business? If she was hallucinating before we got here but isn't now, that means he had to dose her recently. It's been long enough from the time she was taken it should be out of her system if he'd only hit her the once. Her altered state will stabilize quickly; the drug's fairly short-acting, relative to the other medications in the same class." Gunny looked up and shook his head at Mudd's puzzled expression. "What? I do a lot of volunteer work at the horse rescue place north of town. One of the other volunteers got canned because he was rippin' off the ketamine. I did some research."

"Damn, man, you have some odd interests." Mudd turned to Einstein. "You're in good hands, brother. I'm going to check on our fearless leader." Einstein became aware of a jumble of voices and conversation from the rest of the house. "He's sounding testy."

"Getting shot'll do that to a man." Retro shoved Mudd to the side and crouched where he'd been. There was a hole in the left side of his vest, just underneath his arm. Einstein realized his chest was bare, shirt gone, and the exposed skin was stained red. Shaking his head, Retro told him, "Not as bad as it looks, brother. The bullet just caught enough of my side to bounce off a rib. Felt like gettin' kicked by a fuckin' mule, though. I could do without that again in my life."

"Is she okay?" Penrose's question came from nearer the doorway.

"She will be." Retro's expression hardened as he looked away from Marian and towards Penrose.

Einstein returned his attention to Marian, finding her slightly more alert.

"Did you have any inkling what Zipline was planning?" Retro's question encompassed everything Einstein wanted to ask the man.

"No." Low and urgent, Penrose's denial sounded heartfelt. "God, no. He showed up yesterday out of the blue. I haven't seen him since my dad kicked me out of the house years ago. Haven't even thought about Walter. He was just a kid, but his hate ran just as deep as my old man's, so I wasn't about to reach out to him. You can't think I'd have anything to do with them hurting Marian."

"Noah?" Marian squeezed her eyes closed, brow furrowing, and Einstein smoothed the wrinkles away with the pad of his thumb.

"Shhhh, baby. I got you." Without looking away from Marian, Einstein asked, "We need to worry about the cops showing up with the alarm going off like it did?"

"Naw, man. Myron dealt with all that shit." Gunny laughed. "I was on the phone with him when it was goin' on. Found out that man can be sayin' his 'oh fudruckle' in a Midwest accent one moment and then carry a conversation in a Southern drawl the next, explaining how he'd had too much wine and opened a window without thinking. Called it 'dealin' with the wine thweats' until the local cops were laughing along. He's good."

"Zipline?" From Mudd's response earlier, Einstein believed he knew the answer but wanted to be certain.

"Done for." Retro's flat tone went a long way to reassure him. "Mudd made sure of it."

Bane stuck his head in the window. "Nothing, man. He's a fuckin' ghost."

"Jim?" Marian's eyes had opened again, and she was looking around with more clarity in her gaze. "What's going on?"

"The only good thing about ketamine? She might not have any memory of what happened today." Gunny's shoulders moved in a shrug that looked as helpless as Einstein felt. "Mixed blessing, as long as it doesn't leave a fearful gap in her mind."

"I'm going to get her out of here before she has a chance to look around, cement things that are better left unseen." He transferred her to Gunny's arms, then stood and took her again, legs draped over one arm while his other encircled her back. "I got you, baby. Hold on to me now, okay?"

"Isaiah—Hoss is here. He's out front. Go on, I'll be right behind you. Won't be ridin' my bike like this, so I'll drive us to the homesteads."

Einstein acknowledged Retro's words with a nod, gaze fixed on Marian's face as she stared up at him. "You with me, Marian?"

"I...I think so." She twisted, arching her back as she tried to look around the room. "What's going on?"

Hands resting on the sides of the window, Bane offered, "I'll get a couple of prospects to ride your bikes, brothers." He disappeared as Marian's head swung in that direction.

Einstein needed to get her out of there fast, unless he wanted her to see something she wouldn't be able to forget. "We're just going outside. Hang with me, honey."

"I...there was a..." Her eyes widened, and she twisted again, fighting his hold. "Where's Luke? We were... we were at the movies." He didn't let go, pinning her against his chest as he made his way through Penrose's living room to the front door. "This is Noah's house. Why are we in Noah's house?"

"You didn't feel well." The voice approached from the side. Einstein glanced that direction as Penrose came towards them. "Luke's with Myrt and Thad. They're all home. Einstein's going to take you home now." His voice cracked. "I'm glad you're feeling better, Marian." Penrose's gaze never left Marian's face, his eyes brimming with tears. "So, so glad. I'd never want you to be hurt, or be afraid. After how you felt earlier, I think you'll need a couple of days to get better. *Paid*. I take care of my friends."

Sounding lost, Marian whispered, "Okay." Penrose had walked with them to the door and held it open for them. Marian's confused tone remained as she continued, "I'll call you tomorrow, Noah."

"Sounds good."

The door clicked behind Einstein as he carried Marian toward a car parked in the middle of the street. The sides of the road were lined with bikes, packed in as if it were a party. Einstein shivered.

"There's a lot of people here." Marian's observation held less confusion and more certainty. "I didn't just get sick, did I?" She slumped in his arms, curling closer as she rested her cheek on his chest. "Einstein?"

"Yeah, baby?"

"Is it okay if I don't want to know?"

He jostled her, hitching her higher in his arms as he tried to get a look at her face. "What?"

"If I don't want to know what happened, is it okay?"

Einstein sighed. "Luke knows, so does Thad. Part of it at least. I think you should probably know that much, so you aren't blindsided when we walk in the house."

"Okay, that makes sense. If Luke knows, it can't be that bad." Her chin tipped up, and their gazes met. "Oh," she breathed. "It is bad. Oh no." Einstein stopped next to the car, looking down at her. "Will you tell me?"

"How much do you remember of today?" He kept his eyes on her as Hoss opened the car door for them and moved away. Einstein settled Marian into the seat, grabbing a folded blanket from next to her, and as she sat back, he spread the soft fabric over her lap.

"That we have an agreement, you and me. A pretend relationship." The pain that washed over her face pierced his heart, and he had to look away. "It's okay, Einstein."

He forced his gaze back to her, taking in every fleeting expression.

"It. Is not. Pretend. Nothing about it was ever pretend for me, not really." Einstein continued tucking the blanket around her, leaning close. "That was my lie to myself. I don't have an excuse, other than I think it was to ease into the idea. A protection for myself. I don't need it now, though. Not after tonight. I don't want to go slow and easy anymore, Marian."

"But your wife?"

Something pinched his ribs, and he breathed through the pain, not shifting away as it slowly eased. A cool breeze blew across the nape of his neck, and he sucked in a hard breath. He didn't need to pat the front of his vest to know the toothbrush wasn't there anymore, lost somewhere in the terror of the preceding hours or in the rush to get to Marian's side—it didn't matter. It had served its purpose.

"She was a beautiful, sweet woman, who died too early, because of me. That's my truth and what I live with. But before that happened, we had years of happiness. I had so much time with her and never gave her a single reason to doubt my feelings. Tonight—" His throat closed tightly, blocking the words he wanted to say, tears burning the backs of his eyes. Einstein dropped to sit sideways on the seat and wrapped his arms around Marian.

"What happened tonight?" Her arms circled his back, one sliding up to cover the chilled portion of his neck, warming it with her touch.

"I nearly lost my chance of time with you, Marian." He whispered against the side of her head, "Baby, it feels like we've been working towards this for years. Tell me you feel the same, put me out of my misery."

"He came after me, didn't he? The man you talked about today." She laughed, the broken sound muffled against his neck. "That feels like so long ago, but it was just today, right?" He made an affirmative noise, and she tightened her hold. "He did exactly as you predicted and came after me. You were right about what he was going to do." She stiffened, words wavering as she asked, "Is Luke okay? I remember coming out of the movie theater with him, and then nothing until...now, basically."

"Luke's shaken up. He's going to be sticking close to you for a while, I expect, but he's going to be fine." He adjusted his hold, pulling her closer. "You're all right, and that's what matters. You're good, and you're here."

"And you might care for me a little?"

"Me liking you a little? That's like calling a hurricane a thunderstorm. It's more than a little, baby. I know you'll need some time to get used to the idea, but I'm not going anywhere. Already talked to Retro about hanging up my nomad rocker." Her arms spasmed. With fingers clutching at him, she burrowed closer yet. "I figured out that what I want is you, and where I wanna be is wherever you are."

***

Marian

"We're home." Einstein jostled her, and Marian lifted her head from his shoulder. She'd dozed in the car, secure in the knowledge Einstein would keep her safe. "And here comes everybody's favorite protector."

She tried to focus on whatever he was talking about, still peering through the car windows when the door beside her was flung open. Thad's head poked into the car, and he stared at her from only inches away. Lines were etched along his forehead, between his brows, and they didn't ease off as he studied her face. Then his arms were around her neck, and he sobbed against her shoulder, the harsh noises broken with word fragments that contained a mishmash of sounds, mixed in with her name.

The angle was awkward, but she got her arms around him and squeezed as hard as she could. "I'm okay. Thaddy. I'm here, and I'm okay. Everything's going to be all right."

"Can you walk, baby?"

She glanced over her shoulder at Einstein and nodded. The nap on the short drive from town to here had been enough to clear her mind, and she was surprised to find how close to normal she felt now.

"Okay." He smiled at her, the expression turning sad as he watched Thad, who still clung to her neck. "I'll come around to the other side and help you out, make sure you're steady as we go inside."

Without lifting his head, Thad barked out, "I'll help her." His arms were a vise around her neck, clenching through the trembling.

"You can both help me." Marian gave Thad's shoulder a little shove. "Let me out of the car, Thaddy. I want to get inside, check on Myrtie."

"I'm sorry." He didn't release her as he shook, arms tightening around her neck. "I'm sorry. I'm quittin' soccer and football. Quittin' all of it."

"What? Why? Why would you quit? You love playing." Her shove this time was stronger, enough to move him back a few inches. The expression on Thad's face broke her heart. Eyes swollen, he twisted his mouth to the side and shook his head. The tears weren't a reaction to her arrival, but probably the whole ordeal as her family had suffered here, waiting for word. "Thaddy, why?"

"If I'd been there, I could have kept you safe. Between me and Lukie, we'd have taken him down."

Marian's stomach lurched at the idea of her brothers put in that kind of danger. "No."

"Thad, this asshole wasn't someone who would have gone down without a fight." Retro's words from the front seat made her and Thad look at him. He pushed the door open and stood, wavering slightly before he stepped away and closed it behind him. He reached around the open door and, with one hand to Thad's shoulder, guided the boy out of the car, giving Einstein a chance to step in and offer Marian his hand. "Son, it took three men to deal with him, and he still got a shot off and hit me. Man like that? He would have killed you and Luke without a single thought. Your sister is here and safe, and this kind of thing—" Retro sighed, the sound filled with pain and grief she didn't understand. "This is a one in a million. You get me? I understand wanting to keep those we love from getting hurt. Oh man, do I ever get that feeling. This one time, though? If you were there, it would have been the wrong time, wrong place, and your sister who's standin' here smilin' at you would have been cryin' her eyes out instead. You can't put that on yourself, brother."

Thad's shoulders went back, and he straightened at Retro's use of the honorific that meant so much. Thad would know what it meant, Retro calling him that.

"I love you a little bit, Retro." Marian didn't think about her words, and when Einstein's arm around her shoulders jerked her closer, she looked up. "Not like that, Jim. Retro's like Gunny."

"Lord save us, woman. I am not like that man." Retro laughed, sweeping his hair away from his face. "But I understand your meaning." He nodded. "Back atcha. Means this man"—he swooped an arm around Thad's shoulders—"is now officially my little brother. I'm down with that. In fact, it's a great idea. Way I see it, a body can't ever have too much good family."

Somehow having beaten them home from the scene, Bane waited on the front porch with Myrt, and as the four of them walked from the car, Marian looked around for Luke. Thad read her mind, saying with a sigh, "Lukie's sleepin' finally. He's been tore up about everything. He didn't even wake up when Bane came rippin' in here a few minutes ago. Hard asleep."

"No doubt he's upset. It's a tough thing to have happen." Einstein's tension was unmistakable through his connection to Marian. She looped her arm around his waist as he told Thad, "Good thing he's got you to help him through it all."

Myrt's tears were flowing fast as Marian slipped into her arms, holding her little sister close. "I'm okay. Promise. Einstein made sure of it."

"I didn't know if I'd ever see you again." Myrt's trembling grew more pronounced, and Marian squeezed her closer. "I was so scared, Marian."

"I'm good. I'm here." She lifted her head from Myrt's shoulder to see Bane hovering close. With a questioning expression on his face, he raised both hands and made a gesture towards Myrt. Marian nodded. He immediately moved in, winding them both into his embrace. She rushed to reassure him, even though he'd been at Noah's house. "Bane, I'm okay."

"I know. God's blessing, I know. Just fuckin' glad to see you back here, little sister. Real fuckin' glad." He stepped back and unthreaded Myrt's arms from Marian's neck. "Come on inside. Let's get you situated, and then I'll wake up Luke, let him see for himself that you're gonna be just fine." Bane's eyes shifted, his gaze moving to the two men with Marian. "Retro, you're bleedin' again. It'll be a minute before Mudd's here. You're gonna have to suffer through my nursin' skills."

"Or lack thereof." Retro's laugh followed Marian through the door.

There was a bustle of activity around her and Einstein for a few minutes, but she felt detached from it all, as if Einstein's arms were the only things keeping her from floating away.

"I feel funny," she whispered to him. They were seated on the couch, Einstein shoved into a corner leaning back, and Marian draped mostly across his lap.

"Gunny said it could be as much as a full day before the sedative they used was completely out of your system. I'm here, baby. I'll keep you safe. You feel like you need to sleep it off, then sleep." A finger looped under her chin, and he raised her face so they stared at each other. "I'm not going anywhere, baby. Not sure I could stand being away from you right now. You feel like taking a little nap, don't worry about it. I'll be here when you wake up."

"And this isn't a dream?"

Mortified at the words flying out of her mouth, Marian tried to look away, but his grip on her jaw held her in place. That meant that as Einstein's features changed, she got to witness him going from concerned to happy, then a darker expression but somehow still pleased. A flush climbed her neck and settled in her cheeks, blazing hot in an instant.

"No, baby. You might be my dream, but this, what's going on between us? Definitely our new reality. You and me, we're going to ride this out, take it as far as it will go. Decades from now, you'll tell our grandkids about the day your old man finally pulled his head out of his ass and laugh at the effort it took. We're going to live out this dream together."

She nestled closer, and his hold fell away, arms encircling her tightly.

"Sounds good to me."

She didn't know how long she slept like that, perched across Einstein's thighs, but the sun was high in the sky outside the windows when she opened her eyes again. Still upright, Einstein sat with his eyes closed as his head rested against the back of the couch. She marveled at him sleeping with her in his lap. Also asleep, Luke was sprawled across the rest of the available cushions, one arm outstretched so his fingers linked with hers.

Marian tilted her head, gaze moving across Einstein's features. He was all man, as he always had been, but with him resting, she got to see that the hardness cast on him by life had fallen away. Marian suddenly realized there were smile lines that curved through his cheeks, tiny crescents around each corner of his mouth. His inked arms had stayed curled around her even though he was unconscious, and she traced a fingertip across the dark images. This was a quiet, intimate moment with him, and she held it close to her heart. *Even better than I could have imagined.*

She'd begun falling for him the first morning he'd shown up at the house, working easily alongside her in the kitchen. Joking and talking— even then it had been as if they'd always known each other. The way he interacted with Thad and Luke had always been supportive, and his positive affirmation for the boys had fed into her admiration of the man. Always from a distance, because she might not have known the details of what had happened, but Bane had long ago told her that Einstein was damaged by something.

Yesterday seemed like a dream, one of the best, that had then morphed into a nightmare.

Learning what his lips felt like against hers, hearing the sweet words directed her way—it hadn't felt like a gambit or trick, and hadn't been fake on her side of the equation. She'd spent the afternoon trying to figure out how to come out the other end of their deal with her heart intact, Whitney and Noah remarking more than once on her absentmindedness. In the end, Marian had decided to go forwards with Einstein's proposal, willing to take what he offered. *I just never intended for him to know what it would mean to me.*

No matter how deeply she dug, her recollections of leaving work and picking up Luke were thin, wispy. She couldn't remember where they'd eaten before the movie, and the holes in that period were frightening. Scar, the man who had hurt Einstein so badly in the past, had stolen that from her. A whole block of time was simply missing, the memories empty as if time had bent, skipping an entire section of the day.

Jagged edges of something nagged at her, the images in her mind as tantalizing as a word on the tip of her tongue. There, close, but not really within reach. The only thing she was certain of was her deep-seated knowledge and belief that Einstein would keep her safe. It had been as if he were with her all along, the thoughts of him giving her a sense of peace even in chaos.

Still trying to deconstruct the day, she tracked backwards from this moment to them walking up the steps of the porch. Catching at the foggy memories, she pieced them together as best she could, to further back, the moment Einstein had put her in the car. The words he'd spoken swam back into focus, and she tucked them away to scrutinize later. Beyond that, the memories were broken images and sounds, some terrifying and some not. Then a dark hole that led nowhere.

Einstein stirred, and she shook free from her thoughts, gaze on his face as he woke. His arms tightened, pulling her close with a heavy sigh that eased out of him alongside a happy hum. When he opened his eyes, he immediately found her face, and a line appeared between his brows as he studied her. Then that fell away, and a smile took over his expression, those lines she'd noticed in full view now, deep slashes across each cheek a testimony to the depth of his emotions.

Daring greatly, she leaned closer and lifted her chin. He didn't make her wait, immediately bending his neck to brush his lips chastely against hers. They touched once, twice, then he groaned, and a hand slipped up the back of her neck, fingers tangling in her hair as he angled her head for a deeper kiss. They were both breathing unsteadily when he pulled back and pressed their foreheads together. As Marian opened her eyes, she found him staring at her, a softer version of the smile still curving his lips.

"Morning, baby." His lips pursed, and he pecked another kiss at the corner of her mouth. "You're so fucking pretty."

"I slept in your lap."

"Mmhmm."

"Are you comfortable?"

His arms squeezed as he nodded, then pecked her mouth again. "Very. Altogether comfortable like this. Did you sleep okay?"

"Feels like it." She stretched her shoulders up to her ears. "You don't mind me using you as a cushion?"

"Baby, not only do I not mind, but I'm also gonna encourage it as often as you might want. I'm entirely on board with us sleeping together from here on out. Cozied up like this." He tightened his grip on her hair and gave a tug. "Or in a bed. Wherever you are, that's where I want to be."

A dish rattled behind them, and she twisted to look over Einstein's shoulder. Gunny and Sharon were near the stove, an array of dishes on the counter in front of them. Gunny noticed they were awake and lifted his chin in his typical manly greeting. He called out softly, "Mornin'."

Sharon's head whipped up, and she bustled around the island towards the couch, bending over to slip her arms around Marian's neck. Mid-hug, she asked, "Hey, honey. How are you feelin'?"

"I'm good." She squeezed back, marveling at how her life had changed from only a few years ago. She'd gone from no friends and only a single, unhappy relationship with her father, to this. Seated in the lap of a man she loved, with good friends going out of their way to do what they could to ease the burden of what had happened.

A tap at the side door preceded a few men coming inside, some faces she knew well mixed in with some she barely recognized. That small group turned into a trickle, then a stream, and finally a flood, until the room was wall-to-wall bikers, black vests next to denim ones, boots discarded near the door or worn inside—it was overwhelming. Sharon pulled back and released her hold, squealing as she raced towards one of the men, leaving Marian to bury her face against the side of Einstein's neck.

His hand cradled the back of her head, fingers threading through her hair as he pulled her close. "Shhhh, baby. It's okay. These are all friends."

A tug at her fingers had her peeking out to see Luke sitting upright, looking around in amazement. "Hey, Monday," he greeted one of Bane's men, then brightened even more. "Blackie! Hey!" He gave her fingers a final squeeze, then was off the couch and darting towards the burly national president of Bane's club, disappearing into the man's arms.

"Marian?" She glanced up to where Monday was standing close. "When you have a minute, I'd like to chat." He shook his head as his gaze moved to Einstein. "Nothin' bad, brother. I have a message from Noah for her, that's all."

"Why isn't Noah here?" Forgetting to be afraid, she shifted to better face Monday. "Is he okay? Scar didn't hurt him, too, did he?"

"Not Scar, no. His stepbrother, Zipline, bashed him in the head."

Marian's heart raced as fear for her friend flooded her system.

Monday's palms patted the air. "He's okay. Bit of a headache is all. He's resting—" Monday hesitated, his gaze flicking between her and Einstein. "He's resting at my house. I didn't want him to be alone last night." Pointing a thumb over his shoulder at the door, he took a step backwards. "I'll be here for another thirty if you have time. Otherwise, I'll come find you tomorrow. No rush."

"Is it personal?" At Einstein's question, Monday shook his head. "Then now is good, brother."

Monday grimaced and glanced around the room, his gaze coming back to rest on Einstein. "Might not be best."

"Now, or nothing." Einstein's muscles tensed under Marian's bottom, his arm around her waist tightening. His other hand still played in her hair, and she relaxed against him, hoping he'd unwind, too.

"Aww, man. You sure?" Monday crowded closer and sat on the edge of the couch, perching in what looked like an uncomfortable position. "So...Noah, he didn't know Zipline was headed here, had no idea the man was in town. The two of them were waiting for him when he got home yesterday, pushed their way into his house. From what he said, Scar held a gun to his head while Zipline asked questions. The men asked about all kinds of things, and from the sounds of it, nothing was specifically directed towards anyone, so other than the gun and fearing for his own life, it didn't raise any alarms for Noah. Then Scar and Zipline left in a van that had somehow appeared in front of Noah's house. He'd chalked it all up to another weird encounter with his peculiar stepbrother until they came back and hauled you"—he indicated Marian with a lifted finger—"inside."

"And then? Why didn't he pick up the phone and dial? Three buttons." Einstein flicked up a finger. "Call." A second finger joined the first. "Nine." His hand formed the salute best known for a national boy's club. "One, one. Isn't hard. She was there for hours, brother." The arm around her waist hitched her closer. "You're telling me that in all that time, he didn't have a single chance to make a call?"

A memory swam up, clouding Marian's vision. A needle, flashing in the light. "They dosed him too, didn't they? I remember a shot, like a syringe."

"Yeah. Yeah, they dosed him, too. Not as heavy, but enough it sidelined him for too long. He was trying to get help when we showed up. That's what earned him the pistol-whippin'. Trying to get you safe, Marian. 'S what he wanted me to tell you. He'd never hurt you, never let you be hurt, if he could help it." Monday's face twisted. "He couldn't help you quick enough."

She stared at Monday, taking in his posture and expression, and let a tiny smile slip. "You like him."

"Well, I don't dislike him." He looked around the room, avoiding her gaze. "Not even after what happened. I don't think it's any fault of his, honestly."

"I don't either." Einstein sighed heavily and shifted under Marian. "Much as I'd like to. Man was losing his shit. Took me a minute to realize it wasn't on his own behalf, but on hers."

Heat pressed against her temple, and Marian turned around to see Einstein moving back. It dawned on her that he'd kissed her, a gentle thing, showing tenderness. *I like when he's affectionate.*

Looking at Einstein, she told Monday, "Let him know I'll be in tomorrow, just like the schedule says." Like with Einstein's sweet kisses, actions would speak louder than words. She glanced over her shoulder, frowning. "And no arguments."

Monday's mouth snapped closed, and one corner of his lips quirked up. Gaze fixed on Einstein, he said, "Anything, brother. Don't matter I'm wearin' a different patch, you know you can call on me for anything."

"I do." Einstein's answer rumbled through his chest, vibrating Marian. "And I appreciate it more than you can know."

With a wave, Monday stood and walked away, his place on the couch immediately filled by Sharon, who was leading a man by the hand. Sharon leaned close and noisily bussed Marian's cheek. The man stared down at her tolerantly, and Marian looked between them, recognition blooming in her head.

"Are you…?"

"This is my brother, Jason." Sharon's interruption only confirmed what Marian had suspected.

"You're Jason Spencer." Glancing down, Marian futilely attempted to straighten her clothing. Her cheeks were hot, and she felt Einstein's attention shift to her. "You, uh. You played for the Mallets."

"I did. That was long ago and far away." He tousled Sharon's hair, dodging her half-hearted swat at his hand. "I'm only on the margins of hockey these days." He turned a multi-watt smile at Marian. "You a fan?"

"I wasn't." *How much to say?* She knew Einstein was listening closely, so she decided to stick with the truth, albeit glossed over slightly. "Growing up, I didn't have a chance, not really. According to my daddy, sports were a man's world. But I have a sports-crazy brother, and we spent about six months last year going through tons of old videos on the internet. He focused on the Tridents first, and after that began tracking back to where the players had come from. He applied to your foundation, but there wasn't a team close enough." She shrugged. "It's all right. He's got football and soccer to keep him busy. Seems happy enough with what's here."

"Oh, no. That ain't gonna do at all." Jason lifted his head and glared around the room. "Gunny! Lane Robinson, get your ass over here, man." He tromped away, each stamping footstep helping communicate his ire.

The patch on his vest was the one Gunny used to wear, and Truck. *Jason Spencer is in the RWMC?* "This is a travesty!"

"Now you've done it. He's on a mission." Sharon's giggle was light and sweet. "We've got food. I expect you'll want to visit the necessary room before y'all come over to eat." As soon as Sharon mentioned it, Marian became aware of the pressure low in her belly. "My brother has two passions. Family, and hockey. He counts the RWMC and all their friends as family, so if anyone needs him, that man'll turn himself inside out to make it happen. And with hockey, he pours himself into his foundation because, for him, when he steps on the ice, he's just as excited as he was the first time. Jase wants that for every kid he meets. How old is your brother?"

"He's a teen." She shook her head. "He really is happy with what he has. Keeps his schedule full." Turning to Einstein, she shifted, stilling when his hand at her waist clamped down. "I do need to...you know."

"I gotta piss too." Both hands to her waist, he lifted and held tight until she was steady on her feet. Pushing off the couch with a groan, he looped an arm over her shoulders. "Shar, we'll be back in a few. Tell folks not to come looking for us." Sharon's light laughter filled the air as they walked away.

Keeping close to her side, Einstein steered them through the crowd, pausing only briefly to speak to men, nearly all of those conversations consisting of him thanking them and promising to talk later. The men who also knew Marian acted differently than normal, not looking at her unless Einstein called their attention specifically. Even then, their words were brief and respectful in a notable way.

Finally on the other side of the room, Einstein tried to steer her up the stairs, but Marian resisted. "Where are you going?" Gesturing towards her room, she informed him of something he should already know. "My room's this way."

"Baby." His knuckle curled under her chin and lifted. Einstein was leaning close, his mouth only a fraction of an inch away from hers. "Your room is literally feet from this entire crew. I've been holding you for hours now, and I'm almost convinced that this is real. To seal the deal, I'm gonna kiss you in ways I couldn't in that damn diner. You want everyone to hear what you sound like when I'm doing that?"

"Um. Probably not?" Her stomach dipped, and she swayed on her feet, his arm tightening around her in an instant as he pulled her closer.

The corners of his eyes crinkled, and he whispered, "That's what I thought."

Chapter Seventeen

Einstein

He scanned the group as he led Marian up the stairs, and the pair of matching scowls from Bane and Gunny caught his eye. Einstein offered each a serious nod, an acknowledgment of the silent message. He, more than any of them, knew how fragile Marian was right now. *Logically they know I won't do anything to hurt her, but after the last twenty-four hours, I can't say I blame them for the warning.* What they didn't understand yet was how precious Marian was to him. How she'd already been his for the past three years.

Fucking hate I didn't pull my head out of my ass before now.

He couldn't change the past though, as much as he might want to. The idea of having so much lost time with her ate at him, and when he allowed himself to consider how things might have ended differently, it was enough to twist him into knots. Her fingers gave a squeeze, and he realized he'd tightened his grip.

Can't focus on that.

Glancing down, he noted the questioning expression on her face and hopefully doused her doubts with a grin that had to nearly split his face. Not because he wanted to reassure her, even though he did. But mostly because she was following his lead and was instinctively tapped into him in a way he'd never had before.

Guess that's what happens when you build a connection first.

He and Lauren had fallen into bed quickly, those first months together rotating around their time spent naked and horizontal. He'd seen the physical side as one of the more critical aspects of their relationship. *More fool was I.* Not that things hadn't evolved and grown into an emotional love. He absolutely had loved his wife. Loved her, missed her when they weren't together, and profoundly grieved her death. She'd been his best friend well before the end, and the hole she left behind in his heart probably would never be filled.

The thing was...Marian didn't seek to fill that gap. Without even trying, she'd found her own space in his heart, shoring up his fragile walls in the process. She'd intuitively known what he needed every step along the way and given it selflessly. That desire to see him happier and settled was the basis for what they had, because he felt the same way, and had spent these years working to give her opportunities to grow, building her into an even stronger version of the woman he'd first met.

Taking the final step upwards, he turned to face her, walking backwards towards the room Bane kept set aside for him. There was a connected bathroom to the nursery, with a door that locked. Capturing both her hands, he pulled her close enough so she had to tip her chin up to keep her gaze on his face. Einstein couldn't wait and stopped abruptly, arms closing around her as she stumbled into his chest. He bent his neck and pressed their mouths together, lips working against hers until she sighed softly, giving him an opening he took advantage of, slipping his tongue inside to touch hers gently.

The sigh turned into a moan as her arms wound around his neck. Einstein had a fleeting thought of privacy and cupped her ass in both hands, lifting so her knees were cocked on either side of his waist. He turned them and made his way the few steps to the door, backing against the surface to push it wide.

Every sound she made went straight to his cock. Each breathy moan he captured in his mouth, the keening whine at the back of her throat, and her whispered rendition of his name when they broke apart for the barest of breaths.

She squirmed against him, and he pulled back to stare down into her lust-drunk face, eyelids drooping to half-mast not doing a thing to hide her beauty. The sight of her kiss-swollen lips filled him with pride and a sense of possession—*I did that to her.* "Baby?" He whispered the question, and when she squirmed again, he suddenly remembered the why of them vacating their place on the couch. "Oh, sweetie, I got you."

Einstein slowly relaxed his arms, and she went with the movement, the trust she had in him shining through her eyes. The moment her toes reached the floor, she lunged upwards again, crashing their mouths together, and he kissed her deeply. Hands to her waist, he set her away from himself, grinning and shaking his head when she pouted prettily. Still breathing unsteadily, he prompted her, "You had to pee, remember?"

The blush that crept across her collarbones to her neck and then up to her cheeks was endearing.

"Yeah." She tipped her head towards the door. "I'm just gonna." Marian rolled her eyes. "You know." Her hands flew up and covered the bottom part of her face, eyes wide above the too-late barrier. "I mean, I don't want you to know."

"Baby." He curled a hand around the back of her neck, thumb brushing along the edge of her jaw. "I know." Bending closer, he waggled his head, whispering, "And I don't care."

"Well, I do." She straightened and pulled out of his grip, the rosy color on her cheeks deepening. "I'll be right back."

"Baby, just so you know—" He waited for her to look back at him. "I'm gonna need the room next, and I don't care if you know. Wanna stay in there and chat with me? I'm cool with that." Lifting a hand at the adorably horrified expression on her face, he grinned. "Not that I'm expecting that level of comfort with you yet. But just saying, when you get there, it'll be no biggie."

"Oh my God." The scandalized whisper was tossed over her shoulder as she darted into the bathroom.

The door closed quietly. A moment later, the lock clicking was one of the loudest sounds he'd ever heard.

She'd locked him out.

With his jaw clenching tightly, he rubbed at his sternum where his chest burned.

She locked me out.

Frown creasing his brow, Einstein moved to the hallway and into the nursery, all set up and ready for Myrt and Bane's newest addition. Quietly testing the knob on the connecting door, which turned easily in his hand, he nodded in satisfaction and waited for the tell-tale sounds to cease, followed by typical louder water noises. When the faucet for the sink turned on, he opened the door and pushed inside. Spots of water and soap suds dotted his shirt and vest when Marian whirled to face him, mouth open in shock as her wet hands rose in a protective gesture.

"Einstein—"

"Don't lock me out, baby. I'll always respect a closed door." He tried not to let her see how he held back a sigh, chest still aching as he pushed down disappointment. "The fact you don't already know that tells me a lot of things."

"I didn't—"

"I know, sweetie. I know." He stepped across the small room and thumbed the lock, then opened the door, only then closing the way he'd entered. "Finish washing your hands. I'll only be a minute, and we can go downstairs to get some food."

Her head came up, mouth snapping closed as her jaw firmed. Einstein watched as she swallowed hard before turning back to the sink. Dashing her hands under the still-running water, she locked her gaze with his through the mirror's reflection as she rinsed off the remaining suds. "It's not like you to be cruel."

"What?" He didn't understand, but a gut-twisting feeling of guilt rushed over him.

Grabbing a hand towel crumpled on the countertop, Marian methodically wiped at her hands as she spoke. "Punishing me for something I didn't know was a test isn't fair. For the past few years, I've shared bathrooms with growing boys and grown men, and locking the door is a habit, not a statement. Before then, it was survival." She tossed the towel back to the side of the sink as she turned to face him, head still held high. "The fact you don't already know that tells me a lot of things."

After throwing his words back in his face, she stepped backwards through the door, grabbing the edge. Just before it latched into place, she hesitated and broke the pose, head dipping. "The way you decided we couldn't discuss it tells me more. Maybe I don't know you like I thought I did." Then the door closed as softly as it had before.

When he exited the bathroom a minute later, it was to find an empty room, no one waiting.

Chapter Eighteen
Marian

Three weeks later, Marian was not surprised to find that nothing about her life had changed.

She slept in the small downstairs room, alone.

She ferried the boys to their events, freeing Bane to stay with Myrt as she closed in on the last few days before the birth.

She worked, and the not changing thing had been harder here, because Noah wasn't the same.

Marian had tried talking to him, the most recent time this morning when she arrived to find no customers inside the store. As before, he'd shut her down patiently and sweetly, but still relentlessly. From the expression on Monday's face lately, she guessed she wasn't the only one Noah was closing out.

Hands on her hips, she surveyed the workroom, satisfied with what she saw. All orders that had come in this morning were already filled, just waiting to be picked up or delivered. She dusted off a few stray pieces of greenery from her clothes and walked through to the front of the shop.

Noah stood near the window, a dusting rag in his hand that seemed to be forgotten. He was still and quiet, gaze pointed outside. Marian groaned, already knowing what had captured his attention.

Okay, maybe something *had* changed.

Stepping up beside him, she sighed. Noah wrapped an arm around her shoulders and tugged until she leaned against his side. "Your date's here."

Einstein was still in town, not having ridden out yet. *He will, though. Given enough time, he'll leave.* As he always had.

"That's his new usual."

A bike was parked across the street, a familiar form still astride the seat.

"You need to let the man in, Marian." She snorted, and Noah shook her lightly. "I'm serious. I don't know what he did to anger you, but that man has more love and loyalty in his little finger than most people get to experience in a lifetime. At least talk to him."

"I do talk to him. He's just not interested in what I have to say."

Since their argument the day after the kidnapping and subsequent rescue, an amalgamation of things Marian had dubbed *The Event* in her head, Einstein had been different. Initially Marian had been shocked at herself, at the outburst aimed at him, every sentence something her father would have dubbed back talk, a smack-worthy offense.

She'd gone downstairs and found Gunny, staying as close to him as possible. Even when Einstein had trailed down the stairs a few minutes later. The floaty feeling had been back, and Marian hadn't tried to join any conversations, not liking how things wavered around the edges.

Having successfully avoided Einstein all day, she'd gone to bed early and, when she woke the following morning feeling completely normal, realized she must have still been feeling the effects of the drug.

Staying in the same house with him had been hard. But the alternative was unacceptable. Last week when she'd overheard him suggesting a move to Truck's house instead, Marian had stormed around the corner and stalked right up to him. Finger poking into his chest, she'd let him know in no uncertain terms that he wasn't going anywhere. Turning on her heel, she'd run in her retreat, moving fast, but not fast enough to miss Bane's laughing response. "There's your answer, brother. You're stayin' here."

"Then show him how you feel without words." Noah's arm tightened when she would have moved away. "Marian, a blind man can see how much the two of you love each other. It breaks my heart that you'd let my stepbrother—" His voice broke, and he had to clear his throat before continuing. "That you'd let those assholes destroy something so beautiful. Don't let them win, darling. Take your own life back."

Watching Einstein as he guarded the shop, and by extension her, it occurred to her that Noah had a tiny bit of truth in his statement.

Before Scar had shown his hand and forced a reaction, she and Einstein had already been moving towards each other. Their relationship—and she didn't try to deceive herself they weren't in one—wasn't built on lies, not at all. He had long been her best friend, someone she trusted with all her heart. Maybe *The Event* had pushed things onto a faster trajectory, but where they'd ended was the direction they'd been going all along.

She just needed to rewind them to where the pain between them wasn't as prickly. They needed to regain the ease and friendship they'd shared.

"He's my date." Fingers playing with her bottom lip, Marian considered her options.

"That's what I said." Noah pushed her away playfully. "Go get your man, girlfriend."

"Maybe I will," she sassed back, a smile breaking across her face, what felt like the first in weeks. "I need the afternoon off."

Whirling on her heel, she ran to the workroom and grabbed a couple of things from her purse before stashing it under her normal station. She called out, "I won't have my keys, so I can't open in the morning." Dashing off a quick text to Myrtle, she stopped in place, running her quickly devised plan back through her head. "I love him." That last was a whisper, a reminder to herself of what was at stake. Softer, she repeated a version of Noah's words, "Take my own life back."

She gave Noah a wave as she moved through the shop and out the front door, the sweet tinkle of bells announcing her departure. Glancing left and right to ensure traffic remained nonexistent, she continued moving straight across the street. Einstein was seated on the bike, and the instant he appeared to realize her destination, his bootheels dropped from the highway bar mounted to the frame. They hit the ground at the same time she stopped directly next to him.

"Hi."

"Hey, baby." Over the past weeks, each time he'd slipped and used a sweet nickname for her, he'd looked hesitant and regretful. So this time, Marian's eyes dipped closed to hide his expression, and she let the affection in his tone wash over her, bringing confidence and a resolve that this was what they needed.

She leaned towards him until his hand landed on her arm, steadying her. Blinking against the sunshine, she opened her eyes to find his gaze fixed on her mouth. *Good.* As she pressed closer, it was clear he didn't realize her intention until her mouth touched his, the startled expression quickly morphing into that heated desire she wanted to see again and again.

Hand cupping her cheek, he murmured against her lips, "What are you doing, Marian?"

"We're going on a date." Choosing her words deliberately, she pulled back and moved to the saddlebag. Opening it, she brought out the helmet still stored there. *For me.* He'd turned to watch her, so she gave him a tiny smile as her fingers worked the clasp underneath her chin. "If you don't have anything else to do?" She already knew he didn't, because if she hadn't approached him, he would have stayed here until closing time and then followed her home. That had been their routine for the past twenty-two days.

Mouth quirking to one side, he shook his head. "Not a damn thing worth doing. Where you wanna go?"

Darting from one side of the bike to the other, she used a gentle push with the toe of her shoe to lower the foot pegs. Back beside him, she refastened the latch on the saddlebag before climbing on. In stark contrast to their first ride, and many of the ones between then and now, she slipped extra close, spreading her knees wide to fit alongside his hips and thighs.

"Doesn't matter." Hands on his waist, she leaned close and rested the side of her helmet against his spine. "Long as I'm with you, I don't care where we go, Jim."

Silence spread around them, broken only by voices in the distance, children shouting as they played in the park. Tension slowly bled out of his muscles, and her body molded to his as he took in several deep breaths.

His muttered, "Alrighty then," sounded loud to her ears. The bike engine started, rumbling noisily as Einstein gave the system a minute to warm up. His hands covered hers, fingers curling around to grip, and he tugged. She released her hold, following his lead, and when he placed them against his belly, low, just above his belt, she clutched at the fabric of his shirt. "Ready?"

Knowing he'd feel the movement, she simply nodded in response to the question called over his shoulder, then tightened her hold as they eased out into the street.

They rode for hours, not dismounting the bike even during refueling, Einstein maneuvering the beast close enough to the pump to conduct the entire transaction from his position between her legs. She liked the intimacy, liked even more his clear distaste for breaking their connection. Random thoughts threaded through her head as the wind and scenery rushed past. How she loved that this could become their normal, and how much she'd missed him helping her in the kitchen, the memory of his mouth against hers, chaste today, more erotic only a few weeks past.

Consciously setting aside the tiny bit of hurt that still hovered in the back of her mind, she focused on the feel of his muscles underneath her hands. If she wanted him to move past *The Event,* that meant she needed to understand things had also happened to him, and she needed to do the same. She'd lain in her bed and imagined his terror as Myrt had described it. How frantic he'd been, and the words of blame aimed at himself. The farther they rode, the more relaxed she became, making it easier to consider those terrifying hours.

For Marian, most of *The Event* was still a muddle of dark holes and vague memories, growing more tenuous as time passed. It was as if everything had happened to someone else, and Marian had only learned of it through a retelling. Einstein wouldn't have that same buffer in his mind. Marian wondered if she'd somehow gotten the easier end of the deal, because with the amnesiac features of the drug, so much that should have been scarring was just nonexistent.

It was nearly nighttime when she popped her head up and looked over his shoulder just in time to see a county line marker approaching in the bike's headlight. They were entering Blount County, and that triggered a tiny memory, something she'd heard from Retro. Holding tight to Jim's waist, she leaned close and over the sound of the wind called out, "Where are we going, Einstein?"

His head turned enough she caught the gleam of his eyes from behind his shades. Mouth curved in a relaxed smile, he said, "Going home."

A few minutes later, they were off the county highways and onto streets leading into a residential area. Marian sat up straighter, looking from side to side. In the rapidly falling darkness, she could make out only a few details of the houses, but they all looked occupied. Lived in, with piles of kids' bikes in the front yards, swing sets in the back, and close clusters of chairs crowded around firepits. Their speed dropped to a crawl, and she turned to look at the house where they were stopping. There was a pristine yard, well-tended flowerbeds, and a tarp-covered vehicle under the carport. It stood in stark contrast to those lived-in homes on either side.

Unsure what they were doing, she didn't dismount the bike while he parked it as she normally would have, clinging to him like a limpet instead. He didn't remark on it, simply maneuvered the bike until it was positioned as he wanted, then killed the engine.

Marian's heart pounded as he lifted a hand, and she placed hers against his palm, accepting the offer of assistance, which was as second nature as riding behind him had been. Her shoes scuffed swept concrete, and as she removed her helmet, she gazed around with more curiosity than before, certainty building inside her. *He brought me to his home.* She just didn't know yet what it meant.

Einstein looked around much as she had. As he hung his helmet on the handlebar, his muttered, "God, my brothers," didn't make sense, because they were there alone. Marian decided it didn't matter when he reached for her, fingers curling around her hip as he tugged her close.

He punched a set of buttons on a box near the door, the click of the latch loud as it released, and then he led her inside. They paused inside the door as low lights turned on automatically. He chuckled and shook his head, looking around like he had outside.

Toeing off his boots, he told her, "I haven't been here in years. Last time I was in this room, it was a wreck. I'd trashed everything, furniture, cabinet doors—anything that could be broken was. Blind drunk and raging. Retro pulled me out of here, and I camped in the clubhouse for months." She stumbled out of her shoes, pushing them against the wall as he had. His hand at her waist urged her to walk with him, so she did. Lights flashed into existence as they moved, and he led her through a door into a small sitting room, then via another door and down two steps into a much larger living area. "This is all new. A while back, maybe six months ago—I asked Mudd to get me a contractor who'd be willing to work with an absentee homeowner. Took the old bedrooms out, extended the foundation, and made this. It's not half bad." He huffed a soft laugh. "Not too shabby. I like the furniture they picked."

Everything was earth tones and neutrals, scattered rugs leaving plenty of slate floor exposed. The couch, love seat, and chair were leather, the furniture dark and heavy-looking, giving an air of masculinity to the room. The window treatments were brighter, colored in contrast to the rest of the room, and behind one set of blinds, she saw a window seat that just begged for a book, a blanket, and a rainy day.

"This is the first you've seen of the work?"

He was still looking around the room as he nodded. "Yeah. Oh, I saw pictures of course, but in the flesh? First time." He tugged her sideways towards a door set in a far wall. "Let's check out the rest of the work, baby."

They walked into a short hallway with a single door at the end and stepped through into a huge bedroom. The bed was the largest she'd ever seen, but it fit the room well. To one side of the doorway was what looked to be a closet, and the other had a sliding door that opened into a bathroom. Low lighting had preceded them here, as well, and she could see as much of the detail as was needed to know it had a large tub, and a larger shower.

"Looks even better than the pictures." His voice was filled with satisfaction, and she glanced up to find a pleased expression curling the corners of his mouth upwards. "They finished a few weeks ago. Just before all the shit went down in Baker."

The Event.

Pulling her to face him, he bracketed her sides with his arms, fingers finding their way into her back pockets as he tugged her close. "See, I'd been fighting it for a while, how I feel about you. I'm a stupid asshole, trying to deny something so beautiful. Still, seems my subconscious knew I'd want to bring you back here and knew I needed to make changes to be okay with it. The bedroom I shared with Lauren is gone." His head jerked towards the door leading back to the living area. "It's not that I want to forget her. I don't, and I trust you to understand what I mean when I say that. I'll never forget her or my daughter. But…" His chest rose and fell with a heavy sigh. "I think it's time to find my way back to the land of the living."

"You shouldn't forget them. They'll always be part of you." Glancing from him to the bed and back, she asked, "So the furniture is new, too?"

"Yeah, baby. Nobody's been in that bed before us." His mouth worked and he swallowed. "And that statement is wildly presumptuous of me."

"No." She crowded closer, the hot bar of his erection pressing against her belly. "You're not being presumptuous. And I think deep inside, you know that." Her hand curled around his bicep, felt the muscles flex under her hold. "We both have ideas about what happens next, I think." Sliding her other hand up his chest and under his vest, she curved her fingers around the top of his shoulder and lifted to her toes. "Would you kiss me? Again? Like the first time?"

His head descended, and their mouths touched, pressed, and moved, a series of tender kisses that fanned those flames inside her that never seemed to quiet when around him. His tongue laved her bottom lip and she rocked back, heels thudding against the floor. Chasing her mouth down, he pressed inside, gentle touches of his tongue prodding her to respond in kind, until they were gasping for air.

"Please." She panted the plea, eyes opening to slits to find him watching her closely. "Oh, please."

She shivered with a brief chill as his hands left her skin, then he shifted, his vest and shirt vanishing like magic. Welcome heat hit her belly, his hands sliding up and around in a single movement, and she lifted her arms as he relieved her of her shirt.

She bent her head and got to work on his belt, leaving it dangling from the loops as she moved to his pants. Hers loosened, and then one of his hands slipped inside the back, large palm curving over her ass as he pulled her against him.

"Einstein," she complained, then gasped as her bra fell away just as she got the zipper of his pants down.

"Come on, baby. I want you in this bed. My bed." He steered her backwards towards where she knew the bed was, so it wasn't a surprise when it hit the backs of her legs. "*Our* bed." He lifted and tossed her, and as she bounced on the mattress, his clever hands had her pants and panties stripped away, socks too. "God damn. I'm a fucking lucky man."

He froze in place, and she stared at him, taking in everything about him.

That crooked smile and the way he stood with shoulders squared, ready for anything. The tattoos extended across his chest and belly, the dark lines and symbols covering so much of that satin skin over hard muscles. He looked unbelievably sexy as he looked down, his gaze roving every inch of her. Heavy scruff defined his jaw, and the furrow that was so often between his brows had faded, leaving him looking lighter and happier. With his jeans hanging off his slim hips, he looked like a conqueror, and she smiled at the thought as she curled onto her side.

"I'm lucky too." He smiled at her words, cheeks lifting so his eyes narrowed, the expression of delight such a novelty she marked it, branding it on her brain. "Don't leave me alone."

"Never again, Marian. Never gonna leave you again." He bent and, with efficient movements, finished stripping before putting a knee to the mattress. "Never again." He grasped an ankle and tugged, shifting her on the bed. As he moved to rest between her legs, he straightened on his knees, and she saw the rest of his body for the first time. Thick thighs rose in strong columns to the juncture of his body, where a rigid shaft of flesh lifted proudly from a nest of curls. "Neither one of us will be alone. I've got you, baby." The heat along her leg was his hand traveling from ankle to knee, then up her thigh to caress the curve of her hip, leaving behind an indelible trace of his touch in sparks and tingles. "Gonna take care of you."

"Promise?" Trembling sounds joined to push that one word out, her throat closing around the rest of the plea.

His body soared over hers, held up by one stiffened arm as that skillful hand continued its blazing trail along her skin. "Always take care of my baby."

"Please." She didn't know exactly what she needed, but from the gleam in his eye, she thought he might. "Einstein, please?"

"Gonna take care of you." His mouth touched hers, this kiss sweet, reverent, and brief as his lips slid to her cheek, then near her ear. His soft whisper was a gentle, "Wanna make love to you, Marian. I won't hurt you. Won't ever hurt you." Teeth nipped at her lobe, and she gasped, her hands flying up to curl around his back. Palms flat on the broad expanse of skin, she explored as kisses rained down her neck, interspersed with warm, wet passes of his tongue, mixed in equal measure by sharp bites and nips. "Make you ready for me."

"I'm ready now."

His gentle laughter at her words was accompanied by gusts of air across her chest, and she shivered as his mouth met her breast. Soft lips closed around a nipple and tugged, a movement that had a direct line to her groin, the swell of want pushing her hips up against nothing.

"Einstein." Chin to her chest, she watched his face as he pulled more of her into his mouth. With his eyes closed, he looked like he was concentrating hard, and as he sucked firmly she gasped again, sighing, "Jim." He smiled, lips still tight around her flesh.

His tongue lapped a wide swath across her pebbled nipple. "Need you wanting, baby." He shifted to his forearms as he moved down the bed, mouth leaving a wet trail along her skin, tongue working back and forth until he encountered her navel, where he paused. Dipping inside, then curling around the perimeter, the innocent touch made her hips jerk again, this time his chest there to confront the movement. The pressure felt good, so good she repeated the action, groaning when his hand landed on her hip and pinned her to the bed. "Want you desperate for me."

"Jim." When he didn't look up, she studied what she could see of his face. Brow furrowed, he was concentrating on her every reaction, reading her body like a book, and she knew it wouldn't take long for him to register her sudden hesitancy. Sure enough, his eyes popped open, and he rested his chin just above her mons, staring up at her. "I've never done this before." He didn't respond verbally, but the way his pupils dilated told her the words had registered. "I don't know what to do for you."

"You shouldn't worry about that." Mouth quirking up on one side, he blinked slowly. "What we're doing right now has me hard enough to pound spikes." Shifting, one of his hands disappeared underneath him, and she watched the muscles of his arm bunch and move. *He's touching himself. Talking to me and touching himself.* "Me wanting you is never going to be an issue, Marian. And I thought it might be the case, but you not having taken anyone into your body before isn't a turnoff, so just wipe that idea from your mind. The knowledge that you've never trusted anyone like this makes me want to crow."

"I understand the mechanics." She shrugged, feeling silly at having this discussion while naked and half underneath him. "Can't grow up in the country without having some idea of what sex is about."

"Yeah, but we aren't going to have sex." He surged up the bed and kissed her hard, forcing his tongue between her lips as she caught up to and met his movements. He broke away, and with his mouth next to her ear, whispered, "I'm going to make love to you, baby."

Goose bumps erupted over her skin, drawn there in an instant by the heat and truth in his words.

"It'll never be anything else between us. Even if it's hard and fast sometimes, you'll know—I'm always going to be making love to you."

***

Einstein

He kissed her again, insistently, fingers curled in her hair to tug her head backwards as he traveled from her lips to the satin skin of her throat. Moving back down her body, this time faster, he reconnected with all the places she'd enjoyed on the first round, until he reclaimed his place between her legs.

Without hesitating, he lapped at her center, tongue laving slowly up to focus on the button of nerves that made her gasp and writhe. Every sound was music to his ears, telling him she wasn't banking her passion. With his palms scraping up the inside of each thigh, he curled a firm grip around her hips and applied pressure, holding her in place. Then he made out with her lower lips, not turned off that they'd been on the bike all day because she smelled and tasted of arousal. Slippery wetness met his probing tongue when he speared inside, and the moan she gave at the barely there entrance had his balls drawing up tight to his body. Einstein angled his knees wider, not giving himself any room to find friction, knowing he'd come at the first touch right now.

He shifted and met his tongue with a finger, getting it wet enough it slid inside her without resistance. Curling and thrusting, he let her sounds and movements guide him, and soon enough, he slipped in a second finger, adding scissoring to the motions in his arsenal. Marian gave him a flow of constant feedback in sighs and moans, gasps scattered and separated by drawn-out cries of his name, by turns low and quavering, or high and demanding.

With her thighs tensed on either side of his head, he played with all the sensitive areas he could reach, sucking and tonguing her clit until she quivered, then mouthed his way along the juncture of thighs to her body.

"Jim." His name came from her mouth on a rising wail, and her body tightened. Mouth to her core, he felt the pulsing of her orgasm through the clenching hold her channel had on his fingers, the jerking of her body under his.

Pulling back, he kept two fingers inside, thrusting in the same steady rhythm as he brushed his thumb sideways across her clit. Marian's head was pushed backwards into the pillow, eyes closed, mouth open as she trembled. Her hands roved side to side across her belly, and he tracked each movement, noting each sensual pass over her skin. Nipples peaked, muscles and tendons flexing, and he took it all in. She was a study in beauty laid out on the bed in front of him.

When he fumbled for the condom he'd tossed to the bed earlier, she seemed obvious to the crinkle of the wrapper. The beautiful torment of taking himself in hand to suit up turned him into the one groaning, and he gave himself a hard grip around the base before counting it done. Maybe the agony of that makeshift cock ring would let him get all the way into her before blowing.

Wiping his lips and chin against the inside of an elbow, he levered himself into place above her and lowered his mouth to hers. Gratification spread through his gut when she gasped and met him motion for motion, clearly as eager for the connection as he was.

Then he was inside her, the barest tip of his cock nudging between her lips. A curl of his back, thrust of his hips, and he sank in halfway, holding still for an eon before pulling back slowly. Her heels thudded against his ass, strong legs keeping him in place, and Einstein opened eyes he didn't know he'd closed to see Marian's brow furrowed.

Mouth open and panting, she mouthed, "Please," as her arms lifted to curl around his shoulders.

He pushed inside again, finding that halfway point and surpassing it before he again retreated. Her worry was lessened this time, body finding the same rhythm as her hips rose and fell. A final long glide had him buried deep, the base of his cock grinding against her clit in a way that set her body shuddering. The movement transferred directly to his dick, and he froze with eyes wide open, panting as he held back his orgasm by will alone.

"Please, baby." Her mouth touched his, words whispered against his lips. "Please move. Please."

Finding a rhythm between them was easy as breathing, and the silken glide of her sweat-slickened skin against his ratcheted up the need, the desire. They moved, coming together and falling apart, joined intimately. His mouth found hers often, and hers matched the motion.

Propped on one forearm, Einstein drifted a hand along her side. Arms circling his upper body, Marian slid her palms across his back. He caught her off guard when his hand slipped between their bodies, thumb working her clit as he used short, deep, sharp thrusts of his hips that seemed to stoke her passion. When she tightened around him and came again, it felt like he'd won a victory. Burying his head against her neck, Einstein breathed out the truth he'd held inside for a long time.

"Love you, baby. Not gonna be without you. Mine, you're mine, you get that? You and me, we belong together." Each word strengthened the flames of his own desire, and he went with the demands of his body, moving faster, driving deep, burying himself inside her over and over.

"Love you too." As if his words gave hers permission to exist, she repeated them. "For a long time now, I've loved you. Want to be with you. Want you always. Don't leave me alone."

He pushed up enough to crash his mouth to hers, each sobbing sigh of breath joining them until he couldn't tell where he ended, and she began—they just were. Then he was coming, the crashing wave of passion lifting and rising over him until it tumbled him under. Collapsing on top of her, he buried his face against her neck, each surge of pleasure rolling up and through him almost painfully. Gradually it receded, and he came back to himself with a realization that she'd wrapped him up. Arms and legs, even her head was pressed tightly to his, as if she were trying to keep him from flying apart.

An apt metaphor for Marian's very existence in his life.

Nothing in recent memory had ever felt as right as Marian in his arms. Einstein deliberately didn't make his mind shy away from thoughts of Lauren and Makayla, because being with the woman he loved now wasn't disrespectful to their memories. This, what he had with Marian, wasn't moving on; it was just simply living.

Bringing her here had been easier than expected, and most of that had to do with the construction that had transformed the house completely. That had taken a conversation with Vanna and Sharon to understand, and when he'd finally voiced the anxiety he carried, their simple solution was brilliant. Don't want to take his new love to his dead wife's house? Change the house.

The whole ride had been his subconscious way of purging out any residual pain, seducing him with the pleasure of her wrapped around him on the bike. While instigated by her, it had been a way to join them tighter.

Her here, in this bed with him, no one else in the house—perfection.

He rolled them to their sides, chuckling when she clutched him closer. "Not going anywhere, Marian. Just need to take care of the condom." Backing his hips away, he reached between them, pausing to stroke the slope of her breasts before continuing across her belly and down to his softening cock. Rubber off, tied, and thrown on the floor, Einstein turned back to her and cupped a hand over her sex. Not playing, just tracing the creases, watching her face for any flinches of pain. Finally satisfied he hadn't hurt her, Einstein forced an arm underneath her head and angled to his back, pulling her with him so she was splayed out half on top of him. Already tight against his side, she snuggled closer still, head fitting perfectly into the hollow of his shoulder.

She shuddered suddenly, teeth chattering lightly, and he realized his sweat-cooled skin was growing colder too as the air conditioner kicked on. It took a few moments, but he maneuvered them underneath the covers, sheets crisp and smelling like sunshine.

"You doing okay, baby?" His question was met with a quiet hum, and he grinned up into the darkness. "Hungry, or wanting for anything?"

She hesitated for so long he wasn't sure what was going on in her head and had opened his mouth to ask again when she spoke. "Is Birmingham home? Is that why you had the house remodeled?"

"It could be, in the right situation."

"What's the right situation?" Her teeth clattered together briefly, and he wrapped her tighter in his arms.

"Retro's my president, like Bane is for Gunny and Truck, and Blackie is for Bane."

"What?" Marian looked up at him, her features wrinkled into the most adorable frown he'd ever seen, and Einstein pressed a kiss between her brows. "No, seriously. What does that have to do with this house?"

"I don't want to be without you. Never again. Do you get me?" He curled around her. "I'm wholly enamored of you, Marian. This isn't a flighty feeling, not some beer bravery. This is real as it gets, yeah?"

"Okay." Drawing the word out, she angled so their gazes clashed, hers full of confusion.

"How attached are you to your little room at the compound?" He shifted uncomfortably. "To your job there?"

He saw the moment understanding came over her, the expression on her face blanking. Hiding her true feelings seemed second nature to Marian, and he made a mental note to circle back around to that.

"You're moving back here." There was no nuance to her words, just a flat statement.

Oh, that won't do at all, honey.

"Following the most direct route, it's three-plus hours. Not even half a day back down to Baker." Einstein dusted kisses along her cheek and across the bridge of her nose before angling to her mouth. "Retro's put up with a lot from me over the past years. Man's one of the most loyal I've ever met, and I love him like a true brother. But you tell me Birmingham is a no-go, then he's going to have to be more patient. Me with you is not negotiable. The rest of it? We have lots of time to figure it out."

"You'd put this on hold so fast? The house, what I saw of it, looks gorgeous. A remodel isn't cheap, either. You just sunk all that cost here, and you'd turn your back on it?"

"Baby, for more than three years I've been in orbit around you without really realizing it. When I opened my eyes and saw what I'd been doing, the feeling that hit me sure wasn't being pissed. My heart's known for a long time that you were important to me, that I needed, as well as wanted…you. That's all that matters. This?" He gestured around the room and brought his hand back to rest on her cheek, cupping her face, heat from her skin sinking into him in familiar ways. "It's a place. A house, baby." Her lips were giving and soft against his gentle kiss. "You're my home."

Chapter Nineteen

Einstein

Light filtering through the curtains woke him, and Einstein looked around the unfamiliar room groggily. The chirping of birds outside was muted, those worm-chasing early ones being considerate of the rest of the world. Nothing could compete with the soothing cadence of quiet breathing from beside him, and he turned his head to see Marian, still resting on his shoulder. She fit him as if she'd been made for him, every curve slotted against his shoulder and hip, her thigh thrown over his.

Unable to believe the reality of what he held in his hands, he stared at the beauty sleeping next to him—tousled hair a testament to their activities last evening.

After hunger had driven them from bed, once sated on that front, they'd tumbled back between the sheets, and the second round had been as unrushed as the first, savoring each other's bodies.

She'd been determined to be a more active participant, and the concentrated expression as she'd touched him was so endearing he hadn't held back in his reactions. Everything they did was as comfortable as if they'd been together forever, but the thrill of exploring and learning her, having the chance to teach her what he wanted...had been a pounding thought in his head.

His first time with her.

Her first lover ever.

Stroking a curled finger against the apple of her cheek, he was rewarded by a soft sigh and the armful of woman snuggling even closer.

This is my life. From here on out, it's her.

The thought wasn't unsettling at all. He pulled in a deep breath and, as he blew out the air, felt his shoulders and neck relaxing. From the first time he'd laid eyes on her, Marian'd had this effect on him. Through the years, they'd slipped into an easy ritual. Both early risers, they'd meet in the kitchen and share a quiet cup of coffee before tackling making breakfast for the household. And through the years, every time he'd rolled up to Bane's house, his first thought was Marian. When he'd ridden away, if she were home, her waving hand would be the last thing in his mirror.

It really has been her all along.

The passage of time had helped, he knew. If he'd gone to Florida in the early days of his grieving, he'd have been locked away, unable to react to her. Even with the distance between the shattering past and watching her in the kitchen that first time, he hadn't considered anything other than she was sweet and nice, and he didn't hate getting to know her. The decision to remodel the house had followed the realization that if the home continued to echo with his and Lauren's lives, he wouldn't return. Of course, he had taken another full year to be comfortable with the idea of having his patch brothers cleaning out Lauren's and Makayla's closets, handling their belongings. Retro's wife had stepped in at that point and had promised Einstein that everything would be handled respectfully. Somewhere in the attic were boxes of keepsakes she and the other old ladies had saved for him. And someday, with Marian's help, he'd go through them.

Easy and gradual. Wasn't that how river stones were worn down into interesting shapes, though? Through the constant exposure to whatever was passing them by? Life had buffeted him unmercifully, yet somewhere along the way, she'd become that sheltering curve where things didn't pound at him so hard. Where the water calmed and went deep.

"What are you thinking about so hard over there?" Her voice was low and sleep-filled, startling in the quiet of the room.

"How you're my still water, peace for my soul, baby. Made for me in so many ways, I can't even begin to count them." Throat tight, he blinked fast. "I fucking love you, Marian Threadgill."

"Then it's a good thing I love you right back, Jim Dancer."

Chapter Twenty
Scar

Hissing through his teeth as the forceps of the black-market doc painfully dug into the hole in his shoulder, Scar kept his eyes fixed on the clock hanging high on the wall in front of him. Every minute that passed was a chance for one of the men who'd been inside that house to track him down, find him and bring him back for their brand of justice.

Tonight all his plans had gone to shit.

First Zipline had kidnapped Dancer's woman. Fuckin' kidnapped her, after everything Scar had told him *not* to goddamned well do.

And in doing so, he'd also drugged her. The stillness of the bitch's body as Zipline had carried her into the house they'd commandeered had been terrifying. Caused Scar to flash back to another time, years in the past, when a miscalculation by a different associate had cost the lives of a woman and child.

He'd ripped Dancer's old lady out of Zip's arms, not believing the man's protests until he'd heard with his own ears she was still breathing. Felt the slow cadence of her pulse through the skin of her neck.

And then, everything still went to hell.

Good thing he had ideas not yet tapped for how to climb back out of that hole. Ideas that didn't depend on his old familial ties.

Or that old bastard Dolph.

When Dancer had moved to nomad status, it had seriously fucked with Scar's plans of migrating to a decent club away from the East Coast. A man couldn't make a case for an old friend if he wasn't near the leadership to make those arguments on a regular basis.

Now Scar needed to shift plans and set his sights on a different person to leverage. He might not have a history with the man, but he'd never seen someone as well connected.

Scar just needed to figure out the individual vulnerabilities, take the time to map the opportunities across the multitude of clubs. Then he would fully engage with an eye towards his final goal.

It'd take time, but he had proven he could be patient when he needed to be.

And somewhere in the future, there'd be a point where he'd be able to leverage Gunny's relationships to gain access to a vibrant, growing club, join them, move up the ranks. And then?

He'd take over.

Fini

THANK YOU FOR READING
Tangled Threats on the Nomad Highway!

ABOUT THE AUTHOR

Raised in the south, *Wall Street Journal* & *USA TODAY* bestselling author MariaLisa learned about the magic of books at an early age. Every summer, she would spend hours in the local library, devouring books of every genre. Self-described as a book-a-holic, she says "I've always loved to read, but then I discovered writing, and found I adored that, too. For reading...if nothing else is available, I've been known to read the back of the cereal box."

Want sneak peeks into what she's working on, or to chat with other readers about her books? Join the Facebook group! **bit.ly/deMora-FB-group**

deMora's got a spam-free newsletter list she'd love to have you join, too: **bit.ly/mldemora-newsletter**

~~~~~

ADDITIONAL SERIES AND BOOKS

</div>

Please note that books in a series frequently feature characters from additional books within that series. If series books are read out of order, readers will twig to spoilers for the other books, so going back to read the skipped titles won't have the same angsty reveals.

Rebel Wayfarers MC series

A motorcycle club can be a frightening place, filled with hardened men and bad attitudes. Rebel Wayfarers is a club with their own measure of hard and dangerous, led by their national president, Davis Mason. This book series follows members as they move through their lives, filled with anguish and heartache, laughter and love. In the club, each of them find a home and family they thought long lost to them.
~~~~~

Mica, #1
A Sweet & Merry Christmas, #1.5
Slate, #2
Bear, #3
Jase, #4
Gunny, #5
Mason, #6
Hoss, #7
Harddrive Holidays, #7.5
Duck, #8
Biker Chick Campout, #8.5
Watcher, #9
A Kiss to Keep You, #9.25
Gun Totin' Annie, #9.5
Secret Santa, #9.75
Bones, #10
Gunny's Pups, #10.25
Not Even A Mouse, #10.75
Fury, #11
Christmas Doings, #11.25
Gypsy's Lady includes *Never Settle* (#10.5), #11.5
Cassie, #12
Road Runner's Ride, #12.5

Occupy Yourself band series

Stardom doesn't happen overnight. Hell, it doesn't even happen after a decade in the business, as the members of Occupy Yourself have found out. But, with the right talent and the right representation, they might still have a chance to make it big. As long as they can keep their lead singer sober, keep their drummer focused on the music, keep their guitarist out of trouble … well, you get the idea. Come and join us, stand side stage for a close-up view of the backstage happenings in a rock-and-roll band. It's guaranteed to be a show you won't ever forget.

Born Into Trouble, #1
Grace In Motion, #2 (TBD)
What They Say, #3 (TBD)

Neither This, Nor That MC series

Legends are born from moments like these. Folktales spun around a single point in time so perfect, you can almost hear the click resonating through the universe as things align. Meet Twisted, Po'Boy, Retro, and Ragman, good old boys from southern states who have many things in common. First, is a bone-deep love of the biker lifestyle. Second, would be their love of the brotherhood, and knowing that you trust the man at your back. Finally, these men have the love of a good woman. None of these come without a price, and it is our pleasure to journey along with them as they discover the blessings that can be won, and lost along the way.

This Is the Route Of Twisted Pain, #1
Treading the Traitor's Path: Out Bad, #2
Shelter My Heart, #3
Trapped by Fate on Reckless Roads, #4
Tarnished Lies and Dead Ends, #5
Tangled Threats on the Nomad Highway, #6

Rebel Wayfarers crossover stories

Enjoy these stories that tie the different worlds of my MC universe together, bringing Rebel Wayfarers MC and clubs like Neither This Nor That and other series into glorious alignment.

Going Down Easy
No Man's Land
In Search of Solace

Mayhan Bucklers MC series

The Mayhan Bucklers MC has been part of the rolling hills of Northeast Texas for decades. Now, new life is being breathed into this reborn club, a legacy resurrected by grandsons of the founder. The MBMC is set to surpass its original glory, fortified with an honorable purpose: Helping wounded warriors reintegrate back into society, gifting those who've given so much with a safe place to land.

Learning how to navigate life while war still echoes inside you isn't easy, but with solid brothers at your back, anything is possible.

Most Rikki-Tik, #1
Mad Minute, #2
Pucker Factor, #3
Boocoo Dinky Dau, #4

Borderline Freaks MC series

When you can't count on anyone else to save you, there's only one real choice. Borderline Freaks MC is a series of books about the men of the club and their brotherhood — and of course the love they have for their women. Take a trip along with Monk, Blade, Wolf, and Neptune, and feel for yourself the connection these men have for each other.

Service and Sacrifice, #1
More Than Enough, #2
Lack of In-between, #3
See You in Valhalla, #4

Alace Sweets series

Dark romantic thrillers, these books are not light reads. Filled with edge-of-your-seat suspense, these intense stories command the reader's attention as they drive towards their explosive endings. Alace Sweets is a vigilante serial killer, with everything that implies and is sure to trip all your triggers. Be ready.

Alace Sweets, #1
Seeking Worthy Pursuits, #2
Embarrassment of Monsters, #3
All the Broken Rules, #4 (TBD)

With My Whole Heart series

Sweet as pie and twice as delicious, these romantic love stories are a guaranteed happily-ever-after read.

With My Whole Heart, #1
Bet On Us, #2

If You Could Change One Thing:
Tangled Fates Stories

When threads in the tapestry of life are cut short, inexorably changing the future for those you love, would you be willing to tempt fate to set things right?

There Are Limits, #1
Rules Are Rules, #2
The Gray Zone, #3

Other Books:

Hard Focus
Dirty Bitches MC: Season 3

~~~~~

deMora's Rebel Wayfarers MC and the Neither This Nor That MC series do cross over, along with the Occupy Yourself band books, so readers have a couple of choices. The series can be read independently beginning with RWMC, OYBS, and then NTNT without too many spoilers. There's also a crossover between deMora's RWMC world and Lila Rose's Hawks MC world. Or they can be read intertwined—in chronological order.
~~~~~

Here's the recommended reading order if you want to follow according to timing:

Mica, RWMC #1
A Sweet & Merry Christmas, RWMC #1.5
Slate, RWMC #2
Bear, RWMC #3
Born Into Trouble, OYBS #1
Jase, RWMC #4
Gunny, RWMC #5
Mason, RWMC #6
Hoss, RWMC #7
This Is the Route of Twisted Pain, NTNT #1
Harddrive Holidays, RWMC #7.5
Duck, RWMC #8
Biker Chick Campout, RWMC #8.5
Watcher, RWMC #9
Treading the Traitor's Path: Out Bad, NTNT #2
Living Without, Lila Rose's Hawks MC: Caroline Springs #4
Shelter My Heart, NTNT #3
A Kiss to Keep You, RWMC #9.25
Gun Totin' Annie, RWMC #9.5
Secret Santa, RWMC #9.75
Trapped by Fate on Reckless Roads, NTNT #4
Bones, RWMC #10
Gunny's Pups, RWMC #10.25
Not Even A Mouse, RWMC #10.75
Road Runner's Ride, RWMC #12.5
Never Settle, RWMC #10.5
Fury, RWMC #11
Christmas Doings, RWMC #11.25
Gypsy's Lady, RWMC #11.5
Tarnished Lies and Dead Ends, NTNT #5
Going Down Easy
No Man's Land
In Search of Solace
Tangled Threats on the Nomad Highway, NTNT #6
Cassie, RWMC #12
More information available at **mldemora.com**.